Un. Love

SUE FORTIN

Harper*Impulse* an imprint of
HarperCollins*Publishers Ltd*
77–85 Fulham Palace Road
Hammersmith, London W6 8JB

www.harpercollins.co.uk

A Paperback Original 2013

First published in Great Britain in ebook format by HarperImpulse 2013

Cover Images © Shutterstock.com

Sue Fortin asserts the moral right to
be identified as the author of this work

A catalogue record for this book
is available from the British Library

ISBN: 978-0-00-755974-9

This novel is entirely a work of fiction.
The names, characters and incidents portrayed in it are
the work of the author's imagination. Any resemblance to
actual persons, living or dead, events or localities is
entirely coincidental.

Automatically produced by Atomik ePublisher from Easypress

Chapter One

It was her hair that caught his attention first: short cropped and blonde. White blonde. It was her neat little figure second, and it was the car coming up the road as she stepped backwards off the sidewalk that he noticed last.

Tex Garcia felt like he was moving in slow motion as he lunged towards her, grabbing her arm and hauling her out of the car's path. She slammed into his chest, and in a reflex gesture he engulfed her in his arms as the car sped by, missing her by inches.

'Whoa! You got some sort of death wish?' He looked down at her. Staring back up at him were two startled and confused mossy-green eyes. 'You just nearly got yourself run over.'

She looked up the road at the offending vehicle as it disappeared out of sight. 'Th...thank you,' she stammered. 'I didn't see it.'

'You don't say.' He crooked a smile.

'Well, I think the danger is over now, so maybe you could...' She regarded his arms still firmly around her. 'Perhaps release me?'

'What? Oh, sorry.' Tex dropped his hands and took a step back. Then, as a precautionary measure, put a hand on her arm and drew her away from the edge of the sidewalk and into the forecourt of the church building. He looked up at his new business premises, wondering what had distracted her. She had been gazing up at the building, poised with a camera in her hand.

3

She followed his gaze. 'It's going to be a pizza place.' He didn't miss the derogatory tone in her voice.

'Really?' He stole a glance at her from the corner of his eye.

'Hmm. Apparently some Italian chef has bought it. Nico Garcia. Although I have to admit, I thought Garcia was a Hispanic name.'

'You don't sound too impressed.'

'Ignoring the potential for noisy scooters whining up and down with their delivery boxes full of pizza, I dread to think what will happen to the building itself. I just hope that the planning department doesn't let this Nico Garcia ruin it.'

Tex sucked in the corners of his mouth to repress the grin that was threatening to erupt. 'What makes you think it will be ruined?'

'Not being British, he may not appreciate how old this building really is. It's got so much history and, okay, it hasn't been used as a church for a long time now, but it has always retained its dignity.' She wandered over to the entrance and reached out to touch the solid oak doors. 'It would be awful if these were changed to some modern glass ones, or those gorgeous leaded and stained glass windows swapped for big, white plastic, double-glazed ones.'

This time Tex couldn't censor his grin or the small chuckle. He had actually been thinking about changing those old windows with plain glass to let some more light into the place. She turned and looked at him, her eyebrows darting together. He swallowed down his laugh and put on a straight face.

'You're quite passionate about it, aren't you?'

The frown lifted as she shrugged. 'I love Arundel. This town's got so much history. I work part-time as a tour guide so I suppose I've grown quite fond of some of the buildings, even if they don't warrant a mention on the tours.'

He nodded, and as she looked up at the building again, he took the opportunity to appreciate a different view: her neat butt. She swung round too quickly for him to avert his eyes, and for a moment he wondered whether she was some sort of feminist who was about to slap his face. To his relief, it appeared she wasn't. Instead, she began to inspect her camera and presumably the photos she had taken of the church.

He leant over her shoulder, peering at the small digital screen, taking time to breathe in the soft vanilla fragrance that floated around her hair.

'What are the photos for?'

'I like to keep a record of the town. Before and after shots of how things change and develop. I might make a book of them all one day.'

'Social history in pictures.'

She turned to look at him. 'Yeah, something like that.' Switching off her camera, she moved slightly away. 'You're American, right?'

'Sure am,' replied Tex, tipping his forehead with his fingers in a slack salute.

'On holiday?'

'No. Actually, I've lived in the UK for five years now.' He drove down the churning in his gut. It always happened when he thought about his move here and what he had left behind.

'Oh, I see. If you were a tourist I was going to sign you up for a guided tour.' She smiled at him. 'My boss is always nagging me, so at least today I can say I tried. And speaking of which, I had better get on. I've got a tour in five minutes and I've got to get up to the cathedral yet.'

Tex was aware that a slither of disappointment eked its way through him as she made to head off.

She paused. 'There's an open evening here tonight. Get to meet the new owner.'

'You going?' he asked.

'Too right. I need to check out the competition.'

Tex raised his eyebrows in question. 'Competition?' She looked so sincere, he almost felt guilty for his deception. Maybe deception was too harsh a word. More like withholding information.

She pointed vaguely in the direction of a building further along the road. 'I also work in the tea rooms down there a couple of days a week, so I'm curious to find out if we have anything to worry about and what exactly this Nico Garcia has planned.'

He grinned. 'You never know, you might be pleasantly surprised.'

'I'm not holding my breath.'

'I'll be there tonight. Will be interesting to see your reaction.' Had he blown it? She was looking at him strangely. He held out his hand, hoping to distract her. 'My name's Tex, by the way.'

'Anna.'

As she put her hand in his, he couldn't help noticing how small it looked and how soft it felt against his own rough fingertips.

Something akin to an electric shock zipped right through her when she shook his hand. The same something she had been fully aware of when he had leant on her shoulder to look at the camera. It was unnerving. Aware, too, that her heart was now doing its usual skippy thing it always did when she felt attracted toward someone. Anna made a supreme effort to walk calmly away from Tex. It only took several paces before her resolve weakened and she found herself turning round to look at him. He was standing there, hands stuffed in his jeans pocket, watching her.

'Oh, by the way,' she heard herself call out. 'Thank you for saving me!'

He tipped his forehead in that lazy, mock-salute way he had done earlier and treated her to what she could only describe as a laconic Paul Newman smile.

As Anna walked away, she was already mentally going through her wardrobe wondering what to wear that night, and then chided herself. Of course, had he, Tex, not been going, she probably wouldn't even be thinking about it, but now it seemed incredibly important that she looked nice. 'Get a grip,' she said out loud. 'You're thirty-five, separated from your husband and definitely don't need another relationship just yet.'

Despite this pep talk, throughout the guided tour that afternoon, no matter how hard she tried to dismiss thoughts of him, her mind kept conjuring up images of the tall American. The dark brown eyes encased in thick lashes, the dark hair brushed back from his face, a few strands falling forwards. And all set off against a honey-toned complexion.

The main hall of the old United Reformed Church was beginning to fill up with guests, mostly local traders. It was probably out of curiosity rather than any real desire to welcome him into their community with open arms, but Tex wasn't worried. This way he hoped he would be able to win them over. He had hired in a local outside catering company to organise the food and drinks, as a gesture of his willingness to fit in and support his new neighbours. The fact that the church kitchens were so primitive and in no fit state for him to be able to do justice to any food he cooked, was neither here nor there.

'You all right, mate?' It was Jamie, a long-established friend and former colleague of his. 'Not a bad turn out, eh?'

Tex nodded, thinking yeah, sure it was going okay but shame there was no sign of the little blonde from earlier. Anna. Before he could commiserate further, Yvonne, Jamie's wife, skipped over.

She gave him a kiss on the cheek before picking up a vol-au-vent from her plate and biting into it. 'Hiya, Tex. I have to say this food is really lovely. I think this company could give you a run for your money.'

Tex gave her a look of mock reproach. 'You hush your mouth there, little lady,' he said, exaggerating his southern drawl.

Yvonne laughed. 'I do love it when you go and get all cowboy on me, Tex.'

Jamie gave Tex a nudge. 'That bloke over there, the one looking at your plans.' He nodded towards the centre table where the architect's drawings had been carefully laid out around a scale model and cross section of the new premises. 'See him? I think I overheard him saying he was from the local Chamber of Commerce. Didn't know if you needed to go and sweet-talk him.'

Tex followed his friend's gaze, and sighed. 'I suppose I'd better.'

Tiresome as it was having to suck up to the local hierarchy, he knew it was a necessary evil and so headed off towards the middle-aged, bearded man that Jamie had pointed out. It was then that he saw Anna coming in. He felt himself draw breath. She looked good – her hair styled a bit more choppy, fresh make-up, pretty soft blouse that showed off her tiny frame, skirt resting just above her knees, revealing a fine pair of legs.

She spotted him, broke into a smile and waved. He was aware that he waved back in some klutzy high school way. Damn it! Not only that, but she had noticed, judging by the giggle she made no attempt to hide. He walked over to greet her.

She was still smiling. 'You made it then?'

'Sure. Had no choice.' He really should tell her, before it all got out of hand and she found out for herself.

'Mr Garcia!' Tex heard a voice behind him and groaned inwardly. Too late. Anna was peering about, no doubt trying to work out which one was Mr Garcia.

'Mr Garcia!' There it was again, except closer this time. Then Tex felt a tap on his shoulder.

'Argh, Mr Garcia, sorry to interrupt. I just wondered if we could have a quick word. I'm Richard Harrington, Arundel Chamber of Commerce.' He was by the side of Tex now, holding out his hand.

Tex shook hands. 'Pleased to meet you.' He turned to Anna

whose mouth was working but no sound coming out. 'Could you just excuse me a moment, Anna? Maybe we can talk later?' Her eyes hardened as she nodded. Computation complete. Oh yeah, she'd worked it out.

'We certainly can talk later, Mr Garcia,' Anna said, the smile now nowhere in sight.

So he thought he was clever did he? A proper smart-arse. Nico Garcia or Tex, or whatever his blasted name was. Anna glared at the American's back as he chatted to the Chamber of Commerce guy. Despite her bad temper with Tex, she couldn't fail to acknowledge the broadness of his shoulders underneath the crisp, dark suit. He looked even more attractive tonight, all spruced up, shirt and tie. He really did scrub up well. Stop! She must stop thinking like this about him.

'Hello, Anna.' It was Andy Bartholomew, the curator of the museum at Arundel Castle.

Great, just what she needed. Handy Andy, as he was unaffectionately known amongst the female tour guides, and it was certainly nothing to do with his DIY skills.

'Hello, Andy,' she replied politely as she shifted around him, looking for an escape route, someone else she could suddenly develop the urgent need to speak with.

Unfortunately, luck wasn't on her side. Everyone's attention now appeared to be focused towards the stage where Tex stood with a microphone in his hand. Feeling obliged to stand still and pay attention, Anna was dismayed to feel Handy Andy brush up alongside her.

'Could I have your attention for one moment please?' Tex began, flashing a killer smile around the room. Anna could almost hear the collective swoon of all the females there, his soft drawl was practically X-rated.

'First, I would like to thank you all so much for turning up here this evening, it means a lot. Second, I must thank Forresters Outside Catering for the fabulous buffet they have provided. And my thanks also go to local architects Hanson & Williams for the excellent scale model in the centre there. Perhaps you could join me in a small round of applause.'

Everyone seemed more than happy to join in, Anna noted. Tex had obviously been working the room well leading up to this little speech.

'You will see from the display,' Tex continued, 'that I intend to open a contemporary restaurant: high-class food for the working man's pocket. Not a pizza delivery service with a horde of mopeds 'whining up and down' the road, as some of you might fear.' A little ripple of laughter circulated.

Anna felt a flush race to her face as he fixed his eyes on her, a hint of amusement playing at the corners of his mouth. He so knew what he was doing. To her relief, he looked away and carried on speaking, telling the attentive listeners how he was looking forward to being part of the community, that there was enough room for everyone, and how pleased he was to be putting something back into the local economy, jobs for local people, and so on.

God, he was good. By the time he had finished, the whole audience was clapping and smiling broadly at him. Mission complete it would seem.

'So thank you again for coming,' he said as the applause died down. 'I'm looking forward to getting to know you all much better.' His eyes swept the room, coming to rest at Anna, as another flutter of clapping spread throughout the guests.

'Smarmy Yank,' muttered Andy, leaning into Anna and snaking his arm around her waist.

She resisted the urge to point out the irony of this statement, and attempted to wriggle free.

'What say me and you slip away for a quiet drink at the Kings Head?' Andy suggested, tightening his grip on her waist and running a finger down her arm.

Anna shuddered but tried to retain a degree of professionalism. 'I don't think that's a good idea, Andy. Thanks all the same.'

'You're not knocking me back again, are you?' A frown folded over his face. 'I wouldn't want to have to complain to Howard about the lack of service.'

'Andy, can you stop this please?' He had been trying for the past six months, on and off, to get her to go on a date with him. It just wasn't happening. Ever. Purposefully, she took hold of his hand and prised it from her waist. 'As I've said before, I don't mix business with pleasure.' Not that he would be a pleasure by any stretch of the imagination.

'Oh, come on, Anna.' He went to take hold of her again, but now that everyone was milling around once more, Anna seized her opportunity.

Spinning on her heel to avoid his groping hand, she propelled herself forward and found herself running straight into the chest of Tex.

Chapter Two

Tex wrapped his arms round her as she bundled into him. He couldn't have planned it better if he had tried. Hugging her tight to his chest, he appreciated the feel of her curves against him. He grinned down at her.

'We seem to be making a habit of this,' he said.

'Maybe. Trouble is, this morning, I thought I had bumped into Tex. Now I seem to have bumped into Nico Garcia.'

'And which one do you prefer?' He noticed she hadn't tried to wriggle free.

'I'm not sure yet. Although I do know someone who isn't a contender.' She jerked her head backwards.

Tex had already spoken to the castle curator earlier in the evening and had also clocked him pestering Anna. In fact, he had just been on his way over to rescue her. Again.

Releasing her from his hold, but catching her hand in his, he smiled politely at the brooding curator. 'Would you mind excusing us, I need to speak to Anna about the tour guides. Thank you.'

He didn't wait for an answer, instead plucking a glass of wine from a passing waiter's tray, he whisked her away through the guests to the back of the hall.

'I had it all under control there, you know,' she spoke, after a rather large gulp of her wine.

Tex nodded. 'Of course you did.'

'I did!' She took another sip, trying to hide a small smile of embarrassment behind the glass.

Tex didn't miss it. 'Look, I wanted to speak to you anyway,' he began. 'About earlier. I didn't say anything because I was curious to hear an unbiased and honest opinion of what folks were feeling around here. I was going to tell you. Honest!'

She eyed him sceptically. 'Okay, so what if I tell you I'm not really Anna but my name's Sheila and I'm the local planning officer? I was just preparing a report to uphold an objection against the development of this building.'

What the…! He felt himself draw back to look at her again through fresh eyes. 'You serious?' Jeez, she looked it.

Then she broke into a huge smile and laughed out loud. Tex felt the air expel from his lungs, and found himself laughing too.

'Oh, your face,' she said once she had calmed down. 'Got you going there for a moment. Serves you right.'

Tex shook his head. He was in no position to complain. He deserved that.

'You two look like you're having fun,' came Jamie's voice as he wandered over with Yvonne.

'Don't ask.'

'Do you and Tex already know each other?' Yvonne asked Anna, accepting the glass of wine Tex had summoned over.

'Not really. We did briefly meet this morning. You could say he saved my life.' Anna gave Tex a grateful smile.

'Twice,' Tex added.

Jamie patted Tex's back. 'The all-American hero.'

Tex shrugged. 'Hey, what can I say?'

'So do you work around here?' Jamie asked.

Anna repeated what she had told Tex that morning, adding, 'I also do a bit of work from home, translating electronic manuals or legal documents. Nothing particularly exciting, but it's all work.'

'You're a busy lady,' said Tex, surprised. She hadn't mentioned all that this morning.

'Just three small jobs, no different to working full-time at one.'

'So as a tour guide, do you speak any other languages?' asked Yvonne, exchanging a glance with her husband.

'German and French.'

Tex gave Anna a little nudge, whispering theatrically in her ear, 'Watch out, he'll be trying to employ you next.'

'Interesting,' mused Jamie. 'I run a relocation company, primarily for clients who are moving to the UK from overseas. It's a sort of handholding, fix-it service for foreigners working, visiting or relocating here. I use bilingual staff as some of my clients, especially their spouses, can't speak enough English to deal with things like banking, property purchases, schools for their children etc. We basically help them in any way they need it where the language might prove a barrier.'

'That sounds interesting. Have you got clients locally then?' asked Anna.

'That will be me,' put in Tex.

'Oh, I thought you were just friends.' Anna looked a mixture of confused and embarrassed.

'We're both. BFFs, as you girls would say,' grinned Jamie, putting his arm round Tex and pretending to plant a kiss on his cheek.

'Sometimes I feel like the gooseberry,' said Yvonne.

'A real bromance then.' A small giggle escaped Anna.

While Jamie and Yvonne laughed at the joke, Tex looked blankly at the three of them, which just made them all laugh even more.

'Think of it as brotherly love,' explained Jamie. 'Bromance. Girls find it highly amusing.'

'Oh, not amusing,' teased Anna, 'more like sweet.'

'Yes, sweet,' agreed Yvonne. 'You two are so cute.' She gave it her best coochy-coo voice.

'Hey, don't knock it,' winked Jamie.

As the four of them chatted easily for a while, discussing the local town of Arundel, nearby Chichester and Goodwood Racecourse, which Jamie had attended recently, Anna seemed relaxed and at ease in their company, Tex thought, aware that he was glancing at her more than was necessary.

He felt the familiar buzz he always got when the chase was on. First though, it looked like he still needed to get rid of the castle curator who had just sidled up to Anna.

'Apologies to interrupt, but have you finished here now?' The curator's hand rested on Anna's back. Tex felt himself bristle unexpectedly at the gesture. He was about to tell this slimeball to back off when Anna spoke.

'Is it important, Andy? Can't it wait until tomorrow? I could call over to the castle in the morning, if you like?'

They were speaking in low tones but Tex could just about make out what was being said. He studied her face. He couldn't tell from the expression whether she meant it or was just trying to get rid of him. He checked himself and said nothing.

Andy now looked irritated. 'As I said earlier, I'm sure Howard wouldn't want to find out you've been neglecting me.'

Tex studied Anna's face for an indicator. He still couldn't read her, although he did notice she was fiddling with a couple of rings on her right hand, rapidly twisting them back and forth.

'But this isn't work's time, so I don't think it counts,' she replied firmly.

'Let's make it count.' The impatience in Andy's voice was thinly disguised, the leer in his eyes even less hidden.

Something inside Tex snapped. He'd had a bellyful of this Andy guy already. He stepped forward, his arm cutting between Anna and the curator, then hooked the surprised man away.

'I think the lady doesn't want to be bothered and I've still got some business to discuss with her, so why don't you be a good boy and take a hike.'

The surprised look on Andy's face and his mouth flopping open in astonishment sent a feeling of satisfaction through Tex. He gave Andy a shove towards the exit and watched him disappear out of the door, before turning triumphantly to Anna.

Damn it! She did not look impressed.

'Very caveman-like,' she said evenly. 'I was handling it myself actually.'

No, she definitely wasn't impressed. 'He's a jerk,' he replied.

'That's as maybe, but he was my jerk, and I could do without him complaining to my boss.' She looked at him reproachfully. 'And you could do without making any enemies, which is what I thought tonight was all about.'

She had a point, but he didn't think some nerdy castle curator was too much to worry about.

'Will you get into trouble? With work, I mean,' asked Yvonne.

Anna shrugged. 'I'll find out Monday when I'm next in the office.' She gave Tex a small smile. 'I suppose I should say thank you. Again.'

He wondered if it was necessary for him to smile so widely, but he seemed to have lost control of his facial muscles. 'This is becoming a habit.'

'Look, Anna,' said Jamie, 'if you have any bother at work and fancy a change, give me a call.' He took his wallet out from his inside pocket and extracted a business card. 'Here, take this, it would be good to chat.'

Anna took the card. 'Thanks, I might just do that.'

'I was going to say I don't have any lecherous clients,' said Jamie, 'but then I remembered him!' He nodded at Tex, who was relieved to see Anna grin, the awkwardness passing.

'I suppose I had better go. I've got to get back to Chichester,' said Anna after a while.

'I'll walk you to your car,' said Tex.

'Don't forget my offer,' Jamie called after her.

There was a chill in the night air as they stepped outside. Anna shivered, wishing she had brought a cardigan with her. As if reading her mind, Tex slipped off his jacket and draped it over her shoulders. She could smell the citrus-fresh fragrance of his aftershave on the collar.

'You don't have to walk me. I'll be fine.'

Tex smiled. 'I know I don't have to, but I want to.'

She could feel his hand resting between her shoulder blades as he ushered her across the road, and he kept it there as they walked.

'Well, this is my car,' said Anna as they reached her battered old blue Fiesta. As she stood in front of him, she suddenly felt self-conscious.

He cast an acknowledging eye over her vehicle before turning back to her. Anna didn't know what to say next. Meeting his steady gaze, she felt tongue-tied, like a teenager on her first date. She had forgiven him for tricking her earlier and had enjoyed his company this evening, very much aware that she had been unable to stop herself looking at him. A couple of times when he had caught her watching him, it had caused her to look hurriedly away, embarrassed. Despite this, she had looked back again and again. Like an addiction, she couldn't help letting her gaze linger on him. Those eyes were so welcoming, they seemed to be able to smile all on their own, and as she had listened to the timbre of his soft drawl, it were as if her eardrums were being caressed by his voice. It was enough to give her an eargasm.

Realising that she was doing much the same again now, she quickly turned her attention to her feet. This was awkward.

Sneaking a look back up at him, she saw that Tex was now peering at her feet too.

'What?' she said worriedly.

'Nothing. I was just wondering what was so interesting on the floor.' For a second or two he looked deadly serious then, looking up, his whole face broke into a broad grin.

Anna laughed. He had such a lovely smile that seemed to reflect in his eyes. 'Thanks for... well, you know... rescuing me...'

'Can I see you again?' he asked gently, interrupting.

She caught her breath. He wanted to see her again – yay! The feeling of joy competed with the nervousness in her stomach.

Since Mark had left a year ago, she had only been on two dates, courtesy of Zoe, her sister-in-law. Neither date had been her choice, but Zoe had gone through a matchmaking phase last year and decided that the two candidates were just perfect for Anna. Apparently. Apparently not, as it turned out. Anna had soon got rid of them by pointing out that she was still married and had a teenage son. It was a good tactic to deter any undesirables.

Tex must have misread her silence. 'It's okay, you don't have to say yes.' He lifted her left hand and ran his thumb along her bare third finger. 'Sorry, I assumed you were single.'

'I am. Well, sort of. Oh God, I'm making a mess of this.' She took a deep breath. 'I'm separated, have been for the past year and I have a teenage son.'

'Okay, separated is good,' smiled Tex, still holding her hand. 'As for a son, that's not unusual, so why do I feel you are still hesitant?'

'I don't get out much,' she said, then catching the look of amusement in Tex's eyes, found herself laughing again. 'Oh, that sounds bad.'

'Hey, that's cool. We should remedy the situation though.' Letting go of her hand, he took out his iPhone. 'I'll ring you, if that's okay with you?'

'It's very okay.'

Anna slipped his jacket off her shoulders as he tapped the number into his phone, double-checking he had it right.

'I'll call you,' he said smiling, taking the jacket. He paused as his hand brushed hers, his face still, his eyes even more still as he gazed at her. Anna felt her stomach knot as for a moment she held her breath, willing him to kiss her. He seemed to have the same idea, and in an instant, he was drawing her towards him. When his lips made contact with hers, it were as if she had been tasered, a shockwave shooting through the very core of her being.

'Are you sure you have to go home?' he murmured when he eventually pulled away.

She nodded. 'Sorry.' That didn't even begin to cover it.

He let out a long sigh before stooping for another kiss.

'Oh man, this is no good. I'm gonna have to go,' he groaned as he disentangled himself.

As she drove home, Anna's tummy was performing all sorts of gymnastics at the thought of a date with Tex. She hoped he would ring. He hadn't seemed too bothered about her ex, Mark, or the fact that she had a son, so that was a good sign.

Not that Mark should be a problem; he was over five thousand miles away building a new life for himself. Her and Mark were very much separated, her marital status a mere technicality.

Chapter Three

Anna was thankful that the last group of foreign exchange students hadn't wanted to ask any questions at the end of their guided tour of Chichester Cathedral. Spurred on by the thought of a chilled glass of wine at the Fish and Fly tonight with her sister-in-law, she picked up her bag and headed towards the main entrance.

It was then that she saw him. He was just standing there, grinning at her obvious shock. For a moment she thought her legs would give way.

'Hey,' Mark murmured, as if stroking her with the word.

Anna stared back, went to speak but her mouth and throat had completely dried up. What the hell was *he* doing here? He was still as good looking as the day he had left, all six foot of him. His blonde hair, the tips now white from the LA sun, tanned complexion and Wedgwood blue eyes. The teeth, however, weren't quite as Anna remembered. Now they seemed whiter, and possibly straighter.

'Hi,' she finally managed to say.

'You're looking well. You cut your hair.'

Anna's hand automatically went to her now short hair. Her break-up haircut. Of course, Mark hadn't seen it. She knew he preferred long hair, that was part of the satisfaction of getting it cut.

'It's nice,' he continued as he took a step closer, his arms slightly open.

Anna stiffened. How do you greet your estranged husband? A full-on embrace? Definitely not. Handshaking? Too formal. Maybe a quick hug and an air kiss. Before she could decide, Mark was upon her. Hands holding hers, moving in closer for a kiss on the cheek, a quick hug, before looking directly into her eyes.

'It's good to see you,' he said.

For a moment neither spoke. It was Anna who broke the gaze first and took not only a physical step back, but a mental one too. She didn't like the way Mark could almost put a spell on her, even after everything that had happened. She needed to pull herself together. He may still be able to melt her with his looks but she needed to remember what was underneath.

'What are you doing here?' She hoped she sounded more confident than she felt.

'Came to see you, of course.'

'No, *here*. How did you know I'd be here? Why didn't you phone? Does Luke know you're back?' Her mind was on overload. As the questions came tumbling out like an upended jar of marbles, she was barely able to keep up with her thoughts.

'Hey, hey, slow down,' Mark gave her a small grin. 'One question at a time.'

'Well?'

'I called at the house. Spoke to Luke.'

'Oh God, Mark, why didn't you wait for me before you saw him? I could have warned him in advance.'

'I don't think you have to warn my own son about me.'

She ignored the edge in his voice. 'You know what I mean.'

'Yeah, I do. Anyway, he was delighted to see me, as it happens. He told me where to find you.'

'And your reason for coming back?'

'Didn't know I needed one. But seeing as you asked, I thought I'd come over and see you and Luke. I thought I could spend some time with him.' He flashed a boyish grin at her. 'Thought I would surprise you.'

'You thought a lot of things,' said Anna before walking out through the glass doors. Like a pit pony coming out into daylight, she squinted as she was momentarily struck by the brightness. She popped her sunglasses on. She could hear Mark's footsteps quicken to catch up with her, falling in next to her as she hurried across the flagstones, up the steps, past the statue of St Richard, around the bell tower and down the path that ran along the side of the cathedral.

'Where are you staying?' she asked, without breaking her stride or looking at him.

'Err, well, there's a bit of a problem there. Everywhere's really busy. I didn't decide to come until the last minute so didn't make any arrangements.'

'Unfortunate.'

'I thought I could stay with you. At the house,' he said casually.

'Stay with me?' echoed Anna, stopping dead. They were at the Market Cross in the centre of Chichester, where the four pedestrian roads met. A great meeting spot, a favourite with teenagers, and today foreign exchange students in particular. Anna could hear the gabble of French and Spanish, mixed in with the English voices of other tourists and shoppers. She took off her sunglasses and looked at Mark. Was he being serious?

'It will give me a chance to spend some quality time with Luke,' said Mark, a defensive tone creeping in. 'I haven't seen him in ages.'

Anna bristled. 'A whole year.'

'I do my best,' said Mark lamely, 'but let's not get into all that now. I'm here to try and make up for lost time. Come on, it'll be fine.'

'I don't think it's a good idea. I haven't got enough room anyway.'

'I can kip on the sofa, not a problem,' replied Mark Then

winking, said, 'Failing that, I'm sure we could both still share the same bed, in a purely platonic way of course.'

'There must be a B&B somewhere, or what about a Travelodge?' said Anna, choosing to ignore the last comment. Replacing her sunglasses, relieved that her feet responded, she headed down East Street towards home.

'Come on, Anna. What's the big deal? Besides, you know Luke will be really pleased if I stay with you and him.'

'You can't just waltz back into our lives, acting like everything is hunky-dory,' said Anna, looking straight ahead, still walking. 'You haven't exactly been the greatest advertisement for fatherhood. The occasional phone call or sometimes an email.'

'I was hoping you'd be a bit more understanding.' There was a coolness in his voice. 'I didn't want to have to force you to agree but you seem to be forgetting one tiny detail. It is actually *my* house. I don't think you've got a lot of choice. I am entitled to stay in my own home, you know.'

'Your house, but my home. It's never been your home. You bought it for me and Luke. No, you're not staying. In fact, let's go back into town and find you a B&B.'

'You'll have to pay then. I can't afford it. Money's a bit tight.'

'Money's a bit tight yet you've managed to afford a flight here! Don't give me that, Mark. You're not broke and you're not staying with me.'

'Thing is, my case is already there. Let's go and get it and tell Luke you're kicking me out.'

She knew that he was fully aware she didn't have the heart to do it, not because she felt sorry for him, but because Luke would be hurt. Anna let out a sigh and ground to a halt.

'You're such a shit at times.' She paused before finally agreeing. 'Okay, but you're on the sofa.'

'That's my girl. You know it makes sense.' He had the effrontery to grin and then hug her. An embrace that he held just a moment too long for her liking. 'Come on then, let's get home. I'm starving. What's for tea?'

'You're letting him do it to you again,' grumbled Zoe. Anna could hear the irritation in her voice over the phone. Zoe was more than just the wife of Anna's brother, she had become a friend and confidante over the years, especially so when Anna's marriage was in its darkest hour.

'I don't have a lot of choice,' said Anna in a low voice, looking over her shoulder to make sure her bedroom door was shut properly.

'You're letting him take control. Christ, he's only been back for ten minutes and already he's calling the shots.'

'It's not like that, honestly,' protested Anna, dropping her skirt and blouse into the linen bin. 'He's Luke's father, I can't get in the way of that. Hang on one sec.' She put the phone on the bed as she quickly pulled on a fresh t-shirt from the drawer. 'Okay, I'm back.'

'Well, don't pretend you're happy about him staying,' said Zoe.

'I'm not. Look, I'd better go, I've left him downstairs while I've nipped up to get changed out of my work clothes. I'm really sorry about tonight.'

'That's all right. It's karaoke night at the pub, so we won't be missing much.'

'I'd say we've had a lucky escape then,' said Anna, as she tucked the phone under her chin and wriggled into her jeans.

'Look, you do what you feel is best, but please don't let Mark walk all over you. Do it because *you* want to, not because he wants you to,' said Zoe. Her voice softened. 'All I'm saying is to be on your guard. You know what a sweet-talking charmer he can be.'

Having had a rather restless night's sleep, Anna woke early and tiptoed downstairs. Mark was still fast asleep on the sofa but she was surprised to find Luke already up and sitting at the kitchen table.

'Morning.' Anna dropped a kiss on top of her son's head. 'You okay? Thought you'd still be tucked up in bed, fast asleep.' She pushed the kitchen door closed and spoke softly so as not to disturb Mark.

Luke shrugged. 'Couldn't sleep.'

Anna filled the kettle and flicked it on to boil. 'Are you okay with your dad being here?' She took a seat next to him so they could speak quietly.

'Yeah,' course I'm pleased to see him. It just feels a bit odd.'

'He's been away for a year now, it's bound to feel a bit strange him being around.' Anna could identify with that feeling. It felt quite surreal last night as the three of them sat around the kitchen table sharing a Chinese takeaway.

'He seems different,' continued Luke. 'A bit more interested in things, maybe.'

'It's been just you and me for a long time now, I suppose it's bound to feel a bit odd, but it's good he's taking an interest in what you've been doing, isn't it?'

Luke nodded and gave his mum a small smile. 'Yeah. I mean, even when Dad was still living with us, it was almost like he wasn't. Even then it was just, like, me and you. It was always you who gave me lifts, always you who came to parents' evenings, sports days, that sort of thing. Dad was always too busy.'

Anna nodded. She couldn't really deny it. Mark's involvement with Luke had been sporadic. He was there when it suited him and him alone. More times than she cared to remember, she had felt like a single parent. When Mark had decided to move to America, it hadn't really changed anything. Her and Luke had carried on as they were.

'I don't know how long your dad is back for,' began Anna. She didn't want Luke getting his hopes up that Mark would be around for any length of time. 'Just try to take a day at a time with him. He may have to go back for work or something, you know that, don't you?'

Luke gave wry smile. 'It's all right, Mum, I know what you're trying to say.'

'Do you?'

'I know I can't depend on him totally, not at the moment anyway,' replied Luke, slowly spinning his mobile round on the table with his finger. 'But I want to give him the chance. You never know, things may be better now.'

Anna slipped her arm around Luke's shoulder and gave him a squeeze. 'Okay, just don't get your hopes too high, that's all I'm saying.'

The sound of raised voices and shrieking seeped out through the front door as Anna stood on the doorstep, waiting for her knock to be answered.

'Morning, Titch,' smiled Nathan, opening the door and standing to one side so she could come in.

'Morning, Lofty.' It was a joke they had shared since childhood.

At nearly six feet tall, her brother Nathan took after their father with his athletic physique, fine-tuned by his career in fitness training. Anna, on the other hand, at five feet two, with a small petite frame and waiflike in her appearance, took after their more delicate mother.

'Sounds fun in here this morning.' Anna headed towards the kitchen where the noise of squabbling children seemed to be reaching fever pitch. 'Morning everyone,' she said as she poked her head round the door.

'I don't want Coco Pops,' whined Alex, one half of Nathan's

seven-year-old twin boys. 'I want Boulders.'

'Just eat them now,' sighed Zoe as she held a warmed bottle of milk in Emily's mouth with one hand, and with the other began pouring another bowl of Coco Pops for Jake, the other half of the duo. She glanced up as Anna walked in. 'Well, good morning to you. What are you doing here so early?' Then with a sudden anxious look on her face, 'Everything all right?'

'Fine, absolutely fine,' said Anna reassuringly. She took the box of cereal from Zoe and finished pouring them into the bowl. 'Here you go, Jake. Where's the milk?'

Jake wasn't paying attention, instead embarking on a tug-of-war with his three-year-old brother, Henry. Jake wanted the milk, but so did Henry. Giving the carton one final tug, Jake managed to pull the milk free from Henry's grasp. The momentum took Jake by surprise and the milk flew out of his hand, splashing all over the table and sending a cup of tea into Zoe's lap.

'Oh, for God's sake!' Zoe cried. 'That's so naughty, look what you've done!'

Baby Emily began screaming in protest at having her breakfast whipped away as Zoe dropped the bottle while trying, and failing, to avoid the tea.

'Hey! Hey! Hey! Boys!' commanded Nathan as he strode across the kitchen. 'That's enough.'

The boys exchanged a look and immediately sat quiet, as did Henry. Nathan picked up the bottle of milk and ran it under the tap to clean the teat before quickly popping it back into Emily's mouth. Peace.

'Could have done with you down here five minutes earlier,' muttered Zoe, simultaneously trying to mop up the milk on the table and sponge out the tea from her dressing gown. 'I expect you've got to rush off to work now.'

'Here, Zoe, let me clean that up,' insisted Anna. 'You sort yourself out.'

'So how's your house guest?' asked Zoe as she dabbed at the tea stain.

'We had a Chinese last night and then he pretty much fell asleep. Jet-lagged. Left him asleep on the sofa this morning.'

'I think you're asking for trouble,' grumbled Nathan, looking at his watch. 'Oh Christ, I've got to go. I'm going to be late for my client. We've got a five-k run this morning. Here, Zoe, take Emily.'

'Always rushing off,' complained Zoe, lifting Emily from Nathan's shoulder. She popped a kiss on her daughter's head and put her back in her baby chair. 'You sit there, darling. Mummy's got to sort out those brothers of yours. Daddy's clearing off again, just when I could do with his help. Perfect.'

Anna glanced at Nathan who gave a small shake of his head, tension etched in his face.

'I'll be back at lunchtime. Bye, love.' He went to kiss Zoe but she turned away, busying herself with filling the kettle.

'Right. Fine.'

Anna waited until she heard the front door close. 'I'll make the tea, Zoe, you sit there for a bit. Is everything all right?'

Zoe looked thoughtfully out of the window for a moment before answering. 'The official party line is yes, everything is fine. Nathan's personal training business is really taking off. I'm busy looking after the children and the house, sipping coffee with girl-friends and flicking through glossy home furnishing magazines.' Zoe let out a big sigh.

'And unofficially?' prompted Anna.

'Unofficially, Nathan's working all the hours God sends to keep a roof over our heads so I don't have to go back to work. We hardly see each other. I just feel so tired all the time, it's a struggle to do anything.' She tucked a strand of hair behind her ear. 'I am a complete wreck, suffering from sleep deprivation, who can just about manage to pull on my baggy tracksuit and tie my hair in a ponytail.'

'Is it really that bad?'

'Most of the time. When you cancelled last night my first thought was, oh good, I don't have to bother getting all done up, I can just have a bath and go to bed. I was asleep by nine.'

Normally, Zoe was upbeat and positive but since Emily had been born, she had seemed less so, thought Anna as she looked at her sister-in-law. Her eyes looked heavy and the black circles underneath them were highlighting the bags that were beginning to become part of her daily feature.

'It's natural to feel a bit run-down. You only had a baby four months ago.'

'Some days I don't even want to get up. I feel like it's Groundhog Day most of the time.' Zoe pulled her dressing gown further around her, retying the belt. 'When Nathan gets in all I want to do is go to bed to sleep.'

Anna sensed that a 'pull yourself together' team talk wouldn't help Zoe at this precise moment. A more practical approach would probably be best, Anna thought. In her head she began to formulate a plan of action.

Chapter Four

Anna was convinced Mark was up to something but she couldn't for the life of her think what it was. She had woken up on Sunday morning to the smell of bacon and eggs cooking. Mark had made brunch for all three of them, something hitherto unheard of. Then, later, they had wandered down to the Fish and Fly pub and sat out in the courtyard garden sharing a bowl of chips. She had a glass of wine, while Luke nursed a coke. The conversation up until then had been easy-going, mostly involving Luke: his schoolwork, his band and his GCSEs that were looming in a couple of months. On the whole, it had been okay until Mark took a phone call. He had moved out of earshot, leaving her to watch him pace the car park with animated gestures. That was thirty minutes ago, and ever since he seemed agitated and restless, drumming his fingers or tapping his foot.

'You okay, Mark?' asked Anna, feeling uneasy by his mood change.

'Of course I am. Why the hell wouldn't I be?' he snapped back.

'Sorry, you just seem a bit on edge…'

'Just drop it, Anna.' He got up and strode off towards the toilets.

'What's got into him?' asked Luke, exchanging a look with his mother. 'He was all right until he took that call.'

Anna shrugged. 'I've no idea. Best not say anything again.'

Mark came back a few minutes later and sat down, smiling at them. 'That's better. All okay? Good. Another drink?'

At home after returning from the pub, Anna felt even more troubled about Mark and his sour mood swing. Yes, he used to fly off the handle from time to time throughout their marriage, but she had never known it to be so sudden, or such a dramatic swing.

Late on Monday morning, Anna was sitting in a coffee shop in Chichester, phone in one hand and Jamie's business card in the other. She hadn't heard from Tex yet and she couldn't help feeling disappointed.

She flicked the business card over and over again in her fingers. Jamie had sounded like he'd meant it when he had said she should give him a call about work. She didn't actually have much choice. Not after her meeting with Howard earlier. She should have just kept her mouth shut. She should have just let Howard give her a roasting over her behaviour towards Andy. She should have just nodded and apologised. What she shouldn't have done was to tell Howard just what a creep Andy was and that Howard should be backing up his staff. She also shouldn't have said words to the effect of 'over her dead body' about taking Andy out to lunch. And she most definitely shouldn't have told Howard that if his attitude was her word against Andy's then he could stick his sodding job.

Ten minutes later and with a feeling of trepidation, Anna left the coffee shop. It had been a successful call. Jamie had sounded genuinely pleased to hear from her. They had agreed that she should travel up to his home in Surrey tomorrow.

'Most of my work is done over the phone,' he had explained. 'Any meetings are usually at the client's house or hotel. I tend to go to my clients rather than them come to me, it's part of making the service professional and elite. I use my office at home to co-ordinate my staff. Yvonne helps out with the paperwork.'

31

It occurred to Anna that she should have done a bit of research about Jamie's company before she had phoned. She would have a look at his website when she got home, then at least she would be better prepared when she met him tomorrow. She also had a document waiting to be translated by Friday, so she'd have to make a start on that this afternoon, because Wednesday and Thursday she was working in the tea rooms. She could see a few late nights of translating coming up. Still, she shouldn't complain, especially not now she'd just lost one of her jobs.

When she and Mark had separated, they had sold their bigger Southampton home and Mark had bought this one for her and Luke. She hadn't wanted to stay in Southampton, she'd only gone there with Mark because as a professional footballer, he needed to be near his club. Once his career had been deemed over, due to an accident, they no longer had any ties with the city. Anna had chosen to return to Chichester, where she had grown up, needing to feel she belonged somewhere, getting comfort from familiar places and people.

It was only a two-minute walk from the centre of Chichester to her little, two-up two-down, mews cottage. No matter whatever the weather – be it a bright April morning like today or a cold, dark winter's afternoon – the sight of her blue wooden door at 2 Coach House Cottages always made her feel happy.

She approached her front door, and as usual her neighbour Mrs Meekham twitched her net curtain. Anna waved and smiled, thinking if you looked up the expression Neighbourhood Watch in the dictionary, it would simply say 'Mrs Meekham'. She put the key in the lock and turned it gently before creeping in. The front door opened straight into the living room and she didn't want to disturb Mark.

Much to her surprise, he was actually up, showered and dressed, judging by the two wet towels tossed idly on the back of the sofa, and was now in the kitchen, talking on his mobile.

'Yes that would be great. I'll give you a call when it's convenient to come round. I just need to make sure…' He stopped in mid-flow as he turned and saw Anna. 'Err, look, can I give you a call back? … No everything's fine... not at the moment… Yep... Yep... that's right… Okay, cheers then. Bye.' He slid his phone shut and thrust it into his pocket.

'You didn't need to hang up on my account,' said Anna as she picked up the towels.

'I didn't.'

'Really?'

'Yes. Really.' The slight irritation in his voice didn't go unnoticed. 'Just business. Nothing for you to worry about.'

Famous last words, thought Anna suspiciously. He was definitely being shifty. Perhaps he was planning to dash off back to America, something that she would be most happy about, but on the flip side, Luke would be crushed.

'How long are you here for?' she asked.

'Not sure, a couple of weeks,' responded Mark vaguely. 'Thought I'd go and see my parents at the weekend.'

'That'll be nice. You could take Luke with you.'

Mark looked slightly startled at the suggestion. It was obvious the thought hadn't actually crossed his mind.

'Yeah, I was just about to suggest that myself,' he said rather too brightly.

'Good, that's that sorted,' smiled Anna. Then changing the subject before Mark could think of an excuse to wriggle out of it, she said, 'I have an appointment in Surrey tomorrow, so you and Luke will have to look after yourselves. I just need to sort out a few things about work.'

'Okay, no problem.'

Towels put away, Anna sat down at the kitchen table and

typed Jamie's website address into the laptop. The company logo appeared, a fancy hand drawn with wavy lines reaching out across an image of the world. She skimmed over the homepage, speed-reading. Relocation packages, various different levels of service – Silver, Gold, Platinum. Specialising in international relocations and assistance.

Anna flicked around the website, jotting down some things she thought she should remember. It might help to impress at tomorrow's interview. Then she clicked on 'About Us'. There was a picture of Jamie smiling easily at the camera, his fair hair cut short with a slight side parting. Scrolling down, there was a picture of a footballer in a red and white kit standing next to Jamie. She read the caption underneath it. *Patrick Ardoin, Arsenal FC.* Anna assumed that Jamie had links with football clubs; it would make sense, as there were so many foreign players these days. She vaguely remembered Mark talking about Ardoin, saying what a good defender he was.

As a pro-footballer in his younger days, Mark had always been appreciative of Arsenal's 'rock solid back line'. Unfortunately, Mark's premiership career had only consisted of six first team starts.

Anna felt that familiar pang she always experienced when she thought of the accident that had not only brought about the end of Mark's playing career, but had also caused her to miscarry what would have been their second child. Another little boy. She closed her eyes and tried to shake the thoughts out of her head. She hated thinking about the last few years of their marriage; it was too painful. She turned her attention back to Jamie's website and clicked on 'Testimonials and Clients'.

'What you looking at?' asked Mark, peering over Anna's shoulder.

Anna jumped, unaware that Mark was there. She snapped the lid down on the laptop.

'Trunky want a bun?' she teased, well, half-teased.

'That's a pretty impressive CV,' said Jamie, putting down the printout of Anna's résumé she had emailed the day before. 'I was particularly impressed by the fact that you completed your Modern Languages degree through the Open University. That couldn't have been easy with a young child.'

'No, it wasn't at times,' acknowledged Anna. 'But going to a brick uni wasn't an option.'

'Work with the tour company is definitely over then?'

'Well, put it like this. My P45 landed on the doormat within twenty-four hours of the meeting. So I think it's pretty safe to say I no longer work for them.'

Jamie leant back in his chair, his fingers steepled. 'I can't guarantee work day in, day out initially. It quite often depends on whom you're assigned to, where they are located, whether it's a one-off assignment or an ongoing working arrangement. For example, you could be assigned to a family who are relocating from abroad and need lots of things sorting – moving home, schools, bank arrangements and so on – in which case you would be with them for several weeks or even months. On the other hand, it may be a one-off business meeting, or you may be needed to translate or help interview a live-in nanny or gardener. Something like that could be one day or a few days.'

'It sounds fine. I've still got the couple of mornings I do at the tea rooms midweek.'

'The work here doesn't always involve translating. Sometimes it's a bit more like PA work. Are you okay with that too?'

She nodded. 'Absolutely. It sounds great.' She genuinely liked the sound of it. She may even be able to give up the two mornings at the tea rooms.

'Okay, let's give it a go, shall we?' Jamie sat forward and tapped at the keyboard on his laptop. Then he paused, as if struck by a thought. 'The PA work I mentioned, you all right working for Tex?'

Anna felt a little flutter in her stomach. Working for Tex? Could she work for him? Then again, could she say no to Jamie? Would that jeopardise her chances of getting this job? She realised Jamie was waiting for an answer.

'Err… yes, that's okay by me.'

'You sure?'

'Absolutely. He seems nice enough, I'm certain we can work together well.' She wasn't sure if Jamie was convinced.

'I can always assign you to someone else, it's just that Tex thought someone with local knowledge would be ideal.'

'What, he asked for me?'

'Pretty much. I told him I was interviewing you today and that's when he suggested it.' Jamie looked evenly at her. 'I must admit, I have my reservations. You know he can be very charming.'

Anna felt the flutter in her stomach turn into a knot. Jamie was warning her Tex was a charmer. A ladies' man. She looked directly at Jamie. 'I'm sure he can be, but don't worry, I never mix business with pleasure.'

A timely knock at the door brought the conversation to a halt. Yvonne poked her head in the room and smiled when she saw Anna.

'Hi! How are you?' she enquired.

'I'm fine thanks. You?'

'Great, thanks.' Waving some papers in her hand, Yvonne looked over at her husband. 'Thought you might need these. Time sheets, expenses forms, personnel form.'

'Excellent! What would I do without you? Actually, while you're here perhaps you can go through them with Anna. You're much better at that sort of thing than me.' Jamie gave Yvonne his best angelic smile and fluttered his eyes at her.

'Quit with the puppy dog eyes, Dixon,' joked Yvonne, then coming into the office, beckoned Anna. 'Come on, you're with the Queen of Forms now. Let's sit over there on the sofa and go through them.'

'Thank you, darling.' Jamie grinned at his wife.

Anna dutifully followed Yvonne over to the black cube sofa and began going through the various personnel questions with her.

'Okay, that's all done,' announced Yvonne after fifteen minutes. 'All explained and filled out as necessary.' She put the form Anna had just completed into a wire tray marked 'filing' on Jamie's desk.

'Thanks ever so much for this,' said Anna as she was leaving. Funny how it now seemed to be a double-edged sword. And one she didn't want to get cut by.

Chapter Five

'So there you have it. I am now going to be working for a relocation company and my first job is in Arundel. How ideal is that?'
Anna said to Mark and Luke as the three of them sat at the table,
having finished their evening meal. 'Thought it was about time I
did something different. A new challenge.' She crossed her fingers
under the table at the lie, well, manipulation of the truth.

'Well done, Mum.'

'All I've got to do now is finish translating that document,' said
Anna, eyeing the green folder on the bookshelf. 'I'm not going to
put all my eggs in one basket. I'm still going to keep the translating work going.'

'Perhaps I should do something like this Jamie's doing,' mused
Mark as he broke off a piece of garlic bread. 'Sounds like he's
doing all right. A nice house in Surrey that must be worth a bob
or two. Working from home, just organising people. He must be
raking it in.'

'You're doing okay though, aren't you?' asked Anna. Somewhere
in the back of her mind alarm bells were ringing.

'Oh yeah, everything's fine,' responded Mark, then changed the
subject swiftly. 'Thought I'd visit my parents tomorrow.'

'Oh, right,' said Anna trying to keep up with the turn in conversation. 'What about Luke?' Mark looked blankly at her. 'You were

going to take him with you but he's got school tomorrow.'

'I can have the day off,' interjected Luke. 'Well, that's if Dad doesn't mind me going with him.' Luke looked at his dad expectantly.

'Of course you can, son. Not a problem at all,' said Mark.

'But, Luke, I don't know if that's a good idea,' began Anna.

'Come on, Mum, it's only one day,' argued Luke. 'How is one day going to hurt? It's hardly likely to affect my future career prospects, is it?'

Anna looked at Mark for some moral support, but he just shrugged and said, 'Don't look at me. I don't want to be brought into your row.'

'Mum! Why are you being so difficult and starting an argument?' said Luke grumpily. 'You always do it. Anyway, I'm going with Dad tomorrow and that's that.' To show that as far as he was concerned the matter was now closed, Luke clattered his cutlery down onto his plate and stood up. 'Don't spoil everything.' With that, he stormed off to his room, stomping on every stair as he went.

'Luke!'

'Just leave it, Anna,' said Mark frowning, agitatedly tapping the table with his fingers. 'It's only one sodding day.'

The following morning Anna saw Mark and Luke off. Well, just Luke really. She hated any bad feeling between her and her son and always liked to wipe the slate clean at the beginning of each day. She had rung Luke's school earlier that morning, excusing him on the pretence of illness. Thank goodness she could leave a message on the answerphone, it was much easier to lie to a machine than a real person.

'Give my regards to your grandparents,' said Anna, as Luke followed Mark out the door.

Luke gave his mum a smile and brief hug. 'Yeah, sure. See you later.'

Closing the door behind them, she turned and looked menacingly at the laptop and the electronics folder containing the document that she was translating.

'Right, here I come,' she said, marching purposefully over to the offending items.

Often the thought of the work was worse than the actual act, and quite soon, she was working steadily through the text. The morning was productive but the afternoon proved less so. Not only was she feeling tired after yesterday's travelling and interview, but the phone seemed to be on a personal mission to disrupt her concentration as many times as possible. Four times it rang within an hour and each was a complete waste of time. Fed up with so many interruptions by people trying to sell her something, the last one being from an estate agent wanting to make an appointment – Anna rudely slammed the phone down on him – she pulled the phone out of the wall to make sure no one disturbed her again.

She did, however, receive a text message on her mobile.

Hey! Looking forward to seeing you next week at work. Maybe we could get some lunch? Tex.

She looked thoughtfully at her phone while wrestling with conflicting feelings. She was happy she had a job and she was happy that Tex had messaged her, but on the other hand, she was disappointed that the job involved working with him. Much as she liked Tex, now he was going to be a client she couldn't afford to get involved. Beautiful eyes and an orgasmic voice or not. In the end, she didn't reply. It would be easier if she explained face to face.

'That's really great, sis,' said Nathan after Anna had finished telling him about her new job. 'A bit sudden though. I didn't know

40

you were looking for a change.'

'I wasn't really. It just came up. A great opportunity,' said Anna, holding her mobile to her ear as she looked out between the Venetian blinds at her living room window. She watched the Saturday evening shoppers and workers rush by, her road a convenient shortcut to the car park on the north side of the city walls. 'Anyway, I was just ringing to see how Zoe is. We were supposed to be going out tonight.' Anna wandered over to the sofa and began fluffing the cushions.

'I'll pass you over.' There was a slight pause and a rustling sound while the phone exchanged hands, then Anna heard her sister-in-law.

'Hi, Anna, I'm really sorry but I can't make it tonight. I feel dreadful.' Zoe sniffed. 'I can't shift this cold I picked up from the kids.'

'You don't sound too good,' consoled Anna, trying to hide the disappointment.

'I'm so tired, I really wouldn't be any fun tonight. Aitch-choo!'

'Bless you.'

More sniffing. 'Thank you.'

'Well, you get yourself dosed up and into bed. I'll come by in the morning and take the boys out to the park or something.'

'Oh, thank you, Anna. You're a star. That would be a great help. Nathan's working tomorrow, as usual. I'll see you in the morning. And sorry.'

'Don't worry. Not a problem. We will get a night out sooner or later.'

Anna ended the call and flopped down onto the newly fluffed cushions. She had been looking forward to a girlie Saturday night. Something that she felt Zoe needed as much as she did herself. It had been a funny week, and she really wanted to chat to Zoe and get her take on the turn of events. That was the trouble when you lived alone, you didn't have anyone to sound out your ideas and thoughts with. Someone to reassure you that you were doing the right thing or, indeed, the wrong thing. That was something she really missed.

Anna was now faced with an evening alone. Luke had gone to one of his friends after school and was staying the night as they were having band practice followed by an X-box evening. Mark was going to Southampton that evening to see his old friend Gary. Mark had somehow managed to talk Anna into letting him borrow her car. Just as well she had never changed the insurance details when Mark went to America; her tired old blue Fiesta was still insured for any driver over twenty-five. This did have an upside too, mused Anna, trying to cheer herself up. Mark would look pretty funny in it, his six-foot frame scrunched up like a locust. So not cool.

'Penny for them?' Mark asked, coming into the living room. He was carrying two glasses of wine and passed one to her. 'Been stood up?'

'Mmm. You heard then. Should you be drinking if you're driving tonight?'

'I might go over to Gary's in the morning instead.'

'Why's that then? Won't he mind?' Anna took a sip of wine.

'No, he'll be fine.' Mark smiled at her. 'Cheers. I just thought seeing as Luke isn't here and you're all alone, that maybe we could go out tonight.'

'Me and you? Out? Tonight?' The suggestion had taken her completely by surprise.

'Yeah,' nodded Mark slowly. 'That was the general idea of what I said.'

Anna eyed him carefully. Was this a good idea?

'What's the harm in it?' asked Mark, as if sensing her apprehension. 'We've been eating together all week. It's just the same except we'll be at a restaurant instead.'

'I suppose you have a point,' said Anna, trying to reason with the thought.

'Of course I do. Come on, get your glad rags on. It'll be just like old times.'

Anna couldn't make up her mind if the butterflies she felt in her stomach were excitement or nerves. She couldn't ignore the feeling that going out for dinner with Mark wasn't one of her best ideas.

'Wow, you look lovely!' he exclaimed as Anna came downstairs and into the living room.

It was the response she had hoped for. Had she been going out with the girls tonight, she may have just worn her jeans and one of her casual tops, but as it was Mark, she wanted to show him that she could still look good and hadn't fallen to pieces without him. She had opted for a black shift dress with bold, purple and red embroidered flowers around the neckline and hem, teamed with black patent high-heeled boots and a purple cardigan.

'You look nice, too.' In fact, Anna thought Mark looked gorgeous. She had always liked him in a dark suit and open neck shirt. Whether he remembered this and had purposefully dressed that way, she didn't know.

It felt odd walking through the town centre, side by side. It had been so long since they had done that. Before, Anna would have automatically slipped her arm into his, or he would have put his arm around her shoulders or held her hand, but those days were long gone now. Having said that, Anna had gradually felt herself relax around Mark as the week had gone on. She was still unsettled as to what he was doing back in England, but actually having him physically present wasn't as unnerving as it had been originally. Maybe tonight, on neutral ground, they both might relax even more, and she might be able to wheedle out of Mark why he was here.

The restaurant in South Street was busy but they managed to get a table. There was plenty of noise and a good atmosphere, which would help fill any awkward silences between the two of them, Anna thought. But she needn't have worried, she realised, as the conversation flowed pretty easily, although Mark seemed to be asking most of the questions and avoiding talking about himself and America. The conversation had started off very generally, almost politely, as they talked about how much new housing was being built around Chichester, the recession, Luke, his school and, of course, in true British style, the weather.

'Talking of the weather,' said Mark, 'do you remember that time we went camping, when Luke was about three or four? We went to Cornwall.'

'Oh, will I ever forget it,' chuckled Anna. 'I've never known so much rain. I thought tents were supposed to be waterproof.'

'They are, except someone didn't zip it up properly and left all my clothes by the door.'

'That wasn't me!' she exclaimed, laughing at the memory. 'Oh, but weren't they soaking that morning? Every single thing was dripping wet. Oh God, and then Luke did a wee on your sleeping bag. Do you remember?' Anna was really giggling now. At the time, Mark had been horrified.

'How can I forget? He must have been saving that wee up all night. It soaked straight through the bag.' Mark was laughing too.

'It was such a horrendous night that we packed up and came home the next day.' Anna was shaking her head and still grinning at the memory.

'We were so Ray Mears, weren't we?' said Mark smiling at her.

'See, I told you that one day we would laugh about it.' Anna was aware that she had had too much to drink. She wasn't really sure how much, as Mark had just kept topping her glass up. Time to abandon caution she thought, it was now or never.

'Mark,' she began, nervously twiddling the stem of the wine glass in front of her. 'What are you really doing back here?' She looked up at him for a response but he just looked back at her, studying her face, as if he was deciding whether to tell her something or not. Anna raised her eyebrows questioningly. 'Well?'

'Well…' Mark moved his hand across the table until his fingers were touching the base of the wine glass Anna was still fiddling with. 'Let's go home. I'll explain there, where it's more private and less noisy.' He stroked the tip of her finger with his.

Somewhere at the back of her mind she knew her sensible voice was telling her to move her hand away, however, it appeared the hand was ignoring the distant advice. Her hand stayed exactly where it was, letting Mark's fingers slide the glass away to hold her hand fully.

'Can I get you anything else? Sir? Madam?' The waitress broke the silence, and Anna felt herself snap out from the spell she was under. Feeling flustered, she snatched her hand away from Mark's. The wine was sure making it difficult to think straight. Coffee. Yes, that was what she needed.

'Can I have a coffee please? Black. Strong.' Hopefully, that would sort her out a bit as she felt decidedly squiffy.

Despite the coffee, Anna didn't feel much better when they left the restaurant. Her brain and feet seemed to be having trouble communicating effectively.

'Steady,' laughed Mark, catching Anna's arm as she stumbled on the path. 'Here, hold onto me. Big deep breaths. That's it. Come on, let's get you home.'

Anna had to admit that linking her arm with Mark's was making the art of walking slightly easier. A pair of flat shoes would have made it even more so.

Anna dropped back onto the sofa and unzipped her boots, relieved Mark had managed to get her home in one piece.

'Here, let me,' said Mark, kneeling down and gently pulling each of her boots off in turn.

Anna put her head back into the headrest and closed her eyes. It felt like her brain was swaying all on its own to the James Blunt track *You're Beautiful* that Mark had just put on. She was aware that Mark had sat down on the sofa beside her, but she kept her eyes closed and hummed to the music. Mark began humming too, which was most unlike him. She opened one eye and glimpsed sideways at him, sitting back in the same position as her. He looked at her and a big grin spread across his face. They looked at each other for a second and then they both burst out laughing.

'Stop it,' Anna grinned. 'If I didn't know you better, I'd think you were taking the mickey out of me.' She gave him a playful tap on the arm.

Mark caught her hand in his. 'As if I'd do a thing like that.'

There, her hand was doing it again; it wasn't paying any attention to the warnings. Her hand was certainly being defiant. Anna closed her eyes again but opened them as Mark lifted her hand to his lips.

For a second, all the years of heartache fell away and a brief image of them on their wedding day, happy and smiling, flitted in front of her. Love and treachery went hand in hand with Mark, as immediately this image was replaced with the memory of his betrayal. This was certainly a sobering thought, in more ways than one.

Quietly and with an apologetic smile, Anna withdrew her hand. Mark gave a resigned half smile.

'You're probably right,' he said softly.

Anna nodded, shifting slightly in her seat to face him, resting her head on her hand.

'Why *are* you back, Mark?'

Chapter Six

Anna awoke the next morning with a thumping headache. It felt as if the whole cast of *Riverdance* were performing in her head, and her mouth tasted like it had an old sock stuck in it. It was a few seconds before she remembered the events of the previous evening. She groaned inwardly as she began to put together fragmented memories that came to mind, not necessarily in the order of events, but it didn't take her long before she got to *that* moment on the sofa with Mark.

'Shit,' she said aloud as she remembered him saying that he had come back for her. That he missed her, and could they possibly give things another try? It had poleaxed her. She hadn't known what to say, but somehow through the haze of the alcohol she had managed some clarity and had suggested they talk about it when they were both sober. Okay, she was buying time, but she needed headspace.

She reached over for her mobile and saw a message from Luke. It had come in last night, after she had gone to bed. A simple message saying goodnight and that he loved her. Anna sent one back, asking if he was okay, and to let her know if he needed picking up later.

Tentatively, Anna swung her feet onto the floor. She needed a cup of tea. It was then she remembered she was supposed to be taking her nephews out that morning. 'Oh no,' she groaned, but knew she couldn't let Zoe down.

Pulling on her dressing gown and making her way downstairs, Anna was relieved to find Mark had already left. She didn't want to face him yet.

Zoe opened the front door to a rather delicate looking Anna.

'Blimey, you actually look worse than me,' Zoe croaked through her soggy tissue. She stood to one side to let Anna come in. 'I take it whatever you ended up doing, you had a good night?'

Anna grunted and began to shake her head but stopped abruptly. It hurt too much. Her barely intelligible response to Zoe reminded her of Luke. Hell! When did she morph into her teenage son? 'My head is killing me,' she groaned and looked at herself in the hall mirror. 'God, my eyes look like burn holes in a blanket.'

'I'll put the kettle on.'

The clattering of feet on the wooden floor and the shrieking of three excited boys pierced the air.

'Aunty Anna! Aunty Anna!'

'Yay! We're going to the park!'

'Can we go now?'

Anna was nearly bowled over as Jake, Alex and Henry threw themselves at her for a group hug.

'Sshhhh! Boys! Sssshhh!' pleaded Zoe, trying to calm them down and prise them away from their aunt. 'You're going to wake Emily up.' Too late. Emily didn't want to be left out of the fun and began crying. 'Thanks a lot, boys.'

Anna looked at Zoe who was now pulling a crumpled tissue from her sleeve. She wasn't sure if Zoe was dabbing her eyes and nose because of her cold or because she was upset. This wasn't good.

'Come on, boys,' cajoled Anna. 'Why don't you go in the garden for ten minutes? I'm not quite ready yet. Come on. And you, Henry. Here, I'll carry you. There we go. Come on, Jake. Alex. Let's go outside for a bit.'

Zoe looked at her gratefully before disappearing upstairs.

'There's a cup of tea for you,' smiled Anna as Zoe came back down carrying Emily. 'Ooh hello, Emily darling. Did those boys wake you up? Never mind. Come here for a cuddle while mummy has a cup of tea.' Anna took Emily before either mother or daughter could protest, and gently bobbing the child up and down, she wandered over to the window. 'Look, can you see your brothers? There's Alex and Jake and little Henry. Aren't they having fun?' She turned to her sister-in-law. 'You okay, Zoe?'

'Thanks, Anna. That's the first time someone's made a cup of tea for me in ages.'

'Why don't I take Emily out as well? She doesn't seem too full of cold this morning. As long as you wrap her up warm the fresh air will do her good. What do you think, Emily? Want to come to the park? Mummy can have a nice, long soak in the bath, or sleep in bed, do whatever she fancies. Veg out in front of some cooking show.'

Zoe didn't even pretend to make a 'oh, you don't have to' or 'it'll be too much for you' type of protest. She didn't have the energy or the inclination, it seemed.

Having spent a good couple of hours at the park with the children then walking into town, treating them all to a McDonald's, Anna was glad to be back home. She really could do with a sleep. A boozy night, followed by an early morning and all that running around in the park had worn her out.

Any notion she had of a quiet afternoon was shattered pretty much as soon as she walked through the front door to her house. Luke jumped up from the sofa and turned to face her angrily.

'What did you say to Dad?' he demanded.

'Oh, hello, Mum. How are you? Want a cup of tea? Oh, I'm fine thanks, Luke. A bit tired but I'd love a cup of tea,' she said, annoyed at the abruptness of Luke's greeting.

'Sorry,' mumbled Luke. He went out to the kitchen and reappeared a couple of minutes later with a cup of tea.

'Thank you.' She took the cup from Luke and put it on the coffee table in front of her. 'Now, what's up?'

Luke flopped down into the chair by the fireplace. 'Dad! He was supposed to be taking me out for a curry tonight and then we were coming back to watch the football.'

'And now?'

'He phoned to say he wasn't coming back tonight because of you.' Luke glanced up at Anna before reverting his gaze to the television.

'Me? What have I done?' What had she done to make Mark leave? She had no idea. 'Did he say anything?'

Luke let out a sigh. 'No, just that he thought it was best if he stayed out of your way for a bit.'

Anna could see the disappointment Luke was trying to hide behind his sullen expression. So it hadn't taken Mark long to let Luke down. Selfish pig. And as for using her as an excuse! Right, where was her phone? She was going to phone Mark and get to the bottom of this.

He answered on the fifth ring.

'Mark, I just wanted to check if you were coming back tonight or not? Only Luke doesn't seem to think so.' She tried to sound as nonchalant as possible.

'No, that's right. Thought I'd stay over here the night. Why, is there a problem? I didn't think I had to clear things with you these days.' Mark's response was terse. Then, as if catching himself, he spoke more cordially. 'I just thought I'd give you the headspace that you asked for. Give you time to think about us.'

Anna sighed, glancing at Luke before she walked into the kitchen and spoke in a quieter voice. 'Mark, there hasn't been an "us" for a long time now.'

'So last night was your way of getting a bit of revenge then?' The terseness was back. 'Giving me the green light then switching to red at the last minute. Is that your way of getting your own back at me?'

'Do you really think I've been waiting all this time to get my own back? Besides, what happened last night could hardly be considered as like for like.' God, now she was being drawn into an argument with him about their marriage. Hadn't they done all this a year ago?

'Mark, please just listen to me a minute. This isn't getting us anywhere. Last night I had, well, we both had, too much to drink. I thought we could just have a nice evening out, which was at your suggestion. We were both a little worse for wear. We both knew it wasn't the right way to go. If you thought otherwise, I'm sorry.' Damn, somehow she had ended up apologising. 'We can't take our misunderstanding out on Luke. It's not his fault.'

'Which is exactly why I'm giving us a bit of space,' said Mark.

'Perhaps you can spend some time with him tomorrow then. Give him a call later. It will cheer him up.'

'Yeah, okay. I've got to go. Me and Gary are just on our way out. Gary says hello, by the way.'

'Say hello back,' said Anna, somehow feeling like the villain. 'See you tomorrow. Do you know what time?' Too late, Mark had hung up.

Anna leaned back against the worktop and closed her eyes. Her head was hurting again. At least tomorrow was a bank holiday so she would have a full day to recover before beginning her new job. She wanted to make sure she started off well, to impress not only

Jamie but Tex also. She was going to be totally organised – her clothes, her work bag, check the directions, go over some basic building terms and procedures in case she needed to sort anything out. She wasn't going to leave anything to chance.

Chapter Seven

It was not the best start to the first day in her new job. To begin with, Mark had extended his stay in Southampton, much to her annoyance and Luke's disappointment. It was now Tuesday, and because of Mark's change of plans, she didn't have her car today to drive to Arundel. She took the train instead and walked down from the station into the town to Tarrant Street. The walk itself wouldn't have been too bad had it not been raining, and even less had the wind not been so strong it had turned her umbrella inside out.

Peering out from under the hood of her parka coat, the old United Reformed Church stood back from the row of shops lining Tarrant Street, with a paved area at the front used as outside seating for when it was a coffee shop. Today, instead of tables and chairs were three vehicles: a white transit van, a Volvo estate and a Ford Ranger pick-up style truck. The builder, the architect and Tex, she concluded.

Anna wasn't sure if she should just go straight in, whether she should knock, or try to find a side door. However, her dilemma was solved when the door opened and out stepped a man.

'Are you here for the meeting?' he said, popping his glasses into his shirt pocket. He sidestepped her and sprinted over to the Volvo, from where he removed three large cardboard tubes from the back seat.

'Yes, that's right,' she called, holding the edge of her hood up a bit so she could see him properly.

He nipped past her, back through the door he'd left open and into the dry. 'You'd better come in then,' he said, gesturing. 'You'll get soaked standing out there.'

'Thanks.' Anna was grateful to get in from the rain. She entered into a small hallway. Through a set of double glass doors she could see the main hall.

'I'm Graeme Roberts, by the way,' said the man, just managing to stick his hand out as he struggled to keep the cardboard tubes from falling. 'Mr Garcia's architect.'

'Anna Barnes. Mr Garcia's PA.' Anna shook his hand, and then held one of the internal glass doors open for him to get through.

The trestle table with the cross-section model of the restaurant had been moved to the side of the hall. Graeme scurried over to it, dumping his things on the floor before beginning to examine the plans.

Anna could hear the dull tones of voices coming from one of the rooms at the back and assumed it was Tex and the builder. She walked over to the table and took off her wet coat, which she hung on the handle of the window. Taking her phone from her bag, she switched it on to silent.

The door at the back of the hall opened and a large burly man, dressed in jeans and a sweatshirt, came out.

'Hello, Rod. How are you?' said Graeme. He turned to Anna. 'This is Rod. He's one of the building contractors tendering for the project. Rod, this is Anna, works for Mr Garcia.'

Rod shook her hand. 'Pleased to meet you. He won't be a minute, he's just taking a phone call.'

'Anna, would you mind giving me a hand with these?' asked Graeme, indicating the large sheets of drawings for the renovation works he had removed from the tubes and was now attempting to lay out. 'Got some more detailed plans to look at today. Could you hold the ends while I tape them down?'

'Sure. It looks complicated,' said Anna, popping her phone onto the windowsill. 'I mean, the drawings, not the taping.' She stretched her arms out and held down each edge of the drawing as Graeme unpicked the end of the masking tape.

He smiled and looked as if he were about to answer, when his attention was caught by the sound of one of the doors at the back of the hall opening and closing.

'Good morning.' The rich accented voice sounded out, flirting with Anna's eardrums.

Still leaning over the table, arms outstretched while Graeme seemed to take an age finding the end of the tape, Anna looked back over her shoulder and smiled at Tex. 'Hi!'

With more than a hint of amusement on his lips, Tex raised his eyebrows slightly. 'Nice view.' Then he seamlessly moved on to greet Graeme.

Anna felt her face burn hot with embarrassment and stood up abruptly, letting go of the drawing, which pinged back into a roll and fell to the floor. By now, Tex was by her side and stooped to pick up the drawing, placing it back on the table.

Anna was grateful for the few seconds to compose herself before Tex turned to her.

'You okay?' He cupped her upper arms with his hands and kissed her on the cheek.

'Yes. Yes, I'm fine. Thank you.' Right, she must remain professional and concentrate on the job in hand and stop acting like a lovestruck teenager. Briskly, she turned back to the table and resumed holding the large sheet of paper in place, this time by taking one edge in turn, while Graeme taped it down as he fell into discussion with Tex. Rod sauntered back across to join them.

Meeting commenced, thought Anna. Good.

Initially, she made notes on her pad in case anything needed to be clarified afterwards. All the while she tried not to let her gaze linger on Tex for too long. It was hard though. She liked the way his hair casually fell forwards, not long enough to fall in his eyes, but enough to touch the top of his dark eyebrows. He had remarkably long, thick eyelashes for a man too, framing those deep brown eyes of his.

Anna wasn't entirely sure what Tex was expecting her to do, so she continued taking notes as the three men discussed technical issues, such as beam splicing and loading, engineers' reports and calculations.

'I would like the staircase to start at this side and curve round to the first floor,' explained Tex, walking over to the right-hand side of the hall. He made a sweeping motion with his arm to emphasise his point.

Anna couldn't help admiring him as he stood there explaining and gesturing. Dark trousers, expensive-looking, black shiny leather shoes, pale blue shirt open at the collar, his sleeves rolled up. That fresh showery, citrus smell of his aftershave tantalising her senses.

'You would lose quite a bit of floor space downstairs if you want a curving staircase,' said Rod, 'and then you have to take into consideration the rise of each step and how far it carries. It will take a fair bit of working out.'

Rod went on to explain how each tread and riser was calculated and how much something like that would cost. He rambled about kites and winders, newels, spindles and strings. Graeme was furiously pecking at his calculator as Rod reeled off numbers and measurements.

Anna had no idea what they were talking about. She looked over at Tex and had to stifle a giggle as he gave an exaggerated, confused look, unnoticed by the others. Rod carried on, more or less discussing it with himself, correcting and contradicting himself along the way, and Graeme continued to tap at the calculator like some sort of demented woodpecker.

She stole another glance at Tex who, catching her eye, mimed a yawn, tapping his mouth with his hand, which just made Anna want to giggle again. When he silently acted out a noose round his neck and then made out to shoot himself in the temple with his fingers, Anna couldn't hold the burst of laughter in. Rod and Graeme stopped and stared at her. She quickly fashioned the laugh into a small series of coughs.

'Sorry, tickly throat,' she said apologetically, not daring to look at Tex.

'Hey, come out back and I'll get you a glass of water,' Tex piped up, and before she could protest, he was gently leading her away by the arm. Once inside the kitchen he closed the door and they both laughed quietly.

'Jeez,' groaned Tex. 'Death by numbers.' He took a step closer. 'Now, where did we leave off the other night?'

Anna took a step back. Oh, this was hard. 'I think it's best to leave it there,' she said.

He was standing in front of her. 'Huh?'

'I'm sorry, Tex, but I think it's best if we just keep things professional now that I'm working for Jamie which, by default, now means you. It's a rule of mine never to mix business with pleasure.'

'You serious? Damn it, you are!' Tex cursed. This wasn't going to plan. 'What about if I fire you then? Tell Jamie I've changed my mind.' He saw the alarm on her face. 'I was only joking. I wouldn't really.'

'Good, because I could do with this job,' replied Anna.

'What about if you give me a chance to change your mind?' He fixed her with his killer smile, the one that he usually got his way with. She was shaking her head. She wasn't buying it.

Before he could plan his next move, there was a knock at the door and a female voice calling his name. It was Christine.

The door opened and in she wiggled, smiling widely at him. Then she clocked Anna, and instantly Christine's smile disappeared. 'Oh, hello.'

'Anna, this is Christine,' said Tex. 'She works in the art gallery across the way. Christine, this is Anna, she's my PA.' He watched Christine's hostile eyes look Anna up and down. Anna would have to be downright stupid to miss that, he thought.

'Hmm, I see,' responded Christine.

Tex had been so busy checking Anna's reaction to this unfavourable greeting that he was totally caught out when Christine draped herself over his shoulder and kissed him on the cheek. Without barely moving her mouth away from him, she said, 'I just came over to see if you were free for lunch, but I don't want to interrupt anything.'

'You weren't,' said Anna tersely. 'I'd better get back to Graeme and Rod. Don't want to miss anything.'

Tex cursed to himself yet again as Anna left the room.

'Sorry, did I upset someone?' cooed Christine.

'Hmmm,' grunted Tex, then gathering himself, 'I'm sorry, but I'll take a rain check on lunch. I've already got a meeting.'

'Oh, come over later then. I've got some pictures that I thought would look good in the restaurant.' She smiled sweetly and wiggled her way back out.

The rest of the meeting ran smoothly without any problems, although Tex noted that Anna didn't look at him once this time. She definitely had a businesslike air about her. Professional, almost to the point of being curt. She really did mean it when she said she wasn't mixing business with pleasure.

'Okay, that's me done,' said Rod as the meeting drew to a close. 'I'll need a couple of days to price this, so I will get back to you by the end of the week.'

As Rod left, Graeme looked expectantly at Anna. When it appeared she wasn't taking the hint, he said to Tex, 'Have you got a minute? I wondered if I could have a quick word.'

'Sure, but I do have another appointment at midday,' replied Tex, glancing at his watch.

'I'll leave you to it,' said Anna, still avoiding eye contact with him. 'If there's anything you need to clarify, you can get hold of me through Jamie.'

'Anna…' began Tex.

'I've got to go, my train will be here soon. Nice to have met you, Graeme.' Anna walked towards the door.

'Anna! One moment please,' called Tex.

'Sorry, got to go,' she called back, as Graeme anxiously tried to retain Tex's attention.

Chapter Eight

'Tex. It's about my daughter's wedding. Would you give her some advice on the menu?'

Tex looked from Graeme to the door and back again. Much as he wanted to tell Graeme that his daughter's wedding menu was the last thing on his mind at that moment, and that it was something he really should be asking the caterers, he couldn't be rude.

Making polite but short work of discussing the best dishes for large parties, Tex managed to usher Graeme out of the building in ten minutes with the promise of putting some ideas down on an email for him. As soon as the door closed behind the architect, Tex took out his cell phone and called Anna's.

She wasn't answering it. Perhaps it was in her handbag and she hadn't been able to get to it in time. Listening to the ringing tone and willing her to answer, Tex wandered over to the trestle table where Graeme had left a revised set of drawings taped to the table. It was then that he heard a vibrating sound coming from the direction of the window. He looked over and saw a phone jiggling away on the windowsill. Anna's.

Tex checked his watch. She could only have just made it to the station by now. If he was quick he could be there in five minutes, hopefully before her train arrived. He patted his back pocket. Yes, his keys were there. Without looking for his jacket, Tex dashed out to his car.

It was still raining as he drove out of Tarrant Street and over the bridge towards the train station. Within a few minutes, he pulled up outside the ticket office, and abandoning his car, sprinted through the unmanned office and out on to the platform. Tex scanned the deserted platform up and down; there was no sign of Anna there or in the waiting room. He looked over at platform two on the other side of the tracks. That appeared empty too.

Then he saw her, stepping out from the plastic waiting shelter there, looking at him. Intrigued? Curious? He wasn't sure. They walked towards each other on opposite platforms.

'Can we start again?' Tex called across the tracks. Anna said nothing as she stood there studying him, as if wrestling with herself as to what she should say or do. 'You can't leave yet anyway. I have your phone. You left it on the window ledge.' Ah, now that got her attention.

Looking concerned, Anna stuffed her hands in her coat pockets and then rummaged through her bag, obviously up until that point not realising she didn't have her phone with her. Tex waved the Nokia in the air.

'So it would seem,' she said finally. 'I suppose you want me to come and get it?' Tex grinned as Anna made her way over the bridge and walked up to where he was standing. 'I forgot I'd left that. Thank you.' She reached out to take the phone.

Tex popped the phone behind his back. 'There's one condition.'
'Which is?'
'Have lunch with me.'

She sighed and her shoulders drooped. 'I don't think it's a good idea. Under any other circumstances I would love to, but not when you're my client. It's a bad idea. Really bad.'

'Would it be bad if it was a business lunch?'

She appeared to be contemplating what he had said. 'Just

business you say?'

'Just business,' repeated Tex. Personal business, he added to himself.

'Okay, I accept.' She smiled a shy smile up at him.

'Thank you. I am now a very happy man.' Tex fought the urge to kiss her there and then. He was going to have to work his charm to win her over. Still, he liked a challenge. Then her brow furrowed and she had a confused look on her face.

'I thought I heard you say to Graeme that you had a lunch appointment.'

'I was hoping that would be you,' said Tex, a sheepish grin crossing his face.

'That was rather presumptuous of you,' said Anna, folding her arms and raising her eyebrows playfully.

'Not presumptuous. More like hopeful.'

'That will do,' Anna smiled. 'So can I have my phone back now?' Tex nodded. 'Well, that's the only reason I'm agreeing. That, and it being a business lunch. You do understand don't you?'

'Yes, Ma'am.' He gave a quick salute. 'I understand completely.' He wasn't entirely sure he did, but she had agreed to lunch, which is what he had wanted. He didn't usually have to work quite so hard. Normally it was much easier and much more straightforward – a bit of flirting, a little bit of fun, nothing serious, no obligation. He liked it that way.

He drove her back to the hall in silence, cranking up the car's heated seats to help dry Anna's coat which was soaked from her walk down to the station. Having just spent five minutes standing on the platform with no jacket and the rain blowing under the canopy, Tex wasn't faring much better himself.

'Not very nice weather for public transport. Do you always travel on the train?' he asked, as they pulled up outside the hall.

'No. I have the car but I let Mark, my sort of ex, borrow it. He was supposed to come back at the weekend but didn't.'

Tex ushered Anna through the internal doors into the main hall and then guided her to the room on the left at the back of the hall. There was a small square table in the middle of the room with a simple white linen tablecloth on it, at its centre, a vibrant red gerbera in a tall drinking glass. The table was set for two people.

'Presumptuous,' said Anna as she took in the scene.

'Hopeful,' corrected Tex. He walked up behind her and gently rested his hands on her shoulders. 'May I take your coat?' He took a deep breath as he momentarily flirted with the idea of kissing the back of her bare neck, before checking himself. Slipping Anna's coat from her shoulders, he hung it on the back of the door before pulling out the chair for her to sit down.

'I'll be back in one minute,' he said and disappeared into the adjoining room to warm up the soup he had prepared that morning. Whilst that was heating, he cut some French stick then took the bread together with a bottle of Perrier water back into Anna.

'It's nearly ready. Just some humble soup. I only have two gas rings at the moment,' he said as he put the bread down and poured a glass of water for each of them.

'I'm sure it will be lovely.'

Tex switched the radio on. Hopefully, a bit of background music would help her relax.

'This isn't looking very businesslike,' commented Anna.

'Let's talk business if it makes you feel happier.' Hmm, this was going to be harder than he thought.

'Have you always been a chef?' she asked.

'Yes. I never wanted to be anything else.'

'Where did you train?'

'France, of course. That is where the best chefs in the world are and I was fortunate enough to have some very good teachers.

I worked for some of the great chefs in France.'

'Any I would know?'

'Edward Le Manquais. You have heard of him no doubt?'

'Of course. He's a bit more than just a chef now, he's something of a celebrity in his own right,' said Anna. 'Didn't he do a reality restaurant show on TV recently?'

'Ahh yes, the celebrity chef. I am afraid that is not for me.'

'By choice?'

'By choice,' Tex affirmed. 'Does that make any difference to you?'

Anna looked surprised by the question. 'To me? No. No, it doesn't make any difference. That doesn't worry me the way you think.'

'What way do I think?' probed Tex. He waited patiently whilst she took a sip of water. He wasn't letting her off the hook that easy. Experience told him if he said nothing for long enough, the other person would carry on speaking.

'Okay, here goes,' she said. 'You probably think I would be impressed and pleased that I had landed a famous client. That I would be imagining fancy parties, champagne, rubbing shoulders with the rich and famous, but the truth is, I couldn't be less interested in that.'

'Go on, I'm still listening,' coaxed Tex.

'Don't say you didn't ask,' said Anna with wry smile. 'Mark was a professional footballer. We married when we were very young; I was pregnant. Mark had a lot of temptation in the female stakes. He hasn't got much willpower. Part of it was because he was a bit famous, and as a footballer there were plenty of offers from a slew of female fans. So my experience of being with someone well known isn't a particularly good one.'

'You said the other night that you were separated but not divorced.'

'That's right. He went off to America and we have just never got round to it. Part of me doesn't want to become a statistic, but to all intents and purposes we might as well be divorced.'

Tex smiled reassuringly at her. There was obviously a lot more to it but now wasn't the time. He'd established that Mark wasn't a threat.

'How did we get onto the subject of my personal life?' asked Anna. She leant back in her chair. Tex couldn't help noticing the button of her blouse had come undone, revealing a glimpse of white flesh encased in black lace. He forced himself to look at her face, keeping his eyes level with hers to answer her question.

'It's important if we are going to work together that we know each other properly. It's not a regular sort of office job, there may be times when you have to accompany me on social events. It's real important that we know each other well so we're comfortable together.'

Anna didn't look convinced, but didn't challenge him either.

'When do I get to find out about you?' she asked.

'I will get the soup and then you can ask me anything you like.'

Tex returned to the makeshift kitchen. Leaning against the work surface he took a deep breath as he recalled her open blouse. Reappearing a few minutes later with two bowls of soup, he placed one in front of Anna. Her blouse now done up, he ignored the self-conscious look on her face.

'This looks nice,' she said, picking up her spoon and dipping it into the thick, orange liquid. 'Tastes good too. Let me guess. Carrot and... mmm... not sure. There's definitely another flavour but I'm not sure what it is.'

'Coriander.'

'Ah yes, I recognise it now. It's lovely.'

'Thank you.'

They ate together in silence for several minutes. A comfortable silence, with just the radio to fill the space between them.

'So, in the interest of fairness and Anglo-American relations, I think I'll take you up on your offer,' said Anna. Tex looked blankly at her. 'Exchange of information. Background information. It's your turn,' she smiled.

'What do you wanna know?'

'You tell me. If you were me, what would I want to know?'

Tex made an act of looking thoughtfully up to the ceiling, as if he were recalling any relevant information. 'Where to begin,' he mused.

'Why the name Tex?'

'That's an easy one. Short for Texas, where I'm from. Brenham to be exact. When I went off to Europe, I was something of a novelty. You don't get many cowboys from Texan ranches wanting to learn how to cook.'

She smiled. 'Okay, what else?'

She'd seemed pretty unfazed by that, which was cool. 'I am forty-five years old,' he continued. 'I have one daughter. Julie-Ann, she's twenty-two. Lives in Paris.'

'And Mrs Garcia?'

He was used to that sort of question. They all asked sooner or later. It was still difficult to say, nonetheless.

'Estelle, Julie-Ann's mother, my wife, she died six years ago.' He watched the surprise flicker across Anna's eyes, quickly followed by a look of concern. She went to speak, probably to offer her condolences, but he raised his hand slightly. She didn't need to say anything, it wasn't necessary.

'She was ill for a short time,' he continued. 'Liver cancer. There was nothing they could do for her. Afterwards, I promised I would make a success of the restaurant, just as we had both planned, except I didn't stay in Paris, I came to England. Jamie and Yvonne helped me a lot, both professionally and personally.'

'And since then?' Anna spoke gently.

Tex knew what she was asking, and in a strange way he found it refreshing. Most women avoided the question once they heard about Estelle.

'And since then I haven't had any meaningful or long relationship.' He had answered honestly, and hoping to retrieve the light tone the lunch had started out with, said buoyantly, 'I've been too busy opening the restaurant and working hard to get my first Michelin star at my Guildford restaurant.'

'Do you always let work rule your personal life and stop relationships?'

'Do you?' responded Tex immediately, eager to steer the conversation away from Estelle.

Anna looked slightly startled by his response, then gave a little laugh. 'Touché. I asked first.'

'The truth is...' Tex hesitated, putting his spoon down and pushing the near empty bowl away. 'The truth is, my work is my true love.'

'And no one could ever mean as much as your work?'

'No one has meant enough yet.' He gave a small laugh to himself and shook his head as he leant back in his chair. 'I have no idea why I'm telling you this. Any sane person would not want anything to do with me and here I am in danger of scaring you off.' He paused and then spoke more softly. 'Which is something I really don't wanna do.' The chase was well and truly on.

Anna, straight-faced, looked directly at him. 'Why would you scare me off? Our relationship is purely business.'

'So why do you let business get in the way of your personal life?' Tex held her gaze until she looked away.

'You really want to know?' she asked, fiddling with her napkin.

Tex nodded but said nothing so Anna would continue.

'Okay. When my son, Luke, went to school, I got a part-time job working in the offices at the football club Mark played for.

Trouble was, after a while I started to hear rumours about what Mark was doing, what he was getting up to when he and the other lads were out. Naturally, I was upset, suspicious, and began questioning him, which caused quite a few arguments.' Anna paused to have a sip of water.

Tex remained silent, his feeling that there was more was confirmed as Anna began to speak again.

'As if that wasn't enough, Mark was jealous if any man spoke to me too much, that included any member of management and any of his team mates. Needless to say, I handed my notice in after just three months, it was more trouble than it was worth. So that is why I don't mix business with pleasure.'

'And you think that every business and pleasure encounter will end the same?'

Anna shrugged in response.

Tex decided it was best to keep off the subject of their personal lives. Anna must have thought the same when she changed the subject by asking, 'So how come you ended up here in England?'

'Jamie and I were at catering college together but it didn't take him long before he realised being in the kitchen wasn't for him. Instead, he put his organisational skills to good use and started working for a PR company arranging work placements in the UK for chefs from France and vice versa. This gradually expanded through word of mouth and soon Jamie was helping foreign nationals to settle in the UK. Such was the demand, he had the foresight to leave the PR company and set up his own relocation company.'

'Good that you remained friends though.'

'Yes. Through his help I was able to open my first restaurant. That was five years ago. I've been looking for premises in this area for a long time to open another and finally came across this place.' He gestured in the air with his arms. 'Next week I need to start looking for an apartment so I can keep a closer eye on the refurbishment. The Guildford restaurant runs itself mostly.'

Anna wasn't quite sure where the two hours went, but when she glanced at her watch she was shocked to see it was gone two o'clock.

'I'd better go, otherwise I'm not sure what time I'll get back. I think there's a train in about half an hour. I'm supposed to ring Jamie when I get home. He'll think I've resigned before I've even started.'

Tex dropped his napkin to the table. 'I'll take you home.'

'Oh, you don't have to.'

'I know.' Tex paused as he pushed back his chair. 'Or does it go against your no business with pleasure rule?'

'Probably,' said Anna, 'but a lift would be nice all the same.' She silently tutted at the desertion of her willpower. It was very difficult to say no to Tex Garcia.

Twenty minutes later Tex pulled his car to a halt outside Coach House Cottages. Anna noticed both Mrs Meekham's curtain twitching and her car parked in the resident's parking bay a little way up the road. Mark was obviously back.

'Can I see you again?' asked Tex, as he turned in his seat to face her.

'You'd better check with Jamie. He said something about me going to Brighton next week to help a family who want to look at schools.'

'Not business,' smiled Tex.

Anna gulped and reminded herself to breathe. His voice was giving her all sorts of problems. 'Pleasure?' It was almost a whisper.

Tex nodded. 'Are you free Friday evening? Me, Jamie and Yvonne are coming down for the weekend. I have a few things to sort out to do with the refurbishment, and Jamie's got a client he wants to see in Sussex. As it's also Yvonne's birthday, we thought we would go out for a drink. Maybe you'd like to come too?'

'Did you not listen to anything I said about not mixing business with pleasure?'

'I was hoping I may have changed your mind and that maybe you weren't so goddamn stubborn.' Tex let out a sigh of resignation.

'It's hard work being this stubborn. Sorry.' Anna looked apologetically at him, her sigh matching his. 'I can't anyway; I'm going out with my sister-in-law. We were supposed to go out last week but couldn't for one reason and another, so we rearranged for this week.'

'I understand. Where are you going? Anywhere nice?'

'Just the Fish and Fly, our local haunt.'

'Perhaps we could all meet up there? Just for one drink.'

'I think this is where I'm supposed to say no,' said Anna, feeling her resolve weaken. 'That would be against my no business with pleasure rule.'

'Think of it as, how do you say, a work's do.'

How could she resist that smile, those eyes and that voice?

Anna felt as if she were floating as she walked up to her front door. Funny how she could suddenly justify her actions, relegating her work ethics to the back of her mind. Like Tex said, if they were going to work closely together then it was inevitable that a few social occasions would arise.

Her feeling of happiness didn't last long. In fact, within seconds of walking through the front door it was totally eradicated.

Chapter Nine

Mark was standing at the window, glaring at the Ford Ranger as it drove away down the road. As Anna closed the door, he turned to her. From the look on his face, Anna could instantly tell he was in a bad mood. She gave an involuntary shudder as it immediately took her back to the dark days of their marriage.

'What's with the bloke and the pick-up then?' Mark said stiffly.

'Not that it's any business of yours but, if you must know, that was my client today. He kindly gave me a lift home because someone didn't bring my car back in time.'

'You still got there okay, and got a lift back in style.'

'No thanks to you.' Glaring at him, Anna dropped her bag to the floor and threw her coat onto the back of the sofa. 'You could at least apologise.'

Mark gave a sideways look. 'I'm sorry.'

He didn't sound particularly sincere, Anna thought, but at least he had apologised.

'I was just hoping you would have time to think about us. I didn't expect you to be getting it on with your client.'

Anna let out an exasperated sigh. 'I wasn't getting anything on with my client. It's just business.'

'So that answers one question. What about the other? Did you think about us?' His voice was calm and soft now.

Anna sighed sadly. 'Mark, I think we're better off apart. In fact, I *know* we are.' She really didn't want to have this conversation. She almost felt sorry for him, guilty even, until she remembered how she had felt during their marriage, and what he had done. The pain might not be so real now but she couldn't forget how much hurt she had endured back then.

'Listen, there's something I want to tell you,' began Mark. 'I...'

Anna shook her head fiercely. 'No. Not now, Mark. Please.' Picking up her bag, she made for the stairs. 'I'm too tired and I still haven't finished work yet.'

Leaving Mark standing open-mouthed by the sofa, she went upstairs to ring Jamie.

'Tex was really impressed with you,' enthused Jamie. Anna wondered whether Tex was referring to her skills as a PA or in being able to say no to him. 'I'm really happy and confident about giving you more work if you want to carry on,' Jamie continued.

'I'd be delighted,' answered Anna, a morass of feelings swirling round in her head, half of her hoping the work would be with Tex, the other half hoping it wouldn't. She didn't know if she would be able to resist him for too long.

Home from school, Luke grinned with delight at seeing his father seated on the sofa. 'Hi, Dad! You're back then.'

'Yeah, I'm back here with the Ice Maiden. She's not in a good mood with me.'

Anna ignored Mark's comment, the atmosphere between them as stilted as it had been all afternoon. She continued preparing the evening meal. Jacket potatoes tonight. Nice and easy. And she knew Mark didn't really like them.

Luke headed straight for the fridge. 'You still fed up about the car, Mum?'

'Don't start picking, tea will be ready soon.' Anna tapped Luke's arm and closed the fridge door. 'And as far as your dad is concerned, just ignore him.'

'I don't know why you're being so pissy, you're not usually,' frowned Luke, stealing a pinch of cheese Anna was grating.

Mark appeared in the doorway and lounged against the wall. 'I was thinking of going back to the States,' he announced. 'I'm not sure if it's working out me being here.'

'What?' exclaimed Luke. 'You've only been here a couple of weeks. He doesn't have to go does he, Mum?'

'Well... it's up to your dad,' said Anna, totally surprised by this apparent U-turn. What was all that about getting back together then?

'Of course I don't want to go, but...'

'Just stay, Dad,' pleaded Luke. 'It will be okay. Mum's just having a couple of stressy days. Aren't you, Mum?'

'It's not quite that simple,' Anna said.

'I think maybe my coming back was a mistake.' Mark looked over at Anna as he spoke. If he was hoping for her to refute this, then he was out of luck. Anna said nothing.

'It wasn't a mistake, Dad. It's a good thing. I've really enjoyed you being here. It's just like it used to be. I wish you could stay, you know, for good. Here.' Luke dropped his gaze to his trainers. 'Just stay for now, please.'

'All right,' said Mark after a lengthy pause. 'I'll hang about for a bit longer, just as long as your mum doesn't mind.'

'You don't mind do you, Mum?' said Luke looking eagerly at Anna.

'Well, I... err...' began Anna. Yes, she *did* mind wasn't what Luke really wanted her to say.

'Why don't you just say yes?' her son snapped. 'Why don't you just say, "I think it's a great idea? Your dad is more than welcome."'

Anna looked at Mark, hoping for a bit of support. Wrong. Mark just shrugged in a nothing-to-do-with-me sort of way. Not for the first time, she sensed that Mark was manipulating everyone around him.

'Don't you need to get back for work?' she asked Mark, hoping he would take the hint.

'Oh no. They can manage without me for a bit longer. Well, that's that sorted then.' Mark pushed himself upright from the wall and grinning at Luke, gave him a playful punch on the arm. 'Cheers mate.'

Luke beamed back.

Anna had to marvel at the laser-precision, pincer movement Mark and Luke had just executed. Attack from both sides. She never stood a chance. Now it looked like she had Mark here indefinitely.

'Just give him a chance, Mum,' said Luke after Mark had gone upstairs for a shower. 'Everyone deserves one. You always say that yourself.'

'It's not that simple,' said Anna reticently.

'Of course it is. You're just making it difficult.'

Anna sighed. How much did you tell your son about your marriage? 'Listen, Luke. You know I wouldn't say anything bad about your dad to you, but you have to understand lots of things happened between me and him, things that you wouldn't know about.'

'I'm not stupid,' grumbled Luke. 'I remember the arguments. Dad being out late or all night. You crying.' He paused, looking at her before dropping his gaze. 'I know about the baby and the other women.'

Anna gulped. She had often wondered if he knew more than she or, indeed, Mark gave him credit for. 'I'm sorry you do. I guess I never protected you from it as much as I thought.'

'But you could still give him another chance. Now that he's had a year to sort himself out. Couldn't you?'

Anna gave Luke a hug, which felt slightly ridiculous as he was several inches taller than her already. 'Let's just worry about you and Dad getting to know each other again. That's the important thing.'

Jamie had asked her to step in at the last minute to cover for another member of staff who was sick. She was to accompany a German woman and her two children on a school visit in Brighton and help with the interpreting. Anna had really enjoyed this assignment. It was great to be able to practice her German and the family were very charming and polite. An unexpectedly busy week as it had transpired, as a small document concerning a property transaction in France had also come in for translating. However, Anna was glad to have Friday free, which meant she could implement phase one of her 'Help Zoe' plan.

'Just be ready in half an hour,' said Anna down the phone to Zoe. 'Both you and Emily.'

'Can't you just tell me what we're doing? Just a hint?' pleaded Zoe.

'Nope. Bye.' Anna hung up before her sister-in-law could delve any deeper. She checked through the two bags on the kitchen table to make sure everything was there. Satisfied, she placed them by the door ready for action.

The gym was quiet. When Zoe protested she didn't have any sports clothes with her, Anna produced the bag from the boot of her car. 'All your stuff's in here. Nathan got it for me the other day,' she said, grinning triumphantly. 'And before you say anything about Emily, she's booked into the crèche, which Nathan has checked out, so you have absolutely nothing to worry about or any reason to duck out. Come on, girly, we're getting you sorted.'

Picking up the car seat with Emily still strapped in, Anna strode off across the car park, leaving Zoe little alternative but to follow obediently.

Anna called back over her shoulder. 'Anyway, I could do with your advice about something. Come on.'

Anna had been grateful to get out of the house a couple of times in the week. There had definitely been a shift in dynamics since Mark had wrangled what seemed to be a pretty much open invitation to stay. She didn't want to seem paranoid but, as she explained to Zoe while they strode side by side on the treadmills, it was like Mark and Luke had their own little club now, one that she was excluded from.

'Luke's bound to be a bit like that,' puffed Zoe, turning the speed setting down. 'For the past year all he has really wanted is to have a relationship with his dad. Now Mark's here, he has finally got it. The only thing that would top that is you and Mark getting back together. It's only natural he doesn't want to upset Mark. Luke knows that you will always be there for him and that's why you're getting the brunt of everything. It's a familiarity thing.'

'I know you're right,' sighed Anna, taking her lead from Zoe and slowing the speed down, 'and I do try to put Luke first in all this but it's very difficult. I wish Mark wasn't living under the same roof as us though. It's not like I've even got the space really. I feel quite claustrophobic at times.'

'And he hasn't said how long he's staying for?' asked Zoe, as she pressed the red stop button and wiped her face with her towel.

'No. I just wish he could stay somewhere else. Things may start to get a bit more complicated at home now.'

'Oh yeah? What's this then?' Zoe eyed her sister-in-law with interest. 'Come on spill the beans.'

'Well, I have sort of met someone,' began Anna. 'Hang on, let me get off this thing. I can't concentrate.'

'What do you mean "sort of"? You either have or you haven't.'

'Okay, I have met someone, but he's a client.'

'What, through your new job?' They wandered over to the water fountain so Anna could refill her bottle. 'You kept this quiet. Come on then, I want all the details.'

Within the quieter weights and exercise room, which fortunately was empty, and whilst laying on the floor holding Zoe's ankles while she did sit-ups, Anna relayed her two encounters with Tex.

'So there you have it,' finished Anna. 'We might bump into each other briefly on Friday evening.'

'Well, good for you,' said Zoe warmly as she lay flat out on her back. 'I have to stop, my stomach muscles are hurting already. Oh, that's better. Look people meet each other through work all the time. I can't see a problem. Besides, it's about time you started going out and finding someone. I mean, I've done my best over the past year to fix you up with eligible bachelors.'

'I think you need to work on your matchmaking skills a bit more. Some of the men you lined up for me, well, they were just terrible.' Anna laughed at the look of mock indignation on Zoe's face. 'What about at that barbecue for your birthday last year? You introduced me to Evan. I mean, where did you find him? His idea of stimulating conversation was to recount the past twenty Eurovision Song Contest winners, complete with songs title and total points.' Anna eased herself backwards over the blue exercise ball.

'Sorry, that was Nathan's idea actually. A friend of a friend,' grinned Zoe.

'Okay, I'll let you off Evan, but what about the New Year fancy dress party and the Chinese Elvis lookalike? I couldn't believe it when he told me his name was Wai Ling. How funny is that? He really did sound like he was wailing when he got up on the karaoke machine.' The memory of this sent her and Zoe off into fits of giggles. Anna rolled off the ball and onto the floor to attempt some press-ups.

'I was only trying to help,' chuckled Zoe, who seemed to enjoy just resting on the mat. 'So this Tex, he's got a few tough acts to follow.'

'Doesn't he just.' Five press-ups were enough. Anna sat up on her heels. 'Joking aside though, it's all a bit scary. I mean, it's exciting, as I haven't been remotely interested in getting involved with anyone since Mark and I split up, but now suddenly I feel like a sixteen-year-old, all nervous and giggly.' Anna gave a quick look round the room to make sure it was still empty. Zoe, attention piqued, sat up. Anna continued. 'Ignoring the fact that he's a client for a minute, do you know what really worries me about getting involved with anyone?'

'Mark?'

'No. Well, a bit, but that's not what I was thinking of. What actually makes me nervous is sex.'

'Now you really do sound like a sixteen-year-old.'

'No seriously, Zoe. I haven't slept with anyone since Mark and I split up. I mean, I haven't slept with anyone other than Mark since I was nineteen! I know I'd be so nervous if it actually came to it. I'd be such a disappointment. A real let-down you could say.'

Zoe giggled, then looking sympathetically at Anna said, 'I really think you're worrying about nothing. Don't go getting yourself all worked up about it. Don't do anything until you feel it's right and then everything will just come naturally, all your worries will vanish. You'll be lost in the moment and everything will be okay. Correction, everything will be beautiful.'

'You're such a romantic.'

'You should try it again sometime,' smiled Zoe kindly.

'Maybe I should, just not with a client,' sighed Anna. 'Do you think we should go somewhere else tonight and not meet them?'

'It's up to you but it's not like a date or anything. It's just you and me possibly meeting your boss, his wife and your client for a friendly and brief drink. What could possibly go wrong?'

Chapter Ten

Anna closed the blinds to her living room as the City Car taxi pulled up and Zoe got out.

'Right I'm off.'

'Where are you going again?' asked Mark, looking up from the TV.

'Just out with the Zoe into town.'

'Yeah, but where?'

'Not sure yet. The Fish and Fly maybe. We'll probably go to a couple of different places. Why?' Anna eyed Mark suspiciously.

'No reason, just asking,' said Mark defensively. 'I might go out for a pint tonight. Didn't want to bump into you and cramp your style. Besides, sitting with you two isn't exactly my idea of fun. *Witches of Eastwick* or *MacBeth* spring to mind. "When shall we three meet again, in thunder, lightning or in rain."' He gave Anna a wink.

'That might have been funny if there were three of us,' said Anna dryly as she buttoned up her navy duffel jacket and made for the door. 'See you later. Don't wait up!'

The Fish and Fly was a popular pub that had recently been refurbished with low tables and several deep-seated leather sofas, as well as the more traditional table and chairs and high-backed bar stools. What Anna liked about the pub was that it attracted all sorts of people and ages, with a nice party-like atmosphere in the evenings but relaxed enough that you didn't have to shout in each other's ears to have a conversation.

As she walked in with Zoe, Anna scanned the room, looking for Tex, although he did say eight and it was only seven thirty. Having arrived early, the pub wasn't too busy yet and there were plenty of empty tables. Anna ushered Zoe to one that gave the perfect position to clock who came in.

'I would just love to swap places with Nathan for the day and see how he copes,' Zoe regaled. 'The organisation it took was second only to the D-Day Landings. I took Henry and Emily to the park for well over an hour after nursery to wear them out, then settled Henry in front of a Fireman Sam DVD so I could shower, having Emily in her bouncer chair in the bathroom to entertain her with funny faces and stupid dances whilst washing my hair.'

'The things we do,' said Anna absently, looking towards the door for what seemed like the one-hundredth time.

'I was just glad it didn't rain. Even remotely damp and my hair frizzles up.' Zoe smoothed her hair down, as if checking her worst nightmare hadn't turned into a reality. 'And the car journey home was as fraught as ever with all three boys trying to talk to me at once. I'm trying to concentrate on driving whilst appearing to take a keen interest in the twins' day at school. Things like the latest Club Penguin collectors' card, or who had played "It" at playtime, what they had for school dinner, and why the whole class had to miss Golden Time because Callum Jones had cut the end off Rebecca Mosley's plait. Anna? Anna? Anna, are you even listening?'

'What?' Anna winced inwardly and forced herself to look away from the pub entrance.

'Only you seem very interested in the door. I know I don't

get out much and may be a bit boring, but surely it hasn't come to the point where a lump of wood is more entertaining!' Zoe feigned a hurtful look.

'Sorry.'

'Willpower alone won't make your new boyfriend turn up any quicker.'

'He's not my boyfriend,' protested Anna.

'Yeah, but he soon will be, I can tell,' said Zoe, giving Anna a dismissive wave of her hand.

Out of the corner of her eye, Anna noticed Tex, Jamie and Yvonne arrive. Perfect timing. As her gaze was met by Tex when she turned round to acknowledge them, she felt her heart give a little flip. She was aware that she was smiling broadly and although Tex smiled back, he didn't look relaxed. There was a tension in his face and an apologetic expression as they came over to the table.

Tex bent down and kissed Anna on the cheek, then spoke quietly into her ear. 'I'm sorry, but we seem to have picked up an extra guest. It's not what you think.'

Confused, Anna had no chance to reply. Jamie stood before the table smiling brightly at her, but Yvonne's warm greeting was followed by the briefest of grimaces as she moved aside so Anna could see.

'Hello everyone,' said Christine, stepping out from behind them both. She looked very glamorous in her high-heeled stilettoes and tight white jeans, a floaty sheer blouse and undulating brunette hair. Christine gave Anna and Zoe an appraising once-over, stroking her hair over one shoulder and then puffing the ends with perfectly manicured hands.

'This is Christine Bennett, you met her the other day,' Tex reminded Anna.

'Hi, again,' Anna said, not sure what was going on.

'I'm Zoe, Anna's sister-in-law.' Zoe held out her hand towards

Jamie's wife. 'And you must be Yvonne? Anna mentioned it was your birthday. Many happy returns for the day.'

'Anyone like a drink?' asked Jamie rather too cheerfully. 'What are you girls drinking? Wine? I'll just get a bottle and we can all have a drink to toast the lovely birthday girl. Come on, Tex, you can give me a hand.'

'Just water for me,' said Tex. 'I'm driving.'

'I didn't realise you were meeting friends,' said Christine. 'I wouldn't have gatecrashed if I'd known. I'd only popped round to show Tex some more samples.'

'Oh, there wasn't anything definite arranged,' explained Anna, trying to ignore the strange agitated feeling rolling around in the pit of her stomach.

'So, you're working for Tex,' asserted Christine, tossing her hair from her shoulder.

'We've just taken Anna on,' explained Yvonne.

'Oh, I see.' Christine directed her comment to Anna. 'That makes two of us working for him.'

'Four actually,' put in Yvonne. 'Technically, Jamie and I work for Tex too.'

'He's got himself quite an entourage then.' Christine pursed her lips. 'All trying to please him, no doubt.'

'Looks like I'm the odd one out,' said Zoe with a little laugh.

With a look that Anna could only describe as withering, Christine raised her eyebrows at Zoe. 'Quite.'

Jamie returned with wine and drinking glasses. Tex brought a couple of stools over, passing one to Jamie, and was about to put his next to Anna, when Christine shuffled her chair along instead, indicating to the gap between herself and Yvonne.

'Here we are, Tex. There's space here for you. I'll budge up next to... err... Sorry, I can't remember your name.'

'Anna.' There was something about Christine that Anna didn't like. Call it women's intuition but she felt sure Christine was trouble.

Zoe excused herself to go to the Ladies'.

Moments later, Anna could feel her phone in her bag vibrating against her leg. She bent down and discreetly looked at the message she had just received.

Awkward or what?!!!!

It came from Zoe, who at that moment returned to her seat.

Anna had to make a deliberate effort not to laugh out loud, and avoided looking at Zoe. She knew she wouldn't be able to control herself if she did. Instead, she let her gaze wander across to the bar where a hen party had just gathered. The bride-to-be was bedecked with fairy wings, tutu and L-plates, and her friends, similarly attired and giggling noisily, were already lining up vodka shots.

'Oh, before I forget, Anna,' said Tex. 'Are you free on Monday for work? I need help looking for an apartment to rent.'

'Oh, I could help you,' piped up Christine, her hand resting on Tex's arm. 'I have an eye for that sort of thing, as you know.'

'That's very kind of you, Christine, but I need Anna to help me with all the legal stuff, words and terminology, the...'

'Jargon?' suggested Anna, looking back at Tex.

'Exactly! Jargon. See what I mean? I need to make sure that I am not taken advantage of.'

Anna doubted very much that Tex would let himself be taken advantage of, business wise or any wise for that matter. She looked questioningly at Jamie.

'That would be great if you could,' confirmed Jamie. 'I know it's short notice but that's how it is sometimes.'

'Monday? Yes, that's okay.' Anna smiled, satisfied that she had

83

muscled Christine out.

'Great. I'll pick you up at eleven o'clock.' Tex looked as if he were trying to supress a grin when he picked up his glass of water.

'No, it's okay, I'll drive. I'll meet you at the church,' said Anna quickly, not wishing to be told what to do. She preferred to do things herself these days.

'Fine. Good.' Tex looked at her thoughtfully for a moment before smiling.

Christine let out a scoffing sort of noise. The look on her face could only be described as poisonous, and Anna decided this was a good moment to nip to the Ladies' and head off any more talk of her meeting up with Tex.

Leaning back against the sink, Anna took a couple of deep breaths. To her, it was obvious that Christine, whoever she was, didn't approve of her working with Tex. She couldn't help feeling that there was history between the two of them. Recent history. A thought which deflated any elation she felt.

The door opened and in came Lucifer's daughter herself. Christine.

'Oh, hi,' said Anna.

Christine joined her at the sink and opened her bag. 'You and Tex, just a working relationship is it?' she said, before dabbing at her lips with Dusky Pink No.7.

'Yes it is. Why do you ask?'

'I was just wondering, that's all.' Christine stopped applying the lipstick to smile condescendingly in the mirror at Anna. 'Have you got a boyfriend? Husband?'

'Ex husband, sort of ex. We're separated,' replied Anna, unsure where this conversation was going.

'Not divorced then?'

'No, it's complicated.'

Christine then took out a small, white, round bottle of perfume.

Christian Dior, *Pure Poison*. How appropriate, thought Anna, watching as Christine sprayed herself on her neck and on each wrist, rubbing her wrists together.

Putting the bottle and lipstick away, Christine said, 'Tex and I… People assume we have just a working relationship, but then when we go out as a couple they think otherwise.' She whisked the zipper shut on the bag and looked directly at Anna. 'It's complicated.'

With that, she left the toilets.

Anna stood there trying to process the information. Okay, was Christine implying that she was actually in some sort of relationship with Tex? The sudden feeling of jealousy that seemed to come from nowhere surprised her.

Instead of going straight back to the table, Anna went through the door at the back of the pub and out into the courtyard garden. At the far end stood a small gazebo sheltering several people who were sitting around a table and smoking. Leaning against the wall of the pub, Anna rested her head back, took a deep breath of fresh air, and tried to work out exactly what Christine had meant. Perhaps Christine was staking her claim over Tex. Warning her off. And still the niggling feeling of jealousy and mistrust wouldn't completely go away; it kept nudging its way to the forefront of her mind.

Anna was just thinking she ought to get back when the sight of Tex coming into the courtyard made her stay put. She was getting used to the little skip her heart gave every time she saw him. She watched him walk over to her. He didn't make eye contact or say anything as he stood beside her. He copied her stance, and still without speaking, just stared straight ahead at the opposite wall, as if contemplating the departure board at Victoria Station.

'There is nothing between Christine and myself,' he said quietly after a few moments. 'There was something at one time, but not anymore.'

A sensation of relief zinged in Anna's stomach. So, she had been right in suspecting there had been something between the two of them. But it was in the past, apparently. A voice at the back of her mind was saying she shouldn't really let it bother her – he was her client, nothing else.

'It's not really any of my business, you don't have to explain,' she said, although she so didn't mean it. 'It doesn't affect our working relationship.'

Tex turned to face her. 'No, that is true, it doesn't affect our working relationship. But it *does* affect our personal one.' He took a step closer and drew her into his arms.

Anna couldn't quite bring herself to resist, even though she knew she should. Sinking into him and closing her eyes, she let herself be held, her head resting under his chin. It felt good. He felt good. She pulled away slightly so she could look up into his deep brown eyes.

'But we don't have a personal relationship,' Anna said without conviction. She knew she should be disentangling herself. This was highly unprofessional. But, God, she so wanted to kiss him again. Tex seemed to have the same idea as he slowly moved his mouth closer to hers.

The moment was broken by a commotion in the doorway as the sound of high heels on the flagstone coming to an abrupt halt, accompanied by 'Argh!' and 'Oops!' made Anna and Tex look round. Despite herself, Anna couldn't help laughing. Zoe had obviously come looking for her. On seeing her and Tex in an embrace, Zoe must have stopped dead in her tracks, but in so doing, lost her footing on the wet floor and stumbled across the step.

'Sorry!' Zoe pulled an eek sort of face at Anna before spinning around and half hobbling back into the pub.

Tex grinned at Anna. 'Perfect timing.' He shook his head, letting Anna go, but as he slid his hand down her arm, he held onto her hand.

Anna could feel the electricity running between them. 'Sorry, we'd better go back in or there'll be another search party out looking for you.'

She let her hand drop away as they went back inside. She laughed to herself at the thought of never washing her hand again now that Tex had touched it, a bit like those fans who had been able to touch Elvis!

Jamie, Yvonne and Christine were putting on their coats. Christine looked decidedly unhappy at the sight of Anna and Tex together.

'Could you take me home please, Tex?' Christine asked. 'I'm really not feeling well.'

Tex looked at Anna. 'Sorry but I am driving. I will have to go.'

'It's okay.' Anna ran her hand down the top of Tex's arm and touched him again with her other hand. That was two hands she couldn't wash now. 'You'd better go.' As she spoke, Anna caught sight of Zoe. The look of concern on her face alarmed Anna immediately. Almost within a nanosecond Anna felt a tap on her shoulder. She looked round and up, and then gasped.

'Mark! What are you doing here?'

Chapter Eleven

'Hello, Anna,' replied Mark casually. 'Fancy seeing you here. Hello, Zoe. Lovely to see you.'

'Likewise,' said Zoe, who clearly didn't mean it.

Mark moved to Anna's side and smiled at everyone. 'Hope I'm not interrupting anything, but I just popped in for a drink and saw my wife here. What a coincidence.' He grinned at Anna and, putting a proprietorial arm around her shoulder, pulled her towards him. Anna tried to wriggle away but Mark's hand was holding her firm.

'Oh, so you're Anna's husband,' said Christine.

'Certainly am,' said Mark with satisfaction, then to Anna, 'We need to talk.'

'Here? Now?' Anna jerked her head away from Mark and glanced at Tex.

Tex watched silently, his face impassive, and although he was neither smiling nor scowling, there was an unmistaken hardened look to his eyes that matched the tension in his voice. 'Don't let us interrupt you. We are leaving anyway.'

Anna couldn't help but feel disappointed at the rather warmer goodbye Tex directed at Zoe than the mere nod of the head proffered at her. She watched as the quartet left, Christine flashing a self-satisfied smile in her direction. Anna found herself looking daggers in response.

'Hope it wasn't anything I said,' grinned Mark, with what Anna could only describe as temerity.

'What's with introducing yourself as my husband?' Irritated didn't even come close to how she felt towards Mark.

Mark finally released his hold, looking all innocent. 'What's wrong with that? I am your husband, after all.'

'You know perfectly well what's wrong with that. Anyway, what's so important that it can't wait until I get home or tomorrow? I am actually having a night out with Zoe.'

'It looked more than a night out with Zoe. Who's that bloke you came back in with?'

'Just my client.'

'Just your client, eh?'

'Yes.'

'If you say so.'

'I do.'

'Not the same client that gave you a lift home the other day by any chance?'

'Piss off, Mark,' she snapped.

Mark held her gaze for a moment before turning to Zoe. 'You couldn't give us a minute, could you?'

Zoe looked questioningly at Anna, who rolled her eyes. 'I'll just be at the bar then.' Zoe picked up her bag and edged past her brother-in-law.

'Well?' said Anna, impatiently turning on Mark.

'Let's sit down.' He gestured towards the seats. 'That's better. Look, I was just out for a drink. I forgot you said you'd be here, but when I saw you with *your client*, I was, well, hurt.'

'Hurt?'

'Yeah, like shocked. Jealous, I suppose.'

'Jealous?'

'Blimey, Anna, it's like having a conversation with an echo.' Mark let out a sigh. 'You know how I feel about you, I told you the other night. You said you were going to think about things. Since then you've avoided me like a dose of the clap.'

'Mark, this isn't the time either,' said Anna gently.

'See, you're doing it again. You're avoiding the issue. Avoiding us.'

Anna took a deep breath. 'There is no "us". I told you that the other day. Getting back together just isn't an option anymore. If anything, we should be looking to make our separation official. Taking it a step further. Divorce.'

'Divorce?' Mark sat back, as if the word had been spat at him. 'You want a divorce? Where the fuck did that idea come from? We've never talked about divorce before. Never.'

'Maybe it's about time we did,' said Anna carefully. She could see a muscle beginning to twitch in his jaw, tension visible in his neck, spreading down through his shoulders, reaching his hands as he balled and unballed his fists. A familiar sign that an explosion of temper was on the way.

'No!' Mark shouted the word. People at a nearby table turned round to look briefly. His next words were quieter but still as forceful. 'I'm not agreeing to a divorce.' With that, he stood up and marched out of the pub.

'Do you want me to come in with you?' asked Zoe as they came to a stop outside Anna's house later that evening.

Anna shook her head. 'No, I'll be okay, but thanks anyway.' She looked towards the house which was in total darkness. 'Either Mark's not back yet or he's asleep. Either way, I'm glad. I have no intention of getting into a row with him tonight about anything, least of all a divorce.'

'It's about time you divorced him anyway,' said Zoe. 'Neither Nathan nor I can understand why you've never pursued it.'

'I know. I know,' replied Anna ruefully, well aware how keen they were for her to divorce Mark. 'It's just, well, it's like admitting you've failed at something. When you get divorced you even get a certificate to prove that you've been a total failure. It's been easier to ignore it than to confront it. Not only that, but I've never felt it necessary.'

'So you definitely don't want to get back with Mark?'

Anna shook her head. 'It won't work. We've tried before but it never has. I don't know why this time would be any different. I was going to speak to Mark but I wasn't quite ready. It just sort of came out tonight.'

'It's amazing what a new love interest can do for you,' smiled Zoe, ignoring Anna's protests that Tex wasn't a love interest nor could possibly be one. 'Oh look, this must be my taxi. Thanks for tonight. I really enjoyed getting out for a couple of hours, although I am seriously knackered now.'

Fortunately, Mark was asleep on the sofa when Anna crept in and upstairs. As she reached the landing, she could see the flickering light of the TV coming from under the door of Luke's room. Anna gently knocked on the door. No answer. Luke must have fallen asleep watching it. She crept in and switched off the television.

'I wasn't asleep,' came Luke's voice, slightly muffled by the duvet.

'Oh, sorry, I thought you were. Do you want the telly back on?'

'No,' said Luke abruptly, sitting up and flicking on his bedside light. 'Dad said you were out with a man.'

Anna eyed her son carefully. Impossible to tell what he was thinking.

'What else did he say?' she asked, giving an inward sigh. Mark had obviously come home and stirred things up already. Luke shrugged. Anna chose her words carefully. 'I went out with Zoe and we briefly met my boss, his wife, my client and another woman.'

'Dad didn't seem to think it was just that. I think he was a bit upset to be honest, seeing you with another man.'

'It wasn't exactly like that,' said Anna patiently. She sat down on the edge of Luke's bed. 'You know we've always been honest with each other. If there was anything significant to tell you, then I would.'

Luke nodded. 'I know.'

'There may well come a time when I meet someone else. I wouldn't like to think I'll be on my own forever.' She rested her hand on Luke's shoulder. 'Your dad could just as easily meet someone too.'

'I suppose so.'

'Now you really should go to sleep, it's late. I'll see you in the morning. We can always talk more then, when we're not so tired.' She gave Luke a hug and a kiss. 'Night. Love you.'

'Love you too, Mum.'

Saturday morning was tense, the atmosphere between Anna and Mark positively Arctic.

'This is pleasant. Not!' said Luke, sitting down at the table. 'What's that saying about cutting the air with a knife?'

'Just what I was thinking,' commented Mark as he continued texting without looking up. An awkward silence followed and then Mark spoke again, this time more brightly. 'Hey, Luke, fancy going to watch Chelsea play Wigan tomorrow? A mate of mine's got some tickets. It's at Stamford Bridge. We can meet him and his son there.'

'Definitely,' said Luke without a moment's hesitation. 'That would be brilliant. Cheers, Dad.'

Anna couldn't help feeling slightly peeved at Luke's enthusiastic response to Mark's suggestion. She then checked herself. She wanted Luke to have a good relationship with his father, so she should be pleased they were getting along.

'That will be nice,' she forced herself to say.

'It will be brilliant. I'm going out now,' said Luke, getting up from the table. 'Going to meet Jacob. See you later.'

Anna waited until Luke was safely out of the house before she spoke.

'Mark. Can we talk?'

'Before you say anything, can you just listen to me first?' Mark put his phone down and pushed his plate to the middle of the table. 'I know I've been a shit in the past and I am sorry. You know that, don't you?'

Anna nodded. 'Yes, I know.' She knew that Mark was sorry, he had always been sorry, but ultimately it had never changed anything. He had continued to behave the same.

'I've done a lot of thinking while I've been in the States,' Mark continued, his fingers twitching. 'At first, I was glad to be away. Things were so difficult between us, it was a relief to be several thousand miles away. But I never stopped thinking about you, Anna, never stopped loving you. I've missed you. I meant what I said when I first came back. I've changed. I'm not like I used to be. I've grown up. I really want us to try again.'

He looked and sounded so sincere, Anna felt she could almost believe him, but she knew they couldn't go back to how things had been. That was too awful to contemplate. Maybe Mark had changed, but so had she.

'When you first went to America, I wasn't sure how I was going to manage,' said Anna gently. 'I hadn't been on my own since I was nineteen. I was devastated our marriage was in the state it was, it was the last thing I wanted. But after you left, I discovered I was more capable than I thought. I like where I am now and I don't mean in the physical sense. I don't want to go backwards. Us getting back together would be doing that. I just want to go forwards, and that means divorce. I'm sorry, Mark.'

Anna stood up and rinsed her cup in the sink. She felt awful saying that but it was true and she had to be honest with Mark. She couldn't let him think there was any chance of them getting back together, that wouldn't be fair.

Mark came and stood beside her. 'I'm not agreeing to a divorce. You'll have to divorce me.'

'Why are you being so difficult? Why do you want to stay married?' Anna waited for a response but was met with silence. She looked thoughtfully out of the window at the buddleia bobbing in the spring breeze, before adding defiantly, 'I'll get some advice. I'm sure I have grounds for divorce whether you agree to it or not.'

'Do you really want to drag our marriage through the courts? Do you really want Luke to find out all the details? Do you really want it splashed across the papers?'

'What are you on about, the papers?' Anna turned to face him. 'The newspapers aren't going to be interested in a divorce between an ex-footballer and his wife. Remember, I pre-date the WAG scene. No one's interested in me.'

'No, but they might be a bit more interested when they find out the co-defendant is making a name for himself in the restaurant world, has a Michelin star, and is hoping to open a restaurant in Arundel.' Mark spoke with a coolness that made her shudder involuntarily. 'Yes, Anna, the papers might take a bit more of an interest then and I don't know how that will affect his business. Wouldn't want it to have a negative effect, would we? And in case you're wondering how I know all about Mr Garcia, it's amazing what you can learn from a file being left lying around on the table for anyone to read. That and Google.'

'I can't believe you did that!' Anna cried. 'You've been looking at my work files. They are confidential.'

'If they were that private you should have put them away.'

Anna took a deep breath. 'Mr Garcia is a client. Nothing else.

Besides, that sort of news isn't really headline is it?'

'True, but there is a bit of a hoo-ha about his restaurant. You know, locals opposing it. This will just taint his reputation a bit further.'

'You need to do your homework better, Mark. Most of the locals are for the restaurant now. Anyway, it's all publicity and will only get people talking about the restaurant all the more. In fact, people will be dying to see who this notorious chef is, so your plan may well backfire.' Anna couldn't keep the triumph out of her voice. Now she had him on the back foot. She took another deep breath, hoping to install some confidence in herself before she spoke again. 'I don't want you living here anymore. There's plenty of bed and breakfast places around or you could go and stay with one of your friends. But I think your staying with me has run its course.'

'I'm not going anywhere,' said Mark. 'It's my house and I'm not leaving. Besides, I don't think Luke will be happy if you kick me out.'

'Don't you dare bring Luke into this,' Anna snapped. She fought hard to keep her breathing under control so she didn't stammer over her words. 'You've done enough damage. Don't you even think about trying to set me up as the bad one. I've always been very decent about you to our son. I've never once run you down to him, so don't you try and play games with me and make out that I'm letting him down. I did everything I could to make our family work. I didn't ruin our marriage.'

'No, but you ruined my career.' There was a hard, callous tone in his voice. He stood up, towering over her. 'Because of you, I had to give up football.'

'That's so unfair,' cried Anna. 'I was only driving because you were too drunk. I didn't even want to go to that party but you insisted. If I'd known before it was only because you were shagging the hostess, I would never have agreed to go in the first place.'

'And if you hadn't been so bloody miserable and insisted that we had to leave the party because you were worried about being late for the babysitter, then we could have stayed the night and I could have driven back the following morning. Safely. But no, we had to leave, didn't we?'

'We had to leave because you were so drunk you were practically fawning over Melanie Wilson in front of her husband. You made it so obvious that you and her were at it.' Anna held on to the side of the worktop. 'Anyway, that's typical of you, that you can only think about yourself. That car accident put me in hospital for five days, killed our unborn baby and meant that I could never have children again. Don't you think I've relived that evening over and over again. Thinking if only? What if? Wishing I could change what happened. Don't you think both of us have suffered because of that night? It was a combination of events and decisions. So don't you dare lay all the blame at my door.'

Anna was fighting back the tears now. She had always felt guilty about the car accident even though she knew it wasn't her fault. The car had slid on wet mud at a sharp bend in the road. Sliding across the tarmac. Careering through the fence. Rolling over and over down the embankment. The hedgerow at the bottom of the slope catching the broken and battered BMW. It had been an accident. A dreadful accident with awful consequences, but an accident nonetheless. The tears were stinging her eyes and she blinked hard to keep them from falling. 'You can't blame me for everything, Mark. You can't punish me forever.'

'I'm not punishing you, Anna.' Mark exhaled deeply. 'Anna, please, I'm sorry. I don't want to argue, I don't want to upset you. And I don't want to divorce you. In fact, I refuse to divorce you. I love you.' Mark rested his hand lightly on her back. 'There's something else.'

'I don't want to hear it.' She shrugged his hand away and rushed from the kitchen, seeking solace in her bedroom.

Anna sat silently on the edge of her bed, trying to catch her breath, concentrating on regaining her composure. On hearing the front door close, she went to the window, tipping the blinds so she could see out. She saw Mark pause as he closed the garden gate and then look up at her. Did he know she would be watching? He gave a half smile before walking down the road, heavy-footed and head bowed. It wasn't until he was out of sight that Anna's resolve finally gave way and she sank to the floor, letting the tears fall.

The tears weren't just from the pain of the past that had been brought back to the surface – the pain of her broken marriage, her lost child and lost chance of more children – she cried for the frustration and anger Mark had invoked within her, and for the hurt she seemed to be inflicting on him now. All the times she had wanted to hurt him, to make him suffer, to crush his love as he had done to hers, and now that the tables seemed to be turned she didn't feel any satisfaction whatsoever. Just sadness.

Chapter Twelve

Tex checked his watch again. It was nearly eleven and Anna would be arriving at the premises any minute now.

Despite his best attempts over the weekend to dismiss any thoughts of Anna from his mind, he had found it a futile exercise. It had annoyed him more than he cared to admit when her husband had turned up on Friday night. The way Mark had put his arm around Anna's shoulder with such familiarity, and the fact that Anna didn't move away, had irked him further. It was a surprising feeling that sat uncomfortably with him. He knew he hadn't been very magnanimous towards her when he'd left the pub, barely saying a word, and now he felt regretful.

Then to top it all, he had arrived at the restaurant this morning to find that the main door and windows had been damaged. Several of the small leaded windowpanes had been smashed and the front door had been daubed in green paint with the words 'Yank Out'. Had it been senseless vandalism he might have not been so concerned, but the fact that 'Yank' referred directly to him was unsettling.

The sound of knocking at the door and his name being called out sliced through his ruminating. She was here.

Walking out into the main hall of the old church, Tex drew breath at the sight of Anna, and realised he was involuntarily casting a barely disguised appreciative eye over her. She was wearing a white t-shirt that clung in all the right places, with a crewneck, pale pink cardigan and a tailored black skirt which finished just on her knee. Her slender legs, encased in skin-toned glossy nylon, looked gorgeous and her high black heels gave her an extra couple of inches in height.

'Hey, there. How ya' doin'?' said Tex, regaining his equanimity and going over to her, kissed her on each cheek. He felt the tension in her shoulders.

'I'm fine,' Anna replied.

She sounded very businesslike today, Tex thought, and felt like kicking himself. Having got her to relax and open up a bit last time she was here, now, after his behaviour on Friday evening, the barrier was back in place.

'What happened to the front of the building?' asked Anna.

'Vandals.'

'That's terrible. Why would anyone do that? Have you managed to sort someone out to clean it off? I can organise it, if you need me to.'

For now, Tex decided to bide his time before apologising about Friday. 'Thank you, but I've arranged it already.'

'Is it just this place that's been attacked?'

'It would seem so.'

'So they've singled you out. Who do you think would do that?'

Tex shrugged. 'Local competition. Local people. Who knows?'

'Well, I don't think any of the locals would do it, not after the party, and if you think it was the tea rooms, then you are seriously out of touch.'

She seemed riled by his suggestion that the tea rooms, as competition, might be involved, so he let it go. Perhaps now was a good time to mention her brother. She had given him one of Nathan's business cards the other day over lunch when Tex had said he

99

really ought to check out the local gym.

'I… erm… spoke to your brother this morning.'

Anna looked at him in surprise. 'My brother? What for?'

'To ask him if he could give me a couple of mornings each week to keep me in shape. A bit of jogging, gentle exercise.'

'Oh, right. What did he say?'

'He's coming over tomorrow.' He smiled at her. Was she pleased? Had he done enough yet to win her over? 'Would you like a coffee?'

Anna shrugged. 'Don't you want to get on with finding somewhere to live? After all, you are having to pay Jamie for my time here.'

'I could tell you what I'm looking for over a coffee. Let's go to the coffee shop by the river,' suggested Tex, keeping his sigh of frustration in. She wasn't making it easy for him, that was sure. Maybe she'd feel more relaxed on neutral ground. He rested his hand on her back to shepherd her towards the door and noted that she increased her pace just enough so that he couldn't maintain contact.

Ten minutes later they were seated in the Riverside Coffee Pot positioned by the River Arun, looking out towards the three-arched bridge that spanned the water.

'So, what are your requirements?' asked Anna, retrieving a notebook and pen from her bag. She didn't look up as she spoke. 'Number of bedrooms? Location? How much do you want to pay? How long do you want the tenancy for?'

Tex decided to play it straight for now, keep things on a business keel until the time was right.

'Two bedrooms. Needs to be here in Arundel. Can be a house or an apartment. Parking is a must, as is internet connection.' He paused, waiting for her to write these points down. 'I am flexible on the rent and I want the tenancy for at least six months.'

'We could begin by looking online, or we could go to the

estate agents this morning,' said Anna, taking a sip of her tea, still avoiding eye contact. 'It might be easier to go direct actually, as not all estate agents keep their webpages up to date, especially where rentals are concerned. Stride & Hunter Lettings would be a good one to start with as they are quite up-market, with some very exclusive properties to let.'

Tex watched her gaze flit to the window and then back to her notebook, pen poised. 'Okay, I will take your advice.'

Stride & Hunter's offices were only across the road. Tex let Anna lead the way. An elderly gentleman looked up from behind his desk as the couple came in, giving the briefest of smiles before greeting them.

'Good morning, sir, madam. How can I help?' he asked starchily.

'We are looking for a two-bedroom property to rent in the town,' said Anna.

'Please sit down. My name's Arthur Hemmings,' began the estate agent, gesturing to the two seats in front of his desk. 'If I can just take your names?' He picked up his fountain pen and opened to a blank page in his notebook.

'Garcia,' replied Tex, then spelt it out.

'Mr and Mrs Garcia,' said the estate agent as he wrote.

'We're not a couple,' corrected Anna. 'Mr Garcia is my client.'

'Client?' Arthur Hemmings peered over his glasses at Anna and then at Tex, raising his eyebrows slightly. Anna looked as if she was about to say something but Arthur Hemmings spoke again. 'Right, first things first. Are you living permanently in the UK, Mr Garcia? It's just some of our landlords aren't too keen on foreign nationals. We require two UK references.'

'Mr Garcia has been here for over five years,' replied Anna, not allowing Tex time to answer. 'References won't be a problem either.'

'Professional references.' More peering over the top of his glasses.

101

'As I said, that won't be a problem,' replied Anna firmly.

'Good. What about benefits? Do you work? Full-time? Most of my clients prefer professionals, no one on benefits, I'm afraid.'

'Self-employed actually,' replied Anna again. Tex noticed there was an edge to her voice.

'Arr, self-employed. That can be a bit tricky. Again, most of my landlords prefer tenants to be in paid employment. Makes it easier all round.'

'I'm sure the company's accountant can provide you with the necessary supporting paperwork,' Anna said.

Tex sat back and folded his arms as he observed the duel with interest. Anna was definitely riled, probably fuelled somewhat by her bad mood with him, but she was certainly holding her ground.

'Yes, I appreciate what you are saying.' Arthur Hemmings put down his pen. 'It's just with the economic climate being the way it is, landlords want more reassurance, they need to be certain that the rent will be met. Being self-employed these days isn't particularly secure.'

'You know nothing about my client's business, his finances or his creditworthiness; you are making assumptions. And on that basis, I don't think I can recommend your services to my client.' Anna stood and tapped Tex's arm. 'Come on, Tex, let's go. We're wasting our time here.'

Tex followed Anna out of the office and then watched with great amusement as she stuck her head back round the door.

'And just for the record, my client is a professional and highly successful chef with his own Michelin-star restaurant, and is about to open another one in the town. Your loss, I do believe.' Letting the door slam behind her, Anna marched off around the corner.

Tex jogged to catch up. He regarded her for a moment.

'I'm sorry,' she said, looking sheepish. 'He just really annoyed me.'

'Hey, that's cool. Thank you for defending me. I don't think anyone other than my mother has spoken up for me like that.'

'I'm sure you are capable of looking after yourself but he was being so pompous.' Anna let out a sigh. 'I hated the way he just jumped to conclusions.'

Tex stopped smiling and spoke softly. 'Like I did the other night?'

'Yes. No. Maybe…' Anna looked down at her feet. 'What conclusion did you jump to?'

'That your marriage wasn't quite as over as you said.' Tex moved Anna over to the side of the pavement to allow some sightseers to pass by. 'Was that the wrong conclusion?' He hoped it was.

'From my perspective, yes.' Anna's breathing was heavier.

Tex could see her chest rise and fall quickly as she took shorter, quicker breaths. He moved closer, resting his shoulder against the wall next to hers, their faces only inches apart.

'Then I am sorry,' said Tex gently. He dipped his head to look up under her eyelashes. When she bit her bottom lip, he felt a deep desire settle in his bones. He had to fight every urge not to lean in and kiss her.

She glanced up at him. 'There's something else.'

'I'm listening.' Jeez, what else could there be?

'He's staying at my house. On the sofa.'

'On the sofa,' Tex repeated. Okay, this wasn't ideal but then again, it could be worse. Exhaling long and hard, he leaned back against the wall, looking skyward and briefly closing his eyes. Why did he get the feeling he was getting involved in something that he would probably regret? Then pushing himself upright, he took hold of Anna's hand. 'Let's go.'

He strode off up the hill towards another estate agents', keeping a firm hold on Anna's hand so she had no choice but to follow. That in itself was something to be marvelled at, he thought, considering her choice of footwear today.

At the next agency, Anna had rather more success and managed to secure two viewings for that afternoon. One was a Grade II listed house at the top of Arundel, near to the cathedral, and the other an apartment overlooking the River Arun.

'I really like the look of this one,' said Anna, holding up the apartment details as they walked back down the hill. 'It's also closer to your restaurant than the other one, nicer views, and you have an allocated parking space. With the house you need a parking permit, I don't think you get an allocated space, just permission to park on the road.'

'It would be nice having views of the river rather than the street,' said Tex. 'Are you hungry? Shall we have some lunch in one of the pubs?' He was pleased that Anna seemed far more relaxed since her outburst earlier and their clearing of the air about her marital status.

'Let's just quickly nip over to Johnson's Estate Agents,' said Anna, pointing to the bay window opposite them. 'They are quite a big chain and have branches in Bognor and Chichester. They might have something we haven't seen before.'

'Okay, but then lunch,' agreed Tex, again taking her hand as they crossed the road. He noted with satisfaction that this time, Anna actually held his hand rather than just leaving it limply in his, as she had done earlier.

'I think it's mostly houses for sale. I can't see any for rent,' commented Anna, as they edged gradually along the shopfront, studying the photos and brief descriptions. Then, she suddenly gripped his arm tightly with her free hand. 'Oh my God!'

'What?' chuckled Tex, expecting her to say she'd found a perfect home for him. However, when he looked down at her, the ashen look on her face told him something different. 'Anna? What's wrong?'

The power of speech seemed to have deserted her. Letting go

of his arm, Anna pressed her finger against the glass, pointing at a property hanging at the edge of the bay window, the words 'For Sale' in striking red across the corner of the photo. Finally, with a tremulous voice she managed to eke out a coherent sentence.

'There must be some mistake. That's… that's *my* house.'

Chapter Thirteen

Anna's initial reaction had been to tear into the estate agents' and demand to know why they had her house on the market and that they remove the advert immediately. Fortunately, Tex had a much more pragmatic and subtle approach to dealing with it. Having safely seated Anna in a nearby coffee shop, harbouring a skinny latte in her cupped hands, he went into the estate agents' posing as a potential purchaser.

Anna glanced at her watch. Tex had been gone a good twenty minutes, surely it couldn't take that long to get the details. Just as she toyed with the idea of going to find him, Tex walked back in carrying an armful of leaflets.

'I didn't realise how difficult it was just to get one set of details,' he commented, flicking through the papers. 'They want to put you on their mailing list, try to get you to put your house on with them, offer financial advice, and take all your personal information before they even make a move towards the filing cabinet for the property information.' He pulled out a sheet. 'Have a look at this while I get us both another drink.'

Anna looked at the piece of paper and read the address twice, just to check it was definitely her house and not the one next door. No doubt about it, 2 Coach House Cottages, Chichester it was.

The picture had been taken recently, she noted, as the pink

clematis that crept over her door, across to the window and flowered in April, was in full bloom. She turned the particulars over and staring back at her were two photos of the interior of her house. The first was of the living room, the fireplace being the main focal point, with the wooden hand-painted letters spelling out 'HOME' on the mantelpiece, the antique gold-leafed mirror hanging above.

The words *charming, delightful, good decorative order* and *original features* jumped out as she scanned the description. The second photo was of her kitchen, taken from the doorway, a vase of lilies on the windowsill, her Shaker cupboards and Belfast sink in the background, her table and chairs in the foreground. Anna looked closer at the photo. Something had caught her eye that was out of place. There on the table was a black and red mobile phone. Mark's mobile phone.

'The bastard!' fumed Anna as Tex sat down next to her. 'The complete and utter bastard. He never goes anywhere without his phone. He must have been there when they took the pictures. He's put the house on the market.'

'I assume you are referring to Mark,' said Tex.

'Who else could it be? Maybe there's been some mistake.'

'Sorry. No mistake. The agent told me that Mr Barnes, the owner, was moving abroad and wanted a quick sale. That there was no forwarding chain and that the property was vacant possession.' Tex took a sip of his espresso. 'Mark obviously didn't say anything to you about it then?'

'Obviously,' said Anna, rather more acidly than she had intended. It wasn't Tex's fault, he was trying to help. She looked apologetically at him. 'Sorry. It's just a shock. No, he never said a word to me. He must have organised this pretty much as soon as he turned up. Look, see those flowers on the windowsill? Well, he bought those for me the first weekend when he cooked us a meal.' Anna rubbed her brow with her fingertips. 'I knew he was up to something. I remember now. On the Monday when I got back from Chichester, he was on the phone and as soon as I came in, he hung up. He's been planning this all along.'

'What about the estate agent? Has he not contacted you with viewings?'

A few moments passed as the realisation dawned upon Anna. 'Oh my God! I am so, so stupid,' she groaned. 'I had a phone call later that week from an estate agent. I was in the middle of translating a document and had already had a couple of time-wasting phone calls. I assumed it was a wrong number. I didn't wait to hear what they had to say, I put the phone down.'

Anna buried her face in her hands and then ran them through her hair, amazed at the level Mark was prepared to take his perfidy to.

'Is the house in both your names?' asked Tex.

'No. I wasn't working at the time so there was no way I could get a mortgage. Besides, Mark bought it outright from the sale proceeds of our house in Southampton.' Anna twirled the spoon around in her latte.

'You need to get some legal advice. I can arrange for you to see my solicitor tomorrow? I can ring him now.' Tex reached into his pocket for his phone.

'No. Don't ring them, I've got my own solicitor. I am capable of sorting this out.'

He pursed his lips and then slipped the phone back into his pocket. 'Yes, of course.'

'Sorry,' said Anna, knowing she had sounded churlish. 'It's kind of you to offer, but I'll be okay. Thank you anyway.' She gave him what she hoped was a friendly smile. Although at present she didn't feel quite in control of her emotions.

An hour later, having made a half-hearted attempt at eating a jacket potato with tuna mayonnaise – lunch that Tex had insisted she should have – Anna had stopped picking up the details of her house and muttering things like 'unbelievable' or 'bastard'. Now a more belligerent and defiant mood began to inhabit her.

'If he thinks I'm going to agree to sell the house just like that, without even talking to me about it first, then he can think again,' she announced as she pushed her plate away. 'He's got to at least provide for Luke until Luke's eighteen. We had this all agreed before he went to the States. I *knew* he was back for something else other than…' Anna trailed off and then waved her hand dismissively. 'Sorry, ignore me. You don't want to hear all this.'

'What did he say he was back for?' asked Tex quietly.

'Oh, nothing. Don't worry about it.'

'When you said earlier your marriage was over from your perspective, you didn't say what his perspective was. What's he really come back for?' Although Tex's voice was soft, the hard look in his eyes betrayed him. Anna wished she hadn't said anything, but Tex didn't look like he was going to be fobbed off.

'He said he wanted us to get back together,' she replied after a few moments. 'I've told him it won't work. It's not what I want.'

'And has he accepted that?'

Anna shrugged and shifted in her seat. She decided not to mention Mark's reaction and threat to her suggestion of a divorce. Tex didn't need to know. She'd deal with it.

Looking up at Tex, she couldn't quite hold his gaze. She felt as if his eyes could see right into her heart and mind. Could he see how much her heart fluttered when he looked at her like that with those intense dark brown eyes? Could he read the thoughts and images her mind involuntarily conjured up of him kissing her? Like he had nearly kissed her the other night at the Fish and Fly. Or how she was sure he was going to kiss her earlier that morning? This really wasn't good. He was her client; she couldn't

109

possibly get involved, but if she was honest, she didn't think she could possibly resist. Feeling herself blush, she tore her eyes away from his, studying her watch, trying to hide her embarrassment. 'We're going to be late for those viewings.'

'We could always rearrange if you wanted to go home and sort things out,' suggested Tex, standing up and easing Anna's chair out for her.

'That's nice of you to offer but I'll be fine,' said Anna as they headed for the exit. 'Anyway, we can't have us both homeless!' She gave a little laugh, which she guessed was probably unconvincing.

When Tex slipped his arm around her shoulder as they walked across the bridge towards the apartment, Anna found herself snuggling into him, as if it were something they had done a hundred times before, although the fluttering sensation in her stomach told her otherwise. And when he then dropped a small kiss on the top of head, squeezing her gently, her stomach felt as if it could give the spin cycle on her washing machine a run for its money.

'It will be okay,' he said reassuringly.

Anna wasn't entirely sure what Tex was referring to. Maybe he was just being kind.

When they paused on the bridge to admire the renovated apartment buildings lining the banks of the River Arun, Tex took his hand away and rested his arms on the edge of the stone parapet.

'The apartment we're going to look at is one of those on the top floor,' said Anna, trying to refocus on what she was there for as she pointed to the blue shiplapped façade of the new development on the other bank of the river. The buildings consisted of what looked like five flats on each of the three floors. Each apartment had its own balcony overlooking the water and across to the main hub of the town.

Due to the tidal water and close proximity to the sea, Arundel had been a very busy shipping town in the past. Now, however, the old buildings that had stood empty and run-down for so many years were part of a regeneration project. A lot of them had been converted into apartments or, indeed, pulled down and new buildings constructed in their place, such as these, she explained to Tex.

'And is there parking?' he asked.

'Yes, it's underneath the apartments. You have your own designated bay.'

The apartment was stunning and Anna was pleased that Tex seemed to be of the same opinion. It had an open-plan living area, the kitchen being separated by a breakfast bar, and the double sliding doors opening onto the balcony from the living room were a noteworthy feature. The main bedroom, with a small Juliet balcony, also looked over the river, while the second bedroom and bathroom were at the back of the property where the entrance door was, looking over at the buildings behind.

'That second bedroom will be very useful for when my sister visits,' commented Tex as they wandered back across the bridge. 'She's coming in a couple of weeks with her husband and two children.'

'Ooh, that will be a bit of a squash,' said Anna. They paused again at the bridge to admire the view down the river.

'I can always sleep on the sofa, assuming I have one by then.' He turned and smiled at her. 'That will be your next assignment. Furniture shopping with me.'

'People will start thinking we're an old married couple.' Anna gave a small laugh.

'Not old and maybe not married but...'

There he was doing that smiling with his eyes thing again, and Anna knew she was doing that stupid, embarrassing looking away thing in response.

The afternoon ended by looking around a Georgian house at

the top of the hill. Tex agreed it probably wasn't as ideal as the apartment by the river. The lack of private parking was as big a drawback as the river by the apartment was a major attraction. So with Anna's help, he paid a deposit and completed the application form for a six-month rolling tenancy on the apartment.

'Are you always as decisive as that?' asked Anna as she unlocked her car and got in the driver's seat. They were now back at the old church building. 'You didn't think about the apartment for too long.'

'I know when I like something, so I cannot see the point in wasting time looking elsewhere,' replied Tex.

Anna went to close the door but he had somehow managed to position himself in the way, one arm casually resting on the roof, the other on the top of the door. He lowered his head so their eyes were level.

'Thank you for your help today.'

'All part of the service,' replied Anna, her hand still on the door handle.

'I hope you manage to sort everything out with your... err... with Mark,' said Tex. 'Make sure you get some legal advice and try not to get upset about it. You will achieve a lot more if you can stay calm.'

He moved out of the way so she could close the door and stood there with his hands in his pockets, a brooding look on his face, watching her as she drove away.

Anna knew what Tex had said was right. She definitely needed to speak to her solicitor, and she also needed to stay calm when she confronted Mark about the house sale. However, now she was nearing home, her lovely little flint cottage that she loved dearly, she could feel the anger rising up inside her again, the pure impudence of what Mark had done stirring her fury once more. No way was she going to be able to stay calm.

Chapter Fourteen

'Please, Anna, let me explain,' pleaded Mark, walking across the living room towards her. 'Sit down. Let's talk about this civilly.'

'I don't want to sit down and have some cosy chat about it. I want to know what's going on.' Anna could feel anger raging through every part of her body. She actually felt like she could be violent towards him. 'Tell me!'

Mark nodded his head slightly as if conceding defeat and capitulating to her demand. 'Just hear me out before you say anything.'

'Get on with it then.' Anna folded her arms and jutted out her chin.

'I was going to tell you. No, I was. Don't raise your eyebrows like that. I tried to tell you a couple of times, but you didn't want to talk. Every time I said there was something else, you avoided getting into a conversation.'

Anna sighed inwardly as she took in what Mark was saying and realised that he was right. 'You could have told me when you first came back. It would have been easier.'

'I didn't want to upset you as soon as I got here.' Mark moved closer and put his hand on her arm. 'Come on, Annie, let's sit down.'

Anna shrugged off his gesture, ignoring the pet name he used to call her. She wasn't that much of a pushover. 'You can't just sell the house. Where are we supposed to live? More to the point, why? Why are you selling it?'

'It won't be that bad. There are loads of places to rent in Chichester. I won't leave you and Luke homeless, give me some credit.'

'Rent! We're going to have to rent? Luke needs security. We can't just rent, we could be asked to move in six months. No, that's not on, Mark.'

'People rent all the time. You can get twelve-month tenancy agreements. I'll make sure everything is sorted. Like I said, you won't be left homeless.'

'You still haven't answered me. Why are you selling?' Anna closed her eyes and exhaled, suddenly feeling tired, physically and mentally. She needed to sit down. Her emotions were taking a hammering today. 'Please, Mark, just tell me.'

Mark sat down on the opposite sofa to which Anna had slumped into, leaning over, he rested his elbows on his legs, clasping his hands together. He was like a chameleon, thought Anna, one day aggressive and spiteful, the next subdued and sorrowful.

'Mark?' she asked again, this time more gently.

'Things aren't going so well in the States with the football academy. I need the money from the sale of the house,' his voice vacillating. 'The bank's starting to get twitchy for its money and I need to put cash into the business to develop it. Selling the house is the only way I can raise more funds. I know you can't afford to buy it.'

'What makes you so sure?'

'Well, can you?'

Anna shook her head and swallowed down her pride. 'No, I can't. I wish I could but I just don't earn enough to get a mortgage.'

'Exactly. Why bother saying that?'

'You still should have asked though,' said Anna, although she knew she was only point scoring. 'Isn't there any other way, any other way at all?'

'No.'

'What about your business partner? Your parents?'

'No. I've tried everything. I need a lot of money and the house proceeds are the only way to do it.' He looked up at Anna. 'I'm sorry, I know I should have told you sooner. I tried. I wish there was some other way, I really do.'

Anna looked at Mark sitting there. He didn't look his usual confident, some might say arrogant, self. Instead, she saw a vulnerable, forlorn and humiliated man. How could she hate one man so much and yet still feel compassion for him? It was madness. She couldn't fathom it out at all.

'Will the money actually save the business or will it just get you out of a hole for now? What I mean is, are you sure you're not just throwing good money after bad? Is the academy actually a viable business?'

'Fucking hell, Anna, you sound like my sodding bank manager!' Mark leant back, looking up at the ceiling. 'Of course it's viable, but if I don't put the money in now it will be closed within six months, twelve tops.'

'Couldn't you get a mortgage on the house? That way you could free up the equity without selling it.'

Mark shook his head. 'No UK bank is going to lend to a US resident whose business finances are in the shit, and likewise no US bank is going to lend on a UK home. Not these days with the way the economy is for everyone.'

'I'm sorry, Mark, but you got yourself into the financial mess you're in, it's up to you to sort it out without it affecting Luke, and selling the house is taking away any security I have for him.' Suddenly she felt empowered. She was standing up to Mark, something she should have done before. 'You've got a responsibility to him until he's at least eighteen. You have to provide a home for him. I'll fight it in the courts if I have to. I'm not agreeing to you selling the house.'

Mark stood up, looking at her for a few seconds, his lips pursed. When he finally spoke, the menace in his voice sent a slither of alarm snaking down Anna's spine.

'In that case you don't leave me with any choice. I was hoping to avoid this.'

He went to his briefcase by the side of the fireplace, and from the inside pocket pulled out a white envelope which had his company logo printed in the top left-hand corner. He tipped the contents onto the coffee table. The half a dozen or so photos that scattered the surface made Anna recoil in horror.

She looked at Mark, not daring to say what she was thinking. She had forgotten all about them. Intimate photos of her, taken by Mark, one very drunken night probably over ten years ago now.

'I didn't know you still had those,' she ventured at last, crouching down at the table, turning them over one by one before attempting to gather them up.

Mark's hand clamped down on hers. 'Oh no you don't. They're mine. I took them. They belong to me.' Before she realised what he was doing, Mark had swooped them up and dropped them back into the envelope. He smiled smugly. 'Great night that was, don't you remember?'

'You know I don't,' snapped Anna. 'I was so drunk I didn't know what I was doing. You, on the other hand, knew exactly what you were doing. Now give me the photos.'

'I don't think so. You see, they are my insurance policy.' Mark popped the envelope back into his briefcase, shutting the lid firmly and ensuring it was locked.

'What do you mean?' Anna struggled to keep the tremor from her voice.

'If you stand in the way of selling the house, if you persist in applying for a divorce, I may just be forced to send copies of these out to your friends and colleagues, oh, and pop them on Facebook.'

Anna gasped. 'You wouldn't!'

'You wanna bet on that?'

'That's blackmail.'

'Blackmail is a rather unpleasant word.' Mark cocked his head to one side. 'I much prefer to describe it as encouraging you. Encouraging you to see things from a different angle.'

'And you wonder why I want to divorce you!' Anna could hear herself screeching at him. 'It's because you always want things your way, on your terms. You only ever think of yourself and satisfying your needs. Never mind about anyone else and what they want.' She couldn't stop herself from screaming at him. The words just continued to flow as the panic took hold. 'You're just being difficult about the divorce because you're not in control. It's not me you really want, it's just the money from the house.'

'It doesn't have to be like this, Anna,' said Mark calmly. 'There is another solution.'

Anna sat bolt upright. 'What's that?' She knew there must be a way. Thank God!

'I could let the business go, move back to the UK. Back here.' He jabbed his finger towards the floor several times. 'If you agreed, if you wanted to, we could make a fresh start. You, me, Luke. A family again.'

'Oooh! Who's the new boy then?' crooned Christine as she swanned into the business premises. 'And look at you in your lycra. Very nice. Both of you actually.'

'I wasn't expecting you,' said Tex. 'We didn't have a meeting booked in, did we? This is Nathan Palmer, my personal trainer.'

'Hello, Nathan.' Cooed Christine as she shook hands with him. Tex didn't miss the coy smile and fluttering of eyelashes that she did so well. 'No, no meeting, Tex, not at all. I just thought I would pop in. It's been a bit quiet from you. I just wanted to make sure you were happy with all the arrangements.'

Tex wasn't entirely sure if Christine was actually talking about the artwork he was buying or whether she was talking in code, referring to their short but sweet merger. After that evening at the Fish and Fly, he thought he had made it clear he wasn't looking for any sort of relationship with her, he thought she had understood this. Now though, he wasn't so sure.

'I could pop back in half an hour, if that helps at all,' suggested Nathan.

'No, it's fine…' began Tex, but was interrupted by Christine.

'Actually, if you could just give us five minutes, Nathan, that would be great. I just need to speak to Tex about something.'

'Sure, no problem, I'll just wait in the car.'

'No need for that,' interjected Tex. What the hell Christine was playing at he didn't know. 'Me and Christine will go into the office.'

As soon as the door was shut, Christine pounced on Tex, wrapping her arms around his neck. 'I was hoping you might want to reconsider your decision about us. I've missed you. I don't like just having a professional relationship.' She let go momentarily to make quotation marks in the air, before replacing her hands around his neck and moving in for a kiss.

Tex moved his head backwards out of reach. Taking hold of her hands, he unhooked them.

'Look, Christine, I'm sorry but I meant what I said. It's better this way. Believe me. I'm sorry if you expected more.'

'Let me get this straight. I didn't actually mean anything to you, it literally was just a couple of shags. And now you've got Little Miss Bilingual in your sights, you don't want me. I saw you and her the other day, trotting around the town. I thought you two looked a bit cosy, which is what made me come over today. I thought to myself, Tex's not the shag-them-and-leave-them sort. No, he's more of a gentleman. I was obviously wrong.'

'I'm sorry, Christine. I thought you knew it wasn't anything serious.'

'Well, you were wrong. I may have thought that myself initially, but after spending time with you, Tex, I really liked you.' She held up her hand. 'And don't apologise again. I understand this time.'

'I hope this doesn't affect our working relationship,' said Tex, which he really did mean, as Christine had a great eye for art and had negotiated a very good deal for him. 'I would hate to lose you from this project.'

Christine looked at him thoughtfully. 'I don't have any choice in the matter.' She paused in the doorway. 'I will see you at the end of the week for our meeting then.'

After she had gone, Tex let out a deep sigh. That had been awkward, but Christine seemed okay about it in the end. For a moment there he thought maybe Anna's belief about it being dangerous to mix business with pleasure would be proved right. Since Anna, he had not given his fling with Christine another thought. In fact, the resistance and intrigue surrounding Anna was too much of a distraction. For some reason he felt a strong pull towards her and everyone else just fell by the wayside. Quite strange and quite different to anything he had experienced before.

Anna wasn't particularly looking forward to furniture shopping with Tex, but Jamie was paying her, and as Tex was officially her client now she couldn't really refuse. She knew Tex would ask her about her confronting Mark over the house sale, and she also knew that he probably wouldn't be impressed with the outcome.

'Sorry, but am I understanding you correctly?' frowned Tex as he and Anna wandered around the local furniture shop looking at the beds. 'Mark needs to sell the house to support his business, and you are going to let him because you feel sorry for him? Not only that, but you have not been to see a solicitor?'

'Pretty much,' bristled Anna. 'What about this bed? Is this the sort of thing you're looking for or is the bedstead a bit girly for you?'

'I don't like the metal frame. I would prefer a leather headboard. And you are changing the subject.'

'There's nothing else to say and I am actually here to find you a bed.' Anna walked off towards some more king-size beds. 'What about this one? It's got the headboard you like and the mattress is really deep.' She pushed down on it with her hand. 'Quite firm.'

Tex stood on the opposite side of the bed. 'The only way to tell is to test it.' He laid down on the bed, stretching his jeaned legs and trainered feet out, putting his hands behind his head. 'Come on, lay down. What do you think?'

'It's up to you. You're the one who will be sleeping in it. Not me.'

Anna could have sworn he was trying to supress a grin, those eyes of his dancing mischievously behind his thick lashes.

He patted the bed. 'I'd still like your opinion. Do you think it's too firm?'

Deciding to play him at his own game, Anna lay down on the bed next to him. She was glad that she had worn trousers and a jumper, much more modest for clambering onto beds with Tex.

'It feels fine to me. What you've got to bear in mind though is moving around, you have to try all different positions.'

As if to demonstrate, Anna bounced her body up and down a couple of times, then rolled onto her side so her back was to Tex, more fidgeting before rolling over onto her other side, only to find that Tex had rolled over too, and they were now face to face. She gave a little yelp of surprise but decided to brazen it out. A game of brinkmanship.

A smile played at the corners of Tex's mouth. 'Well, would it be comfortable enough to spend the night on?'

'From a purely hypothetical point of view, yes. It would be very comfortable.' Anna wasn't sure if she'd be able to hold her nerve as she stifled the sudden urge to move closer and kiss him.

'You really should see a solicitor,' said Tex softly. He reached across and held her arm so she couldn't move away. 'You may be agreeing to this because you feel sorry for him but he still has a responsibility to his son. And so do you.'

'Thanks for the advice but I am capable of looking after myself and my son. I've managed fine for the past year.'

Tex let go of her arm and, taking umbrage, Anna hoiked herself off the bed. He'd touched a nerve bringing into question her responsibility towards Luke. Being a good single parent had been her top priority, something she prided herself with having carried out successfully. She wasn't about to let anyone cast doubt upon that.

Tex's comment continued to niggle away at Anna for the rest of the afternoon, despite her endeavours to disregard it. Now, with the atmosphere between them uneasy, she kept the exchanges purely professional, only discussing Tex's requirements for furnishing his apartment.

The king-size bed and two single beds could be delivered within the week but the sofa was on a back order of four weeks.

'We could see about hiring a sofa and dining suite if that will help,' suggested Anna, aware that Tex needed these items for next weekend as his sister wasn't wasting any time in visiting.

The rest of the afternoon was spent browsing and selecting the necessary furniture from a hire store in nearby Worthing. Anna hadn't enjoyed the starch atmosphere, or the stilted and awkward exchange of goodbyes that rounded off the day.

'If I'm honest, I have to agree with Tex,' said Zoe matter-of-factly as she slipped off the stool at the workbench of Nails by Natasha.

'Mark has a responsibility to Luke and can't just make him home-less. I really don't know why you won't seek legal advice.'

'I'm still working on the alternatives,' grumbled Anna as she admired her newly manicured nails.

This little treat was part of Anna's plan to bring the old Zoe back to life. Zoe had protested that beautiful nails and nappies didn't exactly go together, but Anna had been adamant and refused to let her sister-in-law off the hook.

'I can't see what the alternatives are, other than you and Mark getting back together, which actually isn't an alternative at all.' Zoe turned and raised her eyebrows at Anna, in the way that mums do when they correct their children for saying something rather silly.

'Don't worry, that's definitely not an option,' Anna remarked as she headed for the reception desk. 'Put your purse away, Zoe, this is mine and Nathan's treat.'

'Really? You two are becoming quite a pair of schemers.' Zoe smiled at her sister-in-law.

Anna carried on the conversation once they had left the nail bar. 'I asked Mark for a divorce, but he's not playing ball. In fact, he's threatening to blackmail me.'

'Blackmail! Why does that not surprise me? And how exactly is he planning to do that?'

'By not agreeing to a divorce, making me go through the courts to get one, where he's threatening to counterclaim and name Tex.'

'Oh, he's ridiculous,' snapped Zoe. 'What does he think this is, the 1940s? Who honestly today would really give a hoot?'

'He could make things very difficult though.' Anna felt too embarrassed to mention the photos – it made her cringe just to think about them.

'What does Tex say about it all?'

'I've told him I'm trying to work things out, but I just can't think straight at the moment. Mark has totally thrown me by turning up and wanting to sell the house, and then I've got Tex driving me mad.'

'Why's that?'

'Whenever I'm around him I just feel like I'm on the brink of losing control of my senses. It would be so easy to become involved with him, yet I know it will be asking for trouble.'

'Get a grip of yourself,' scolded Zoe as they reached the car. 'You won't be the first person to have a relationship with a work colleague. It happens all the time. You need to relax and stop worrying. You're so stubborn at times. You and your silly self-imposed rule of not mixing business and pleasure.'

'There's a reason why it's a saying,' retorted Anna. 'Everything is complicated enough as it is. Remember, you heard it here. I. Am. Not. Getting. Involved. With. Tex.'

Chapter Fifteen

Not getting involved with Tex was going to be a real test of her willpower, thought Anna as she strolled around Swanbourne Lake in Arundel with Tex and his nephew and niece. Eight-year-old Toby was running ahead, clambering up the surrounding chalky hills littered with spindly trees, their exposed roots acting as great foot and handholds. Meanwhile, little Josie was happy to hold hands with Anna and Tex as they swung her up off her feet and into the air every now and again. Tex had looked over at Anna a couple of times, and grinned at the delight of his five-year-old niece. His whole face seemed to light up with enjoyment, almost as much as Josie's, thought Anna. He looked very relaxed, and very wantable.

Jamie had phoned and asked her to help Tex out on the Friday. Tex's sister Gabriella and her husband were spending the day sightseeing in London, and Tex was on babysitting duties.

Anna had gone with the intention of keeping things very formal and businesslike but it really wasn't appropriate with two young children, not to mention pretty near impossible with Tex in such a relaxed and happy mood. He was obviously pleased to be seeing his sister, who had greeted Anna warmly.

Like Tex, Gabriella was charming and friendly. Tex had already warned Anna that his sister wore a hearing aid, due to losing her hearing completely in one ear as a child, but she still liked to lip-read. As they had sat in Tex's sparsely furnished apartment drinking coffee, Anna had given a lot of her attention to Gabriella's two young children, chatting earnestly with Toby about Power Rangers, and Josie about Barbie.

'Thank you for coming today,' said Tex as Josie ran ahead to join her brother at a rather large tree that, like the others, seemed to cling to the side of the hill. Anna remembered Nathan's boys spending many a happy time clamouring around on the thick and rambling roots that looked like a heap of spaghetti which spread out at least two metres in diameter around the tree.

'All part of the service,' grinned Anna, laughing as Tex shook his head at what was becoming her catchphrase.

By the time they had completed a full circuit of the lake and arrived back at the kiosk, Toby was in need of the toilet. Anna and Josie waited on a wooden bench, watching the ducks and swans vying with one another to peck the birdfeed being thrown into the water by families with young children.

'I want to climb the hill over there,' said Josie, tugging at Anna's arm and pointing.

Anna looked over her shoulder at the white embankment behind the kiosk. 'It's a bit too steep.'

'Toby did. Why can't I?'

'I have a better idea, why don't we feed the ducks instead?' suggested Anna, hoping to distract the child. 'Come on,' she coaxed, taking Josie's hand.

They stood patiently in the line waiting to be served while a family group ahead of them placed their seemingly never-ending order of ice-creams, lollipops, teas and coffees. Anna rummaged around in her bag for her purse, eventually finding it at the bottom, and checked she had enough change. As she did so, Tex came up and standing close by her side, slipped his arm around her shoulders, giving her a quick squeeze. Anna felt herself catch her breath as she breathed in the delightful citrus waft of Tex's aftershave.

'We were just getting some food for the ducks,' she forced herself to say.

'Great,' smiled Tex as he looked around him. 'Where is Josie?'

Anna looked down by her side where Josie had been standing just moments earlier but who now seemed to have disappeared. Anna scanned the group in front of her and the queue behind her.

'She was here just a second ago,' she said. 'She can't have gone far.'

'She's not here now though,' responded Tex in alarm.

In unison, they looked towards the lake, searching for the little dark-haired child. Anna's mouth began to dry up and she could feel a tightness encompassing her throat.

'Oh shit,' she murmured when she couldn't see Josie anywhere. She looked at Tex. 'She was right beside me.'

'Jeez!' exclaimed Tex. 'How can you just lose a child?'

They broke from the queue and began hurriedly searching through the visitors. Where on earth was she? Dark thoughts began to swarm Anna's mind – images of drowning, going out onto the road, abduction. What if she had fallen into the water unnoticed? Rushing to the edge, Anna scanned the surprisingly clear water. Nothing. She could hear the words *stay calm* in her mind, she mustn't panic. Looking towards the exit, Anna now studied the people coming and going, checking each one to see if Josie was with them.

Nothing.

Tex, holding tightly onto Toby's hand, was circling the area, calling out Josie's name, and asking people if they had seen a little girl in a blue jacket with dark bobbed hair. All he got was shakes of heads.

Anna felt the panic and desperation beginning to take hold of her. She had lost a child! Tex's niece. A little five-year-old who didn't know where she was.

She blinked hard, this wasn't the time to start crying and going to pieces. She had to find Josie. Her eyes met Tex's and she could see his own panic there but she could also see anger. Anger directed her way. He marched over.

'How can she have just disappeared? Why weren't you watching her? Why weren't you holding her hand?' Agitated, he ran his hand through his hair and down over his face. 'Damn it, Anna!'

'I'm sorry. I just let go for a moment to get my purse out. I thought she was right by my side.'

'Obviously not,' he snapped.

Anna gulped. His words, his tone, his look were like a physical slap.

'Okay, look, you wait here with Toby,' she said, 'in case she comes back or someone finds her. It will be you she wants. I'll start walking back the way we came.'

'Shouldn't we call the police?'

'Let me just have a quick look. I'm sure we'll find her.'

Anna felt physically sick. She'd lost Tex's niece just like that, in a blink of an eye. If only that family hadn't taken so long with their order, she wouldn't have been in the queue for so long waiting to buy bloody duck food. Josie hadn't even really wanted to feed the ducks anyway. Oh God, this was a nightmare.

She began to jog back along the footpath, calling out Josie's name, peering up through the bushes and trees, berating herself. She should have just let Josie climb the hill behind the kiosk then all this… The hill! Anna stopped dead in her tracks. Of course, the hill!

She raced back along the footpath, stumbling slightly as she veered off onto the uneven grass at the bottom of the hill. She called out for Josie and paused to listen for a response, then began scrambling up the chalky, muddy incline.

'Josie! Are you there?'

She heard a faint noise.

'Mommy, I want my mommy.'

It was coming from higher up the hill. It could only be Josie. Grabbing branches and roots, Anna clambered higher until through some overhanging greenery, she could see Josie's pink trainer.

'Thank God,' gasped Anna, relief flooding through her.

If Anna thought she was going to receive a hero's welcome, having redeemed herself by finding his niece, then she was very much mistaken.

Tex had been overwhelmed with relief as he hugged a sobbing Josie, scooping her up into his arms easily, carrying her in one arm and firmly holding hands with Toby with the other. Tex walked as quickly as Toby would allow him, back towards the town. Anna trailed behind feeling like a disgraced schoolgirl who had been sent to Coventry. Only when they reached the car park below Tex's apartment did he turn and speak to her.

'I can manage on my own now.' His voice was tense, his eyes hostile.

'I am sorry.' She'd said it enough times, surely he had calmed down by now.

'All you had to do was watch her for five minutes. What was so difficult?'

'Oh Tex! I've told you, I only let go of her hand for a second. Everything was all right in the end and I have apologised. Lots.'

'It is only by luck everything is okay. She could have fallen down that hill and broken her arm or leg. She could have gone into the road, been taken… Anything.'

His accusational tone igniting a defensive anger in her, Anna snapped, 'I know. But she's fine. Anyway, I'm not a childminder.'

'No, but you work for Jamie who offers a PR service which includes a variety of things. You are being paid to help me and I needed help looking after the children. If you don't like your job…' He waved his hand dismissively, his eyes hard as he looked at her. 'Go home, Anna. I'll see you next week.'

He strode off into the apartment building, leaving Anna with the feeling she had been well and truly dismissed. She couldn't believe Tex was overreacting so much after the event.

As she drove over the bridge, she pulled over to wipe the tears from her eyes. Tex was cross with her, more than cross, and that hurt. An unexpected feeling, not one of anger anymore, but one of sadness that she had upset him, she had let him down. She didn't like it and she didn't like the implications of her own reaction. Tex Garcia was getting under her skin, somewhere in a no man's land of her feelings, somewhere between professional and personal. Gradually advancing towards personal, she suspected.

Chapter Sixteen

The weekend passed unexceptionally. Anna had half hoped Tex would ring her but she didn't hear a word from him. Jamie had emailed her with the details of her client for Monday and hadn't mentioned anything about Friday. Perhaps Tex hadn't told him.

Mark had tried to coax her to come to the pub with him and Luke for Sunday lunch but Anna had declined. She was having a hard time just looking at Mark. Every time she saw him, images of those photos came flooding back.

Luke came out to the garden where she was picking at a few weeds, just really as a diversional exercise, anything to keep her away from Mark.

'Are you staying here then?' Luke asked, sitting himself down on the edge of the raised flowerbed.

'I think so. The garden could do with a tidy up.'

'Looks all right to me.'

Anna sat back on her heels and brushed her gloved hands together. 'You go with your dad, it will be nice for you two to have some time alone.' She regarded Luke's raised eyebrows. 'Unless, of course, you'd rather I came. If you don't want to be on your own, that is.'

'No, I'm fine, I want to go. Just thought it would be nice if we all went.' Luke got to his feet.

'Sorry,' replied Anna, looking apologetically at him.

'It's okay, don't worry about it.' He bent down and kissed her on the cheek. 'See you later.'

It had been a long day, longer than Anna had expected. Her Monday client, the German family, had wanted to be shown around Brighton and the surrounding areas to see where they would like to base themselves. A tour of where the schools were in relation to desirable residential areas had also been on the agenda, together with a visit to the seafront and walk along the pier. Nevertheless, it had been a successful day, and Anna was pleased that they had appeared genuinely grateful for her help.

Heading back home, Anna dashed into the local Tesco Express, emerging a few minutes later with a can of energy drink in one hand and a bar of chocolate in the other. Naughty but nice, she smiled to herself as she wandered up towards the station. She had twenty minutes to kill before her train got in, plenty of time to indulge herself. What first? Drink or chocolate?

'I hope you're not really gonna eat or drink any of that stuff.'

Anna looked up and there was Tex leaning against the side of his 4X4, his arms folded and a lazy smile on his mouth.

'It really isn't part of a healthy diet,' he added.

Anna eyed him sceptically, not answering immediately. Her heart was doing that skippy thing again and her stomach suddenly didn't feel it could take any food. She wished she could think of a clever or funny answer but her mind seemed to have frozen as well.

Tex eased himself from his resting point and walked over to her, standing well within her personal space. Slowly, he took the can and bar of chocolate from her hands and, with the accuracy of a Harlem Globetrotter, tossed them onto the flatbed of his Ford Ranger. Then he took her hands in his, holding them close to his chest.

'I'm sorry for behaving so badly last week. I had no right to speak to you the way I did.'

Anna nodded. 'It's okay. I am sorry for what happened too.'

'Shhh. Don't. It wasn't your fault. You were right. I was wrong.' He smiled and led her towards the truck. 'I'll give you a ride. And I'll buy you something healthy to eat.' He nodded with distain at the can and chocolate bar.

In Arundel, he stopped the car and escorted her into the local pizza restaurant – just to check out the opposition, he told her.

Inside, Tex told her about his weekend with his sister and her family, who had now left to visit some friends in the north of England, and Anna recounted her day with the German family. An easy exchange of pleasantries which made Anna feel relaxed and happy again. When they left the restaurant and headed back to the car park where he had parked his 4X4, Anna couldn't help noticing that Tex seemed a bit quiet, a small furrow in his brow.

'Is everything all right?' Anna asked.

He seemed to be struggling how to answer for a few moments, until they came to halt by the car.

'There was something I wanted to say, about what happened at the lake the other day.'

'Let's just forget about it. Honestly, Tex, there's no need to go through it all again.' Anna stopped as Tex looked at her. There was a sadness in his eyes. Something told her this was important. Perhaps he was going to sack her. Maybe he had already complained about her to Jamie. 'What is it?' Why did she feel like she wasn't going to like what he was about to say?

'There was a reason for my overreaction at Josie going missing.'

'I thought there probably was,' she replied gently.

'The ranch, back home, where I grew up. My parents have lodges that they rent out, you know, supplement their income.

132

They've always done it, still do. Anyway, when I was fourteen my mom asked me to look after my sister, Gabriella, she was only three. My grandma was ill so Mom was going to visit her. It was a lovely summer's day so I took Gabriella out towards the lake on the ranch. There's a small play area there for the guests. She was quite happy playing on the little slide and climbing frame while I just sat on the bench watching her.' Tex paused, looking across the car park and then back at Anna. He took a deep breath. 'There was this family staying in one of the lodges. They had a daughter about my age, who I kinda took a shine to.'

Anna felt it was probably inappropriate to make some remark about Tex always having an eye for the girls.

'Anyway, she was swimming in the lake,' Tex continued, 'so I decided to go for a swim too. You know, dive in off the jetty, impress her and all that. I was so busy showing off, I forgot all about Gabriella. It was about fifteen or twenty minutes before I remembered her. When I looked over, the play area was empty. She had wandered off.'

'Oh Tex,' sighed Anna. She took his hands into hers. 'Is that why you were so upset the other day?'

Tex squeezed her hand. 'That's not all,' he said, his voice quavering slightly, shame in his eyes. 'Eventually we found her in the woods that ran alongside the park. Unconscious. She had fallen and hit her head on a tree trunk. I remember seeing the blood and not being able to work out where it was coming from, it was all over one side of her head and face. I was so scared. So very scared.'

Again, Anna could feel the pressure of his hand squeezing hers. 'But she was all right though?' she ventured softly.

'Yes and no. It obviously wasn't fatal but the bang to her head damaged her eardrum. All the blood was coming from her ear.' Anna could see Tex gulp. 'That's why she's deaf in one ear. She lost her hearing. For a long time I blamed myself. Of course, nobody accused me, nobody blamed me but I have always felt responsible for what happened. I should never have gone swimming, I should never have left her. If I had stayed in the park none of that would have happened.'

'Tex, you poor thing,' whispered Anna. She understood now why he had been so cross when Josie went missing. It was only because he was frightened, it must have brought back all those terrible memories. She also totally understood his feeling of guilt even though the rational part of him knew it wasn't his fault. It was exactly how she felt about the car accident involving her and Mark. 'I understand, I really do,' she said in a hushed voice. She wrapped her arms around his neck, pulling him into an embrace as, on tiptoes, she rested her head against his shoulder. 'It's really okay, Tex, really okay,' she said as his head sunk against her neck.

Anna felt Tex's hand touch her hips tentatively at first, then the tension in his shoulders began to dissipate as she continued to hold him, until finally his hands slid round her waist and up her back. His lips fleetingly brushed her neck, the sensation making her catch her breath. He kissed her neck again. Without questioning herself, Anna pulled away slightly and turning her head, met his lips with hers. Just his kisses caused a total infusion of her senses. She couldn't focus on anything, just the tingling, zinging, jingling sensation that was coursing through her like a galloping thoroughbred. A small tentative exchange of kisses, followed by a longer, more passionate, deeper one. It was almost too much. Almost.

Groaning, Tex pulled away first. 'I gotta stop. This is not good for my blood pressure.' He held her tightly to him instead, caressing her hair, dropping a small kiss on the top of her head. 'Do you want me to take you home?' he asked at last, looking down at her.

Anna could see the unspoken question in his eyes. Was this the moment when she abandoned all notion of not getting involved with Tex? Was this where she allowed things to go further?

'Probably best if you take me home,' she responded at last. 'Sorry.'

'It's okay,' he said reassuringly, before kissing her gently on the mouth.

Chapter Seventeen

Giving herself one last spray of perfume, Anna deemed herself ready for her date with Tex. She hadn't been sure about the floaty dress that Zoe had encouraged her to buy, but now with her make-up done, high heels on, she was pleased with the result. Zoe was right – it certainly did soften her sometimes boyish look.

Thinking of Zoe, Anna reflected on her mini-campaign to bring back the old, lively and outgoing sister-in-law. So far, her plan seemed quite successful. They were going regularly to the gym and Zoe was happy with the crèche for Emily. They had had a manicure, bought some new clothes and today, Zoe had had the much needed wash, cut and blow-dry. Despite Zoe's half-hearted protests, once reassured that Nathan was paying for it and not Anna, she had been happy to go along, while Anna took Emily for a walk in Bishop Park Gardens. Yes, it had been a successful day so far.

All Anna had to do now was negotiate leaving the house without too much interrogation from Mark. Since their argument over the photos, Anna had barely been able to bring herself to speak to him. Although she doubted he would really stoop so low and do something as despicable as he had threatened to do, she couldn't be certain. He seemed pretty desperate, and desperate people did desperate things. Not only that, she was hurt, outraged that he could even come up with such an idea.

'You look nice, Mum,' said Luke as she came into the living room doing up her watch strap. She had arranged to meet Tex at the restaurant. He had wanted to pick her up from the house but Anna was worried about her husband, albeit estranged, and lover coming face to face.

'Thanks, love, your Aunt Zoe helped choose it. I wasn't sure but…'

'It suits you,' Luke reassured her before returning to plucking at his guitar strings.

Mark strolled in from the kitchen, pausing in the doorway. 'Where are you off to then?'

'Just out into town,' answered Anna.

'You're looking very glammed up for a drink down the Fish and Fly with Zoe.' His mouth was set in a mulish line.

She shrugged. 'I'm going out for a meal.'

Mark took a sip of his beer from the bottle. 'You going on a date?'

'It doesn't really matter, does it?'

'Who you going with then?' Mark put his beer on the table and, picking up Anna's jacket, came over to her. Holding the jacket up, he hung it around her. His hands rested on her shoulders.

'I've got a meeting with one of my clients,' she said with as much confidence as she could muster. It wasn't, after all, a lie. She was aware that Luke had stopped fiddling around with his guitar and was watching them closely. She felt Mark's fingers closing with slightly too much pressure than was necessary.

'The American chef.' It was more of a statement than a question.

Anna nodded, shrugging his hands away. 'That's right. Look, I really must get going.' She dropped a kiss on Luke's head. 'Bye, love.'

'Yeah, bye, Mum. Have a nice…' his voice trailed off as he glanced at his dad, who Anna could see was scowling.

She had just reached the gate when the front door flew open and, slamming it shut behind him, Mark jogged down the path.

137

'I'll give you a lift.' He jangled the keys as he spoke.

'You're all right, thanks. I need a bit of fresh air. I'd sooner walk.'

'Anna, let me give you a lift. I want to talk to you.' Mark ran in front of her and began walking backwards as he spoke.

'After the other day, I don't actually want to talk to you.' She spoke tritely, purposefully striding out.

'Just listen to me. You don't have to talk.'

Anna stopped walking and sighed. 'Hurry up then.'

'I know you're upset with me but I wouldn't be forced into this position if you would just go along with the sale. I really need the money, Anna. Things are desperate. I'm getting calls all the time from the bank in the States and I don't know how much longer I can stall them for.'

Despite her intention to just listen, Anna couldn't help herself speak up. 'What you're doing is despicable, Mark. You know what? The more I think about it, the more I'm upset that you would threaten to do such a thing. How can you think so little of me? I was your wife. I'm the mother of your son. How can you betray me with something so personal and intimate as those photos?'

'All you have to do is agree to the sale of the house, Anna. It's not difficult.'

'But that will leave me and Luke with nothing. No security, just uncertainty. And I still want a divorce.'

'And I want the house sale!'

'See, this is a totally pointless conversation, it's going nowhere, we're just going round and round in circles.' She began to walk away. 'I'm going to be late.'

He ran to catch up with her again, spinning her round to face him. 'Now listen here. I've got to go back to the States for a couple of weeks. Whilst I'm gone, you have a good think about all this because when I get back, I want to you to agree to the house sale. I'm not messing around, Anna. You stand in my way, and I *will* send out those photos. Understood?'

As the maître d' escorted Anna towards the table, Tex rose to greet her. Her smile to him was mesmerising. She looked devastatingly beautiful tonight, and the soft floaty dress showed off her petite frame. He felt a stirring inside him as his body involuntarily responded to both the sight and the thought of her. He kissed her gently on each cheek, lingering as he took in the scent of her perfume and the softness of her skin against his.

'You look beautiful,' he said as they sat down.

It irritated him when the waiter appeared with the menu, and in offering it to him, Tex was forced to look away from Anna for a moment. Any waiter worth his money, and certainly any waiter he employed, would know to wait a minute or two for the guests to settle themselves and exchange pleasantries, especially if they were a couple on a dinner date.

Anna was still smiling at Tex as she took her menu. 'Thank you. You look very nice too.'

It was nice that she noticed, thought Tex.

Anna seemed to take a genuine interest in the new restaurant and how the refurbishment was coming along, the conversation never drying up during the meal. Something which he pleasantly noted. He was about to ask her about her work with Jamie when he noticed her face cloud over and she fiddled with her napkin.

'Is something wrong, Anna?' He couldn't think what had suddenly troubled her.

She looked up at him. 'I'm not really one for raking over past loves,' she began. 'It's just that… well… Christine.'

'What do you wanna know?' He hadn't expected this and it wasn't something he particularly wanted to discuss; however, he was also aware of some deeply buried desire to reassure Anna.

'The other night at the pub, she gave me the impression that…

you and her… you know… had some sort of relationship. I know you said there had been, once. I just need to be sure that it is in the past. I've been through all this before and I can't do it again.'

Automatically, Tex reached across the table and took her hand in both of his. 'I promise you, it is definitely all over between myself and Christine. It was over before I even met you.' He didn't take his eyes away from hers as he spoke, he really wanted her to believe him, to trust him.

She studied him for a few moments, her gaze intent, as if she was searching the very soul of his eyes. Then she nodded. 'Okay,' she smiled. 'So do you think you will settle into the quieter way of life that is Arundel?'

Letting go of her hand and sitting back, Tex returned her smiled. 'Actually, I've found it rather more busy than even I anticipated,' he confessed, glad she seemed to believe him about Christine. 'Of course, I did plenty of market research before investing in the restaurant but Arundel has an amazing nightlife. People seem to love the ambiance of the town.'

'I'm sure the restaurant will be very popular.'

'I hope it will be popular with the customers, at least,' replied Tex, frowning slightly, thinking back to the damage and graffiti incident.

'You haven't had any more trouble, have you?'

'Nothing more since the vandalism.' Tex signalled for the bill.

'I'm sorry,' said Anna, looking embarrassed.

Tex looked at her quizzically. 'Why are you sorry?'

'Well, it's embarrassing when other English people behave like that. We're not all that way inclined but it gives us a bad name.'

Tex let out a laugh, and then when she looked alarmed, he managed to control himself. 'You are very sweet, Anna, but you don't have to apologise for ignorant vandals and I know they are in the minority. I mean, take yourself for example. I know you don't hate me or wish me to go home. At least not alone.' He smiled at the embarrassed flush to her face.

'About that – you going home alone…' Anna began, before she was interrupted by the waiter returning with the bill.

Tex didn't press her any further, he kind of got the message, she wasn't coming back to his place. Not tonight anyway. After paying the bill, he helped Anna on with her coat, and with his hand resting in the small of her back, shepherded her outside. The anxious look on her face told him what she hadn't been able to say back in the restaurant.

'At least let me drive you home,' he said, saving her the awkwardness of having to say anything.

'I could call a taxi,' she answered, letting him draw her towards him.

'I'll drive you.' He kissed her, groaning inwardly, knowing this was as close to her as he would get tonight.

The shrill of his iPhone bursting into life forced him to stop kissing her. Still holding her round the waist against him, Tex answered his phone.

'Yeah, hello,' he spoke, before giving Anna another kiss. She grinned and tapped his arm, as if to reprimand him.

'Mr Garcia?' the voice on the other end of the phone queried.

'Yes. Speaking.' He grinned at Anna and kissed her again. Trying not to giggle, she clamped a hand over her mouth and half-heartedly tried to wriggle free. Tex raised his eyebrows and shook his head at her, only half listening to the woman on the other end of the call.

'Mr Garcia, proprietor of the United Reformed Church, Tarrant Street, Arundel?'

'Yes, that's right,' replied Tex, taking slightly more interest in the call now. This sounded official.

'It's Sussex Police here. I'm afraid we've got some bad news for you.'

Chapter Eighteen

Bad news was something of an understatement, thought Tex as he stood alongside the Chief Fire Officer outside the business premises, waiting for the firemen to emerge from the building. He had come straight over, after insisting that he take Anna home first. What a way to end the night!

The fire had been put out relatively quickly and Tex found himself saying a silent prayer that there wasn't much damage. It was difficult to tell in the dark. From the front, everything looked okay, the fire had been at the back of the building, in the kitchen area. He dreaded to think how much it would cost him to replace all the new stainless steel state-of-the-art appliances that had only gone in that week.

'It could be an electrical fault,' said the Fire Officer, turning to him. 'You say you've just had a new kitchen put in. Could well be some bad wiring.' He paused to listen to his radio as it crackled into life. Tex couldn't make out what was being said. 'Right, well it seems the fire started at the rear door.'

'The door?' Tex puzzled.

'Hmm, it's hard to tell until we have a proper look in daylight but there's the possibility it could have been started deliberately.'

'Shit, this is bad. I'm so sorry, mate. Is it as bad as it looks?' said Jamie as he surveyed the blackened kitchen. Ash and soot covered every surface, the floor by the rear door housed a sludgy pile from the foam that had been used to extinguish the flames. Jamie had rushed down to offer some moral support as soon as Tex had phoned him with the news.

'I've no idea. I have the loss adjuster coming out tomorrow,' sighed Tex.

'And it's definitely arson?'

Tex nodded. 'Apparently. It was started from the outside of the back door. The wheelie bin was moved behind it and some of the cardboard in it was soaked in petrol before being set alight.'

'What have the police said?'

'They are going to make some inquiries. They've asked me all the usual questions, like do I know anyone who has a grudge against me or would want to harm the business? Usual stuff.'

'And you said yes, the tea rooms down the road, the curator at the castle, and not forgetting the husband of the latest member to your fan club.'

Tex looked evenly at his friend. 'No, I said nothing.'

'What! Are you mad? Jesus, Tex. A bit of graffiti is one thing, but this…' – he gestured to the blackened kitchen – '…this is taking it to a whole new level.'

'It may just antagonise the situation if the cops start asking questions,' explained Tex. 'I will go and speak to the coffee shop owner and the curator myself.'

'And the husband? What about him?'

'I would if it wasn't for Anna. I don't want to make things more difficult for her.'

Jamie looked at him, lips pursed.

'What?'

'Nothing,' Jamie began. 'Just that at this point I would expect

143

you to be ditching Anna because of all the trouble it's causing. Yet for some reason, you're not. Wouldn't be because she might mean something to you?'

Tex frowned at his friend. 'You chat shit sometimes, man.' As he went back into the main hall, Tex tried to push down the feeling that there might be some truth in what Jamie had said. No way. He didn't do relationships.

'Thanks for giving me a lift, Mum,' said Luke as he hauled his guitar and rucksack out to the car.

'That's okay,' smiled Anna. 'Here, I'll just unlock it.' Lifting the boot open, Anna was met by the distinct whiff of petrol. 'Ooh, yuk! It really smells in here for some reason.'

Luke lifted out the petrol can. 'It's this. Didn't Dad tell you?'

Anna looked blankly at her son. 'Tell me what?'

'He borrowed your car last night to go and get a Chinese, and ran out of petrol.'

'Ran out of petrol? Where did he go for the Chinese for God's sake?'

Luke looked a bit uncomfortable. 'I dunno. He went out to meet some friends first and got the Chinese on the way home. Maybe it wasn't that local.'

Anna tutted. 'At least he could have taken the can out.' As she spoke something gripped the inside of her stomach and twisted. She stared at the petrol can and thought of the fire at Tex's restaurant. Suspicion snaked its way into her mind. 'What time did he go out?' she finally managed to ask.

Luke shrugged. 'What's wrong, Mum? Look, I didn't mean to drop Dad in it or anything. I didn't think you'd mind if he borrowed your car. I don't want to cause a big row.'

Anna sighed. The last thing she wanted was for Luke to feel guilty for telling her. 'Hey, it's not a problem. Let's put your stuff on the back seat, you don't want your bag smelling of petrol. I'll just put the can inside the front gate.' She smiled, feigning cheerfulness. 'Come on, let's get you to Jacob's and then I must get on to Nathan's for babysitting duties.' She would have to think about the implications of the petrol can when she was alone. Now wasn't the time.

That morning Anna had been up before Mark and Luke and had been over to Zoe's house by nine thirty. She had taken the three boys and Emily out to give Zoe a break, and had offered to babysit, hoping that a night out together would go some way to mending bridges between Nathan and Zoe. Perhaps naively, Anna had thought they would be delighted at the chance of having some time together, just the two of them. However, she now had the distinct feeling that they were going out just to please her. There was definitely an uneasy atmosphere between them. Anna wondered if they had had an argument or maybe the children had been playing up. Having said that, Emily and Henry were already tucked up in bed fast asleep and the twins were behaving themselves. She was none the wiser.

'I hear you were out on a date last night,' said Nathan, coming into the room. 'Zoe mentioned it.'

'I was going to tell you but I haven't seen you much lately.'

'Join the club.' It was Zoe. She stood in the doorway, hands in her coat pockets.

The briefest of scowls crossed Nathan's face at his wife's remark but he carried on talking. 'And it's Tex?'

'That's right.'

'Not ideal, if you want my opinion.'

'Well she doesn't,' butted in Zoe, coming to Anna's defence. 'People meet their partners through work all the time. What's the difference?'

'Oh, is that someone's phone ringing?' Anna stood up, hoping that her comment would head off any argument. Everyone stood still and silent for a moment.

'I can't hear anything,' said Zoe. 'Mine's in the kitchen. I'll just go and check.'

Anna had got the twins off to bed by nine, and when Tex phoned her briefly from his Guildford restaurant, just hearing the timbre of his voice sent a ripple of pleasure through her. The fire dominated most of the conversation but despite this, Anna didn't mention the petrol can. She needed time to think about it properly and to somehow broach the subject with Mark.

'I'm sorry but I need to get back to work,' said Tex after ten minutes. 'Are you free tomorrow? I thought maybe we could go to Arundel for tea and cake somewhere. I know how fond you English are of that.'

After they had hung up, Anna wondered whether tomorrow was going to be the day she and Tex took things further. The thought made her stomach feel fluttery, but she realised that the nervousness had now been replaced by excitement and anticipation.

Anna was surprised when Nathan and Zoe returned home just two hours after leaving.

'You're back early,' she said as Zoe tiptoed into the living room, trying not to let her heels clatter on the wooden floor.

'I'm shattered. I'll be up early with Emily in the morning so I really need to get to bed.' Zoe slipped off her shoes. 'Everything all right?'

'Yes, fine. Not a sound from any of them. Hi, Nathan. Nice evening?'

'If you're referring to the restaurant, wine and food, then yes, it was nice.' Nathan's steely eyes narrowed slightly as he looked at his wife.

'But the company was crap is what he's trying to say,' said Zoe returning an equally bad-tempered look. 'I could say the same myself, actually. Anyway, I'm knackered. Thanks ever so much for everything today, Anna.' She gave Anna a fleeting hug. 'I really must go to bed. Night.'

'Night, Zoe.' Oh dear, this wasn't good.

'So what's the score with Mark at the moment?' asked Nathan, pushing the door shut behind Zoe. Anna quickly brought her brother up to date with events, his eyebrows raising now and again, the occasional tut and shake of the head.

'He's going back to the States this week so that will be a relief. It's been cosy to say the least. It'll be nice to have the house just to myself and Luke again. Bliss.'

'How's Luke taking it all?' Sitting in the chair by the fireside, Nathan flicked through the TV channels.

'Not sure. He hasn't said too much. He's going to miss his dad. Just when they were building up a relationship, Mark clears off. You know he's selling the house?'

'Really? Where does that leave you?'

'I could oppose it or I could let him sell it. I don't know what to do for the best really.' This wasn't that far from the truth, Anna consoled herself. She really didn't know what to do but she didn't want to appear to be giving in to Mark's demands too readily, Nathan might get suspicious and start asking questions, the answers to which she had no intention of sharing with him, let alone mention the photos, the thought of them repellent in every way. So for now she would lay the ground for moving on as if it were her choice. 'I've actually been wondering whether it's about time I got a place of my own. Became more independent.'

'About time you sorted out a divorce as well. Then you can be totally free.'

'One thing at a time, but yes, that will be the next step.' Anna stood up. 'Anyway, I'd better go.' She wanted to get away before

Nathan started digging for any more information or pushing her for a commitment. 'Stay there. I'll see myself out.'

'Okay, sis.' Nathan put out his hand and caught Anna's as she walked past. 'Thanks for tonight. Look, don't worry about me and Zoe. It's been so long since we've been out together, I think we've forgotten how to do it.' He smiled reassuringly and then added jokingly, 'That amongst other things.'

Although Anna did acknowledge to herself that eleven o'clock at night probably wasn't the best time to quiz Mark about the petrol can and the fire, she also knew that she had to at least try and find out if there was any truth in her suspicion.

Mark switched the television off and, placing the remote precisely and slowly onto the coffee table, looked up at Anna from the sofa. 'So, Mr Garcia has had a fire at the restaurant, has he? Too bad.'

'Where did you go last night that would warrant you running out of petrol?' demanded Anna, irritated by his laconic attitude, although it was nothing less than she expected.

'I don't have to report my every move to you,' responded Mark. 'That's something that we might have done as a married couple, but you seem to have made it clear to me that is something we are not.'

What a bastard! He was enjoying this. He knew she had no idea if he were telling the truth or not.

'You have to admit, Mark, it's all pretty suspicious. I think the police would call it incriminating evidence. Beyond reasonable doubt. All that sort of stuff.'

'Now neither you nor your Yankee boyfriend would want to involve the police, would you? You especially. Not when you know what's in that envelope in my briefcase.' He sat back on the sofa looking very self-satisfied.

Anna felt a ripple of fear begin to knot in her stomach. She closed her eyes for a second to salvage her initial thoughts. Opening them again, she said, 'What did you call him?'

'What? Your boyfriend?'

'Yes. What did you just say?'

'Yankee boyfriend?' Mark gave her a look that clearly said he thought she had gone mad.

'Yankee boyfriend,' repeated Anna. 'Don't tell me that was you too.'

Mark shrugged. 'I have absolutely no idea what you're talking about.'

'The graffiti. The vandalism. It said, "Yank Out". Jesus, Mark, you just said the selfsame thing. And Tex thinks it's the tea rooms.'

'So now you're accusing me of vandalism, graffiti and arson. You really have a high opinion of me.'

'Well, you're not exactly crowning yourself in glory, are you?'

'Think what you like, Anna, but if I find out who did the graffiti, I'll buy them a drink.'

Chapter Nineteen

'Have you eaten?' asked Tex as he released Anna from his embrace. 'I've made a light salad.'

'What and spoil the tea and cake you promised me?'

'We could go out later. You should eat. It is not good to miss meals, especially lunch.' He looked seriously at her. 'Come, sit, we will eat now and go out for your tea and cake later.'

Anna allowed herself to be led to the breakfast bar, taking the seat that Tex indicated. She was actually quite hungry. Having avoided Mark this morning by going to the gym and from there getting herself ready before heading over to Arundel, food had been the last thing on her mind.

'If you insist,' she said lightly.

'I do.' Tex opened the fridge, took out a bottle of wine and poured two glasses. He gave one to Anna.

'Only the one for me, I've got to drive home later. Plus I need a clear head for the morning. Jamie's asked me to go to London tomorrow and Tuesday. A client of his has a business meeting and needs me there to help with the translation.'

'Are you staying overnight?'

'No. Can't really because of Luke. Having said that, he'd probably be okay. He is sixteen but I always worry that there's going to be some wild house party or he won't get up for school. Or both! It will be a bit of a pain travelling up both days, but I think it works out cheaper than having a hotel for the night.'

'You can always stay at my apartment in Guildford if ever you're working there. It would cut your journey time down considerably.' Tex put a chicken and bacon salad in front of Anna, along with a basket containing a selection of bread rolls.

'Oh, right. Thanks.' Anna wondered idly if Tex had two bedrooms in his Guildford apartment and found herself hoping he only had the one.

Playfully, Tex nudged her elbow with his as he sat down beside her. 'What you thinking?'

'Nothing.' Anna tried to sound casual but rather suspected a sudden flush of colour to her face was betraying her. She looked intently at her salad.

Tex gave a little chuckle. He leaned into Anna so that their shoulders were touching. 'I have two bedrooms in Guildford.'

How did he do that? Read her thoughts. He was teasing her now, flirting a bit, and Anna was enjoying it.

'That's good to know. Wouldn't want you to be too uncomfortable on the sofa.' She took a large sip of wine, already feeling a bit giggly. Tex topped up her glass. 'You're not trying to get me drunk are you, Mr Garcia?'

'Me? No!' exclaimed Tex in mock indignation. 'A gentleman wouldn't do that.'

'Are you a gentleman then?'

'Do you want me to be a gentleman?' His eyes were dancing with amusement.

Anna cocked her head to one side, as if considering his question carefully. 'Ask me again later.'

Tex insisted on clearing away, shooing Anna out of the kitchen. She wandered out through the sliding patio doors and onto the balcony, which wasn't huge but big enough for a circular metal

151

bistro table and two chairs. Anna leaned on the railings with her glass of wine, gazing out at the river, watching the tourists strolling over the bridge, cameras and camcorders hanging from their necks. They stopped, pointed at, and took photos of the imposing castle rising above the rooftops and the cathedral standing proud over the town from its position at the top of the hill. Anna tilted her face skywards to soak up the warm rays of the sun. She really shouldn't have any more wine, and combined with the lunch, she didn't fancy a walk now, and certainly didn't think she could manage cake.

Tex joined her on the balcony, slipping his arms around her waist, nestling his chin into her shoulder. Anna could feel the warmth of his body against her back. She let out a small murmur of contentment and closed her eyes, leaning back into him and resting her head against his. She relished the feeling of being in close contact with him; it made her whole body tingle. Absently, Anna ran her hand along the bare forearm that held her, seeking out his hand, their fingers entwining.

He kissed her shoulder through her blouse, then her bare neck and finally her ear. She felt the butterflies in her stomach going crazy and her breathing becoming deeper as he squeezed her more tightly, pressing his hips against her. It felt like the excitement was physically creeping up through her windpipe, trying to burst out of her madly pumping heart. This was decision time. This was the moment where she either stopped things before they got out of hand or allowed it to go further. It was a one-horse race really. Every part of her body seemed imbued with a feeling of desire.

Anna twisted around in Tex's arms and, putting one arm around his neck, holding the other out so that she didn't spill the wine down either of them, kissed him on the mouth. Not a quick or tentative peck, but a full-on, open-mouthed, tongue-exploring kiss.

Tex let out a groan and gently pulled away. Anna let him take the glass from her and place it on the table, then as he took both her hands and began to walk backwards into the living room, Anna followed, her eyes never leaving his.

Once inside, Tex began to kiss her again. Anna felt as if her body had a mind all of its own. She arched towards him, offering herself to his now showering kisses. First around her face, then down her neck and towards her cleavage. His hand was warm on her back, keeping her pressed towards him, while the other spread wide at her waist, travelling up her side, thumbing her ribs.

He pulled away looking directly at her. 'Yes?' His voice was soft.

Anna nodded, a small smile of self-consciousness flicked across her face.

Tex held her gaze. 'You sure?'

'Yes, I'm sure.' A whisper.

Again holding his hands, Tex led her into the bedroom.

He stopped at the edge of the bed and cupped her face in his hands. His lips touching hers like little static shocks. He paused, barely breaking contact with her mouth. 'You okay, baby?'

All Anna could do was nod, as a small moan of desire left her throat.

Their lovemaking was passionate and needy. Anna felt as if a wild, wanting alter ego had taken hold of her. It may have been a long time but all her worries seemed to dissolve at once. Her nerves had been calmed and long-forgotten emotions and feelings stirred. She felt like she was a woman again. She wasn't a mum, she wasn't a wife – she was a lover. It felt good. It felt right.

Afterwards, Tex had held her tightly in his arms, their bodies pressed against each other. He had murmured that she was beautiful and had kissed her reassuringly on her forehead and stroked her hair.

When Anna awoke about an hour later, she was still in Tex's arms, his fingers caressing her shoulders and neckline.

They made love again, this time more slowly, taking their time to explore each other's bodies. Caressing, stroking, squeezing, holding, kissing, tasting. All so gently and tenderly. They finally fell, tired but satisfied, back onto the bed, her face buried in his chest, his strong arms holding her tightly. Tex's lovemaking had been so munificent. Closing her eyes, relishing the feeling of contentment he evoked in her, Anna felt cared for and considered, something she didn't think she had ever truly experienced before.

'When you say you didn't do anything on Sunday, do you actually mean you didn't do *anything*, as in nothing at all? Nothing happened with Anna?' Jamie took a large swig of the pint Tex had just put down on the pub table and then smacked his lips together. 'Cheers, salut and all that. I mean, if that's the case, then you're slipping, mate.'

Tex didn't answer, instead leaning back in his chair he surveyed the emptiness of the pub. An old man cradling half a bitter was perched on a bar stool, his Jack Russell terrier dozing on the cool flagstones, dreaming of chasing rabbits, an ear or a leg twitching now and again. A couple of workmen were playing pool, their high-vis jackets and hard site hats bundled on a chair. Tuesday lunchtimes in the Three Bells obviously wasn't the hub of all social activity in Arundel. Or maybe it was. He was, after all, in the sleepy Sussex countryside.

'You're not saying much,' said Jamie. 'You're being unusually quiet about your latest *femme fatale*.'

Tex shrugged indifferently, as if it were no big deal. Normally, he wouldn't think twice about sharing the details with Jamie, sometimes more detail than others, but today he didn't want to.

'Let's just say we did not go out for a walk,' he said at last, more to keep Jamie happy than the need or desire to share the information.

'I knew it!' chortled Jamie. 'Mind you, I give Anna her due, she did hold out on you for a bit. Made you work for it. I hope she was worth the wait.'

Tex gave a small nod in the affirmative. Yes, she had certainly been worth it. He didn't, however, want to share it with Jamie, or anyone for that matter. It had been beautiful and satisfying at many different levels but most of all, Anna had trusted him and he didn't want to break her trust.

'She's not your usual type,' carried on Jamie.

'Which is?'

'Tall. Brunette. Long hair. Sophisticated. Busty. Although having said all that, Anna is pretty hot, in her own sort of elfin way. Nice bum but a bit flat-chested.' Jamie took another swig of his beer, as he considered his summing up.

Tex bristled at the idea of Jamie thinking about Anna in any sort of sexual way. Jamie didn't miss his unguarded expression which screamed 'hands off'.

'Hey, don't look so alarmed. I mean I could, of course, easily charm Anna away from you, but seeing as we've been friends so long and I'm more than happy with my dear wife, I'll leave her to you.'

'That's very kind of you, Jamie. I will be eternally grateful for your sacrifice.'

Tex grinned at his friend. He knew he didn't have anything to worry about with Jamie, who was as madly in love with Yvonne as he was when they had first met. Tex also knew Jamie was only window shopping. Sure, they had discussed the attributes and failings of many a woman, mostly Tex's girl of the moment, but Jamie had never even come close to being tempted. Jamie affirmed Tex's belief in there being a someone for everyone; some people found The One straight away, others took a bit longer, while some never found it. He had, of course, had something like it himself once. With Estelle.

Estelle's smiling face drifted to the front of his mind. He no longer felt the pain, the rawness, that he had known for several years after her death, but there was still a heavy sadness. Forcing memories of Estelle to the abyss of his mind, Tex conjured up images of Anna and yesterday afternoon. Surprisingly, this wasn't quite as difficult as was customary.

'I was going to invite Anna to the awards dinner on Friday,' Tex said, taking a sip of his beer. 'I have a spare ticket.'

Jamie raised his eyebrows. 'You were? I mean, you are?' He nodded in an approving way. 'Good for you. About time you did more with them than just sleep with them.'

Tex shrugged in an attempt to seem nonchalant. 'We get on well. She's interesting.'

Jamie nodded again, this time slowly as he eyed Tex with more than a hint of amusement on his face. 'Interesting. Right. I would probably use the word complicated. In an ex-husband, who isn't really an ex and who happens to be living with her, sort of way. Oh, and let's not forget the teenage son. All that testosterone flying around. Interesting, maybe. Complicated, definitely.'

Tex couldn't actually deny Jamie's summing up, and under normal circumstances he would have kept well away from anyone remotely complicated. Ever since Estelle had passed away he had ploughed all his time and energy into the business and reaped the rewards by gaining a Michelin star. His restaurant was his wife, the women who now passed in and out of his life, his mistresses. So why now having slept with Anna, did he still feel as if his thirst for her hadn't even begun to be quenched?

The Tarrant Tea Room was surprisingly busy when Tex paid a visit the following day. Anna was working there and although he could have called in to chat to the owners earlier in the week, he was conscious that he had purposefully put it off until today.

There she was in her white blouse, black skirt, complete with little black and white gingham apron, looking very cute as she took the order from an elderly couple. As she turned, she saw him and broke in to a broad smile.

'This is a surprise.' She came over, but Tex noticed she stayed just out of touching distance. Perhaps she could read his mind and decided the tea rooms was not the appropriate place for a lustful greeting. He had spoken to her on the phone four times since Sunday, but this was the first time he had actually seen her since then.

'Hey. You okay?' He looked for any sign of unease and was pleased to note the absence of anything resembling regret.

'I'm fine, thanks. What are you doing here? I didn't think English tea and scones would be your thing.'

'I've come to see Brian actually.'

Concern settled on her face. 'About the fire?'

He nodded. 'And to just try to reassure him about the restaurant not being a threat.'

'Okay. I'll go and get him.' She headed off towards the back of the restaurant.

Tex had to force his eyes away from her neat butt that was resurrecting more than just the memories of Sunday afternoon, all of which were highly inappropriate for the current setting.

Anna returned a few minutes later. 'Do you want to take a seat, Brian will be along soon. Can I get you a coffee?'

Tex followed her over to a small two-seater table by the window, purposefully taking the seat in the corner. He rested his hands on her hips as he squeezed behind her, pausing momentarily to breathe in the fresh vanilla smell of her hair that he was becoming increasingly addicted to.

'Stop it,' she hissed, although he could tell she was smiling. 'You'll get me sacked and yourself arrested for lewd conduct.'

He let out a sigh before muttering in her ear, 'It would be so worth it though.'

'I think you need a bucket of cold water.' She smiled warmly, her lovely mossy green eyes sparkling as he held her gaze for a moment, smiling back.

'So you're Nico Garcia,' said the plump man standing in front of the table.

Tex stood up and held out his hand. 'That's right, but people usually call me Tex. Brian is it?'

Brian regarded Tex's outstretched hand for a moment before wiping his own on his apron and accepting the gesture, saying, 'It's Mr Stephens.'

'Of course, sir.' Tex looked evenly at Brian Stephens, thinking it was handy being from Texas at times, as Brian Stephens had no idea if he was being facetious using the word sir, or whether he was just using it in a respectful, American way.

'Well, let's sit down,' he said. Tex observed the older man lower himself into the carver style chair that really was too big to be at such a small table. Bad planning. Once Brian Stephens had settled himself, Tex began.

'I just really wanted to introduce myself properly. I didn't see you at the open evening the other night so didn't have the chance to chat.'

'Hmm, well, I was busy. Lots of customers. Didn't get cleared up until late.'

'That's great that you're busy.' The opening was easier than he thought. 'You know, that was one of the things that struck me about Arundel when I did my market research.' Tex relaxed his shoulders purposefully in a non-threatening manner. 'I could tell immediately that there were enough customers to go round and that your establishment and mine wouldn't really overlap. We

158

wouldn't be competing against each other.'

'Is that right? How did you work that out then?'

'Well, for a start, your tea rooms offer the quintessential British tea and cake. Afternoon tea is such a British thing and so suitable for a historic town like Arundel. The tourists must love it, all the history, the quaint shops, the ambiance of the place. So having afternoon tea just makes perfect sense.'

Brian puffed his chest like a proud lion. 'Oh yes, we offer a beautiful selection of cakes and sandwiches. I'm not saying we're the Ritz but we have our standards.'

Tex smiled approvingly. 'Absolutely, and with that in mind my restaurant, although just a couple of doors down, couldn't even begin to compare or, indeed, compete.' It was hard work, but Tex could see Brian Stephens's initial hostility gradually dissolving, especially when he went on to say that he was focusing on the evening sitting, that's where his main business would be and there'd be no overlap at all. As for daytime customers, he would be offering a light lunch, brasserie style, and he envisaged a totally different clientele to Tarrant Tea Room.

When they parted company with a much warmer handshake, Tex felt he had completed what he had set out to achieve. He had brought the matter of the fire up and, give Brian his due, he had been suitably outraged and sympathetic in a way that a fellow businessman would understand, and Tex was convinced graffiti, vandalism and arson wasn't this man's style.

So, that left two possible candidates. Castle Curator or Evil Ex.

Chapter Twenty

Anna could barely believe her eyes. Coming towards her table at the charity ball was Nathan. Automatically, her eyes looked beyond her brother, seeking out Zoe. If she had been shocked to see Nathan, then she was stunned to see the tall, willowy figure of Christine appearing at his side. Nathan pulled out a chair for Christine to sit down and took the one next to her. Anna looked round the table. Tex on her left, Jamie on her right, then Yvonne. Duncan Hughes, a high-profile chef, and his wife, then Tex's maître d', Edward with his wife. Next to them were Nathan and then Christine, who sat next to Tex to complete the circle. No spare seat. No Zoe.

'Good evening everyone,' purred Christine, smiling round the table to the greetings of the other guests. 'Christine Bennett, art adviser to Tex.' She touched Tex's arm lightly, leaning into him, smiling. Anna wasn't sure if it was a smile or a grimace on Tex's face but, ever the gentleman, he just gave a slight nod in acknowledgement. 'And this is my friend Nathan,' Christine continued. More touching of arms. 'He's also my personal trainer.'

'Christine's date couldn't make it, so she asked me to step in at the last minute,' offered Nathan by way of explanation, not meeting the accusing eyes of his sister.

'He's my knight in shining armour,' said Christine, still with that smug look on her face.

'Isn't he just,' muttered Anna.

Tex reached under the table and squeezed Anna's clenched fist. She could feel the anger and disappointment raging inside her. What was Nathan playing at? Loyal, dependable, honest, married, father of four, Nathan. Never in her wildest dreams did she think he would be unfaithful and so blatant. After everything that she had endured with Mark. All those times Nathan had been outraged by his brother-in-law, surely he wasn't at it himself now. The pain at remembering Mark's infidelity swept through her. Were all men the same? Were all men ruled by what was between their legs? She stole a glance at Tex. Was he the same? Oh, please not.

Anna moved her hand away from Tex's and rested it casually on the table, aware that Tex had turned to look at her. Probably wondering why she had rejected his gesture. He said nothing but took his empty hand away and rested it on the back of her chair. She could feel his thumb gently and slowly caressing her bare back. His touch sent an internal shiver through her. She took a deep breath – she must trust her instincts and believe in Tex. Not all men were the same.

The charity event was being held at Albury Park in Surrey, a beautiful Grade II listed Tudor mansion, which boasted being a backdrop for the film *Four Weddings and a Funeral*, amongst others. For today a large marquee had been erected in the glorious grounds, surrounded by beautiful wooded parkland with the River Tillingbourne tripping along the edge. The evening was to raise awareness and money for hearing-impaired children, a cause close to Tex's heart. It also served as the opportunity to give several awards to local businesses. Tex's maître d', Edward, had been nominated for a customer service award and although he didn't win, Edward said he was pleased just to have been shortlisted. Tex mumbled something about it being a fix and the judges being incompetent, while Jamie laughed that it was probably because Tex hadn't used his charms to persuade the head judge, Heleana Upper.

'You obviously haven't been up her! Get it? Heleana Upper. Oh well, never mind.'

This had earned him a dig in the arm from Yvonne, while she spoke loudly over him, remarking what a lovely dress Anna was wearing. Again there was the reassuring squeeze of her hand from Tex. This time she didn't take hers away. Of course Tex was going to have a history with Jamie and Yvonne that went a long way back, something she had never been part of. She must try to relax. Perhaps have another drink? It seemed to be working for Jamie.

The meal finished and cleared away meant the main event, the charity auction, could go ahead. The donations had been generous and the bidding even more so, the alcohol making the raising of arms and shouting out of amounts more frequent and bolder. Jamie managed to outbid the room on a meal for four at Tex's restaurant, which Tex found highly amusing.

'You, my friend, are one hell of an idiot at times. You have just paid three times the cost of the meal and if you'd come, I wouldn't have charged you a penny anyway.'

'I know, mate,' slurred Jamie, trying to focus properly while dangling a glass between his forefinger and thumb. 'All for a good cause and all that. You never know, I might invite you along as my guest. Now that would be ironic.' He finished his champagne and on finding the upturned bottle in the ice bucket, signalled the waiter for another.

Anna was hoping that now the bidding was over and the band had struck up, she would get a chance to collar Nathan. No such luck. Christine was dragging him up to the already busy dance floor. Anna scowled after them.

'She's just playing games,' Tex said. 'Don't worry.'

'I know that. You know that. I just hope Nathan knows it.'

162

Tex put his arm around her shoulder and pulled her into him, kissing the side of her head.

'Have I told you how beautiful you look tonight?'

Anna grinned. 'Once or twice.'

'Every time I look at you, you are more beautiful than the time before.'

And she did feel good in her short, electric blue dress. One shoulder bare, the satin draping over her other shoulder and a small frill running down and across her bust and round to the back. Most of the women had gone for a long evening dress, but Anna had opted for an above the knee, tighter-fitting one. It suited her small build and height, although the three-inch platform shoes she wore made up for it. Simple and unfussy, but effective.

Tex stroked her bare back again and whispered in her ear, 'What I really want to do is to take you back to my apartment, discard your satin dress and admire your satin skin instead.'

'All in good time,' Anna smiled at him. 'You don't look so bad yourself.' Dinner jacket, hair brushed back, the fringe slightly falling forward in that cowlick way it did. Freshly shaved. Smelling heavenly. Looking downright sexy.

A rather stout chap who worked in the catering industry, his shirt buttons straining at the navel, joined them at the table to talk to Tex. He had obviously been told vertical stripes were more flattering; however, the same person had failed to tell him that the broad blue and white deckchair look wasn't really doing the trick. She feigned interest as he talked about the downturn in the economy. Boring business chat. Anna got the impression that Tex wasn't too interested either but he was being polite, listening and responding just enough so as not to appear rude.

Fortunately, an increasingly drunk Jamie plonked himself down at the table again, telling 'Big Boy' to shuffle up, and tried to make a serious but somewhat unsuccessful contribution to the discussions. Giving Jamie a contemptuous look, Big Boy made his apologies and left.

'I feel I should high-five you for that,' said Tex to Jamie, 'but I don't trust your co-ordination.'

'What was he trying for?' slurred Jamie. 'A free lunch?'

'He looks like he has plenty of those,' replied Tex.

A slower song was now starting up. 'A chance for you all to catch your breath,' the lead singer announced.

'Come on,' said Tex, standing up and taking Anna's hand.

She obliged willingly. It would give her the chance to hold and be held. To feel his body against hers. To feel his broad shoulders under her hands and to feel his touch on her. They held each other closely and danced slower than the music demanded. Lost in the moment, Tex kissed the top of her head. Anna tilted her head back to catch the kisses on her mouth. Small kisses turning into a longer one. A small moment of bliss shattered by a very wobbly legged Jamie bundling into them, Yvonne, not quite so drunk, hanging round his neck like a pendant.

'Get a room,' slurred Jamie, louder than necessary, sending both him and Yvonne into fits of laughter.

'Piss off, Dixon.' Tex grinned back at his friend. Anna gave a small giggle, it sounded funny Tex saying that with a southern drawl.

'What was that? Piss off! How very English of you,' Jamie laughed. 'Did you hear what he just said, Yvonne? He told me to piss off.'

'Oh, the cheek of it!' cried Yvonne.

'Actually that's not a bad idea,' came a female voice behind them.

Anna turned round as Christine, giving Jamie a shove in the back, bustled her way between everyone, attaching herself to Tex while somehow managing to propel Nathan towards Anna. 'Ladies excuse me.'

'It's all right,' said Anna to Tex before he could protest. She was

164

aware that Jamie was drawing attention to them and she couldn't pass up this opportunity to speak to Nathan. Holding on to her brother's arm, she frogmarched him as discreetly as she could towards the exit.

'What the bloody hell is going on?' demanded Anna.

The garland lights that festooned the surrounding trees, lighting a path towards the house, swung gently in the evening breeze. The shadows flicked across Nathan's face, not totally shielding the guilt. He shuffled from one foot to another.

'Nothing's going on. I'm just accompanying my client to an event. Christine was stood up. I'm doing her a favour, that's all.' He jutted his chin out, the way he did whenever he was arguing a point.

'Does Zoe know?'

'Of course she does. Not that she cares anyway.'

'But Christine – she's your client.'

'That's rich coming from you.' The guilty look making way for indignity.

'But you're married.'

'So are you.'

'Only technically.'

'I might just as well be "only technically" married myself.' Nathan stuffed his hands in his pocket and turned away to look at the gardens.

Anna felt a wave of sympathy rush over her, quickly followed by concern. She moved to stand beside him and slipped her arm through his. 'Are things that bad?'

He looked down at her arm and patted her hand. 'That's more physical contact than I've had with Zoe in months.' There was sadness in his eyes.

'It won't always be like this. It's probably because of having a baby. It can make some women feel a bit, well, you know, like they don't want sex for a while. Zoe has got a lot on her plate.'

'So she keeps telling me.' Nathan shrugged off Anna's arm, rubbing his face up and down in the palms of his hands. 'She's not the only one though. Why do you think I'm here? Because I want to shag Christine? No, I'm here to keep my client happy so I don't lose any business. So I can build up a more expensive client base. That way, I can provide better for my family. I may even be able to get some help in for Zoe, if she wasn't being such a bloody martyr, that is.' He sighed loudly. 'Anyway, Christine's quite good company.'

Anna raised her eyebrows and started to refute this but changed her mind. 'Just be careful. Don't be too flattered by it all.'

'I hardly think you're the best person to advise me about relationships. You haven't exactly got a great track record.'

'Below the belt,' retorted Anna as she followed Nathan back towards the marquee. True as it might be, it was cutting.

He paused at the entrance. 'Look, I'm big enough and ugly enough to look after myself. I do the big brother routine, not you.' He smiled warmly. 'Honestly, Anna, don't worry about me. Everything's fine.' He gave her a quick peck on the cheek before turning and milling his way back towards the table, where Christine now sat drooling over Tex. Smiling and giggling. Anna was right, that woman was trouble.

Sitting back at the table with Tex, she made polite conversation with her other dining companions, Tex chatting easily to Duncan Hughes and Edward about some new television programme Duncan was in the middle of filming. Jamie and Yvonne were still on the dance floor. Him entertaining a small group that had gathered around to watch his Michael Jackson dance moves, Yvonne, laughing and shaking her head adoringly at her husband.

When Christine excused herself to go to the Ladies, Anna got up too. Tex might have been in deep conversation, but he didn't miss anything. He caught Anna's wrist as she walked behind him.

Anna leaned forward, draping her arms over his shoulders, linking them round his chest, she dropped a kiss to his ear.

'Don't worry,' she whispered before heading off in Christine's direction.

Anna rested against the vanity unit, arms folded, waiting. Christine looked startled to see her standing there but she regained her composure almost instantly. Flicking her long brunette waves over her shoulder, she sidestepped Anna and stood in front of the basins and began fluffing her hair.

'You look like you want to say something. Cat got your tongue?' She turned the tap on, rinsing her hands without looking at Anna.

'Stay away from my brother.' Anna hoped her voice sounded firm and steady. Christine gave a derisive laugh.

'Or you'll do what? Tell tales on me out of school?'

Anna didn't actually know what the *or else* bit was of her warning, she hadn't got that far in her mind.

'He's married. He has four children. Just leave him alone.'

'Your brother is an adult. What he does is up to him. I didn't force him to come here tonight.' Christine began flicking her hair again, pulling a strand that was on the wrong side of the parting. 'Obviously coming out with me was a much more attractive option than staying at home with his wife and four children.'

'You're just playing games.' Anna's breathing was getting faster as she became increasingly more frustrated and angry by Christine's indifference.

'I don't think your brother needs or wants his little sister speaking for him,' said Christine as she turned and faced Anna, one hand on her hip, the other leaning on the sink.

'Just stay away from him,' repeated Anna.

Christine leaned closer to Anna. When she spoke it was low and almost sinister.

'Stay away from Tex and we might have a deal.' She gave a

smile that turned into a snarl, stood up straight, knocking Anna's shoulder with her own as she walked out of the toilets.

That woman was such a cow. She needed stopping but Anna had no idea how.

When Anna reappeared ten minutes later, Christine was already back. Tex looked questioningly at Anna as she took her seat next to him. She looked innocently at him as he studied her for a moment, her hands clasped together in her lap to try to stop them shaking.

'Do you want some fresh air?' he asked.

Anna nodded and let herself be led out of the marquee. She put her arm in his as they wandered towards the woodland path, away from the noise of the band and a few smokers who were standing under a gazebo.

'There, relax now,' he said, stopping and turning to face her. 'Wanna talk?'

Anna shook her head. 'A hug would be nice.'

'I can do better than that,' said Tex, kissing her. Eventually he pulled away, letting out a small groan before holding her close to him. 'Oh, baby, did I tell you how beautiful you are?'

It felt so right being held by him. She just wanted to go back to his apartment and enjoy him. Leaving all her worries behind her.

Later that night as they laid together naked on Tex's bed, spent, tired, happy and contented, Tex tentatively enquired about earlier. He was sure something had happened, some words exchanged between Anna and Christine, but didn't know what. Anna had definitely followed Christine to the washrooms and both women had come back slightly unsettled. He hadn't missed the trembling of Anna's hands. He hadn't pressured her to say what was bothering her, in case it had put her on edge, which could possibly spoil the build-up to their lovemaking. He had wanted her all night, from the moment he had picked her up from her little house. She'd stepped out in that tight blue dress, high heels, glossy tights, looking absolutely stunning. Seeing her had taken his breath away and aroused him in a heartbeat. Had it not been a charity event or a possible award for Edward, he would have driven her directly back to the Arundel apartment and taken her straight to bed. As it was, he had had to wait several hours and wasn't going to let a spat with Christine spoil it. Christine seemed to be intent on stirring up trouble.

'Do you want to talk about it now?' he asked, pulling the cotton sheet over them.

'Oh, it's nothing,' said Anna. 'Just the whole Christine and Nathan thing, I don't like it.'

'Hey, it's not your battle to fight.' Tex kissed the tip of her nose, hoping to reassure her.

'But I don't feel I can sit back and just let him mess up his marriage. I'm so surprised at him, especially after…' She stopped abruptly.

Tex cursed silently to himself, wishing he hadn't brought this up. She looked troubled now. Still, he wanted to know, maybe he could fix it. He brushed a strand of her blonde hair away before speaking. 'After what?'

'After what I went through with Mark.' She paused and gave an apologetic smile. 'I'm sorry, let's just leave it. I don't want to spoil the evening by talking about my marriage.'

With an immense effort, Tex quelled the sigh that threatened to escape. The mere mention of Mark ignited some crazy feeling of jealousy. Jeez, what was that all about? Jealousy wasn't on Tex's list of emotions and, yet, it sure as hell was trying to make it. He decided not to press her to talk about it; he wasn't sure he could handle his feelings. Pulling her towards him, his hands wandering up and down her bare skin, he went for the distraction tactic instead.

Chapter Twenty One

Anna watched him sleeping, the steady lifting of the dark swirls of hair as his chest rose and fell, the peaceful look on his face, his stubble beginning to show and his fringe flopping to one side. It was nine-thirty in the morning, and street sounds outside were coming to life. Anna knew she was in Tex's Guildford apartment, but where exactly that was in relation to the town she had no idea. She had never been there before. They had stumbled in late last night, or was it the early hours of the morning? She knew that the taxi had dropped them off at the back of some premises, which she had a vague recollection of being retail, and that Tex had held her hand as they climbed the wrought-iron staircase up to his apartment. Once inside, he had simply swept her off her feet and straight into the bedroom.

She liked to think of it as making love, it sounded much nicer than just sex, but it was too early for love. Yes, she really liked Tex, *really* liked him, and she was sure he felt the same, but they had only known each other for a few weeks, and in the cold light of day how could she be in love with someone she hardly knew? She needed to keep things in perspective and not get too carried away. Although she had forced herself to leave the tag of 'client' in the depths of her mind, every now and then it popped up to shake her confidence in her relationship with Tex.

Not only that, but it was her first romance of any description since Mark had left and she needed to take her time, for her own sake as well as not scaring Tex off by appearing too needy, pushy or demanding, and yet still show she was keen. How on earth did you achieve that? Not for the first time did she think that dating as an adult, where you overthought every situation, was much more complicated than when you were a teenager and just got on with it, fearless in love.

'Hey,' said a sleepy Tex, opening his eyes. He reached over and stroked her face. 'Did you sleep okay?'

'Didn't get that much sleep actually,' she teased. 'Someone kept me up half the night.'

Tex grinned. 'Shouldn't I be saying that?' He kissed her nose and ran his hand down her side, over her hip and round to the back of her thigh. His fingertips were like charges of electricity as they moved across her naked skin. Anna's whole body tingled as she responded to his touch.

Afterwards as she showered, Anna's thoughts turned to last night. She smiled at the memory of Jamie and Yvonne being poured into a taxi by Tex, who, while stuffing a bundle of notes into the driver's hand, relayed their address. Duncan Hughes and Edward, together with their wives, had been charming and very good company. Their other table companions though were another matter.

Nathan and Christine had stayed until Tex and Anna left. Nathan was driving Christine home and had offered to do the same for Tex and Anna, adding that he could take Anna back to Chichester with him. He was obviously making it clear to everyone that he had no intention of staying the night with Christine, something that Anna took a little heart from. When Tex had said that it was okay but they were going back to his apartment, she had thought for a moment that Nathan was going to object. For a second the two men locked eyes, each weighing up the other. Nathan in a 'so you think you're taking my sister back to your flat do you?' way and Tex in a 'you gotta problem with that?' way. Fortunately, Nathan must have realised he wasn't really in a position to spout the appropriateness of what was right and had simply kissed Anna goodnight, telling her to ring him if she needed him. Anna gave a half laugh to herself, it was rather ironic that he was questioning Tex's intentions and her morals yet he himself was treading the very fine line of what could and couldn't be considered adultery.

Drying herself and putting on her jeans and blouse from her overnight bag, she decided to put any thoughts of Christine and Nathan out of her mind. To shut them off as she had Luke and Mark. While she was with Tex she didn't want any problems seeping in and tainting it. Whatever the ultimate conclusion of her romance with Tex turned out be, she wasn't going to let worrying about them preoccupy her time. Whilst she was with Tex she was going to enjoy it.

By the time she had finished getting ready and found her way to the kitchen of Tex's surprisingly large apartment, he was busy preparing brunch. Scrambled eggs, salmon, brown bread, orange juice, fresh coffee for him, tea for her. Yummy. It was in a totally different league to the bowl of cornflakes or toast and Marmite she usually had.

Tex's flat was not dissimilar to that of his Arundel one, in that it was unfussy, very white, lots of glass and chrome, very modern and minimalistic. There was a wide, tiled hallway running the length of the property, with rooms leading off either side. Tex's room had an en-suite, so she assumed the doors led to the second bedroom he had told her about, and a main bathroom. At the end of the hall was the living room that Anna had glimpsed as she had come out of the bedroom. The whole apartment had a spacious and airy feeling with its high ceilings and long-paned Georgian windows.

Anna sat down at the table as Tex served brunch. 'Where exactly are we? I know we're in Guildford but other than that, I've no idea.'

'We're above my restaurant. I like to be near, although I do have an excellent restaurant manager. He lives nearby with his wife, who also works for me. She's the other maître d' when Edward is not working.'

'So what made you want to become a chef?'

'My grandma. She used to cook the most amazing Cuban food and I loved helping her. I think that's where my affair with food began.'

'Cuban?' queried Anna. 'Not Italian, then, like some people thought?'

'No, not Italian. It's a common mistake. My father is a second-generation Cuban immigrant to the States. He met my mom, who came from a big ranching family in Texas, and was seduced by ranch life and, of course, by mom. And the rest, as they say, is history. They took over the ranch together with my uncle. My grandma lived with us.'

'You didn't follow in your father's footsteps then?' She was curious; a cowboy from Texas with a Cuban father, training in France to be a chef was unusual.

'My folks never put any pressure on me to work on the ranch. It was probably helped by my brothers all getting involved. I suppose Pa thought three out of four wasn't a bad average. I think they thought me going off to Europe was something I needed to get out of my system and that I'd be back within a year or two.'

'Three brothers? Wow, you have a large family,' commented Anna.

'Yep. Four boys and two girls.'

'You have another sister as well. God, you could start up your

173

own town.'

Tex laughed. 'Well, if I told you that my brothers all live on the ranch with their wives and family, you'd realise that isn't too far from the truth.'

'They all live together?'

'No. They all have their own homes at various different places on the ranch.'

Anna could hear the amusement in his voice. He grinned at her then spoke again. 'Don't worry, it's not Banjo country, nothing like that film *Deliverance*. All my nephews and nieces go to regular schools and mix with normal kids.' He emphasised the word *normal* as he swept her up in his arms, simply, it seemed, just to feel her against him again.

'I wasn't implying that,' protested Anna, looking up at him. 'Just how big is this ranch?'

'Oh, not too big. About one thousand eight hundred acres,' he said in an offhand manner, but grinning at her wide-eyed, and then added, 'I'll take you there one day.'

After breakfast, Tex took Anna downstairs to show her his restaurant, taking her first to the kitchens. Stainless steel, tiled floor and walls, all spotlessly clean and professional looking. Whilst it looked busy, with staff hurrying around and the noise of pots and pans against utensils, there was a definite atmosphere of calm about it all.

Tex greeted his staff, nodding and smiling to their acknowledgements of 'Morning Chef' or just plain 'Chef'.

'This is where you busy yourself on a Saturday night then?' said Anna, stepping out of the way as a kitchen porter scurried past with a tray of individual deserts.

'Yes, I'm usually over there at the *passe*.'

'The *passe*?' Anna had no idea what Tex meant.

'It's where I check the food for presentation. I make sure it has been plated correctly, that everything is as it should be before I let service take it out to the customers. It's the main point of communication between the kitchen and front of house. Come. I'll show you the restaurant.'

The restaurant was furnished very much in the style of his apartments, Anna noted. Clean lines, modern furniture, no frills, swags or tails. Crisp white tablecloths, brown leather chairs, butter-cream walls and wooden floors. All very tasteful, subtle and oozing understated sophistication. They stood at the rear of the room, which was just receiving its first customers. A smart, bright-eyed Edward, showing no signs of a late boozy night, was greeting guests and escorting them to their seats. As he left a couple at their table, he acknowledged Anna with a nod of the head and a small but respectful smile.

'Madame. Chef.'

'Morning, Edward,' replied Tex, as without pausing or breaking stride, the maître d' continued with his work.

A gentleman dressed in a smart dark grey suit approached them. Tex shook his hand.

'*Bonjour, Jean-Paul. Ça-va?*'

Jean-Paul obviously hadn't been expecting Tex and was anxious to know if everything was all right. Anna looked incredulously at Tex. He was speaking French. Afterwards, when Jean-Paul left, she couldn't help herself.

'I didn't know you speak French!'

He grinned. 'Sure. You don't spend several years in France training to be a chef and then marrying a Frenchwoman without picking up the language.'

'Oh, your wife was French. I didn't realise.' She looked at him, trying to gauge whether the mention of his wife had provoked any sort of emotion. She couldn't tell.

Chapter Twenty Two

'So you're a cook then?' Luke flopped down on the sofa, opposite Tex.

Tex nodded. 'Essentially, yes.' He glanced at Anna standing in the kitchen doorway, looking decidedly on edge. He knew she hadn't been expecting Luke back from his friend's so early. He looked back at Luke. 'I learnt to cook from my mother. I learnt to be a chef at college. I learnt to be an artist at work.'

'I thought cooking was a bit girly myself,' replied Luke, putting his feet on the coffee table as he crunched into an apple. 'Only girls do cooking at school.'

'But that was the best bit.'

'How's that then?' Luke eyed Tex suspiciously.

'I got to spend all my cooking lessons with the girls. They thought it was great to have a boy in the class. The fuss they made over me. I got lots of attention. They all were keen to help me after school with my homework. It was great!' Tex winked at the sullen teenager.

This wasn't quite how he had planned the morning. After leaving Guildford the previous morning, they had arrived back at Chichester and, taking advantage of an empty house, Tex had stayed the night. He and Anna had enjoyed a beautiful, long lie-in that morning. Anna had made breakfast, poached egg on toast. They had showered together and gone back to bed again. Fortunately, they were downstairs, dressed and ready for a stroll, when Luke had unexpectedly arrived home.

'You're back early,' Anna had stammered. 'I wasn't expecting you yet.'

'Obviously.' The tone had been scathing, hostility oozing out of the laconic teenager.

Tex was doing his best to be calm and relaxed; he could see Anna was on edge. She was scurrying around making Luke something to eat, being overly cheerful, and trying hard to carry on as if her lover and her son were the best of friends.

'So, you any good at cooking then?' Luke asked whilst turning the half eaten apple round and crunching into the other side. He pushed a bit of apple to the side of his mouth. 'I mean, do you work for a fancy hotel or restaurant?'

'I have trained and worked in some of the best kitchens in Paris and London. Now I have my own restaurant in Guildford.'

'Tex is being very modest,' commented Anna, putting a bacon sandwich down on the coffee table. 'His restaurant has a Michelin star.' Luke looked nonplussed. 'He's also opening a restaurant in Arundel soon.'

Luke ignored his mum and looked over at Tex. 'But you're not famous though, are you?'

'No. Not my style.' Tex held Luke's gaze for a moment. Luke looked away and discarding the half eaten apple, tucked into his sandwich. Tex decided a different tact was needed. He nodded towards the guitar case propped against the sofa. 'You play guitar then?'

Luke regarded the guitar case. 'Clearly. It's not a flute in there, you know.'

Little shit, thought Tex. Anna went to say something but stopped at Tex's slight shake of the head.

'Can I have a look?' Tex continued. He wasn't going to give up yet.

'If you like.'

Tex took the guitar out of its case and gave a long, low whistle as he turned the instrument over in his hands.

'A Fender, electro-acoustic. Nice. May I?' He rested the guitar on his knee, his left hand automatically taking position at the neck, his right arm resting on the top.

Luke straightened up in his chair, a fleeting look of intrigue on his face, quickly disguised by a disinterested one. 'Suppose so.'

Tex strummed the strings once, picked his place on the neck for his fingers and strummed again. A small twist of one of the tuning heads. A chord. Another slight adjustment. Finally seemingly happy with the tuning, he began to play. Luke watched Tex, his face relaxing from the tight jaw and cross eyebrows.

'Oasis,' Luke said, shifting in his seat, his attention apparently caught. Tex carried on playing, half humming, half singing the words.

Tex ground to a halt, plucking at the strings as he found the notes he was looking for. He struck up again. This time a more upbeat song.

'Pulp. *Common People*,' said Luke after just a few bars.

'I'm impressed,' said Tex as he continued to play. 'Didn't think you'd know who Pulp are.'

'Likewise.' Luke raised his eyebrows. He gestured towards the guitar.

Tex gave him a small smile as he passed the guitar over. Cocky bugger, as Jamie would say.

'Luke's got a wide taste in music,' said Anna, sitting on the arm of Tex's chair while Luke played for Tex. 'He likes all the older stuff. Him and Nathan love their music.'

'How come you know all this English music if you're American?'

asked Luke after he finished his last song and then played a scale up and down.

'Training and working in France, there was always plenty of British music. I was in the UK for a few years in the late nineties when the Brit Pop scene was quite new,' explained Tex, relieved that they had finally found some common ground. It was a start if nothing else. Anna seemed to have relaxed a bit as well.

'Okay, I bet you won't know this one,' challenged Luke, beginning another song. As Tex listened, a small smile twitched at the corners of his mouth.

'That's The Undertakers. Can't remember the title of the song though.' Tex tapped his foot in time to the beat.

'*Death Watch*,' replied Luke, a small look of victory on his face.

'Arh yes. The Undertakers came into the restaurant I was working at one night. They were on tour, just played at a small punk-rock club around the corner.'

Luke stopped playing, his eyes wide. 'No way!'

Tex shook his head and chuckled. 'They were crazy. Definitely very drunk and probably stoned. Before they had even finished their starters, they began a food fight across the table at each other. They ended up throwing bread rolls at the other diners.'

'That Kenny was mad. Nathan's told me about him before.' Luke was grinning as he spoke.

Seizing the moment, Tex went on to tell him some more antics that Kenny and The Undertakers had got up to, plus a few other stories of misbehaving guests, some of them famous. By the end, Luke was laughing along with him.

With no more stories to tell and a silence between them, Luke instantly reverted back to morose teenager mode. Tex sighed to himself although unfazed by the sudden change in attitude. Teenage prerogative.

'I'm knackered,' said Luke, standing up. 'Going up to my room for a bit. See ya.'

'Thank you and sorry,' groaned Anna once Luke was upstairs.

'No need for either,' smiled Tex, squeezing Anna's hand. 'Don't take this the wrong way, but it's probably a good time for me to leave. Give Luke a bit of space.'

'And you.' Anna was trying to sound flippant and light-hearted although Tex could tell she was anything but. Was he really that transparent to her? Could she tell that Luke had annoyed him immensely? That kid was a pain in the butt, for sure, but in a funny way Tex thought it was quite admirable of Luke to be loyal to his dad. However, Tex really didn't need this sort of aggravation in a relationship. In fact, did he even need this relationship? It would only end like all the others once the novelty wore off. And Anna was a novelty, right?

She wasn't a fool. She had seen it in his eyes. Annoyance. Irritation. Testiness. She couldn't blame him. Luke hadn't exactly made Tex feel welcome, in fact, he had seemed to relish in being objectionable from the start. Tex had coped admirably with Mark being around but maybe Luke was just that bit too far. Maybe Tex thought, and quite rightly so, that a mother's bond to her child was far greater than a wife's bond to her once husband. Sitting down on the sofa with a sandwich, Anna wondered whether Tex would bother ringing her again. Maybe this was the end. The tears that spiked the back of her eyes surprised her. She didn't want it to be the end.

'Has he gone?' Luke appeared at the bottom of the stairs.

'If you mean Tex, then yes, he's gone.' She blinked hard to banish the tears.

'So you are seeing him then? I thought you said you'd tell me.' He didn't tamper the accusational tone.

'Come and sit down.' Anna put her plate on the coffee table, her sandwich barely touched, and gave Luke a small unreciprocated smile. Nevertheless, he sat down on the sofa, arms folded. 'Luke, up until now, there really hasn't been much to tell. I needed to be sure this was what I wanted before I brought you into it.'

'I'm sixteen, not six,' said Luke. 'I'm not stupid enough that I think he's going to be my new dad just because you've been out with him a few times. It would have been nice just to be warned a bit before I come home and he's sat here.'

Anna couldn't argue with that. He had a fair point. 'I'm sorry. You're right. I should have told you. But Tex staying was just a spur of the moment thing.'

Luke held up his hand. 'Too much information. I get the idea.' He gave her a small smile and raised his eyebrows slightly.

'Yes, okay. Sorry.' Anna could feel herself getting flustered. Some things a mother should just not discuss with her teenage son, no matter how well they got on.

'When's Dad coming back?'

The sudden change of direction flawed her for a moment. 'Erm, I'm not sure. Why? Are you missing him?'

Luke nodded. 'A bit, well, quite a bit actually. It's been strange getting to know him all over again, but he's been like a totally different person. Better, if you like.'

'I'm pleased for you,' replied Anna. What could she say? She couldn't exactly refute this with details of Mark's blackmailing scheme. That was definitely something she wouldn't be sharing with her son.

'Don't you think he's changed, Mum?'

Anna swallowed hard. How to answer this tactfully? 'He definitely appears to have changed with you and I am genuinely pleased.' She gave Luke's hand a squeeze. 'I really am.'

'But he's not changed enough for you,' stated Luke glumly.

Tex's morning jog with Nathan was fast turning into a full-on run. Tex pounded the sidewalk with his feet as he pushed himself harder, trying to work the frustration of the past few days out of his system, together with the cause of it.

It was now Wednesday and he hadn't contacted Anna since the weekend. It had taken a supreme act of discipline on his part. Several times he had nearly called her, had even got as far as bringing her contact details up on his phone, but he had resisted pushing the 'call' button. She was complicated. Her situation was complicated. He didn't do complicated.

Despite this mantra, Tex hadn't been able to exile her from his thoughts. Damn it! She had even invaded his dream last night.

'Let's just slow it down now,' urged Nathan as they approached the bottom of the hill in the High Street.

Tex obliged, although he knew the steep incline of the hill would have done the job anyway. Tex could feel the strain biting into the back of his calf muscles and tried to focus on that rather than on Anna. Reaching the top of the hill, they rounded the corner, passing by one of the entrances to Arundel Castle. Distracted, Tex didn't see the man hurrying out of the castle entrance.

'Ouf! Sorry. Oh, it's you.' He had run straight into the weasel-like curator who was carrying a tin of paint, the green drips of liquid smeared down the side. Tex looked down at his t-shirt. Great, now he had a weird green pattern in the middle of it. 'You wanna watch where you're going with that,' Tex said, looking back up at Andy.

'You're the one running hell for leather up the hill and not looking out for pedestrians,' Andy snapped back.

'What you doing just wandering round with a tin of paint anyway?' Tex went to wipe his shirt, then noticing Andy's paint stained fingers, thought better of it.

'Not that it's any business of yours, but I'm just taking it to Brian at the tea rooms. I borrowed it from him.' The curator scowled.

'You didn't happen to borrow some petrol too?' Tex watched

Andy's face for any flicker of guilt.

'What?'

'Forget it.'

'Well, if you don't mind, some of us have work to do.'

Tex watched him go. 'That guy does nothing to change my opinion of him.'

'Which is?' enquired Nathan.

'Total jerk.' With that, Tex began running again.

'You all right today?' asked Nathan, catching up.

Tex shot him a sideways look and was met by the same green eyes as those of Nathan's sister. Was there no getting away from her? 'I'm okay. Just have a lot of things to think about,' he offered by way of an explanation.

'Nothing to do with my sister then?'

Stepping off the path to avoid an elderly lady walking along with her dog, gave Tex a few seconds before responding, 'What makes you say that?'

'Just wondered. I saw her yesterday and she seemed a bit fed up. Just putting two and two together.'

'She's worried about you,' said Tex. Okay, that was unnecessary but it deflected the conversation away from himself and Anna. He slowed down to match Nathan's pace.

'Worried about me? Why's that then?' replied Nathan.

'You and Christine.'

Nathan stopped running. 'She collared me about it at the ball and I'll tell you what I told her. I went with Christine as a favour. She had a spare ticket and didn't want to go on her own. She's my client, that's all. Everything is professional and above board. Just the way a client relationship should be.' He raised an eyebrow to go with the challenging look he offered Tex, who continued to jog on the spot.

Despite himself, Tex grinned. 'Good. Now what's that saying?

183

Something about doing what I do, not what I say?'

For a moment he wasn't sure if Nathan appreciated his joke, but the other man's shoulders relaxed and a wry smile showed itself. 'Don't do as I do, do as I say.' Then the smile made way for a serious look. 'Anna could do without any more aggro in her life. Don't mess her about if you're not serious.' Nathan held Tex's gaze for a moment.

Tex nodded. Message received and understood.

Then Nathan was off and jogging again, urging Tex to keep up. Big brother chat apparently over.

She was sitting on the steps to the apartment like a child locked out waiting for her mom to come home. Elbow resting on her knee, her hand cupping her chin, while her other hand fiddled with her phone. Tex felt his stomach knot. He had to admit he was relieved to see her there. He had finished his run with Nathan, who was now on his way to meet Christine for her workout. What that entailed Tex didn't care to imagine. After his run and mini-chat with Nathan, Tex had resolved to speak to Anna. He was planning to call by the tea rooms where she should be working today. He needed to apologise. He was acting no better than a petulant teenager himself. His foot scuffed a stone and she looked up at him, a startled expression on her face, swiftly followed by… What? Embarrassment? Unease?

She jumped to her feet, brushed her jeans down unnecessarily, her eyes locking with his.

'Can we talk?' she said at last.

Normally those three words would set alarm bells ringing in Tex's mind. It was never good when a woman wanted 'to talk'. It usually meant they were after commitment, that the light-hearted days were coming to a close and more serious ones lay ahead. Tex was good at anticipating this point and bringing things to a close beforehand, but today he noted those feelings couldn't be further away.

'You'd better come in.' He tapped in the passcode and swung the door open, letting her walk through first, the scent of her perfume drifting under his nose and triggering a whole host of involuntary reactions; his body tensing. It didn't help that the lift was tiny, just big enough for the two of them. Being in such a confined space with her was sending serious adrenalin rushes to every extremity of his body. Finally, they were in Tex's apartment and he could put a bit of physical space between them.

'Do you wanna cup of tea?' She shook her head and went to speak, but Tex cut in. 'I need to take a shower first. Then we can talk.'

The shower was good, cold, but it did the trick. It also gave him the thinking time he needed. He didn't want things to end with Anna, he wasn't ready for that yet. The idea of not seeing her again gnarled at his insides. He didn't know what to make of himself or how one woman could have this effect on him. Then he realised that he hadn't even thought about Estelle once in the past three days. The realisation stilled him. Rooted him to the spot. He mulled over his feelings and was even more surprised when he could find no guilt, not even if he tried to force it out of him. No, it just wasn't there.

All he felt was a need. It had been plaguing him all week and now he finally acknowledged, finally realised, that this need was for Anna. He needed her for his mind, body and soul. He also realised that just thinking about her meant he needed another shower. Another cold one.

When he came out of the bedroom in his jeans and white t-shirt, bare feet and damp hair, Anna thought for one moment that the fizz of excitement would cause her to spontaneously combust. He

185

looked so handsome. All she could do was stare at him while he stared back as he stood in the doorway. She heard herself swallow as her heart tried to throw in an extra beat. It sounded so loud, she was sure he could hear it too.

She gathered her thoughts. Thoughts that had done nothing but circulate her mind since Sunday like a never-ending merry-go-round. She wasn't entirely sure how she felt about him but she was sure that she had missed him and that she wanted to be with him. However, she didn't want to need him. She had needed Mark for many, many years. Far too many. Now she didn't want to have to need anyone again.

She knew she had baggage, otherwise known as Mark, and to a certain extent Luke – the latter she couldn't do anything about nor wanted to. She could make this work though. She could keep her relationship with Tex separate and avoid confrontations like that again.

All she needed now was to know how Tex felt. Did he want her? He had problems of his own. He had never said outright, but she guessed his wife's memory was never too far from his mind. She would just have to deal with that, as he would have to deal with Mark.

Collecting her thoughts, she spoke. 'I just wanted to know, well, to check, how things stand with us. I understand if you want to call things off. I mean, what with Mark and Luke, I know it's not easy.' She twiddled the rings on her fingers, still unable to draw her eyes from his.

'Is it too difficult for you?' he asked gently.

She shook her head slightly. 'No.'

He took a few steps closer to her. Slowly. 'Then if you can bear it, so can I.' A few more steps nearer. 'I'm sorry for walking out on you the other day. I'm afraid I'm not used to teenage boys who are protective of their mother. And their father. But I understand that now.'

'I'm not asking anything of you, Tex. I know you have never…' She paused, this was harder than she imagined, but it needed saying. 'I know you have never got over the death of your wife. I'm not expecting commitment or anything like that. All I want is honesty.'

He took the last few steps, closing the gap between them. Taking her hand in his, he kissed her palm, never looking away from her face. 'That I can give you.' He could just as easily have kissed her very soul, the sensation went to places inside her she never knew even existed, the soft resonance of his voice caressing her when he said, 'And I can honestly say that I want you.'

She thought she heard him say 'forever' at the end, but she wasn't sure and didn't have time to consider it further, as she was engulfed in his arms, his mouth urgently seeking hers. She had her answer and she welcomed him in a way she had never dreamt she was capable of. Intense. Raw. Must-have.

During the following weeks, while Mark was away in the States, Anna found herself happier than she had been for a long time.

Although Tex was extremely busy organising the refurbishment of the new restaurant, interviewing staff and deciding on menus etc, together with keeping an eye on the Guildford restaurant, he seemed more than happy to make time for her. He had phoned her every day, sometimes two or three times on the odd days he hadn't been able to see her. These phone calls made the days when she didn't see him bearable.

Her work was ticking over nicely. Jamie had a regular supply of clients for her and, encouraged by this, she had handed in her notice at the tea rooms. Brian had been disappointed to see her go but said he understood. It was sad saying goodbye to the staff there, but no doubt she would still see them in and around

Arundel. Anna still kept her translation work going, it was a handy extra which she was mindful would help to support herself when the house was sold.

Working for Jamie also had the benefit of seeing Tex on official business too. Today she had to attend a meeting with Tex and his restaurant manager. Apparently, Tex had told Jamie he needed her to help with the translation of the various CVs that had come in. As it turned out, Anna hadn't actually been needed much, and after the manager had gone, Tex admitted to her that he had just used it as an excuse to see her.

'I'm not sure whether to be flattered or not.' Anna laughed. 'You're paying Jamie for my services. It's like he's my pimp!'

'Well then, I had better get my money's worth.' A mischievous glint flickered in Tex's eyes as, nose to nose, he walked her backwards against the wall of his office, his hands now against the wall, either side of her head, barring her escape. Not that she had any intention of escaping. When he paused from kissing her, he nuzzled her neck, his hands cupping her face.

'Come home with me,' he whispered.

'But I need to get back to work,' she replied, but was making no attempt to move.

'I don't mean now. I don't mean Arundel,' he said evenly. 'I mean Texas. Brenham. Moonshadow Meadows to be precise.'

She gulped. 'That's a long way.'

'A little under five thousand miles.' He kissed her again. 'I would love to take you there. Meet everyone. See the ranch.'

Meet his family? Was that a good idea? She'd think about that later. 'When?'

'Soon. Before the restaurant opens. I could do with a break.' He paused, waiting for her to respond.

'I'd need time to clear it with Jamie.'

'Jamie will be cool. I'll tell him it's for work.'

188

'Paying for me again.' Although she laughed, Anna wasn't entirely comfortable with the concept. 'I'll speak to Jamie and arrange some time off. I'd prefer it that way.'

Tex was grinning like a schoolboy. He looked so gorgeous, Anna felt a small frisson zip through her.

'Okay, whatever way you prefer,' he said.

'Then I'll have to see if Luke can go to a friend's, or to Nathan's.'

'You can't leave him on his own?' More kisses.

'I don't know. I have visions of wild house parties. Mrs Meekham. Drunk teenagers throwing up and having sex everywhere. Gatecrashers. Police.' Anna winced at the possibilities.

'Mrs Meekham getting drunk and having wild sex?' Tex chuckled.

Anna laughed too. 'Oh, that's not a nice thought. Although it could put off potential purchasers.'

The words were out before she'd had time to check herself. It was a taboo subject that she had made clear to Tex she didn't want to discuss, and to his credit he had honoured her wishes. She knew it would cause friction.

Chapter Twenty Three

'You're still going ahead and letting him sell the house then?' asked Tex, his face now serious.

'Yes but...'

Tex cut her off. 'I know, you really don't wanna talk about it.' He took a step back from her, no longer in contact.

'So let's not then,' she said firmly.

'Why have you never divorced him?' He took her hand so she couldn't fiddle with her rings.

'Never got round to it. I didn't want to become a statistic, to become an official failure. I didn't want Luke to think it was final.' A well-rehearsed and often-spouted answer. Anna took a deep breath as she added, 'And I suppose, initially, I didn't want it to be either.'

'And now?'

'It's different now.' It was almost a mumble. She wanted to say it was different because of Tex but she couldn't seem to form the words.

'Do you still love him?'

'No. Not at all. Not love,' Anna said quickly. 'Of course I did love him once but not now. We have a bond, that being Luke, but nothing more.'

'Does Mark want a divorce?'

Anna couldn't meet his gaze. She shrugged, unable to lie but unwilling to tell the truth.

'Have you asked him? Anna, have you asked Mark for a divorce? What does he think about it?'

'Tex, please.'

'Well, *have* you asked him?'

Anna could hear the frustration in Tex's voice. Looking at the floor, she nodded.

'And what did he say? He doesn't want one, does he?' Tex paused.

Anna shook her head. She looked up as he exhaled deeply and stomped across the room to the window. 'He wants to get back together, doesn't he? That's why he's back. He still loves you. Jeez! I knew things would get complicated.' He dragged his hand over his face.

'Huh! You knew about Mark from the start, I never tried to hide him from you. And don't start making out as if I've chased you and forced you into some sort of relationship with me. If I remember rightly, it was me who said not to mix business with pleasure. I was the one who told *you* it would be complicated.'

'You have grounds to divorce him. You've been separated for over a year. What's stopping you?' Tex turned round to face her. 'There is nothing stopping you, only you.'

'You wouldn't understand.' Anna could feel tears building up in her eyes. Of course if it was only divorce, she could deal with it, but it wasn't just that. She couldn't bring herself to tell Tex about the photos. The thought of them plastered all over the Internet and turning up on doormats up and down the country was enough to hold her tongue.

'I might understand.' Tex's voice was softer now. He came over to her. 'Please don't cry Anna. I need to know. Whatever it is. Trust me. Tell me.'

'Just be a bit more patient, Tex.' Anna wiped an escaped tear away from her face. 'I'm not very good at this relationship business, it's been so long.'

'I'm trying to be patient. I am trying very hard.' He sighed heavily as he dropped a kiss on her head.

The Pilates class always finished half an hour before Emily's time at the crèche was over, so Anna and Zoe went for a coffee and a chat in the club lounge, as had become their habit.

'You know he had to go out one evening with a client?' said Zoe as she sat herself down on the chair next to Anna.

Anna could have kicked herself for not even thinking that she might have to have this conversation with Zoe. Was this a test? Did Zoe know that Nathan had taken Christine to the same charity event that she had been to with Tex? Nathan did say that he had told Zoe. Oh what to say! Anna didn't want to drop Nathan in it, but at the same time she didn't want to lie to Zoe. Anna had hesitated too long to reply.

'It's all right, I know all about it. Nathan did tell me.'

'Well, I assumed he would,' said Anna quickly. 'Anyway, that was the other week.'

'I know. I wasn't going to say anything but I heard him on the phone last night, talking all quiet and in that way a bloke does when he is so obviously speaking to a female.'

'Did you ask him who it was?'

'Said it was just a client rearranging an appointment.' Zoe dropped a sugar lump into her coffee.

'Well, there you are then.'

'Hmm. Maybe.' Zoe looked up at Anna. 'I must admit, I thought you might have said something about him being at the charity do with someone else.'

'There was nothing to say,' replied Anna, feeling more and more uncomfortable.

'Do you think he slept with her?' Zoe could have been asking what time the swimming pool opened or if rain was forecast that day. 'Well do you?' Zoe's expression cool and detached.

Anna took a moment or two before answering. 'Do you?' Throw the ball back in her court.

'I've no idea, that's why I was asking you.' Zoe turned her attention back to her coffee cup and plopped another sugar lump into the dark brown liquid. 'I thought I'd get an honest answer from you. No point asking Nathan, he's bound to say no. Of all people, you know what it's like to be cheated on, more than once, so I thought you would be hardly likely to defend him.'

Anna winced at the bluntness of Zoe's comment. 'As far as I know, and believe, Nathan hasn't cheated on you.'

'I know he's your brother, but you would tell me wouldn't you, if he was having an affair?'

'I honestly don't think he'd do that,' said Anna reassuringly. 'Nathan thinks the world of you.'

'Really? Maybe he used to.'

'When you've got a business to run and a family and home to look after, sometimes you forget to make time for each other. Maybe you two should try doing things together, just the two of you, without the children. I'll always babysit for you.' Anna sipped her tea.

'Is she pretty?'

'Who?'

'His client. The one he took to the charity ball.'

'Don't wind yourself up about her. Anyway, he didn't take her, she took him because she didn't have anyone to go with.' As Anna spoke, the scene where Christine had confronted her in the toilets replayed in her mind. Was Christine serious? Wasn't it a tad drastic?

'Mmm. He didn't have to accept though,' grumbled Zoe, stirring her coffee swiftly, the spoon clinking against the china.

'True. But I think he's trying to build up his client base and didn't want to...'

Zoe cut her off. 'You sound just like him! Did he give you a copy of his script?'

'Sorry.'

'Stop being such an apologist. You ought to work for the UN. You're so diplomatic and passive at times, it's infuriating.'

Chapter Twenty Four

The flight had taken nearly ten hours and the drive just over another three. Tex's older brother, Al, had driven to Fort Worth airport to meet them and although he had arrived in a pick-up truck, it oozed luxury and comfort with its wide leather bench seat and the much needed air con. Tex had warned her about the heat but, even so, Anna hadn't expected it quite so hot. This, together with the tiring journey, soon had her dozing off, head resting on Tex's shoulder.

'Hey, sleepyhead. We're nearly there.'

Tex's voice woke Anna from her sleep, she felt him kiss the top of her head. Nestled in the crook of his shoulder, she wanted to stay there forever. She couldn't help feeling nervous about meeting his family and wondering if they would be comparing her with Estelle.

As Al pulled off the main road and onto a smaller track, it seemed to Anna that it went on and on, a continuous straight line disappearing into the horizon. The fields on either side were wide open, clusters and rows of trees in the distance, which Anna assumed broke up the land into sections. It seemed as if she had woken up in the middle of nowhere, surrounded on all sides by field after field. Pastures, Tex called them. The truck slowed down at a lone mailbox by the edge of the road. Anna read the wooden sign that formed an archway above a five-bar gate announcing they were now at Moonshadow Meadows.

Al pulled up and Tex jumped out of the truck to open the gate, a procedure they seemed totally comfortable with as neither had to exchange a word. Anna squinted down the drive. It was one heck of a drive, and like the track they had just come down, the end was nowhere in sight. It was another few minutes' ride before the ranch house came into view. A timber, shiplapped construction with a large veranda stretching across the front and several windows each side of the central doorway. The house appeared to be split over three floors, with several dormer windows in the roof.

'Oh Tex, it's beautiful.' Anna was mesmerised by the charm of it. The Stars and Stripes flag fluttered from a pole by the side of the house, together with the Texan state flag. Before she had time to take in any more, there was a flurry of activity as a swarm of people erupted from the front door, their excited shouts and shrieks ringing out.

Anna heard Tex mutter some undetermined expletive, then a 'Did you know about this?' He was speaking to his brother. Anna read the sideways grin, which was remarkably like Tex's, to say that he knew all right.

Tex was no sooner out of the cab when he was lost in the throng of well-wishers. There was much hugging and kissing from the females, and handshaking followed with manly back-slapping hugs from the men.

'Nico!'

Anna looked on, she assumed the older couple now embracing Tex were his parents. It seemed strange hearing them call him by his proper name. Some of the family that Anna guessed were around her own age were calling him Nick. She made a mental note not to call him Tex in front of his family.

Now Tex was extracting himself and coming back over to the truck. Anna took a deep breath as he opened the door to the cab.

A sudden cold fear rushed over her.

'You ready for this?' He raised his eyebrows, but she could tell he was delighted to be back amongst his family. He held out his hand to her. 'Come on. Hey, don't look so worried.'

'Don't go off.' She knew she sounded pathetic but she couldn't help it. 'Don't leave me.'

'Never.' He looked directly at her. 'I'm gonna keep you right by my side all the time. I'm not letting go of you.'

One thing Anna was fast learning about Tex was that he said what he meant. For the next two hours he barely let go of her, constantly reassuring her with a squeeze of the hand, a calming touch to her back or an encouraging smile.

Tex's family were lovely, so welcoming, and the hum of conversation, howls of laughter, and shrieks from children gave such an informal ambiance that Anna could feel herself relaxing with every passing minute. Everyone was very chatty, involving her in the conversations in such a way that she didn't feel like a newcomer.

As they all sat down for dinner at the back of the house around several large, long, wooden picnic tables, Tex made sure he was right by her side. She soaked up the party-like atmosphere, everyone clearly delighted to have Tex home. She learned he hadn't been back for over two years, and although he apparently spoke regularly to them all from the UK, it was obviously no substitute for being there in person.

'Anyone want some chips?' called out Tex as various bowls of food were passed back and forth and up and down the table.

'Chips!' exclaimed one of Tex's brothers, who Anna thought was called Mikey. 'Since when did anyone call fries, chips? Hell, Bro, you sure have been away too long.' The others seated around the table laughed along with Mikey.

'He'll be telling us he's on holiday next,' joined in one of the others.

'Or that he takes the lift,' someone else called out.

'What about soccer? I bet he calls it football now!'

'Hey, you redneck, what would you know?' joked back Tex. 'You've never been out of the county, let alone the country.'

'Tell us, Anna,' said Mikey. 'Has Nick here gone and gotten all English?'

'Oh no, definitely not,' replied Anna smiling. 'I can assure you he still says sidewalk, trash and cell phone.'

And so the banter went on, Tex laughing and joking along with his family. It was lovely to see him so evidently adored – a clearly mutual feeling.

By early evening, exhausted from the travelling and jetlagged, Tex made their excuses to leave.

'Sorry, folks, but I think we're gonna call it a night.'

'You lightweight,' said Mikey, throwing a cushion at his brother.

'Now you leave them be,' Tex's mother reprimanded her youngest son.

'You tell him, Mama,' said Tex, tossing the cushion back at Mikey before going over and giving his mother a kiss on the cheek. 'Night. See y'all in the morning.'

'Night honey.' Then, much to Tex's delight, his mom went over to Anna and gave her a kiss and a hug. 'You pay them boys no mind. You must be exhausted. Get some rest now. Night honey.'

As they stepped out onto the porch, Tex pulled Anna towards him, putting his arms around her. 'She likes you.'

'Who?'

'Mama.'

'She said?'

'No, but I can tell. In fact, they all like you.'

'Well, that's good, because I like them all too. You have a lovely family.' She stood on tiptoe and gave Tex a quick kiss. 'Anyway, what are we doing out here? I thought we were going to bed.'

'We are. Come on.' He led her towards Al's pick-up truck and opened the passenger door for her. 'We're staying at my place.'

'Your place?'

'Creek Cottage. Just over the back of First Meadow, about half a mile away.' He shut the door and nipped round the front of the truck, sliding into the driver's seat. 'We've all got our own place on the ranch. Creek Cottage is mine.'

A few minutes later, Tex was pulling up outside the small wooden cabin. He breathed deeply as he took in the traditional settler type construction. It felt good being home.

'I feel like I've stepped back in time,' marvelled Anna, breaking his thoughts.

'Well, there's no electricity, running water or inside bathroom,' he said as he helped her down from the cab.

'Seriously?'

'Seriously.' He paused, amused at the look of surprise on her face. 'I am only joking.'

Inside, the cottage was simply furnished. A room to the right was the living area and a room to the left was the kitchen and dining room. All the furniture was traditional, rustic. The stairs were at the back of the kitchen and led up to a large double room, a small single and a bathroom.

'This is really lovely,' said Anna as she looked round the bedroom.

'I'm glad you like it.' Tex smiled as he put his arms round her and kissed her. A thought of Estelle flicked through his head. He had never brought another woman here in the five years since Estelle had died. Was it wrong to bring Anna? He raked around in his heart for some sort of emotion. Guilt. Regret. Sadness. But all were absent. It didn't feel wrong. In fact, it felt right. Very right.

'So what have we got planned for today?' asked Anna, coming up behind Tex and wrapping her arms around him while he cooked their breakfast.

Tex's mom had left what he termed as a Red Cross parcel outside the front door, packed with good old home-style provisions. Bacon, eggs, beans, bread, milk and coffee. She had even managed to produce some English Breakfast tea from somewhere.

'Thought I'd show you the ranch. I meant to ask, can you ride?' He gave the beans a stir and shook the bacon in the pan, sending delicious smells into the mid-morning air.

'A bike. Well I haven't ridden one since I was about ten.'

Tex laughed out loud. 'Not a bicycle. A horse.' He turned round to face her. The look of total horror on her face actually made him feel quite sorry for her. 'I take it that's a no. Okay, not to worry, we can take the quad. You just need to sit on the back and hold on tight.'

While Anna went upstairs to get dressed, Tex prepared a packed lunch for them for later, again courtesy of the Red Cross parcel. He was really looking forward to taking her out today, to showing her the Longhorn cattle, the bison, the lakes where he had fished as a child, the places for shooting, the stables and all the things he enjoyed about ranch life.

Anna came back down suitably dressed in jeans and a white shirt. She was looking at him with amusement dancing in her eyes.

'So you really are a cowboy,' Anna said.

'What?'

'The hat. You really must be a cowboy if you're wearing a Stetson.' She walked towards him. 'Come here, cowboy.' She put her arms around his neck and kissed him. Darn it, he could take her right back to bed there and then. She must have read his mind. 'Don't go getting any ideas. Come on, show me your ranch.'

He caught her hand. 'Don't think you're getting away that easy.

Gotta protect your lily white skin from the sun.' From behind his back he produced another Stetson and dropped it onto her head. 'Let's go, cowgirl.' He gave her behind a playful smack.

As Anna climbed on the back of the quad and shuffled forward, Tex was rather pleased that she couldn't horse ride after all. Having her sitting so tight behind him, her arms wrapped firmly around his waist, he could feel every curve of her body against his back and enjoy the sensation of her thighs against his. What more could he ask for?

It had been a glorious day riding around the ranch. Anna couldn't get over how vast it was, and how Tex seemed to be able to find his way around, despite it being over two years since he was last here.

That evening, dining up at Moonshadow Ranch House with Tex's parents, she felt very much at home, and after sitting out on the porch, the relaxed atmosphere and conversation continued.

'You know Buckler's ranch has started farming olives,' said his father.

'Olives? I know there's more of it going on these days round here. How they doing?' Tex asked.

'Okay, by all accounts. You ought to take a drive up there this week and have a look. Quite something to see row after row of olive trees instead of cattle.'

'That's sounds like a good plan for tomorrow,' said Tex.

When they eventually made it back to Creek Cottage, Anna felt happy. Extremely happy. It was bliss just being in Tex's company all the time. She had hardly thought of Luke, who was splitting his time between Nathan and his friend Jacob's house. Anna dismissed thoughts of England, she didn't want to start worrying, there was nothing she could do anyway. No, the two worlds of lover and family were securely compartmentalised. No overlap. She was here with Tex and that was all she wanted to think about.

The following day Tex took Anna out to Buckler's ranch, which the sign at the gate now advised was called Olive Grove Ranch. Not exactly inspiring but hey, it was what it said.

Browsing in the ranch shop, Tex seemed to be taking a keen interest in the local produce. He picked up a couple of jars of olives.

'Green or black?' he asked, weighing up a jar in each hand.

'Eww, neither,' said Anna, wrinkling up her face. 'I don't like olives.'

'You can learn to like something, you know. Before you know it, you love something you once didn't.' Anna gave him a sideways look but Tex carried on. 'I'll challenge you not to fall in love,' he paused before adding, 'with olives.'

'Okay. How do you propose I do that then? Fall in love with olives that is.'

'Every day you must just eat a little bit of olive. Not a whole one, just a small bite. Do that every day for a month and I'll guarantee that you will love them. That is what they mean by an acquired taste. You have to slowly familiarise yourself with the taste, get used to it gradually, without rushing. A little each day and you will learn to love them.'

'I accept your challenge,' replied Anna cautiously. 'I can't make any promises though.'

The week was slipping by too quickly. Anna thoroughly enjoyed their days out sightseeing, and the days spent relaxing at Creek Cottage and exploring the ranch. Tex had attempted to teach her how to shoot, but she didn't even want to hold the gun, so he had settled on giving her a horse riding lesson, which she much preferred.

She was very impressed to watch him haul himself up onto a horse one afternoon, sitting in the saddle looking totally at ease. The thrill that shot through her when he had winked and tipped his Stetson at her was bad enough, but coupled with that seductive smile of his, she truly thought her legs would give way.

'Are you sure you'll be okay without me for a few hours? I don't mind if you would sooner not be left on your own.' He had checked with her earlier and double-checked several more times throughout the morning.

'Of course I don't mind,' she told him again. 'And, anyway, who am I to stop you having some time with your brothers. You go and enjoy yourself. I'll be fine.' To see him so happy and relaxed was lovely.

He gave the reins a tug to the left and immediately the horse responded. As it swung round, Anna saw Tex give a small but authoritative dig with his heels into the horse's flank, a flick of the reins before galloping off with his brothers to help with the herding. She watched him disappear, swallowed up in cloud of dust, entranced at the way he took command so effortlessly and confidently.

It was their last full day before they had to go back to the UK. Tex couldn't help feeling a bit downhearted at the fact. He had loved being home, spending time with his brothers and their families. They had all made Anna feel so welcome and she seemed at ease in their company too. He was grateful that his siblings' wives and husbands were very laid back and easy to get on with. They had all made a special effort to include Anna in everything, yet at the same time managed to make her presence seem perfectly normal. He was particularly pleased to see Gabriella give Anna a big hug, the incident of going missing, forgiven and forgotten. He made a mental note to thank Gabriella in private when he got the chance.

There was a particular place on the ranch – a small cluster of trees by the edge of the creek up at the top pasture – that Tex hadn't yet shown Anna. Creek Corner – his thinking spot. He hadn't been sure until this morning that he would take her there.

After Estelle's funeral, he had come home to mourn. At the time he hadn't thought of it like that, but he had retreated into the heart of his family. It had been several weeks before he was able to face the world again, and for the most part of those long weeks he had spent them up at Creek Corner.

Taking Anna there now was a gamble, but he had to know whether she could weave her magic and cleanse the place of the blackness that he associated with it. Anna was thankfully totally oblivious to the effect she was having on the usual feelings of guilt and regret that plagued Tex whenever he was involved with a woman. It was something up until now he hadn't wanted to share with Anna. With anyone.

As they reached Creek Corner in the late afternoon warmth, Tex felt his stomach churn over. Climbing off the quad and taking the rucksack from Anna, he paused for a moment to take a deep breath. This was it. This was the ultimate test.

'You okay, Tex?' Her voice was gentle, concerned. She was watching him closely, doing that thing where she really studied him, as if she could read the thoughts behind his eyes.

'Yeah, sure I am. Come on.' He took her hand and strode towards the cluster of trees and then along a small path that led to a clearing on the edge of creek. He spread the blanket out, a silence settling between them. He sat down, his knees drawn up, his arms resting on top. Anna sat down beside him and slipped her arm through his. Tenderly, she kissed his shoulder and then rested her head on his arm.

'Is it difficult coming here?' she asked softly.

She deserved an honest answer. 'It was. But you know what? Now we're here, it feels okay.' He looked down at her and she met his eyes with a steady gaze. 'How did you know?'

She shrugged. 'Don't know. I could just tell. As we got nearer and nearer I could sense something in you. A change.'

'I never came here with Estelle.' He swallowed hard. 'I came here after… after she died. It was like a retreat. I could come here and let all my emotions out.'

'To grieve.' It wasn't a question more an understanding. 'We don't have to stay if it's too painful.'

Should he tell her that the pain had stopped? The deep wound left by grief now healed. He didn't want to frighten her but at the same time, he wanted her to know. He gently stroked her cheek before he spoke. 'There's no pain, not today, not anymore.'

Tex was woken the following morning by Anna kissing him softly, her leg over his, her hand wandering up and down his body, the tips of her fingers like tiny shock waves as she touched him.

'Make love to me,' she whispered.

He didn't need asking twice. He loved loving her. As he pulled her on top of him, admiring her beautiful body with his eyes and his hands, he realised how true those words were. He really did love her. She leaned forward, covering his face in kisses, nuzzling his ear, giving him a moment to analyse this notion. He dug deep into his heart but there was no flicker of guilt. No feeling of betrayal to Estelle. Of course, he would always love Estelle, but that was a lifetime ago, a different lifetime. Not the lifetime he was living now.

Anna paused, looking at him with her mossy green eyes. For a moment he thought she was going to tell him she loved him, but she simply smiled and began working her kisses back to his mouth, before sitting up, her back arching, her eyes closed. Tex ran his hands up her thighs, over her hips and around to the small of her back, then pulled her back down on top of him.

Afterwards, he pulled her to him to lie contently in his arms, enjoying the moment of blissful, mutual satisfaction, of peace and tranquillity, making the most of every second, knowing they'd be back to reality all too soon.

That reality hit hard and fast like an intercity express train suffering brake failure.

Chapter Twenty Five

'Where do you want me to put this?' Tex called as he stepped inside 2 Coach House Cottages, Anna's holdall in his hand.

'I'll take that.'

Tex looked up in surprise at the unexpected voice. He was startled to see Mark standing in front of him but tried not to let his surprise or annoyance show. He looked across at Anna, the colour completely gone from her face, concern in her eyes as she twiddled the rings on her finger nervously.

'You okay?' he asked, holding her gaze. She nodded.

'Of course she's okay,' said Mark. 'Aren't you, Anna?'

'Stop it, Mark. I'm fine, Tex. Just a little surprised to see Mark here, that's all.'

Tex felt a vice-like grip inside his gut. 'Do you want me to stay?'

'I'll be fine, honestly. Look, you'd better go. I'll phone you later.' She moved towards the front door but Tex stood his ground.

'I don't like leaving you.'

'Please, Tex, I'll be fine. I promise.' Anna gave a weak unconvincing smile.

'Call me if you need me.' He gave Mark a long hard stare.

Mark, looking totally unfazed and obviously lapping up Anna's dismissal of him, smirked.

'Don't worry. My wife will be fine with me,' called Mark, coming to the doorway as Tex got in his car. 'Have a nice day, now.'

Anna slammed the front door closed as Tex drove off.

'What are you doing here?' She turned on Mark, who had now wandered back into the living room and, picking up his glass from the table, took a slug of the deep brown liquid.

He smiled at her as he topped up his glass from the bottle of Jack Daniels standing on the mantelpiece. Anna gulped. She knew this was coming but she had hoped it would take a lot longer than this.

'I did try to phone you,' carried on Mark, 'but couldn't get hold of you, so I rang Luke instead. Just as well, really.' He took another large swig of whisky.

Anna eyed the bottle. It was nearly half-empty. She could feel her heart quicken. Mark and whisky had always been a bad mix.

'What do you mean by that?' She tried to sound casual, keeping her tone light.

'What do I mean? Huh!' Mark scoffed. He picked up the copy of *Surrey Life* that was folded open at the charity event page, where amongst the many photos of guests, slap bang in the middle was a picture of Anna stood with Tex, Duncan Hughes and his wife. 'This!'

Anna shrugged. 'I've been out. There's no law against it.'

'But with *him*,' Mark's lip curled as he prodded the picture of Anna and Tex, before tossing the magazine disdainfully onto the sofa. 'You told me there was nothing going on between you two.'

'There wasn't.'

'Liar!' Mark shouted, slamming the glass onto the mantelpiece with such force that the tumbler shattered, broken glass dropping into the hearth. As had so often been the case in the past when Mark drank whisky, the venom and aggression came from nowhere. No build up, no gradual mounting of anger, just a sudden outburst.

Anna recoiled. This wasn't good. But she'd be damned if she was going to let him bully her. She had to stand her ground.

'At the time there wasn't.' Anna could hear her voice wobbling slightly. She hated the fact that he could still unnerve her. She took a deep breath. 'Anyway, it's not really any of your business.'

'Course it bloody is!' The rage was bubbling. 'You're shagging some bloke and not only that, but in my house too. Yeah, don't look so surprised. Luke told me that Yankee boy was here one morning.'

'Mark, you're being unreasonable. I can see someone else if I like.'

'Not if you're leaving Luke alone so you can have a dirty week away.' Mark took several steps towards her as he spoke.

'Luke is sixteen. He's old enough to be left. Nathan was keeping an eye on him.' Anna took a step back to keep the physical space between them.

'Might have known he'd be involved in your scheming. Helping you have your sordid little affair.' Mark picked up the bottle of Jack Daniels and took a swig directly from the bottle. He began circling Anna with slow, purposeful steps. Eyes fixed on her the whole time.

Anna could feel her own anger rising. There was nothing sordid about her and Tex. How dare he come back and confront her as if she was having an affair?

'If I want a week away, I can. Anyway, where is Luke?'

'Gone to his mate's. I expect you're really quite disappointed that I'm here.'

Anna could smell the alcohol on Mark's breath as he stopped in front of her, their faces only inches apart. She turned her head away from his breath.

'No comment.'

'Means you can't have Yankee lover boy here.' Another large swig from the bottle. 'Don't know what you see in him anyway, old git.'

'Get lost, Mark.'

'Go on, tell me. What's so great about him?'

209

'Everything,' snapped Anna, looking back defiantly at Mark. 'Everything is great about him. No one could match up to him.'

Mark stared at her, guzzled from the bottle, and slightly staggering, moved to hold on to the bookcase, knocking a couple of books off the shelf in the process. 'Shit, Anna. You really mean it, don't you?' He was trying to look at her but his eyes were jittering around as he tried to keep focus. 'So, me and you getting back together isn't going to happen? You meant that too?'

Anna nodded. 'Absolutely.'

'You seem to be forgetting one tiny detail,' Mark slurred, trying to stand upright but still needing to hold on to the shelf. 'I'm not agreeing to a divorce, and if you divorce me or stand in the way of the house sale, then I will have to go ahead with my threat and publish those photos.' He nodded towards his open briefcase on the coffee table.

Anna followed his gaze. She could see his passport along with some official looking papers, maybe from the bank. On top was an envelope with his company logo on it, just like the one he had pulled the photos from before. Her stomach lurched at the thought of those photos. She looked back at Mark. He was now slouching against the bookshelf. As he lifted the bottle to his mouth again, she seized her chance.

Like a cat, she sprang towards the table and snatched at the envelope. Slowed by alcohol, Mark's reactions weren't as quick. Nevertheless, he lunged towards her as she swerved from his grasp, the envelope firmly in her hand. His fingers caught her blouse and as he stumbled forwards, crashing into the table, the lightweight fabric ripped.

Unfortunately, Anna forgot about the books that Mark had knocked off the shelf and she stepped awkwardly onto a hardback, twisting her ankle over, causing her to crash to the floor. The side of her face took a glancing blow against the doorframe of the kitchen as she fell. She cried out in pain, stunned and shocked, daring not to move for several seconds.

'Anna! Shit. Are you okay?' Mark pushed himself away from the table and crawled over to her. 'Sorry, Anna, I didn't mean to make you fall.'

'Don't touch me!' Anna shouted as she sat up, half over the threshold, the quarry tiles of the kitchen floor cold against her hands. Her cheek felt as if it were on fire. Tentatively, she touched the wet and warm sensation on her skin. Her fingers were bloodied as she took them away. Noticing her blouse was torn open revealing her bra, she quickly pulled the material round her with her other hand. It was then she realised she didn't have the envelope. Her eyes frantically scoured the floor around her.

By the worst stroke of luck, Mark's knee had it firmly pinned to the floor. He reached down and slipped it out from its resting place. He didn't try to hide the triumphant look on his face.

'That was a bit careless of me, leaving it out on view.'

Before she could protest, Mark was putting it back in his brief-case, snapping the combination locks shut. He turned back to look at her.

'Leave me alone!' Anna shied away, the feeling of desolation swamping her. Was it possible to drown in despair? She shuffled further back into the kitchen until she felt the door of the sink cupboard against her back and she could go no further. She wiped the never-ending tears that seeped from her eyes, wincing as she brushed the graze on her cheek.

Across the doorway, the unspoken barrier of the threshold, Mark sat on his haunches, hands sliding down his face and rubbing his chin, as if he were going over what had just happened. A truly sobering moment. The pair of them must look a sorry sight, thought Anna.

They both heard the key in the front door at the same time,

exchanging alarmed looks, knowing who it was.

'Luke,' gasped Anna, suddenly finding strength in her legs as, in unison, her and Mark scrambled up. Mark, trying to look casual, grabbed at a magazine and sat himself in an armchair. Anna sank back into the kitchen, out of immediate eyesight.

'Hi,' called Luke as he came in. 'Where's Mum? Is she here?'

'All right, son?'

'Where's Mum? Mum!' Anna heard his concerned voice nearing the kitchen. 'Mum! What are all those books doing on the floor?'

She turned away from the door and busied herself by looking in the wall cupboard. For what, she had no idea; she just didn't want Luke to see her face.

'Mum? You all right? Tex is here.' Luke was now standing in the doorway.

Anna froze. Tex! Oh no! She couldn't face him either.

'He's outside. Says he wants to see you.'

'Tell him I'm asleep. Having a lie-down,' said Anna, still searching in the cupboard.

'Okay,' said Luke, suspicion obvious in his voice.

Anna strained to hear what was being said in the doorway but the voices were too low, just a murmur. Then, suddenly and quite clearly, she heard Tex's voice calling her name, becoming louder and more insistent as he came further into the house.

'She's in the kitchen,' Luke was saying.

She heard Tex's footsteps stride across the living room and stop on the quarry tiles.

'Anna?' His voice quieter. Concerned.

Oh, his lovely calming voice. How she wanted him to take her in his arms, hold her, stroke her hair, take her into his world where she was happy and could leave all this mess of a life behind her.

He was standing at her side now, turning her around to face him, tilting her head up towards him, their eyes meeting. The tears

212

filling her eyes again. The pain on his face as he registered the graze on hers. She was still holding her blouse together with one hand. Silently, Tex removed her hand, allowing the ripped fabric to fall open. He touched the material as if he needed to physically confirm what his eyes saw, his mind understanding.

'Oh, baby,' he uttered, his voice full of sadness, his eyes full of hurt and compassion for her. Tex pulled Anna towards him, kissing her hair. 'I'm sorry. I should never have left you.' He held her there for a few moments more before releasing her.

It was then Anna saw a look on his face she had never seen before. A steely, hardened look, his eyes narrowing, his jaw fixed, mouth unsmiling, his hands clenching and unclenching in fists. He turned and strode out of the kitchen.

'Tex! No!' Anna ran after him, just in time to see the look of alarm across Mark's face before Tex's fist connected with it, sending Mark stumbling backwards, clutching his bloodied nose.

'Tex! Stop!' cried Anna. Holding her blouse together, she rushed in front of him, pushing against his chest with her free hand.

Tex looked past her, his stony eyes never leaving Mark's face. 'You leave her alone.' His voice was ice cold. 'Don't lay another finger on her.'

'You fucking idiot,' stammered Mark, standing up. 'I think you've broken my fucking nose.'

'Shame it wasn't your neck.' Tex made a sudden movement forward and Mark shrank back. Any further back and he would be in the fire itself.

'Tex, what are you doing?' cried Anna almost hysterical. 'It's not what you think. I fell. I caught my face on the door.' She was aware of Luke running round the sofa and helping his dad to his feet as Tex stood his ground.

'Stop, Anna. You don't have to cover for him just because Luke's here.'

'What? I'm not. You're not helping.' Still standing in front of him, Anna pushed against his chest, jostling him backwards. 'Just get out. Go!' What was he thinking of attacking Mark like that? He had just jumped to conclusions, he hadn't waited for her to explain, and now Luke had witnessed it all.

'Come with me,' said Tex, taking her hand. 'Where's your bag? I'm not leaving you this time. I had a bad feeling, that's why I came back. Come with me.'

'No. Just go. I need to sort things out here.' She ignored the incredulous look on Tex's face and the hurt in his eyes.

'Anna. You can't stay here. Please come with me.' Tex's voice was more desperate.

'I don't think she wants to, actually,' chipped in Mark, trying to regain his lost pride.

'Shut up,' hissed Tex.

'Both of you shut up!' shouted Anna. She covered her face with her hand for a moment, trying to calm down. When she took her hand away, three pairs of eyes were looking at her.

'Anna?' said Tex gently.

She shook her head, wrapping her arms around herself. 'Please, Tex, just go.'

Chapter Twenty Six

Mark had stopped apologising after the first day. It was remarkable how he could just revert to his usual confident self, no tiptoeing around, no signs of remorse. He'd apologised. Okay, Anna hadn't exactly said she'd forgiven him, but the fact that she had stayed, rather than left with Tex, even she had to acknowledge sent the wrong message to Mark. He probably thought the whole incident was forgotten about by now. She didn't have the energy or inclination for another argument. She felt emotionally drained, with no strength to feel anger or outrage, sadness or despair. There was nothing.

Tex had phoned several times on Tuesday, but Anna hadn't picked up his calls. She wanted to be sure that Mark wasn't going to do anything with those dreadful photos, that he was going to agree to the divorce. She didn't want him getting stubborn at the last minute and cutting off his nose to spite his face. He may decide to let the business in the States go under and then she'd end up losing the house anyway as he would have to sell it to settle his debts. She was also spurred on by the unappealing thought of Mark coming back to the UK and living with them! So instead of calling Tex back, she had sent him a message:

Can you give me a bit of time to sort things out? I need some space. Sorry. X

Tex had to fight every urge in his body not to jump up and give Mark another thumping on the nose. Instead, he maintained his cool, calm and collected exterior, leaning back in his office chair as Mark swaggered in.

'So, Tex, this is where you hide yourself,' began a rather smug looking Mark. 'Nice place you've got here. Must have cost a bob or two, not to mention the money you've pumped into the refurb.'

Tex steepled his fingers and watched as Mark sat himself down in the chair on the opposite side of the desk without waiting to be invited.

'Let us not pretend we are having this discussion to exchange pleasantries about my business,' said Tex, meeting Mark's look. 'Just say what you have come to say.'

'All in good time, Tex, my man, all in good time.' The smug smile never left Mark's face. 'Now, I'm right in assuming you are particularly fond of my wife, goes without saying.' He paused but Tex remained silent, not wanting to give him the satisfaction of a response. Mark continued. 'And no doubt she has told you about the small financial predicament I find myself currently in. It's left me in quite a dilemma if I'm honest.'

Again Mark paused and again Tex said nothing. He really had no idea what the purpose of this visit was, although he was sure he was about to find out.

Mark drummed his fingers on the desk. 'All this is putting me under quite a bit of pressure, as you can imagine, and it's having a rather negative impact on Anna. Upsetting her, getting her down, that sort of thing. Well, it suddenly struck me today that you are in a perfect position to resolve her problems.'

Son of a bitch! Tex despised this man but if there was a way, any way, he could get Mark out of Anna's life, then he was prepared to do it.

'Cut to the chase,' said Tex curtly.

Mark leaned forward. 'Convince Anna to sell the house.'

'And why do you think I can do that, or indeed would?'

'She'll listen to you. And if she doesn't, well, I'll have to persuade her, but that would cause her a lot of embarrassment and humiliation. If you care about her, like I think you do, you would stop that happening.'

Struggling to keep his anger in check, Tex tried to appear unruffled. 'What exactly do you mean?'

The look in Mark's eyes changed in an instant, the amusement disappearing, making way for something far more sinister. 'I'll spell it out. From Anna, I want an agreement to sell the house. From you, I want an advance. Fifty thousand pounds. Cash. You'll get it back from the sale proceeds.'

'Fifty thousand pounds,' repeated Tex, somehow managing to keep the incredulity from his voice. 'I don't have that sort of money.'

'No, but you can get it, I'm sure.'

'And if I say no?'

Mark pulled out a white envelope from his jacket pocket and placed it on the desk, then with his index finger, slid it in Tex's direction. 'This will land on every door of every person in Anna's address book and be posted on Facebook, with every single one of her friends tagged so they get to see it.'

The tension in the room was razor-like, menace hanging in the air like a guillotine. Eventually, Tex reached for the envelope, which had what appeared to be a company logo in the corner and, already knowing he wasn't going to like what it contained, slipped his hand in and withdrew a single photograph.

A young woman in her early twenties, looking slightly the worse for wear with heavy, glassy eyes, lay completely naked on a bed, an empty glass of wine in her hand. The face was unmistakable, those green eyes, rosebud mouth and straight little nose. Her hair was blonde, but instead of its usual short crop it hung loose over her shoulder.

Tex felt his stomach contract as the implications of what Mark was saying sunk in. The anger stampeded through his body.

'Beautiful isn't she?' said Mark. 'I expect she still is.'

Yet again, Tex found himself fighting every urge in his being not to beat the crap out of this dirt-ball. He could feel his heart racing as his blood pumped fast through his veins. Somehow, he managed to keep his voice steady. 'Does Anna know you're here? With this?'

'Of course she doesn't. And there's no reason why she should. Let's just keep this between us. A gentleman's agreement.'

Tex locked eyes with Mark, the irony of the last sentence not lost. He had no idea if Mark was calling his bluff or not but he couldn't afford to find out. Anna would be utterly destroyed if he carried out his threat. However, if he was going to capitulate to Mark's outrageous demands, then he needed to make sure there were no loose ends.

'Twenty thousand pounds and a divorce.' Tex maintained eye contact.

'Fifty thousand pounds if you want a divorce.' Mark didn't blink.

'Fifty thousand pounds, a divorce, all the photos and any copies.'

'By the end of the week.'

'It will take me a couple of weeks to raise the funds. I have to arrange for a transfer from the States.'

'A week.'

'Quit jerking off at me. Two weeks.' Tex could get the money sooner, but he needed to buy some time for both himself and Anna. 'I can give you two thousand pounds cash today. Now.'

Mark took the bait. 'It's a deal. Oh, and you can keep the photo. You get the rest of them when I get the money.'

Tex nodded. Now all he had to do was work out what in hell's name he was going to do. He certainly didn't have fifty thousand pounds laying around. He sat deep in thought for a long time after Mark had left before he decided on his course of action.

He looked at the clock. Brenham was six hours behind, someone should be at the office now though. Checking the number in his contacts book, Tex picked up the landline and dialled the States.

'Hello. Moonshadow Meadows.'

Al worked the office most days and Tex was relieved that today was no exception. 'Hey there, Al.'

'Nick? Is that you, Bro?'

'Yep.'

'What's up? You must have only just gotten back to the UK.'

There was no point in any preamble. 'You still keep in touch with Spencer Hogan? He still working the same line of business?'

There was a moment's pause before Al spoke. 'Yeah, sure I speak to Spence from time to time. What's so bad that you need a private investigator?'

'I need him to do a bit of digging for me. Some British guy, lives in the States, California to be precise. Wanna know if Spence can find any dirt on him?'

'California? A bit out of Spence's remit.'

'Yeah, but I'm sure he's got contacts. I'll pay the going rate.' Tex leaned forward on his desk. 'Up front, if necessary.'

'Okay,' replied Al slowly. 'How deep do you want Spence to dig?'

Tex picked up the photo of Anna, folding the corner back and forth with his finger. 'To goddam hell, if he needs to.'

Anna phoned Jamie on Tuesday morning to say she wouldn't be available for work that week as she wasn't feeling too good.

'A week away with Tex and look what happens,' teased Jamie. 'I'll have to have a word with him, making my staff ill.'

Anna decided to use the week wisely and look for somewhere else to live. A flat that she could afford to rent without the need to depend on Mark. If nothing else came out of the whole fiasco which was her life, at least she'd be independent. She should have done this before.

'This is a good size room. Nice high ceilings,' said Zoe, as they wandered into the living room of an empty flat on the outskirts of Chichester.

Luke had called his uncle and aunty the day after the fight. He was upset and didn't understand what was going on, Zoe had explained to Anna when she turned up an hour after the phone call, the little disagreement they'd had the previous week forgotten about in her hour of need, and Anna was grateful.

Zoe inspected the fireplace before she spoke. 'Has Tex contacted you since all this happened?'

'He rang a couple of times on Tuesday but I couldn't face speaking to him. Since then nothing.' Anna sighed, remembering back to that night. 'I was pretty cross at the time so it's hardly surprising, I suppose. Tex just jumped to conclusions without letting me explain. Plus I didn't want him to hit Mark again, well, not in front of Luke anyway. I think I've lost him for good this time. Why would Tex want anything to do with me now? Not after all this. Luke nearly scared him off before. I should imagine Mark's antics have sealed it now.'

'So he's in the wrong for phoning you and he's also in the wrong for not phoning you,' said Zoe, looking out of the bay window onto the street. 'Poor sod, can't win.'

'I just can't believe how wrong it's all gone. I was trying to keep things separate but they seem to have collided with catastrophic consequences.' Anna joined Zoe at the window. 'If I could just pause everything for three or four weeks, that way the house sale will have gone through, the divorce started and Tex's restaurant opened, then start again. It would be perfect.' Anna gulped away the lump that came to her throat. Every time she thought of losing

Tex for good she felt physically sick and tearful. The desperation was so bleak, it was painful.

By Friday, she and Zoe had viewed several different flats and apartments, finally whittling it down to two possibilities. One contender was in the town centre, just a few minutes' walk from Anna's current house. A modern apartment, two bedrooms, a small kitchen, living room and bathroom. Not huge, but it would do for her and Luke. The other was the ground floor of a converted house. Again two bedrooms, but with the added bonus of a small garden and off-road parking. It was the cheaper of the two but it was further out from the town centre.

'I thought I'd let you have a look and see what you think,' said Anna, perched on the end of Luke's bed. He had stopped playing his guitar and was idly plucking at the strings.

'I don't want to move to a poxy flat.'

'Neither do I really, but we don't have any choice.' Anna put on her best cheerful face. 'Anyway, the flats are quite nice. We can have a look tomorrow.'

'But the house won't be sold properly for weeks yet.'

'I know, I'm just getting organised so there's no mad panic at the end.'

'What about Dad?' Luke had stopped plucking the strings, his arms hanging limply over the edge of the guitar.

'What about him?' Her best cheerful face slipping.

'Is he coming with us?'

'Oh, Luke, no. No, he's not.' Anna felt so sorry for her son. He was obviously still clinging to some hope that his parents might get back together.

'Are you still seeing Tex?'

'We're both a bit busy at the moment. I've got the flat to sort out and he's got the new restaurant opening.' No matter how she phrased it or tried to reason it, the pain was as acute as ever. She knew she was probably losing Tex for good, but she didn't see any other way at the moment.

'That's a no then. So you and Dad... could possibly... you know...' There was a small spark of hope in his eyes. Anna knew she had to quash it.

'No.' Her response was firm and unwavering. She got up to leave, signalling the end of the conversation and finality of a reunion between her and Mark.

'Mum!' Luke called after her as she reached the door. 'Dad didn't hit you the other night, did he?'

Anna looked at Luke, seeing the desperation in his face, and knowing he was trying to hide behind the casualness of his voice. He didn't want to believe his dad could do that.

'No, he didn't hit me. I fell and caught my face.'

'Tex hit Dad.'

'A knee-jerk reaction. I'm sorry you had to see that.'

Luke shrugged. 'Tex must really care about you to react like that.'

Anna couldn't answer, the lump in her throat took her by surprise. Nodding, she closed the door behind her.

Just what the hell else was going to go wrong? Tex ran his hand down the side of his Ford Ranger, following the line of the deep scratch. It stretched from the front wing all the way down to the rear light. One deep cut, right through the paint down to the metal. Definitely intentional and definitely malicious. He hadn't noticed it last night when he drove home from work, but this morning as he went down to the car park below his apartment, there it was, clear as anything. It must have happened some time during service last night while he was working in the restaurant. Someone sure as hell had it in for him.

'Hi, Anna, it's Jamie. You okay now?'

'Yes, fine thanks,' she replied, trying to sound upbeat. It had been two weeks now since she had returned from the States. Two weeks since her and Mark's big row. Two weeks without a word from Tex.

'I need you to collect some papers and deliver them. You up for that?'

'Yeah, sure,' Anna replied. She didn't really feel up for it at all but she needed the work. Since agreeing on the flat in the centre of Chichester last week, she was now trying to scrape together the deposit.

'Now before you say anything, just hear me out,' began Jamie. 'You need to pick up some paperwork from Tex's Arundel apartment and take it round to his fitters at the Tarrant Street restaurant.'

'I don't know...'

'No, listen. Tex isn't there, otherwise he could easily do it himself. He's in Guildford but his fitters are crying out for this plan and can't get on without it, so I need you to go like ten minutes ago.'

'Okay, but I don't have a key.' She couldn't really refuse, not if she wanted to keep her job.

'Apparently the neighbour at number fourteen has a spare. Now, the papers are in an envelope on the coffee table. Give the neighbour back the key when you leave, drop the papers off and Bob's your uncle, job done.'

'You make it sound very straightforward,' sighed Anna.

'That's because it is,' said Jamie, then in a softer tone, 'Look, Tex said things between you two are a bit tricky at the moment, but try not to let it affect your work, eh?'

'Sorry, you're right.' She knew he was, but it *was* difficult.

Anna punched in the familiar code to the car park barrier underneath Tex's apartment block. Parking her car, she saw that the space where his black Ford Ranger usually stood was empty. So he really wasn't here.

Miss Purdy, long-time occupier of apartment number fourteen and unofficial keyholder to a couple of the residents on the top floor, greeted Anna at the door.

'Hello, my dear,' she smiled warmly at Anna. 'He's not given you a key yet then? I expect it won't be long though.' She chuckled at her own joke. 'He's a nice young man, you could do a lot worse than him. There you go. I'll leave you to it. Just drop the key back when you're done.'

Anna cautiously opened the door to Tex's apartment. Stepping inside, she called out, just to make sure it was empty. There was a silence and a stillness that only empty properties can generate. A small lump came to her throat. Normally at this point Tex would be greeting her, wrapping his arms around her and kissing her. Oh for those lovely kisses.

She ventured into the living room, looking for the papers. Jamie had said they were on the table. No sign of them. Anna scoured the room and then the kitchen. No, definitely no envelope, no plans. Perhaps they were in the bedroom. She paused at the door, the memories of her and Tex spending loving hours together in bed came flooding back. Oh the pain in her heart as she thought of those beautiful times that would no longer be. Her hand shaking slightly, Anna pushed open the bedroom door.

The bed was immaculately made, as usual, the clock on the bedside table as it always was. Everything neat and tidy. No sign of any drawings in here. She'd have to ring Jamie.

Tex stood silently in the living room, watching her search her bag, presumably for her phone, fishing it out from the bottom as she always did. He had felt like an undercover surveillance cop earlier as, parked out on the street a safe distance away, he had watched her drive in and park up.

She stopped searching her bag, looked up and then jumped and shrieked before a small gasp of relief escaped as she realised it was him.

Chapter Twenty Seven

'Sorry, I didn't mean to scare you,' he spoke softly.

'I was getting some paperwork. Jamie asked me. He said you were in Guildford. I can't find the papers though. He said they were on the table. I was just looking to see if I could find them.' She was gabbling. Tex waited patiently, it might have been amusing under different circumstances.

'There are no papers.' He watched her face as she took in and processed the information. 'Jamie wouldn't have gone along with it if I had told him the truth.' He spoke gently and quietly so as not to make her feel threatened. He had tricked her into coming here and she was on the defensive. 'How are you'?'

'Okay. You?'

Tex nodded. 'Okay.' It was a lie; he hadn't been okay at all. He had been worried sick about her, but he had been patient and given her the space she'd asked for. How much space did she need? He couldn't wait any longer. He looked at her face, no sign of the graze now. She looked so small, so uncertain standing there. He wanted to sweep her up into his arms, take her away, but he knew he had to tread slowly. Carefully. 'Is Mark still here?'

Anna nodded, twiddling the rings on her finger rapidly.

'Has he been behaving himself?' Tex couldn't disguise the tension in his voice that the thought of Mark with Anna brought to him.

'He was drunk.'

'That's no excuse.'

'You shouldn't have hit him.'

'He deserved it.' Hell, what was wrong with her, defending the son of a bitch? Tex was fighting to keep calm, the anger rising inside of him as he remembered the mess he had found her in.

'Tex, please, I don't want to talk about it. It's over and done.' Anna looked hesitant and unsure of herself. Or was she unsure of him? She'd had two weeks with Mark. Had they made up? Was that why she'd been avoiding him?

'So when were you gonna ring me?' It came across harsher than he intended. 'I've been worried about you.'

'I was going to but with all that's been going on...' She looked down at the floor, staring at her feet. 'I just need a bit more time.'

'More time! Why do you need space at all? What is there to think about? We had a great week together, you come home, Mark is there, you fight, you end up with a grazed face and after all that, it's me you need space from. Tell me, Anna, just what the hell I am missing here?' The frustration spilled over as Tex angrily thrust his hands to his head, trying to keep in control. He checked himself as he saw Anna physically flinch at the tone in his voice.

'He didn't attack me. I told you before. I tripped over a book and caught my face.' She didn't look up as she spoke. Was that because she couldn't look him in the eye? Was she covering up for him?

'I'm meant to believe that, am I?'

Now she looked up at him. 'I'd better go,' she said quietly, walking across the living room.

'Don't go, not yet.' He stood in her way, unsure whether he should hold her. Instead, he rested his forehead on hers. He could feel the heat of her skin, smell her sweet scent, almost taste it. 'I've missed you,' he whispered, gently sliding his hands down the

227

length of her arms, feeling for her hands, holding them in his, rubbing the tops with his thumbs. Tex pulled away slightly. Her gaze lowered, a tear trickling down her face.

'We can work this out,' he whispered softly. Just being in contact with her stirred him. He wanted her so badly, in every way. Still she stood there, not speaking, more tears falling.

'Anna, we can make this work. I know we can. You must believe me. Trust me. Put your past, your marriage, *him*, behind you. It will be okay. I promise.' Tex kissed her on the mouth, a small gentle kiss. Another one. He felt her respond, lift her head and return the kiss. Thank the Lord, they were going to be okay. He drew her to him, stroking her head as it rested against his chest. 'I can fix this.'

Well, he could fix the house sale, he just wished Spencer Hogan would hurry up and get back to him. Al had phoned yesterday to say that Spence was working on something, but it was going to take a while longer. Trouble was, Tex didn't have much time left. His deadline with Mark was looming fast.

Without warning, Anna suddenly pulled away. 'I'm sorry, Tex,' she began. 'I can't do this.'

'Can't do what exactly? Trust me? Why can't you trust me? I can fix this for you.' Jeez, what was it going to take?

'How exactly do you propose to fix it?' It was an accusation, a challenge, not really a question.

'I can buy the house myself. That way he gets his money, goes back to America and you and Luke can carry on living there.'

He thought she would be pleased. Delighted even. How wrong he was.

'No! If you buy the house, I will then be in your debt. Don't you see?' She was almost shouting now, pacing back and forth. 'I am in this mess because I am reliant on him for a home. If you buy it, nothing changes for me. What happens when things between us are over? I will be in the same position I am now. I

228

don't want to need anyone. Not even you.'

It stung him to hear her say that and with such conviction. She really meant it. Now he was angry with her.

'What does that mean?'

'It means I'm sorting this out myself. Don't get involved.'

He couldn't keep the anger at bay. The strain of trying to make her see sense, the frustration at her stubbornness and the pain of her rejection cut him to the core. 'I am on your side and yet you push me away.' The frustration surged through his body. He wanted to shake some sense into her. 'I thought we had something special but I was wrong. You clearly don't want me. Maybe it was him you wanted all along.' It was a gamble. He was forcing her hand, leaving her no option but to deny it. He sounded desperate. He was desperate.

Anna looked at him for what seemed an eternity. Staring intently. When she finally spoke, her voice was hard and cold. 'I thought we had something special too. If you truly believe that I was just trying to get back with Mark, then, like you, I was wrong about us. About you.' With that she was across the room, breaking in to a run as she fled down the hallway, dropping the key, not bothering to close the door, such was her haste to escape.

'Anna!' Tex shouted, chasing after her. His gamble hadn't paid off. It had failed, big time. He leaned over the bannister, he could hear her feet pattering on the staircase. 'Anna! Wait!' He hurtled down the steps, stopping at the first floor and again leaning over the bannister as he heard her feet clattering across the foyer, and then the clunk of the door as it shut behind her. She was gone.

Tex didn't think he'd ever experienced the feeling he had now. A feeling of complete and utter helplessness and hopelessness, his feet heavy on the steps as he went back up to his apartment. She's gone. She's gone. The words going round in his mind, tormenting him. He had a vague image of Miss Purdy standing in her doorway, asking if he was all right. He didn't answer. He couldn't answer. Anna was gone.

He stalked around his apartment angry and despondent, as if he were going to find the answers to it all hidden away in one of the rooms. Every nook, cranny, corner and space of the apartment reminded him of her.

She was gone.

'For fuck's sake!' he shouted at the top of his voice. The pent-up frustration no longer under control, he swept his arm across the worktop, sending cups, kettle and coffee pot crashing and smashing to the floor. He kicked them for good measure, scattering them across the tiles.

Desperation and despair overwhelming him, he leaned on the worktop with his hands, dropping his head, taking long, deep breaths in an effort to regain control. The anger was only masking the pain he could feel burning in the pit of his stomach. The more the anger subsided, the more the pain intensified.

Chapter Twenty Eight

Tex tightened his shoelace as Nathan took a call.

'Thank you very much, Titch.'

Tex's attention was immediately piqued but he carried on fiddling with his shoe, not wishing to alert Nathan to the fact that he knew it was Anna on the other end.

'Erm, I'm with a client actually.'

He obviously wasn't going to elaborate. Tex made to adjust his other shoelace.

'Zoe? Something planned? You must be joking. She scribbled her name on the birthday card the kids made but that's about it.' Nathan sighed.

Still Tex didn't look up, but he was sure Nathan was glancing his way. His voice was lower as he carried on, but not low enough that Tex couldn't hear what was being said.

'Lunch sounds great. I could be with you for, say, one o'clock. Is that okay?' Nathan shut his phone and turned to Tex. 'Sorry about that.'

Tex toyed with the idea of asking after Anna, but changed his mind. What was the point? The less he knew, the less it hurt. He had the restaurant to occupy himself with now. The opening was only a few days away, and he had discovered that, sharing his time equally between the Arundel and Guildford restaurant, he was usually too busy or too tired to dwell much on Anna. Although he couldn't avoid the dreams.

'Happy birthday,' Tex said without much enthusiasm as the two men stepped out into the sunshine ready for their morning run.

'You heard then?' said Nathan as they began their stretching exercises. 'Look, Tex, I know it's none of my business…'

'If you know that, then don't bother.' Probably uncalled for but what the hell, this conversation would only go places he had no intention of exploring.

If Nathan was going to protest, he wasn't given the chance, as from across the road, Christine jogged over to them.

'Well, hello you two,' she smiled, standing on the forecourt, hands on hips. 'Now there's a sight for sore eyes.'

Tex nodded a small acknowledgement.

'Hi, Christine,' answered Nathan.

'I have a confession to make,' Christine said to Nathan, giving him a hug. 'I'm really sorry but I forgot your birthday. Sorry Natty.'

Tex couldn't disguise the scoffing noise he made at Christine's pet name. He looked at Nathan, who at least had the decency to look embarrassed.

'That's okay. I'm getting to that age where I don't want too many reminders,' replied Nathan.

'But I'm going to make it up to you,' beamed Christine.

'That's all right, Christine, there's really no need,' said Nathan. Again Tex met Nathan's sheepish glance.

'There's every need and I insist.' Christine tapped his chest with her polished red fingernail. 'When you get back from your run today, I'm taking you out for lunch. No, I insist.'

With that, Christine was back off across the road.

Nathan looked at Tex. 'She's a client,' he said firmly. 'End of.'

The run had done nothing to shake off Tex's bad mood. He

freshened up in the shower room at the back of his office and then sat down at his desk to deal with the never-ending paperwork. Today, however, he couldn't concentrate at all, his mind kept going back to the day before. Something didn't ring true, yet he couldn't put his finger on what exactly. It was just a gut feeling he had.

Not only that, but tomorrow his deadline with Mark was up and he hadn't heard a word from Spencer. Tex had phoned him and left a voicemail, but so far he hadn't even been able to speak to him.

The ping from his laptop told him he had a new email. Absently, he clicked on 'open'. As soon as he saw the sender, he sat bolt upright and clicked on Spencer Hogan's name to open it.

Nick, hope this isn't too late. Had to rely on contacts. Have attached the report. Ring if you need anything explaining. Spence.

Tex clicked open the file and waited while the pdf document downloaded. Slowly. 'Jeez, come on ,' he urged, as he tracked the download percentage bar across the screen He thought he would punch the screen out of pure impatience, but finally the words 'Download Complete' appeared.   Opening the document, Tex eagerly read the contents. A small, victorious smile tugged at the corners of his mouth.

Anna's attempt at not being too peed off with her brother may have succeeded had she only had to deal with him cancelling their lunch, but to have him propped up outside her door by Christine, and so obviously the worse for wear, was asking a bit too much.

'Shorry, Anna,' slurred Nathan as he staggered in, still in his running gear, and fell onto the sofa like a puppet having its strings cut.

'I took him out for a birthday lunch and he got a bit carried away with the red wine.' Christine smiled apologetically but not convincingly.

'And you didn't?' said Anna, irritated.

'No, not my birthday. Besides, one of us had to drive. I had to get your address from Tex.' Christine brushed past Anna and into the living room, where she knelt down beside Nathan. 'I'm off now, my darling. Hope you don't get in too much trouble with wifey.'

Anna scowled at Christine and followed her out to the end of the garden path. 'Why don't you leave him alone?'

'All in good time. Now, I'm not likely to see you at the opening of Tex's restaurant, am I? Your brother tells me it's all off between you two. About time Tex came to his senses and ditched you.'

'I haven't been ditched,' said Anna, indignantly folding her arms. 'We're just having a bit of time apart. A bit of space, that's all.'

'Oh please, we all know what a bit of space means. According to Tex, it's all over. Why else would he invite me to the opening night on Thursday? Anyway, love to stop and chat but I've got to go shopping – need a new dress for Thursday. Oh, and here are your brother's car keys. His car is in the car park behind Tarrant Street.'

Anna stomped back indoors. Birthday or no birthday, Nathan had a lot to answer for. What was he playing at? Standing his own sister up for lunch only to get pissed with Cruella de Vil!

'Nathan? Nathan!' She shook his shoulder. 'Oh, for pity's sake.' He was fast asleep. Just to make matters worse, chuckling away, Mark appeared from the kitchen where he had been lurking. Anna turned and glared at him. 'And you can shut up too.'

Tex made sure the folder was closed, the contents readily available but hidden until he was set to reveal his ace card. Man, was he going to enjoy wiping the smug smile from that jerk's face.

Mark sat down in front of the desk. 'Well, good afternoon. I'm so glad you want to do business.'

Tex sat impassively on the other side, relishing the thought of what was about to happen. Mark Barnes wouldn't have that self-satisfied grin on his face for much longer.

'You got the photos?' He needed to know they were here before he began.

Mark nodded and patted his side pocket.

Tex carried on. 'Put them on the table so I can see them.'

'You can trust me, you know.' Mark took the envelope from his pocket, dropped it on the desk. 'You got the money?'

Tex picked up the envelope and looked inside, counting the five polaroids. He was just about to take them out of Mark's reach when Mark placed his hand over the top of his.

'Not so fast. Let me see your end of the bargain.'

'Sure.' Tex reached down and lifted up a small holdall from the floor. Dumping it on top of the desk, ensuring it covered the envelope, Tex pulled open the neck to reveal bundles of twenty-pound notes.

Avarice oozed from Mark's eyes at the sight of the money, beads of perspiration breaking out across his brow. He went to touch the bag, but Tex pulled it out of reach, relieved to see that the envelope had been dragged from the desk too. As he slid the holdall off the desk and onto his lap, he hoped the envelope had fallen to the floor. He daren't risk looking down. Not yet.

'Yeah, about that arrangement,' began Tex frowning, shaking his head slightly. 'I'm gonna have to renegotiate.'

'What?' The incredulous look was a gratifying sight.

'Let me explain.' Tex put the holdall on the floor, allowing himself the opportunity to glance down. He trapped the envelope under his foot. That wasn't going anywhere.

'Just what are you playing at?' demanded Mark, his eyes darting back and forth, scanning the desk. 'Where's the envelope?'

'Oh, you can quit worrying about the envelope, I have that in safekeeping.' Tex was on his feet as quick as Mark. Both leaning across the desk, their faces only inches apart. Tex's voice was low and steady. 'Sit down.' He wondered for a second if Mark was going to do something stupid. In a way, he hoped he would. Busting Mark's face would satisfy Tex no end. It was, therefore, slightly disappointing to see Mark sit back down.

Mark straightened his jacket, adjusted his cuffs. 'So, would you care to explain?' From the wary look in Mark's eyes, it was all bravado.

Tex picked up a folder he had by the side of the desk. He opened it and lifted up the first sheet so Mark could see.

'Goldings Casino. August last year. A loss of five hundred dollars. Goldings Casino. August tenth. A loss of seven hundred dollars. Goldings Casino. August fifteenth. Oh, a slight win that time. One hundred dollars.' He looked at Mark, who it seemed had a great poker face, but that's about as far as it went. 'Fast forward a couple of months and the losses keep coming. November. One thousand dollars lost. Three thousand dollars lost. You weren't getting any better, were you? But the stakes were rising.'

'And your point of all this?' said Mark tightly.

'I'm just coming to that. I've done a quick calculation and it seems over the past six months, you've gambled away a total of nearly sixty thousand dollars. Now that's a lot of bucks.'

'No law against it.'

'No, you're right.' Tex picked up another sheet of paper. A change of tact. Confuse him. 'Marsha Davenport. Pretty girl. How old is she? Erm, it says it right here, oh yeah, twenty.'

He could hear Mark take a deep breath as he tried to act nonchalant. 'Again, no law against it.'

'No, again you're right, but I don't know what her daddy would say. Now, if I've read this right, Peter Davenport is her father and also an investor in the football academy. He's put up a lot of money. Nearly one hundred thousand dollars.' That got his attention all right.

Mark slammed his hand on the desk. 'Where are you getting all this from? How the hell did you find that out? It's confidential.'

'That's not really important, is it?' Tex took yet another sheet of paper from the file. Was he enjoying this or what? 'You know, under Californian law, embezzlement is punishable by imprisonment.'

'Embezzlement! You're just guessing. You've no proof of that.'

'Well, the thing is Mark, I don't actually need proof. I can just hand this right over to the authorities and they'll do the rest. Of course, they probably won't be interested in you hooking up with Marsha Davenport, but I suspect that daddy will be, and it ain't gonna be pretty.'

Mark got up, clearly agitated, and started pacing the room. 'What do you want? You got the photos. What's this all about?'

'Sit down.'

Mark did as he was ordered.

'I don't plan on doing anything with these,' said Tex.

'What are you talking about?'

'You get that house sold and you repay the company. No gambling it away. You repay your gambling debts with the balance.' Tex fixed him with a hard stare. He could tell Mark wasn't expecting that.

'What, and you won't say anything?' Mark's eyes narrowed. 'Why are you so keen to get the house sold? That's not what Anna wants. What's the catch?'

Tex shrugged. He wasn't about to say that he wanted the house sold so Anna had as few ties with Mark as possible. 'No catch. You repay your debts. Part two of the deal. Tomorrow you go to the solicitors and instigate divorce proceedings. Part three of the deal. You destroy any copies you may have made of those pictures. If I so much as suspect you've shown them to anyone, then I'll be posting this little lot off to the authorities with a copy to Peter

Davenport.'

'You're going to a lot of trouble for my wife.'

Jeez, he couldn't help himself, could he? What Anna ever saw in this slimeball, he didn't know. 'Part four.'

'Part four!' exclaimed Mark.

'Yes, part four. You even think about mentioning any of this to Anna, then I will also tell Daddy Davenport about the termination you paid for his daughter to have.'

That was his ace, his trump card. If Mark thought that once the money had been restored to the business account he was off the hook and free to blackmail or print those pictures again, then he was wrong. Tex watched the colour seep from Mark's face as he swallowed hard. It was a done deal.

Chapter Twenty Nine

The restaurant had been open for business for nearly a week now and so far everything had run smoothly. Barely a problem, certainly none that the customers would notice, thought Tex, as he sat back in his office chair. He picked up the local newspaper that had a feature about the opening. Too bad about the photo, but the write-up was good.

The sound of breaking glass cut through his thoughts. 'What the…?'

Tex jumped to his feet, pushing his chair back but then checking himself. If there was someone breaking in, he needed to be prepared. He looked round the office, nothing obvious to defend himself with. If he could get to the kitchen then he had a whole host of items to choose from. However, the noise had sounded as if it had actually come from the kitchen, which also meant whoever was trying to get in, if they had already succeeded, that they too had the same choice of weapons.

He listened intently, trying to make out if there was anyone in the building. He moved silently out of the office to the kitchen door and, resting his ear against the door, listened again. There was some sort of muffled rummaging noise and then what sounded like metal sliding against metal. Whoever it was didn't appear to have made it inside the premises.

Slowly, Tex opened the door. The kitchen was in darkness but he could just make out the broken pane of one of the leaded windows. Someone appeared to be bending over on the other side of it. Whoever it was must be standing on the wheelie bin to be that high up.

Tex weighed up his options. He could call the police, but by the time they arrived whatever this person had planned to do would no doubt be accomplished by then, and said person wouldn't hang around. The other option was to creep around the back and catch him by surprise. Returning to the office, Tex picked up the front door keys and his cell phone. He made a quick and quiet call to the police and, ignoring their instructions not to confront the potential intruder, Tex made his way out the front of the restaurant, picking up a large black umbrella that had been left by the door. Anything was better than nothing.

Keeping close to the wall of the old church building, Tex made his way to the front corner. Aware that his silhouette would be framed by the street light, he tentatively poked his head round the corner, and seeing it was clear, light-footedly made his way down the side of the building. Before he reached the end came the sound of a man's cry, followed by a thud, the sound of metal crashing to the ground, and then groaning.

Tex took his opportunity and charged round to the back of the building, feeling slightly ridiculous as he brandished the umbrella. He stopped in his tracks at the sight before him.

'Well, I'll be…' said Tex, approaching the man sprawled out in a heap on the tarmac.

'Don't just stand there, call an ambulance, I think I've broken my arm,' demanded Andy Bartholomew.

'That will match the window then,' replied Tex, the adrenalin pumping wildly through him. He grabbed the curator by the collar and went to haul him up, but Andy's screech and cry of pain stopped him. 'Arsehole.' Tex let go and Andy flopped back to the ground, groaning in pain.

It was then that Tex saw a metal cage, the sort usually used for transporting cats to the vets; however, that was no cat looking back at him. A pair of black beady eyes glinted in the moonlight. Jeez, Andy was going to put a rat in the kitchen.

'Son of a bitch.' Tex toe-poked Andy in the thigh. He crouched down and gripping Andy's chin in one hand, turned his head towards him. 'So it's been you. The graffiti, the fire, the scratching up of my truck. It was you all along. Why?'

He released his grip a fraction so Andy could speak. The words were almost spat out.

'You think you're something special. Riding into town, everyone adoring you, including Anna. Making a fool out of me. So in love with yourself. Sleeping with anyone you care and then just dropping them when you've had enough. Well, you don't deserve to be here and Anna would be better off without you. The town would be better off without you.'

Tex shook his head. 'You crazy jerk, what do you think this is, *High Noon*?' He turned at the sound of police sirens and blue flashing lights bouncing off the buildings. 'Looks like the cavalry arrived just in time to save your sorry arse.'

Anna managed to sulk with Nathan for several days. Since her argument with Mark and the break-up with Tex, she had gradually become more and more miserable. She still went through the motions of the day, going to the gym, working for Jamie, but it was all with a heavy heart. Always the blanket of sadness engulfing her. Even the three A*'s, two A's and a scattering of B's and C's Luke got for his GCSE results couldn't lift her mood. She hated Mark living with them but she knew she didn't have any choice it in. The sooner the house was sold and she could move on, the better, and with Tex out of the frame now Mark didn't have any reason to harm him.

Up until Christine's visit last week, Anna still had half a hope that somehow her and Tex would get back together. However, that last shred of hope seemed dashed now; Christine would not have wasted the opportunity of giving Tex a shoulder to cry on, whilst secretly calculating how to win him over. Seemed like her plan was working if Tex had invited Christine as his guest for the opening evening.

The tears still caught her by surprise when she thought about Tex, fantasising about how they could make things work, remembering those glorious days and nights spent together. His sensual touch, his beautiful kisses, his generosity to her feelings, and their lovemaking. Oh how she missed him. The pain she felt in her heart never diminishing.

Today Anna was having a rare day at home alone. Mark was on parent visiting duties and had taken Luke along too, they wouldn't be back until much later that evening. She had agreed a tenancy on a flat and was due to pick the keys up in a couple of weeks. Anna knew she really should be packing some more of her things, but she had been thrown off-kilter when she came across the jar of olives Tex had bought her.

She had put the jar of olives in her bedside table, along with her passport. Why there and not in the fridge, she had no idea, but then again, she hadn't exactly been thinking straight that week. Not after her confrontation with Mark.

Studying the jar of green olives, Tex's words coming back to her. *'A little each day.'* *'You will learn to love them.'* She unscrewed the lid and after a couple of attempts, managed to secure an olive between her finger and thumb. Tentatively, she nibbled the end.

'Yuk!' She scrunched her face up but ate it all the same. Somehow it made her feel closer to Tex, doing something he had wanted her to do. If only everything else were that simple.

A knock at the front door jolted Anna from her thoughts. Popping the lid back on the jar, she jogged downstairs to see who it was.

'Christine!' The last person Anna expected to be standing on her doorstep. The smug look on her visitor's face alarmed Anna immediately. 'What are you doing here?' She looked past Christine towards her car, half expecting to see a drunk Nathan sitting there.

'Don't worry, I haven't got your precious, married, father of four, brother in the car.' Christine waved a newspaper in front of Anna's face before pushing it towards her. 'But I do have this. Page eight.'

Anna rustled through the *Sussex Observer* until she got to page eight. Her heart tripped, surged and fell simultaneously as she took in the picture staring back at her. Tex standing outside the Arundel restaurant, surrounded by his staff, looking handsome in his chef's whites, his beautiful eyes smiling back at the camera, matching his infectious smile. He looked good. The not so good bit was his arm around the waist of a woman. Tall, slim, long flowing waves of brunette hair, immaculately dressed in a little black number. Her arm around Tex, smiling or was it gloating? The same smug smile that Christine now had on her face.

Anna fought every urge in her body to scream out loud. She wouldn't allow herself to crack in front of Christine. No way would she give Cruella the satisfaction. 'And your point in coming all this way to show me?'

'Just thought you might be interested, that's all.'

'So had enough of messing around with my brother and moved on to Tex now, have you? Huh!' retorted Anna, trying to stop her voice from breaking. Tex and Christine! She could barely believe it.

'Oh please! Me and your brother? He was far too under the thumb to be any fun.'

'More like prefers his wife to you.' Childish comment, yes, but Anna felt better for saying it.

Christine's mouth twisted into something resembling a smile. 'Enjoy the paper.' Then turning on her heel, she swaggered back down the path.

Anna spread the newspaper out on the coffee table and, kneeling on the floor, made herself methodically and carefully read the whole article, looking for any clue, any reference as to what Christine was doing in the shot.

The article never mentioned her. Not once. It gave some background to Tex's early career, where he was from, together with details of his restaurant in Guildford. But nothing about Christine. Anna studied the photograph. Tex definitely had his arm around Christine's waist.

The familiar pain of a knife being twisted in her heart and the feeling of sadness in the pit of her stomach began to erupt. Here she was, still grieving for him, still missing him, still wanting him, and there he was happy, smiling, hooked up with someone else. He had got over her, already moving on to a new woman. She must have meant nothing to him.

Anna could feel her heart pounding, a new emotion rising within her. A fierce burning anger that was raging through every part of her body. Tex had well and truly reeled her in, hook, line and sinker. All his comments and condemnation of Mark's behaviour, only to be just like him. Angry and hurt, she screwed up the newspaper.

'You're a fraud, Tex Garcia. A fraud!' she shouted at the crumpled paper. 'A liar! Just like Mark. Do you hear me?'

Of course he couldn't hear her. God, if he were here now she'd give him a piece of her mind. She paused. Everyone was always telling her to stand up for herself, not to let people walk all over her. Well, maybe just this time she would speak up. Nice Anna, who always tried to smooth things over, avoided confrontation – what a loser she turned out to be. Lost her husband. Lost her boyfriend. About to lose her home. Maybe she just would give Tex what for!

Chapter Thirty

Funny how it seemed such a good idea at the time, when her hurt and anger were at their peak. Anna had already driven by Tex's apartment, but when she saw his car wasn't there, now found herself standing outside the new restaurant, hand paused in mid-air as she re-evaluated her wisdom. She dropped her hand to her side. She had been so incensed, not to mention upset, by Christine's visit, Anna had just grabbed her bag and car keys and driven straight over to Arundel. She didn't even remember much of the journey. She had obviously negotiated the A27 between Chichester and Arundel successfully, but her mind had been on Tex and not her driving.

In her blind fury, she hadn't even stopped to consider the timing of her appearance. The restaurant wasn't due to open for another hour, although the main doors to the entrance foyer were open. Through the inner glass doors she could see waiting staff busying themselves in anticipation of the evening service.

Now that her initial rage had subsided to a simmering wrath, she wondered whether she could actually go through with this. Perhaps she should just leave it. Tex had moved on, and she should accept it.

Anna took the creased sheet of newspaper from her bag and looked at the picture of Tex and Christine. It did the trick, fanning the flames of anger that were smouldering in her stomach, breathing new life into it. Stuffing the article back into her bag, she rapped on the glass before she had time to change her mind again. She noticed a waitress make eye contact with her and then gesture to the maître d'. She knocked on the glass again so he was in no doubt that she wanted him to come over.

The maître d' opened the door slightly, just enough so his frame filled the gap, and just enough so that Anna could not mistake it as an invitation into the restaurant.

'I'm afraid we're closed,' he said apologetically. 'Is there something I can help you with?'

'Yes. I would like to speak with Mr Garcia please.'

'Do you have an appointment?'

'No. Look, I know he's here because his car is parked out the front. I really do need to speak to him.'

'Is there something I could help you with?'

'No.'

'Perhaps I could take your name and any message,' suggested the maître d' patiently.

Anna let out a big sigh, give him his due, he was doing his best to protect his boss.

'I really must speak to Mr Garcia, in person, now. Could you ask him to come here? Please?' Anna was unyielding, feeling more and more impatient. She hoisted the straps of her bag up her shoulder and drummed the bag with her fingertips, remembering the newspaper tucked inside it.

'Madam...'

Anna didn't let him speak, instead standing on tiptoe, she shouted over the man's shoulder. 'Tex! Tex Garcia! I know you're there. Come here. I want to speak to you!' She stuck her foot in the way of the closing door. She wasn't leaving without a fight.

'Madam, please move your foot. If you don't leave I will have to call the police.'

'Just get Mr Garcia then. Tex!'

The waiting staff had ground to a halt, watching the scene unfold in front of them, exchanging uncertain looks, while Anna shouted like a termagant. 'Tex!'

Taking the man behind the door by surprise, Anna gave it a sudden push. In an instant she found herself being propelled into the restaurant, stumbling slightly before regaining her balance. She took a moment to straighten herself up, adjust her cardigan and brush imaginary dust from her trousers. Anna looked round the restaurant, aware that every member of staff had stopped to watch her.

The door to the back room opened suddenly and out walked Tex, flanked by two other chefs, a frown on his face. He looked slightly startled to see Anna there but quickly regained his composure. He muttered something to the two shotgun riders and both disappeared back into the kitchen. The maître d' scurried past her, a worried look on his face.

'Chef, I am so sorry. I tried to stop her but...'

Tex held up his hand. 'It's okay, Stefan. Don't worry.' Stefan gave Anna an uncertain look. 'Thank you, Stefan,' said Tex before flicking an enquiring look towards the rest of his staff. Immediately, everyone returned to their work. When he finally turned his attention to Anna, she was sure she saw a flicker of amusement cross his face. Now though, he looked impassively across the restaurant floor at her.

Anna shifted her weight uneasily from one foot to another.

He spoke first. 'So?'

Anna looked uncomfortably around the restaurant.

Tex spoke again. 'I assume you came here for a reason. Shall we go into the office?' His voice was calm and indifferent.

Anna followed him back through to the office.

Entering first, Tex held the door open for Anna, stepping aside so she could walk in. She stood self-consciously in the centre of the room, a desk in front of her and a couple of filing cabinets behind. Tex shut the door and walked over, perching on the edge of the desk, arms folded.

'So what is so important that you have to force your way in to the building, shouting so loud that you could be heard whether I was in Arundel or Guildford?'

Anna recalled her rehearsed speech. Now how was she going to start? Oh yeah, that was it.

'Out of all the people I've ever known, I would have said that you were one of the most honest, considerate and genuine.' Anna took a breath; this had sounded much better in her head than it did now, out loud. Tex's face was still impassive. She carried on. 'I don't know how I got it so wrong. I must be a terrible judge of character. Of men. You even get other people to do your dirty work.'

'And what is this dirty work?' asked Tex.

'Hiding behind your maître d' for a start,' bristled Anna. 'But worst of all, sending Christine to see me.'

'Christine?'

'Don't pretend you don't know what I'm talking about.'

Tex gave a little laugh. 'But I don't.'

Anna snatched the newspaper cutting from her bag and slapped it down onto the desk before retreating a few steps back to the middle of the room.

'You could at least have told me yourself instead of letting her do it.' Anna took deep breaths as the anger and hurt reared up again.

Tex picked up the cutting, looked at it, turned it over and then back again. He looked blankly at Anna. 'I am sorry but I don't understand. Why this? I haven't sent anyone to see you. Why would I?'

Anna flounced her arms against her sides in frustration and

exhaled theatrically. Did she have to spell it out? Obviously!

'I believed you Tex. I believed that you actually cared about me. I believed you were different.' Anna had to stop, her voice was cracking. How could she feel so angry and yet so sad at the same time? She felt swamped by a whole range of conflicting emotions.

'You were right to believe me,' said Tex, standing up. He took a step towards her. Anna matched it with a step backwards.

'No I wasn't,' she snapped. 'If you meant what you said, how come you moved on so quickly to your next conquest?' She gestured towards the cutting in his hand.

'Conquest? Christine?' His voice was incredulous.

'Yes!' Anna was aware her voice was high-pitched as it fought for space in her dry, closing throat. She swallowed hard. 'Yes. You didn't waste any time getting with Christine. As if that wasn't bad enough, you didn't even have the balls to tell me yourself. You let her do that.'

'Do you honestly think that?' demanded Tex, his eyes fixing on her.

'You haven't denied it,' challenged Anna, sticking out her chin defiantly.

'Why should I? You seem to have got it all worked out in your head.'

'I thought I could trust you. You never really cared about me. You got what you wanted and then moved on. You're really no different to Mark.' Anna turned to leave but Tex reached the door first, holding his hand against it.

'You are not going anywhere. You can't come here shouting about how you've been hurt, accusing me of not caring about you, telling me I am like him, and then think you can just walk away.' Tex was struggling to keep his voice calm but Anna could hear the anger bubbling under his words. 'I cannot believe you think I would behave in that way. Of course I wouldn't send Christine to tell you something like that.'

'Tell me yourself then. Tell me now about you and Christine.' If he said it, she could leave. She had made her point.

'There is nothing to tell.'

'Bullshit. I've been here before with Mark. Don't think I'm going to go through it all again with you.'

'I did everything I could to reassure you, to make you trust me. I wanted you to realise that not all men were like him. I was different. I am different. I was with you because I wanted to be, because you made me happier than I had ever been. And now you throw it all back at me. It meant nothing to you.'

Tex closed his eyes and banged the back of his head against the door. When he spoke again, it was calmer and quieter but the anger was still there. 'Tell me Anna, when Christine came to see you, how did it make you feel? The thought of me and Christine together. What did you feel? Hurt?'

Anna nodded. 'Yes.'

'Sad? No wait, sad isn't the right word. Err... devastated?'

'Mmm.' Anna nodded again, not sure where this was going.

'Rejected? Confused? Angry?'

'Yes, all of those things.'

'You felt the same as me. That is how I felt when you chose him over me. That night at your house, when you wouldn't come with me, well, I'm sorry I just don't get it. You tell me to leave. Me, who has shown you nothing but love. Then you come here and tell me you were only a conquest to me. That I used you. Unbelievable! It's me who has been used by you. Used just to make him jealous so you could get back together.'

'No! No! That's not true.'

'What am I supposed to think? You won't even divorce him. I have made it all so easy for you.'

His eyes felt like laser beams, burning into her own. She looked down at her feet, unable to bear the look of anger in his face. Anger directed at her.

'This was a mistake. I shouldn't have come,' she muttered.

'At least we agree on one thing.' His words stung like acid. He opened the door and walked out, leaving her standing there alone in the middle of the room.

For a moment Anna wasn't sure if she could trust her legs to carry her safely out of the building. Everything had gone horribly wrong. She had been so furious and hurt by Christine's visit, her response was a knee-jerk reaction that had desperation written all over it. She suspected she had used her anger as an excuse to see Tex, but what had she expected? Tex to say it was all a misunderstanding, he wasn't with Christine. That he would wait until Mark had gone. That he understood and everything would be all right. Is that what she had secretly hoped would happen?

Truthfully?

Yes. She probably had.

As it happened, he had turned on her, telling her how she had hurt him and used him. What a mess she had made of it all. She needed to get out of here.

Through the open door, she could see Tex chopping vegetables, fast and furiously, sending the knife up and down in swift, small, precise movements. He stopped and looked up at her. Oh the contempt in his eyes, he really hated her.

She was shaking by the time she reached her car and feeling light-headed. She wasn't sure she was in a fit state to drive. She couldn't stay here though. Anna wandered up the road with no real plan as to what she was doing, and eventually found herself walking into the Kings Head pub just along from Tex's restaurant. It wasn't too busy, just several suited men and women, probably taking an end of week drink, looking relaxed, laughing at something one of them had just said, sipping their wines and lagers, de-mob happy with that Friday feeling.

Anna sat in the corner with her white wine. She took a large gulp. Perhaps the wine would help to dull the pain. She felt slightly self-conscious sitting in a pub on her own, drinking. She'd just have this one and then head off home. There was no point hanging around. Tex would be busy with evening service now, and even if he wasn't, what was there left to say? They had said it all.

'Drinking alone on a Friday, that's never a good sign,' a slightly familiar voice said.

Anna looked up. Great! Handy Andy – just what she needed. He put a glass of wine on the table and sat down next to her.

'Hello, Anna. I would ask how you are, but seeing as you look thoroughly miserable there's probably no point.' He smiled and pushed the fresh glass of wine towards her. 'Cheers.'

'No, I'm okay, thanks,' said Anna, pushing the glass back his way and noticing the sling and plaster cast on his arm. 'What have you done to yourself?'

'Fell down some stairs. Anyway, the drink's a peace offering.' Andy smiled and pushed the wine glass back to her.

'Peace offering?' she eyed him suspiciously.

'Yeah. Look, about that business with me and you at that promotional evening.'

'What about it?'

'I was... well... you know…'

'Out of order?' she prompted.

'Yeah, out of order. It was wrong of me. I'm sorry.' He held out his hand. 'No hard feelings?'

Anna studied his face for a moment, uncertain whether that was a sincere apology or not, but realised it was probably the only one she was going to get. Oh, what the hell. Let bygones be bygones and all that. She shook his hand. 'Sure, no hard feelings.'

'Excellent, now drink up. And you can tell me all your problems if you like. Or if you prefer we can just get wasted.' Andy took a long slug of his pint, as if to show he meant business.

'Cheers,' echoed Anna, picking up her glass.

Pouring her troubles out to Andy wasn't appealing; however, getting wasted was an option she hadn't previously considered. She took a second, larger mouthful of wine. Suddenly the idea of going home to an empty house wasn't so attractive. She'd only end up dwelling on Tex and Christine. Misery. No, she'd stay here, have another drink, relax and forget about the whole sorry mess.

Chapter Thirty One

Tex looked up from the soup he was tasting.

'A little more salt, Patrick,' he said to his sous-chef. He turned his attention to the kitchen porter who had just come through the door. 'So?' he asked Gareth.

'She went into the Kings Head and sat down with a drink,' puffed Gareth, his face red from running back down the road.

Tex nodded thoughtfully, rubbing his chin with his hand. 'You gotta phone?' Gareth nodded. 'Go and get it. Quickly.'

'Chef.' Gareth looked bemused, but the eighteen-year-old was in no position to question his boss and scurried off to the staff room to fetch his phone from the locker.

'Right, this is my number,' said Tex when Gareth returned. 'Now, I want you to go back to the pub, buy yourself a drink and just sit in the corner keeping an eye on her for me. If she looks like she is leaving, phone me straight away. Understand? Good.' Tex pushed a ten pound note into Gareth's hand and whipped off the small black cap perched on the lad's head. 'Take your apron off, put a jacket on and go back now. Okay?'

'Yes, Chef.'

'Everything all right, Chef?' asked Stefan, coming into the kitchen, an alarmed look on his face.

'Yes, fine. I think. Gareth is just doing a little job for me. Once service is under way, I have to go out. Patrick will be in charge of the kitchen, and Daniel is on his way in to make up the numbers. So nothing for front of house to worry about.' Tex smiled, and patting Stefan reassuringly on the back, walked him out to the restaurant area.

As soon as Anna had paused in the kitchen earlier and looked over at him, Tex had instantly regretted giving her such a hard time. The look of sadness in her eyes was haunting him. It truly hurt to see her so obviously upset. He could have made it a lot easier for her by telling her nothing was going on between himself and Christine, but his pride got the better of him and he wanted her to know how it felt to be pushed aside for someone else. Although all the facts pointed to Anna being back with Mark, somehow Tex couldn't quite believe it.

Over the weeks he and Anna had been together, she had opened up a lot about her marriage, and through snippets of information and casual comments, Tex had been able to piece together what he believed was a pretty accurate picture of Anna's relationship with Mark.

Earlier tonight, standing in the office, he had pushed her and pushed her, trying to make her tell him exactly what was going on. He had purposefully let her get the impression that there might be something between himself and Christine in the hope that the jealousy would overwhelm her enough and, in an unguarded moment, she would let slip what hold Mark had over her. Unfortunately, his plan had backfired and just left Anna with a look of desolation. Now he wished he had gone for the softer, gentle and honest approach. That he still only had eyes and heart for Anna. That Christine had muscled in on the photograph without warning, and that he hadn't wanted to make a fuss with the press there. That he was more in love with Anna than he ever was and that everything else paled into insignificance. That she was the love of his life.

Almost before she had even left the restaurant, Tex was calling Gareth over, giving him instructions to follow Anna and report back as to where she went. Much as he wanted to, Tex knew he couldn't abandon the kitchen with service due to start so soon. He would have to hang on until Daniel could get in. Tex checked his watch for a fourth time. Service had started and they were fully booked tonight. He needed to pay attention to the orders that would be coming in any minute now. As usual, he was on the *passe*, making sure all the dishes looked exactly right, the sauce was the right consistency, spread in the correct fashion, all the food was presented correctly, there were no drips on the edge of the plates, that the whole plate of food looked like an exquisite work of art.

The Kings Head was beginning to fill up now as Tex joined Gareth at the bar.

'She's over there by the fireplace, Chef,' said Gareth.

Tex followed his gaze. Immediately, there was a tightness in his chest as he saw that Anna wasn't sitting alone as he had imagined, but was with none other than Andy Bartholomew. Jeez, that man had no shame. Tex wondered if he had been too generous when he had persuaded the police not to press charges and just to give Andy a formal warning. He had figured a broken arm and demotion at work to ticket office clerk was punishment enough. He had also made Andy agree to covering the costs of the repairs to the restaurant.

'How long has he been there?' Tex's eyes fixed on Anna.

'About an hour.'

'Okay. You'd better get back to the restaurant now. Thanks, Gareth.' Tex forced a smile of appreciation at the lad. He watched Gareth leave the pub, before walking over to Anna's table.

Anna looked up and swaying slightly on her chair, fought for a moment to focus on Tex.

'Oh look, Andy, it's Tex,' Anna's words were slightly slurred. 'Hello, Tex. Shouldn't you be at work or have you come out for a drink with Cruella?' She wagged a finger at him and went to rest her elbow on the table, but instead it caught the edge and slipped off it. 'Ooops, who moved the table?'

'You have had too much to drink,' said Tex, ignoring the reference to Christine.

'Well, now you come to mention it,' began Anna, her head lolling to one side, her eyelids heavy.

Andy looked up at Tex. 'Me and Anna are enjoying a drink together and you know what they say, three's a crowd.'

Tex returned the glare. 'Party's over. I am taking her home.' He reached over and took the drink from Anna's hand that she was trying to line up, rather unsuccessfully, with her mouth.

'Oh, you spoilsport,' Anna giggled as, swaying again, she nearly fell off her chair. Andy, putting his arm around her shoulder, pulled her back in towards him.

'I don't think she wants to go home with you,' said Andy.

'Too bad. You think I am going to leave her with a shit like you?' Tex's voice was low, each word considered and menacing.

'Oooh, he's being all masterful and in charge. Aren't you, Chef? You are Masterchef. Ha-ha. Get it? No. Oh dear.' Anna's words were in danger of rolling into each other as she concentrated on speaking, trying to sound sober, but failing as only someone drunk can. She sat upright for a second before flopping back against Andy, her eyes half closed.

'Perhaps we should let the lady decide who she wants to be with?' said Andy confidently. 'Anna. Anna! Don't go to sleep. Listen. Do you want to stay here with me or go with him? Anna, what do you want to do?'

Anna sat up again, blurry eyed. 'Well, I am having a nice time here, I must admit...'

'There's your answer,' said Andy smugly.

'But,' carried on Anna, elbow on the table, hand raised, fore-finger pointed, 'I think maybe I should go. I don't feel too good.' She rested her head on her arms over the table.

Tex didn't waste any time, he was immediately at Anna's side, lifting her up under her arm, making her stand. 'Let's go.'

Anna swayed and leaned into Tex's chest. She put her arms around his neck, locking her fingers together, and looked dreamy-eyed up at him. 'What have you done with Cruella de Vil? She'll be in a stew. Ha-ha! Get it? In a stew? Stew, you know, all worked up and stew, cooking stew, you being a chef. Get it?'

Tex looked down at her and shook his head. She really had had far too much to drink. Seems he got here just in time.

'Charming. All that money wasted on wine,' complained Andy.

Tex looked at him with disdain, fished around in his pocket and then chucked a twenty pound note on the table. 'That should cover your expenses.'

Holding Anna upright, he managed to get her out of the pub in a dignified manner. Once out in the fresh air, he could feel Anna slumping, so he simply scooped her up in his arms and carried her down the street. She was so light, waiflike, Tex could feel her ribs through her t-shirt. She must have lost weight, there was nothing to her.

Anna put her arms around his neck, a contented smile on her face, eyes closed, head tucked into his shoulder. 'Richard,' she murmured.

'What?' Tex stopped and looked at her. Who the hell was Richard?

'Richard,' repeated Anna not opening her eyes. 'Richard Gere. *Officer and a Gentleman*. You're my Richard Gere.'

Tex decided it was easier to carry her into his apartment; walking seemed to be a particular problem for Anna. He put her down on the sofa, arranging the cushions round her to try and keep her upright. No sooner had he finished when Anna staggered up.

'I think I'm going to be sick,' she announced, stumbling towards the balcony window.

'Oh no you don't.' Tex grabbed her arm and whisked her down to the bathroom. He held her shoulders as she knelt down on the floor, head hanging in the toilet bowl. 'Okay?' Perhaps she wasn't going to be sick after all. He spoke too soon!

'I'm sorry,' whimpered Anna afterwards as she sat on the edge of the bath. Tex wiped her face with a wet flannel. Tears began to fall silently down her face, rinsing her mascara, black trickles streaking her skin.

'Oh Anna,' comforted Tex softly as he wiped the tears away. 'Don't cry.' He tipped her chin with his hand and looked under her eyelashes, black smudges of make-up gathering underneath.

'I'm sorry,' mumbled Anna, sniffing. 'I've made such a mess of everything.'

'Shhh. It's all right.' Tex was crouched down. She swayed slightly one way and then the other. Tex held onto her to steady her. The earlier drunken high of jokes and laughter now replaced by the drunken low of tears and apologies. She really was a sorry sight. Not for the first time was he so glad that he had got to the pub when he did, any later and Andy would probably have whisked her off. He shook his head to rid the thought of what might have happened to her, he actually couldn't bear to imagine it.

Tex rinsed the flannel out and tenderly wiped her forehead, pushing her hair back off her face.

'Here, have a sip of water.' He held the glass to her lips as she took a small sip. 'Now, here's a drop of mouthwash. That's it. Spit it out, don't swallow it.'

He helped Anna back through to the living room and again

made her comfortable on the sofa, before making some coffee. By the time he had come back though, Anna was half asleep, slumped over sideways on a cushion. Tex wondered whether he should just put a blanket over her, but decided it would be better to get her undressed and into bed. He lifted her with ease from the sofa and took her into the main bedroom, sitting her on the edge of the bed. He knelt down and slipped her shoes from her feet. Anna leaned forward and rested her hands on his shoulders, her head on his. Tex moved his head up slowly, letting out a deep sigh. He couldn't help it, his mouth found hers, familiar feelings stirring within him instantly. He wondered if she felt the same. She wouldn't know what she felt in her current state. With more reluctance than he thought possible, Tex pulled away.

'Richard Gere wouldn't have done that,' Anna grumbled, before falling back onto the bed and passing out.

Tex slipped her jeans off, then noticing that her t-shirt had a suspicious looking stain on it, took that off too. Seeing her in just her underwear, he was even more convinced she had lost weight. She was painfully thin. She obviously hadn't been looking after herself properly these past few weeks.

He lifted her into bed, putting her on her side and pulling the duvet over her bare shoulders. How tempting was it to climb in next to her and hold her, feeling her skin next to his? He had missed her so much and had wanted her back in his bed so often, yet now he had the opportunity, he knew he couldn't. For a start, he didn't know if he would be able to resist her after all this time and secondly, he didn't want her to wake up and assume something had happened. That wouldn't be a good move.

Instead, Tex took the quilt from the spare room and made himself as comfortable as possible on the bedroom chair next to her. He didn't want to leave her in case she was sick again.

When Anna awoke the following morning, she wasn't entirely sure where she was or what had happened. Her head was killing her. She shielded her eyes from the light that was streaming in through the double doors, dappled by the muslin. Funny, it looked like Tex's window in his apartment. She closed her eyes. Then almost instantly her eyes snapped open, her senses bursting into life, suddenly very aware of where she was.

She *was* in Tex's bedroom. His bed, no less. She looked to her left, half expecting to see him next to her, as she so often had. It was empty. She slid her hand across, feeling the smooth, cold sheet, no sign of a crease where a body might have been. No indentation in the pillow either.

Anna took a sip of water from the glass on the bedside table. It was cold and fresh, obviously recently put there. A blister pack of two paracetamols was also there, alongside a little packet of biscuits. The kind you get complimentary with your coffee in a restaurant. The kind that Tex kept in his cupboard.

Gingerly, Anna sat up, swallowed the tablets and nibbled on one of the biscuits. What time was it? She didn't have her watch on. Had she lost it last night somehow? She tried to recall what had happened last night.

It was starting to come back, and although she had a vague recollection of Tex coming into the pub and, oh no, being sick and Tex wiping her face, she couldn't remember much else of what happened in the apartment. Did he kiss her or was that a dream? Had he undressed her? It didn't appear that he'd slept in the same bed so she assumed that nothing had happened.

Then Anna noticed the duvet and pillow bundled on the chair in the corner of the room. That confirmed her thoughts then. Tex must have slept on the chair. She wasn't quite sure how she felt about that. Should she feel pleased that he didn't take advantage of her, or should she feel miffed that he had resisted her?

Then again, why would he want her when he had Christine now? Tall, glamorous, sophisticated Cruella. Anna didn't stand a chance. She lay back on the pillow. She could hear the gentle tones of a radio playing. Tex always had music on in the background. He was probably sitting on the other side of the door, reading, creating new menus, working on the laptop or going through his paperwork. Things she had seen him do so many times before. She could picture him in his jeans, crisp white t-shirt, bare feet, hair towel-dried, smiling up at her as she approached him. He would then push the papers aside, or drop them on the floor, reaching out for her, kissing her tummy, pulling her onto his lap for more kissing. Sometimes he would cuddle her for a bit and as she got up, he'd playfully smack her behind before returning to his work. Other times he would simply carry on kissing her, ease her on to the sofa, kissing, touching, loving her.

The tears pricked her eyes. Anna couldn't face him yet. She'd wait until he went out and then take her chance to leave. That way she wouldn't have to torture herself just by seeing him, being in the same room as him but not being able to have him, not being wanted.

There was a gentle knock at the door. Anna quickly pulled the duvet up, snuggled down and closed her eyes. She heard the door open and Tex walk into the room over to the edge of the bed. She lay perfectly still, willing him to leave. She heard him pick up the empty tablet pack and then drop it back down again. Her heart was beating faster and faster. She could just tell he was kneeling down beside her. He stroked her hair.

'You can't pretend to be asleep forever,' he said. Anna could hear the amusement in his voice. 'I can see your eyes fluttering.' Anna opened her eyes. 'Hey. How are you feeling?' He smiled a soft, loving smile. One she had seen a hundred times before, one that melted her every time she saw it. She stuck her hand out from the duvet and gave the 'thumbs down' sign.

'I'm not surprised. I don't think I have ever seen you that drunk.' Again he stroked her hair. 'Why don't you have a shower? It will make you feel better. I'll make you a nice cup of tea.'

'I borrowed one of your t-shirts,' said Anna as she came into the living room after her shower. 'Hope you don't mind, but I couldn't find mine.' She felt uncomfortable and embarrassed.

'Your t-shirt's in the dryer. You got something down it last night and your watch is here by the sink. It needed a clean' Tex didn't elaborate and Anna didn't ask. She didn't want to know. 'Sit down. I've made you a cup of tea. There's some toast. Try and have some.'

'Thanks.' Anna was grateful for the tea and although she wasn't keen on eating anything, did so, pleased to find that it did actually settle her stomach a bit.

'Mark phoned you last night. He kept ringing your mobile so in the end I sent a message, just to say you wouldn't be home last night.

'You should have just ignored him.'

'I did think about that but then I wondered whether it may be urgent.'

'Yes, of course. Thank you.' Great. Now she'd had Mark chasing her up like she needed to explain herself to him. Get his permission to stay out. Christ it was like being a teenager with overprotective parents. Mind you, she had behaved like an irresponsible teenager. Getting so drunk she had to be taken home and looked after. 'About last night, Tex. I'm sorry. I didn't mean to cause any problems for you.'

'Actually, it's me who should be apologising to you.' Tex sat down next to her on the sofa, putting his cup on the coffee table. Resting his elbows on his knees, he put his hands together as if in prayer, raising them to his mouth briefly. He took a deep breath.

'When you came to the restaurant last night, I wasn't entirely honest with you.'

'Oh?'

'I let you think there was something going on between myself and Christine.'

Anna shot him a sideways look. 'What do you mean?'

'I wanted to make you jealous. I wanted to make you come back to me. I hated the thought of you being with Mark and I wanted you to know what it felt like.' He rubbed his stubble with the palm of his hand. 'When you assumed I was with Christine, I didn't deny it on purpose.'

Anna fixed her gaze on her cup. Her heart had done a double flip when she realised what he was saying. She took her time before responding.

'That was a bit of a shitty thing to do,' she said at last.

'I know and I am truly sorry.' He touched her arm lightly. The surge of excitement that zinged through her, made Anna flinch involuntarily. Tex took his hand away. 'There's something I wanna say to you. Something important I wanna tell you. I don't want you to say anything. Not today. Maybe you could have a think about what I'm about to say, and we could meet tomorrow when you're feeling better.'

Anna looked quizzically at him. 'Okay,' she said, putting her cup down. This sounded serious.

Chapter Thirty Two

So he loved her. He adored her and everything about her. Said he had never felt like this about anyone. She had been on his mind all the time, wondering where she was, what she was doing. He had missed her more than he thought was possible.

There was one thing he had said he needed to ask, about Mark. Had she slept with him? Anna had shaken her head. No, she hadn't slept with him and no, she didn't want to. The look of relief on Tex's face had been apparent, but almost immediately followed by a clouded look. Whatever it was that was holding her back, and he knew it was something to do with Mark, if only she could tell him, he was sure they could work things out. He said he could make her happy. They could be happy together.

He hadn't wanted to discuss it that morning. Said she was too hung-over and he needed to get to work. He wanted to meet her tomorrow, when she felt better and had had time to think things over. Really think about what he had said.

'All you have to do is trust me,' Tex had said tenderly. They had gone out onto the balcony for some much needed fresh air. Standing side by side, leaning on the railing, gazing out across the River Arun and the town beyond, he had turned to face her, gently turned her to look at him when he had said, 'I love you, Anna. Don't you ever forget that.'

Tex had brought Anna's car back from the restaurant for her, parking it in the underground car park. He popped back up with the keys, telling her to go home and get some sleep. He would see her tomorrow.

Anna had nodded. They had stood, awkwardly looking at each other for a moment. It had felt so wrong not having any physical contact. Spontaneously, Anna had put her arms around Tex's neck and hugged him, closing her eyes, feeling the warmth of his body against hers. Tex had hesitated before wrapping his arms around her and pulling her closer to him. They had stood there, clinging to each other, neither wanting to let go. It was Tex who had moved away first. He had stroked her face, smiled an almost sad smile, before turning away and heading off to work.

After Tex had left for the restaurant, she had stayed at the apartment for another two hours, dozing on and off, waiting for the worst of her hangover to subside, thinking about what he had said.

Just being with him again confirmed what she really knew all along. She wanted to be with him. Anna knew she had to be honest with Tex. She didn't want to lose him. He had thrown their relationship a lifeline and she wasn't going to let it slip away. She wanted to make things work between them. He had been honest with her. He hadn't stopped loving her. She couldn't ask for anyone more attentive, more considerate, more patient or more caring. She knew he loved her and, yes, she felt she could finally admit it to herself. She loved him. Anna Barnes loved Tex Garcia.

Admitting this, acknowledging this fact alone, made Anna feel as if the blanket of sadness that had swamped her in recent weeks had slipped from her shoulders. Her heart felt as if it would burst, not from pain as it had felt before, but with unconditional love. She was deeply in love and she was deeply loved.

She grinned to herself. 'Hello me!' she said out loud. She felt as if she had been re-awakened, kick-started back into life. It almost made her forget how hung-over she still felt.

'Oh, you decided to come home then.' Mark's voice was caustic.

Anna scowled at him, although it was no surprise to her that Mark wasn't particularly impressed with her staying out all night, but she hadn't quite expected him to be so cross.

'I don't have to answer to you, in case you'd forgotten,' she said airily. She ignored the surprised look on his face.

'No, maybe not,' replied Mark, 'but when me and Luke get in after being out all day and have no idea where you are, it's perfectly understandable that we may be concerned. Then all we get is a text saying you'd be home in the morning.'

Anna said a silent prayer of thanks that at least Tex had had the foresight to send a message from her phone, to cover for her. 'You knew I was fine, so what's the problem?'

'I expect you were too busy getting laid by lover boy,' sneered Mark.

'Don't start all that, Mark.' Anna went into the kitchen to make a cup of tea and hunt out a paracetamol. Her head was beginning to throb again, she could feel herself relapsing back into full hangover territory. She called back into the room, hoping her voice didn't betray her lie, albeit a white one. 'I wasn't well.'

'Whatever.' Mark appeared in the doorway. 'Don't give me all that. You were getting your knickers off.'

'You're so crude at times,' snapped Anna, 'usually when you're being spiteful and looking for an argument. Like now.'

'I'm not looking for a row actually,' countered Mark, stepping into the kitchen. 'I am pretty pissed off with you and your behaviour though. You're a thirty-five-year-old mother, not a rebellious teenager and yet you insist on behaving like one. What sort of example are you to our son?'

'You've got a nerve lecturing me about not being responsible.

I don't remember it being one of your strong points.'

'Why do you do that?'

'What?'

'Always bring up the past. You can't let it drop, can you? Every opportunity you get you bring it up.' Mark looked accusingly at her.

'So you admit you've been irresponsible in the past. Well, that's a first.'

'You're the one who's looking for a row. You're in a stinking mood,' scolded Mark. Then spitefully, 'Lover boy dump you?'

'Get lost, Mark.'

'Ooh! Touched a nerve, did I?' He was taunting her now.

Anna's response was intercepted by the bleeping of her phone with a message. She retrieved the mobile out of her bag in the living room. It was from Tex.

Hope you're okay. See you tomorrow. X

'So what exactly was wrong with you last night?' The sound of Mark's voice right behind her startled Anna. Christ, he was like a second shadow, every time she turned round he was there. She popped her phone back into her bag and brushed past him, marching back into the kitchen to finish making her cup of tea.

'I was sick, all right? ' Anna dropped the teabag into the bin. Would he ever shut up?

'You two arguing again?' Luke was now standing in the kitchen.

'Oh, hi, Luke.' Anna smiled at her son, disguising her thoughts. He'd better not start either. 'You okay?'

Luke grunted and nodded. Anna took that as a yes.

'I was just trying to find out from your mum exactly what the problem was last night.'

'For God's sake, Mark!' Anna's voice was louder than she meant it to be, she winced. That hurt her head. She closed her eyes for

268

a moment, waiting for the shooting pain to stop.

'Oh, I get it,' Mark said sarcastically. 'You were drunk, weren't you?'

'Give it a rest, Mark!' Anna could hear her voice rising involuntarily, despite her headache.

'I expect you were sick. Not from illness though, but from drink.' Mark looked very pleased with himself.

'You were out drinking?' Luke sounded surprised.

'Of course she was,' replied Mark before Anna had a chance to say anything. 'And she was out with whatshisname? The Yank.'

He was doing it on purpose.

'Tex,' Anna snapped. 'His name is Tex.'

'There, told you so. She's not denying it, is she?'

'Mum?' Luke looked questioningly at his mother.

'It's not quite like that,' began Anna. What could she say? Like Mark said, she couldn't actually deny it.

'No, no, of course it wasn't,' mocked Mark acidly. 'I expect it wasn't anything as sordid as a drunken night with your boyfriend. Well, not exactly your boyfriend, just your shag-friend.'

'Mark!' Anna looked indignantly at him. What was he thinking of, going through all this in front of Luke?

'Listen to you. Trying to sound all prim and proper. Don't like it that your son may find out what you're really like.' Outraged, Anna went to slap him but he grabbed her wrist in mid-air. 'Tut, tut, tut. Violence isn't the answer.' Mark thrust her hand away, then turning to Luke said, 'Sorry you're having to see your mother like this.'

'I hate you!' screamed Anna. 'Absolutely hate you! I can't wait until you clear off back to America. Even then, the other side of the Atlantic won't be far enough away.'

'Mum! Stop!' Alarmed, Luke stood between his parents.

'Yes, why don't you just stop, Anna?' chided Mark.

269

'Why don't you?' she shouted. 'Why don't you just stop making my life a misery? Why don't you just leave me alone? Forever!' She pushed her way past father and son and rushed upstairs, slamming the bedroom door and throwing herself onto the bed. Too angry to cry, she pounded the pillow with her fist.

Tex looked at his phone for the third time, rereading the message. He couldn't quite believe what Anna had sent him earlier.

Tex I dont want 2 c u any more dont contact me again its over from Anna

He passed the phone to Jamie, who held it so that Yvonne could read it at the same time.

'Ouch,' commented Yvonne.

'You can say that again.' Jamie slid the phone back across the desk to his friend. They were seated in the office of the Arundel restaurant, having been to a client's housewarming party in Brighton, and had called in on Tex on their way home. 'Must say, I'm surprised she did it by text. Didn't think that was her style.'

'Nor did I.' Tex flopped back in his chair. 'I thought I understood her. I obviously don't know her at all.'

'Have you tried talking to her?' asked Yvonne.

'What's the point? I think that message says it all very clearly.' Tex gestured accusingly towards his phone. 'Although another part of me says that something is wrong. I'm sure it is something to do with Mark, but I don't know what and Anna has never said.'

'Sounds to me like she can't make her mind up,' said Jamie. 'I don't mean to sound harsh and it's probably not what you want to hear, but maybe she was using you to make him jealous.'

'Jamie, you're supposed to be making him feel better, not worse,' frowned Yvonne.

'I'm also supposed to be his mate who tells him as it is,' corrected Jamie.

'It's okay, Yvonne,' sighed Tex. 'He's right to say that. And, yes, I had considered that she might wanna get back with him. To be honest, I don't know what to think any more.' He had totally misread the whole situation and how she felt about him. She must have gone home, back to Mark. She didn't have the nerve to meet him tomorrow and tell him in person, she didn't even have the decency to speak to him. 'I knew it wasn't gonna be straightforward, getting involved with her, but I think I have to admit defeat. I give up.'

'Anna! Anna!' yelled Mark from the bottom of the stairs.

What did he want now? What time was it even? She cursed, remembering she had left her watch at Tex's apartment. Judging by the chat show now on the telly, she guessed it was around midnight.

Anna peered down the stairwell at Mark. 'What?'

Before he had time to speak, she could tell from the look on his face that something was wrong.

'What is it?' Pulling her dressing gown around her, she hurried down the stairs.

'It's Luke. He's in St Richard's Hospital,' said Mark gravely. 'He's been drinking and collapsed. Suspected alcohol poisoning. They said his condition is serious but stable.'

Tears sprang to Anna's eyes. 'What does that mean?'

'I'm not a doctor. How should I know? Now get dressed. Go on, don't just stand there.'

Chapter Thirty Three

Alcohol poisoning. Tube in windpipe. Help breathing. Pump stomach. Monitor. Serious. Lucky. Dehydrated. Worst case scenario. Seizures. Brain damage.

The words swam round in Anna's head. She could see the doctor's mouth moving, hear that he was speaking, but the words weren't making sense. She couldn't take in what he was saying.

'Mrs Barnes?' The doctor looked at Anna.

'Come on, Anna. Get a grip,' said Mark impatiently, giving her shoulder a shake.

'Sorry.' Anna shook her head. Mark was right. She needed to focus, this was no time to get all flaky. 'What does it all mean exactly? In plain English. How is my son?' She ignored the tut from Mark.

'Mrs Barnes, your son is in a serious condition. He has drunk far in excess of the legal drink-drive limit. He has alcohol poisoning. When you see him, it may be a bit of a shock. We had to put a tube down his throat to flush out his stomach, to try to get as much alcohol out before it is absorbed. Severe cases of alcohol poisoning can lead to problems breathing, dehydration and possible brain damage.'

Anna closed her eyes. Please God, no.

'It's okay, Mrs Barnes, we're not at that stage yet. I'm confident that your son will make a full recovery, however, as I said, he has drunk an excessive amount of alcohol and it's not going to be a pleasant or easy few days.'

'Thank you, doctor,' said Anna. 'Can we see him?'

'Yes, come this way.' The doctor led them into a cubicle of the emergency treatment room.

'Oh, Luke,' gasped Anna, rushing to her son's bedside. The sight of him lying there looking lifeless, as a nurse took his blood pressure, made Anna feel physically sick from shock. Being told was one thing, but seeing her child in that condition, was another. Luke's lips were dry and puckered from lack of moisture, his skin pale, almost grey. His shirt had been cut open for speed. His favourite Fred Perry one, thought Anna randomly. She stroked his blonde hair and kissed his forehead. 'What have you done Luke?' she said bleakly.

Mark let out an incredulous huff. 'Obvious isn't it? Taken a leaf out of your book.' He glared at Anna for a moment before returning his gaze back to Luke.

'Not now, Mark. It's hardly the time or place for point scoring,' replied Anna stonily. She glanced over at the nurse, who carried on writing up her observations, appearing not to have heard the exchange of words. As if, thought Anna, but all the same was grateful for her discretion. The doctor left them alone, saying he'd come back later to check on Luke's progress.

Anna sat in silence by one side of the bed, clasping one of Luke's hand, willing him to make a recovery. Mark, on the other side of the bed, doing the same. Now and again a nurse came in to check Luke's blood pressure, pulse, and lift his eyelids to see if his pupils were responsive to the little hand-light she flashed across his eyes. Anna just sat there, feeling totally helpless, knowing there was nothing neither she nor Mark could do, it was totally out of their hands. Anna didn't know or care what the time was: time seemed to have no relevance. The hospital never slept, a constant revolving door of injured people, some worse than others, some accidental and some, like Luke, self-inflicted. Busy, busy, busy.

At some point during the night, the doctor came back to speak to them.

'The alcohol levels in his blood are still high, but they are showing signs of dropping. He's not out of the woods yet, but I'm confident that we have things under control.'

'Thank you, doctor,' replied Mark, standing up. 'Do you know if there will be any long-term damage? Has he done himself any lasting harm?'

'Unlikely, although we can't totally rule it out at this stage.' The doctor picked up the flip chart hanging on the end of the bed and flicked through the notes. 'There's been no respiratory problems or seizures and although he was extremely dehydrated, none of this leads me to believe there's been any brain damage. Once he's awake we will have a better idea, but I think it's safe to assume that he will make a full recovery. He's a strong, fit, young man, there's no reason why he won't come out of this with just a hangover.' The doctor gave a small smile before adding, 'That'll be one heck of a hangover.'

Heavy-eyed and groaning, Luke eventually came round, rolling over on his side and retching on a now empty stomach, and finally opening his eyes. Anna rushed back in with the nurse she had gone to fetch, and poured him a glass of water.

'Your throat's going to be a bit sore,' explained the nurse as she helped Luke to sit up.

Luke grunted before resting back on the pillows and closing his eyes. Silence descended again as the nurse went through her usual observational routine of blood pressure, pulse and pupil reaction.

'You'll live. Now, we'll be back soon to move you to a ward. We want to keep you in for a bit longer under observation. Need to do some more blood tests too, just to make sure everything is easing off.' Luke didn't respond. 'I think he's beginning to feel the after-effects already.'

With Luke now settled in the ward, sleeping off his hang-over, Mark drove Anna back home. It was nine-thirty on Sunday morning. Anna felt absolutely drained. Not only had she herself been recovering from the effects of overindulgence in the alcohol stakes, but she had not had any sleep. She closed her eyes. What a day! What a past thirty-six hours!

Suddenly, remembering she was supposed to be meeting Tex later, Anna sat up. There was no way she could see him today. She was absolutely shattered, and she needed to be back at the hospital with Luke. She fished around in her handbag, found her phone and sent Tex a quick message.

Sorry Tex but I can't come over today. Luke very drunk last night, ended up in hospital. He's okay but I need to be with him today. I'll be in touch later or tomorrow. Sorry, I really wanted to see you! X

She hoped he would understand. Talk about lousy timing!

'Anyone I know?' asked Mark, nodding towards her phone.

'Just Nathan,' lied Anna. Actually, that wasn't a bad idea to text Nathan and let him know. She rubbed her temples, trying to stave off the headache that was looming.

'You all right?' asked Mark.

'Yes, fine. Just tired.'

'You look pretty rough.'

'Thanks. You don't look that great yourself.'

'Granted. Look, why don't you have a shower and a sleep when we get in. I can go back with some clean clothes for Luke.' Anna looked at him in surprise. Mark smiled at her. 'It's all right, I'll phone you if there's anything to worry about, which I'm sure there won't be.'

'I don't know. I ought to go back and see him.'

'There's really no need us both being there. When I get back, you can go over if you like. That way, there's always someone with him, rather than us both being there some of the time.' Mark pulled up outside Coach House Cottages. 'It makes sense.'

Anna knew it made sense but it was reluctantly that she agreed to it. She felt uncomfortable with Mark's change in attitude towards her, her escapades and that of Luke's. In fact, he was being surprisingly pleasant, understanding and non-judgemental this morning. Very different to the cold, brutal, spiteful person of the previous evening.

Anna's suspicions were roused further when Mark made tea and toast for both of them and then said he was running her a bath. She needed to relax and could do so better in a bath than in a shower.

'Bath's run,' he announced as he came back downstairs.

'Thanks. You're being very nice to me,' said Anna. She couldn't help herself. 'What are you after?'

Mark came and sat down next to her on the sofa, running his fingers across his eyebrows, a pained expression settling across his face. 'It frightened me. Luke. Last night. Sitting there with him, I couldn't help thinking what if he didn't make it. What if he didn't recover or recover fully? The thought terrified me. I could have lost him last night. Lost him, when I had only really just found him.' Mark sank back into the sofa and rested his head against the backrest. 'All I kept thinking was please let him pull through so I have the chance to make it up to him. I've made such a fuck up of being his dad. In fact, I've made a pretty lousy job at everything. Not just being a dad... but being a husband too.

This time Anna didn't reply. He was unnerving her, this change in attitude. Despite the feeling of exhaustion that was gradually seeping through her, her mind was alert. Maybe this was her chance to get the photos back. Instead of making him her enemy, maybe she should make him her ally, or at least allow him to think so. He might be more willing to give her the photos that way. She swallowed hard and forced herself to reach out for his hand.

'We've both made mistakes,' she said. 'Neither of us have been perfect.' She felt him give a small squeeze of her hand.

'Generous as always. Go and have your bath. Get into bed and get some sleep. I'll take Luke some clean clothes and give you a ring later. Go on.'

The message tone bleeping on her phone brought Anna out of her sleep. Leaning over to the bedside table she picked it up and opened the message box, half expecting it to be from Tex or Mark. No, neither. Some random text from someone who wasn't in her contact list as it just came up with 'unknown caller' and a phone number.

Who is this?

Anna deleted it. She couldn't be bothered to answer, it was obviously just someone sending her the text by mistake. Before she could ponder it any further, there was a knock at the front door. Pulling a sweatshirt on, Anna went downstairs to open the door. She was greeted by Zoe, concern across her face.

'Oh, Anna, how is everything? Mark phoned and told me Luke was in hospital with alcohol poisoning. He asked if I could call over and check you were okay.'

Anna raised her eyebrows. 'That's very unlike Mark to be so thoughtful.'

In need of fresh air, the two women decided to go for a walk along the footpath that circulated Priory Park and Anna brought

Zoe up to speed on how Luke was.

'I'm so glad you came,' said Anna, linking her arm through Zoe's.

'Nathan wanted to, but I persuaded him to let me come,' said Zoe. 'He's looking after the kids but sends his love, and says that it goes without saying but if you want anything, you only have to ring him.'

'I know. Tell him thank you. I'll ring him later anyway, when I know a bit more about how Luke is and what's happening.'

'He wanted to go to the hospital himself but didn't particularly want to bump into Mark. He'll come over though, maybe when Mark's not about. Said he wanted to see Luke himself, and you.' They followed the path as it rose up to the level of the city walls.

'That's fine. I'll sort it out with him.' Anna smiled at Zoe.

'So was Luke at a party or something and overdid it, trying to impress the girls?' asked Zoe.

'I wish it were as straightforward as that,' sighed Anna. 'Me and Mark had an argument last night and Luke was pretty fed up. Went out to his mate's house and they decided to raid the drinks cupboard while the parents were out. The other lad, fortunately, wasn't as bad as Luke and had the sense to ring his parents when Luke collapsed.'

'Oh, how awful,' consoled Zoe.

'The parents called an ambulance. The father went with Luke and waited to speak to Mark. I actually don't remember that. I was so upset by it all. I remember Mark talking to this man while we were waiting for the doctor to come and see us, but I had no idea who he was or what they were saying.'

Anna's phone interrupted. It was Mark. Luke was awake and apparently feeling like he was actually dead. He felt sick. His head hurt just to move his eyes, let alone his head itself. His throat felt like someone had put razor blades in it, and his hand was sore from the drip they had put in to rehydrate his body fluids. Apart from that Luke was fine!

'They're keeping him in until this evening at least,' explained Anna to Zoe, slipping her phone back into her pocket. 'They want to make sure his fluid levels are okay. Don't think he'll be drinking again for a while.'

'Must have been a bad argument for him to react like that.'

Anna looked at Zoe and nodded. 'It's a long story.'

'Well, I'm in no rush,' smiled Zoe, giving Anna's hand a squeeze.

Anna checked her phone yet again. Still no word from Tex. Initially she had thought it a bit odd, but with all that was going on, she hadn't had too much time to dwell on his lack of contact. However, it was now Monday afternoon and he still hadn't so much as acknowledged her text. She had sent another this morning, just in case he was holding off until things with Luke were a bit more settled. She had messaged him to say that Luke was coming home that afternoon, and suggested that she and Tex meet during the week. Perhaps she would try and actually call him this evening and speak to him.

'Luke's sleeping again,' said Mark as he came into the kitchen.

'That's good. He seems a bit quiet. Is he okay?'

'Yeah, he's fine. I think he actually feels embarrassed that a) he can't handle the booze and b) he's caused us all this worry and upset.' Mark filled the kettle. 'Cup of tea?'

'Thanks.' Anna watched Mark potter around getting the cups ready. There was a different atmosphere between her and Mark now. She still couldn't be sure if Mark was being genuine though. Was he playing a game just as she was?

Mark put the cup of tea down in front of her. 'Have you got work this week?'

'No. Well, I should have but I left a message on Jamie's answerphone to say I needed this week off due to family problems. I didn't go into detail and he hasn't rung back, so I'm assuming it's okay.' Anna took a sip of her tea. 'I had already booked next week off because I knew I'd be busy with the move.'

'Have you got much packing left to do?' asked Mark.

Anna eyed the stack of taped-up boxes that had been gradually increasing over the last few weeks. All very organised, labelled in black marker pen with their contents and what room they would be going into at the new flat.

'All pretty much done, except for the kitchen things, bathroom stuff and clothes that I can't really do until the last minute. Just hope I can fit it all in. The new flat is quite small.'

'You'll be okay.'

'I have been quite ruthless and been getting rid of lots of stuff that I don't actually use or need. It's surprising how much you can do without when you put your mind to it.' Anna faked a grin.

'I'm sorry,' said Mark quietly, not looking at Anna but sitting down opposite her at the table.

'Sorry? What for?'

'The house sale. The other night when we argued. What I said.' He looked up at Anna and let out a long sigh. 'Being a pig. Letting you down. Everything.'

Anna was taken aback. She hadn't expected this, Mark apologising, and he really did seem genuine.

He gave her a small smile. 'I would say don't look so surprised, but I guess you've got every reason to be.' He reached across and held her hand. 'I am sorry, Annie. For everything. *Everything.*'

For a moment Anna looked down at his hand around hers, swallowing an unexpected lump that had come to her throat. 'We did try, didn't we?' she said, her voice full of sadness.

'You did. You tried really hard. I should have tried harder.' Mark's voice was tender but the shame and regret was etched all over his face. He sounded truly sincere. He held her hand tighter.

'I did love you, I really did Anna. I think I just loved myself more.'

'We were both young, Mark. Very young. Neither of us were ready for the responsibility of being married and having a child. Don't get me wrong, I wouldn't change anything. How could I? Out of all of this sorry mess we had Luke. We still have him. Thank God.'

'I know. That's what I was trying to say that night after the hospital. The realisation of what happened to Luke, the thought of what could have happened to him, brought it all home to me. It's made me see things clearer. It wasn't just the shock of that night, I've felt like this ever since. It wasn't just a knee-jerk reaction, I promise. It put everything into perspective. I realise now how lucky I am to have him. I really regret not being there for him. Not just the last year while I've been in the States, but all the time. I never really put him or you first. I am sorry.' Mark blinked back the tears that threatened to escape. 'I'm going to make it up to him. I'm going to be there for him. I'm not going to let him down again. I wish we could have been a proper family.'

Anna nodded sadly. The remorse was real. It had been all she had wanted when Luke was born. To be a happy family, the three of them. Now she had the opportunity to say it, she knew she couldn't let it pass. This was about more than just the photos now. This was about redemption and atonement. 'I suppose the one thing that defined us as a family, Luke, ultimately wasn't strong enough to keep us together. There were too many differences and pressures for us to work as a couple. We didn't make a very good team.'

'That was mostly my fault,' conceded Mark. 'I could have tried harder but I didn't. I reacted badly to being a father so young. All the other lads my age at the club, they were out having fun. I wanted to be part of that. I didn't want to sit at home with a baby. I think, in a way, I was punishing you by seeing other women.'

'That's what I mean, we were young and emotionally ill-equipped to be married with a child. We hardly had any time together, just you and me. Hardly any time to get to know each other. That's not to say, we didn't have fun and enjoy ourselves, for a short time.' It was so long ago, it seemed like another lifetime.

'And then after the accident, I blamed you for that too.' Mark held his head in his hands, stopping for a moment to regain his composure. 'I punished you in the way I knew would hurt you most. Instead of being there for you, helping you cope with your loss, our loss. The baby, our child...' Mark's voice tailed off. He kept his head in his hands.

Anna wiped away the tears that were trickling down her face. It was the first time he had ever really acknowledged the baby they had lost. He had practically dismissed it at the time of the accident, so wrapped up in his own drama, his broken leg that meant he was out of football, not just for six months or a year, but out of the game forever. Too severe an injury to fully recover from and be the athlete he once was.

'Don't blame yourself for everything,' said Anna at last. 'If I'm being totally honest, I could have tried harder too. When things got bad, I didn't try and work the problems through. I knew you were with other women and I just let you. I didn't even confront you about them after the accident. It was easier that way. I put all my love and attention onto Luke instead. He became the focal point for my emotions. My passiveness towards you and what you were doing, well, that just allowed you to carry on. I'm sorry. So very sorry.'

Anna knew in her heart of hearts that this was true. In the end, she had simply given up on their marriage. In fact, it had been easier that way, not having to care about what he was doing. It had been her defence mechanism to stop her from getting hurt any more than she already was.

'I wonder how long we would have carried on like that if the

282

offer to work in the States hadn't come through?' Mark gave a weak smile. It didn't hide the sadness Anna saw in his eyes.

She shrugged. 'Who knows?'

'Even when I bought this house for you, I was still punishing you. By me owning it, I could still keep tabs on you. Still be in control,' admitted Mark. 'That way I still had a reason to be in touch. When I came back earlier in the year, I knew I had to sell the house, but I also realised I wasn't ready to let you go. That's why I've been...' He paused, as if searching for the right phrase.

'Difficult?' Anna filled in the gap.

'Yeah, difficult,' nodded Mark. 'Difficult about you and Tex. I'm sorry for that too. You deserve to find someone who really loves you. Someone who won't hurt you.'

It wasn't the time for Anna to disagree with Mark about Tex. She'd have to sort that out herself later. She pushed the thought of Tex away.

'It's okay, Mark. It's time to let go. If it's forgiveness you're looking for, then I do forgive you.' She did forgive him for what had happened in their marriage. However, the photos were another matter.

'Thank you,' said Mark. It was almost a whisper. The smile now grateful. 'I know I can't make it up to you now, I know it's too late, but I am definitely going to make it up to Luke.'

Anna smiled. 'Being there for Luke is the best way you could possibly make it up to me. All the heartache and sadness we've caused each other has to have a reason, a purpose. It's not too late to put things right with Luke. Be there for him. Be his dad.'

'I will. I promise,' said Mark sincerely.

Anna sat in silence as she took in and finally understood how their relationship had worked, or not worked, as was the case. Finally admitting to each other where they had gone wrong, the things they could have done better, should have done better.

Offering and accepting apologies. Seeking and receiving redemption and resolution. Cleansing the soul of their volatile relationship.

Anna broke the silence first. 'Mark, about those photos.' She hoped she had picked the right moment. He seemed conciliatory and reasonable.

Mark looked up at her and went to speak, then shut his mouth again. Anna could feel herself tense. Had she misjudged him? She tried again, this time more steely. 'You did say if I agreed to the house sale I could have them back. Mark?'

'I said I wouldn't send them out, not that you could have them back.' He sounded shifty. He looked shifty.

Why did she expect anything else? 'You're a bastard, you know that?'

Chapter Thirty Four

Luke continued to improve and feel better as the week went on, although any mention of alcohol still managed to turn his stomach.

'I think he's learnt his lesson,' said Anna light-heartedly as she sat in the Fish and Fly with Zoe. 'Mind you, I'm not much better. I don't fancy anything alcoholic myself.' She swirled the diet Coke round in her glass.

'And you and Mark have finally sorted things out?'

'Sort of.'

'What does that mean?'

Anna closed her eyes for a moment to gather her thoughts. 'I suppose it doesn't matter now if I tell you.'

'Tell me what?'

'Apart from threatening to try and ruin Tex's business and not agree to a divorce, Mark had something else he was using against me.'

'I knew it!' snapped Zoe. 'I knew there must be something else. What's he been up to now?'

And so Anna told her sister-in-law about the photos, and how even though she had gone along with everything, he still wouldn't give them to her. 'I just can't get past that. I don't understand what's going on in his mind.'

'What do you think he'll do with them?'

Anna shrugged. 'I don't really know what use they are to him now. He's got everything he wants from me, and even managed to get rid of Tex in a roundabout sort of way.'

'Still not heard from him?' enquired Zoe gently.

Anna shook her head. 'No. Seems when things got tough it frightened him off. I should have expected it really. He's not the settling down type. Too many ghosts. I've tried ringing him but his phone is switched off. He must be avoiding me.'

'I honestly didn't think he'd be like that,' mused Zoe, sipping her wine. 'It seems out of character, if you ask me. He always seemed so decent.'

'I don't want to talk about it.' Anna dropped her gaze, drawing imaginary circles with her finger on the tabletop. 'Let's change the subject. How are things with you and Nathan?'

'Much better, thanks.' Zoe took another sip of her wine. 'All this business with Luke has given us both a kick up the backside. We've talked a lot over the last few days. We've been honest and open and realised how much we still love each other, and how important the children are to us.'

'I'm really pleased,' said Anna earnestly. 'I've been worried about you two.'

'We're going to make a proper effort, both of us. Nathan is going to reschedule his diary so that he has two consecutive days at home a week. Me, I'm going to stop trying to do everything myself and let my mum take Emily two mornings a week.'

'Oh, Zoe, that's brilliant. Your mum will love looking after her. It will give you some me-time.'

'I know, and I've already started sorting myself out. No more trackies, which have been more like a tattoo on me recently. I'm joining that slimming class I keep meaning to. Also, Saturday evenings are going to be time for just me and Nathan. Our time.

Even if we don't go out, we're going to try and keep the time just for each other.' Zoe gave an embarrassed smirk.

'Excellent. If you ever want a babysitter on a Saturday, just give me a shout.'

'Thank you. Anyway, enough of that. How's the house packing going? You all set for next week?'

'Pretty much,' replied Anna. 'I get the keys on Monday. I'll be sad to say goodbye to the house but it's for the best. I'll be able to wipe the slate clean of everything and start again. I'm really looking forward to it.' The fake smile and overenthusiastic raising of her glass of Coke as a toast didn't convince her.

Anna sat on the sofa looking stunned at the announcement Mark had just made. Luke wanted to go to America with his dad on Friday. That, in itself, wasn't the shock, and under any other circumstances Anna would have been delighted. Only, Luke didn't want to go for just a week, or even two weeks, as a holiday, he wanted to go for six months.

'It's bit sudden isn't it?' asked Anna, trying not to sound as shocked as she felt.

'We've been thinking about it since Luke came home last week. We just wanted to make sure it was definitely what we wanted before we spoke to you.'

Not known for his tact, Mark was at least trying to be more empathetic and understanding, acknowledged Anna.

'What about your A levels?' Anna looked at Luke, who so far had let his dad do the talking.

Luke looked up from the floor he had been focused on throughout the conversation, obviously uneasy himself with how his mum would react. 'I could just put them back a year.'

'There's nothing to stop Luke studying over there,' said Mark. 'He could help at the academy too, gain some coaching qualifications.' He paused and looked at Luke questioningly. Luke nodded. Mark continued, this time even more gently. 'He might like it out there and want to stay a bit longer. Maybe go to uni, or college as it's called in the States.'

'Move out there permanently?' God where did that come from? One minute they were talking about six months, the next forever!

'It's early days, just a thought really,' said Mark, coming to sit beside Anna. He put his arm around her shoulder and gave her a squeeze. 'Let's cross that bridge if, and when, we get to it.'

Anna got up, moving away from Mark. She knew he had been trying all week to be more considerate and thoughtful, so much so that a few times she had been reminded of the man she had married. However, the thought of the photos that he refused to give up was a great counter-emotion.

As for Luke going to the States, it was a bittersweet pill, that was for sure. Anna was so pleased for Luke that Mark had finally made that bond with their son but, ironically, that bond was now threatening to take her son to the other side of the Atlantic.

'I can easily come back in the holidays. It's not like I'm never going to see you again,' said Luke enthusiastically. 'We can see and speak to each other on Skype all the time. Email. Text. It'll be just like I'm here really.' Anna didn't look convinced, so Luke tried another tactic. 'If I stayed here, did my A levels and was then going to uni in somewhere like Manchester or, I dunno, Wales or Cornwall, anywhere like that, you wouldn't object. It's just the same really.'

In a small, reasonable part of her mind, Anna knew that Luke was right. 'It's just so far away,' she said weakly. She let out a sigh. 'I'm okay about it really. I just didn't have any inkling that you wanted to go. I'm pleased you and your dad are getting on so much better. Really, I am. I'll just miss you, that's all.'

'I know. I'll miss you too, Mum.'

Face pressed against the window, hands cupped to block out the reflection, Tex tried to see through a chink in the closed Venetian blinds of 2 Coach House Cottages. No good, he couldn't see anything, it was too dark inside. He banged on the door for a third time and leaned on the bell. No answer. Surely there would be someone in at nine o'clock on a Sunday morning.

'What's all this noise about?' Mrs Meekham appeared on her path, looking over the garden to her neighbour's property. 'Oh, it's you.'

'Good morning, Ma'am,' replied Tex politely. He really didn't need nosey Mrs Meekham right now. 'Sorry if I disturbed you.'

'If it's Anna you're after, then you're wasting your time,' said Mrs Meekham, folding her arms.

Tex stopped trying to look through the letterbox, and walked across the little paved front garden to the boundary hedge between the two properties. 'Is she out?'

'You could say that,' said Mrs Meekham, revelling in being the holder of crucial information. 'They're all gone. All three of them.'

'All three of them?' echoed Tex.

'Yes. Mark, Anna and Luke. They've all gone. To America.' Mrs Meekham gave a nod of her head, as if confirming what she was saying.

'To America?' Tex couldn't quite comprehend what she was saying.

'So I believe,' said Mrs Meekham. 'New family moving in on Monday. You've only just missed the Barnes's, they went on Friday.'

'Are you sure?' Tex ignored the irritated feeling that shot through him on hearing them referred to as a family unit.

'I may be old but I haven't lost my marbles yet,' scolded Mrs Meekham. 'Told me himself did young Luke. They were moving to America. Anyway, can't stand here gossiping, I've got things to do. Cheerio.'

Tex felt his gut twist. He had been so sure last week that Anna would turn up on Sunday. That she had finally accepted how much he loved her, and he had been equally sure that she would realise she loved him too. At least he thought she did.

As if on autopilot, Tex drove away from the house, away from Mrs Meekham's twitching curtain. He only made it around the corner before he had to pull over. Holding on to the top of the steering wheel, he rested his head on his hands, closing his eyes. This wasn't supposed to happen. She wasn't supposed to go back to Mark. She certainly wasn't supposed to go to America. Tex sat upright, still holding on to the wheel, his arms locking at full stretch. The tension ran from his neck, through his shoulders, down the length of his arms, causing his fingers to curl and uncurl around the steering wheel.

'Fuck it!' he shouted out loud, and with a clenched fist, thumped the inside of the door. Taking a long, deep breath and exhaling slowly, Tex struggled to keep his anger and frustration under control. He needed to think straight. He closed his eyes, dragging his hand down across his face, rubbing his chin, trying to clear his mind and block out the feeling of loss. It was painful, too painful. Just when he thought he had her back, she had slipped from his grasp, like a child desperately trying to grab the string of a helium-filled balloon as it lifted into the sky, up and away, never to be seen again.

The bleeping of his phone brought him out of his thoughts. A message. Anna? He rummaged in his jacket that was lying on the passenger seat and pulled out his phone. No, of course it wouldn't be her. She was in America. With her husband! Just thinking of Mark being her husband made Tex's face contort into a snarl. He looked at his phone. Jamie.

You all right mate? Fancy coming over for brunch?

He wasn't in the mood for being social. In fact, he hadn't been in the mood all week, brooding over Anna and her lack of contact. He had tried ringing her on Thursday, but it had just gone to voicemail. Perhaps he should have left a message, but it had seemed so impersonal, an automated voice telling him to speak after the tone. He needed to speak to her in person. He just wished he could see her one more time. Touch her. Hold her. Tell her how much he loved her.

Tex shook his head. What was he thinking of? He had done all that on Saturday at his apartment. What good had that done? Built his hopes up, only to have them dropped from an enormous height. His hopes free-falling without a parachute. Hitting the ground. Decimated.

He phoned Jamie. Not that he really wanted brunch but he needed to ask him if he knew anything about Anna going to America.

'Sorry, mate, I thought you knew,' said Jamie apologetically. 'She's resigned. Sent me a letter by post.'

'What did it say?'

'Just that she had to resign with immediate effect due to personal reasons. Why? What's up?'

'She's gone to America. With *him*.' The bitterness was all too apparent.

'Ouch!'

Tex could hear Yvonne's voice in the background. 'Make sure he comes over.' Then down the telephone she called directly to him, 'You get yourself over here now, Tex. No brooding on your own. Understand?'

'Yes,' he sighed before hanging up.

He reached for his jacket again to put his phone away and heard a jangle in his pocket. Anna's watch. He took the watch out and held it across his fingers, rubbing the face with his thumb. This was the closest he was going to get to her. He was going to give it back to her today. That and the envelope sitting on the passenger seat.

Tex looked at the watch. What was the point in keeping it? A painful reminder. He didn't know where to send it, and if she was in America, would she ever get it? Then a thought struck him. Jamie would have to wait a bit longer.

'She's not here,' said Zoe after a few seconds' hesitation.

'I know,' replied Tex. 'Can I come in?'

'You can, although these days my breakfast meetings usually consist of Coco Pops, riot control and baby winding.' Zoe stood back, holding the door wide open. 'As it happens, Nathan has taken the boys swimming this morning so I have a relatively free window, apart from Emily, that is. Come in.'

Tex stepped into the hall and waited while she closed the door, then followed her down to the kitchen.

'Coffee? I can't do an espresso but I can do a black coffee.'

Tex nodded. 'Black will be fine. Thank you.'

Radio 2 played in the background, the presenter relaying messages of love. Bob wanted to tell his gorgeous wife Judy how much he loved her, and how happy he had been for the past twenty-five years. Jessica, who was looking forward to seeing her boyfriend today, wanted to wish him happy birthday and tell him he was the love of her life.

Great, just what he needed. Tex closed his eyes momentarily.

'So?' said Zoe, putting the black coffee down in front of him.

Tex took the watch from his pocket, and together with the large envelope he had been holding, slid them across the table to Zoe. 'Can you make sure Anna gets these?' He wondered if he looked as fatigued as he sounded. He couldn't sum up the energy or enthusiasm to even pretend to be upbeat.

Zoe looked at the watch and envelope over the rim of her coffee cup. 'I can, but why don't you do it yourself?'

'I don't know her address.' Tex hadn't meant to sound quite as bitter as he did. His emotions were swinging wildly, from a deep sense of loss to a bubbling anger and all the feelings in between.

'I can tell you where she is,' began Zoe, before being cut off by Tex.

'No. I do not want to know the details.' Tex took a mouthful of the coffee; it wasn't particularly pleasant, but he didn't really care. He spoke again, this time more gently. 'How is she? Have you heard from her?'

Zoe studied Tex's face for a moment. 'She's okay. I haven't spoken to her since she moved but she did send me a message to say she was settling in.'

'Is she happy?'

'What do you want me to say?' sighed Zoe. 'Do you want me to say that she's fed up and miserable or that she's happy and content?'

Tex screwed his eyes up and rubbed his temples. A bit of straight-talking wouldn't go amiss.

Zoe continued. 'Why don't you ask her yourself?'

'What is the point? She obviously doesn't want to speak to me.'

'What makes you say that?'

'Standing me up. Ignoring my calls. Moving to America. I get the message, loud and clear!' Tex could feel the frustration zipping through every part of his body. Zoe was looking at him as if he was talking another language.

'Whooaaa! Wait a minute, Tex,' said Zoe, frowning and holding her hands up. 'Just run that by me again.'

'Forget it,' snapped Tex. He should go. This conversation was just making him more frustrated. He needed to be alone. He really wasn't good company. He stood up to leave. 'Just make sure Anna gets the stuff, please.'

'Anna hasn't gone to America,' said Zoe evenly. She raised her eyebrows slightly and nodded towards the chair.

Obediently, he sat back down again. 'She's not in America?'

'No. Not at all. She's still here in the UK. Still here in Chichester in actual fact.' Zoe crossed her arms in front of her, cocking her head slightly to the left. Another raised eyebrow look.

Tex looked at her, trying to decipher the meaning of the subtly placed eyebrows. They seemed to be saying 'what do you think to that then?' What did he think? He wasn't sure, but he was aware that his heart had done a three-sixty flip.

'But her neighbour, Mrs Meekham. She said they had gone to America. Luke had told her.'

'Luke and Mark have gone to America. Anna hasn't.'

A moment of relief, quickly replaced by the feeling of his heart now dropping to the pit of his stomach. 'She didn't turn up on Sunday. Sent me a message.'

'Under the circumstances, it's hardly surprising. I think you're being unreasonable.'

Tex shook his head. 'What circumstances?' He fished out his phone and scrolled through his text messages, finding the one from Anna. 'I don't think I am being unreasonable.' He handed the phone over to Zoe. She read the text a couple of times, pursing her lips and tapping the table slowly with her fingernail.

'Anna sent you this?'

Tex nodded.

'Did she ring or text you again?'

A shake of the head this time.

'And did you try to contact her?'

'Once. It went to voicemail. Obviously she didn't want to speak to me.'

'And you didn't leave a message?'

'No.' Tex felt like he was being cross-examined by the Counsel for the Defense. Any minute now Zoe would shout 'Just answer the question. Yes or no?' or 'Objection!' or maybe 'Do you honestly expect the court to believe…'

'So you received a text from Anna, dumping you in effect?' Zoe was summing up. 'You received no further contact from her, and you only tried to contact her once.'

Tex opened his hands, palms up, before dropping them back to the table. No words needed.

'Did you notice anything strange about the text?'

Bewildered, Tex shrugged. Zoe was in full courtroom mode, leading him down a path which he had absolutely no idea where it went. The only certainty was that the Defense Counsel was about to trip him up or state the blatantly obvious, dismissing his version of events.

'Look at the text, Tex. When has Anna ever sent a message in shorthand?' She paused. Obligingly, Tex shrugged. 'Never, is the answer,' said Zoe. 'Anna always texts in full. *To* is never the number two. *You* is never the letter u. Come on, Tex. It's obvious. Anna didn't send that message.'

Tex felt like his heart was on a yo-yo string. Shooting up one minute, dropping the next. Case dismissed? Not quite. 'Why didn't she turn up on Sunday then?'

'Luke ended up in hospital. She spent Saturday night there and most of Sunday morning. He had alcohol poisoning. She couldn't just leave him.'

'But he's okay now? I mean, if he's gone to the States.'

'Yes. He's fine.'

'She hasn't contacted me though.' No matter what explanations Zoe could offer, Tex couldn't get away from the fact that Anna had neither turned up nor tried to contact him at all.

'Not for lack of trying. She's adamant that she sent a message and phoned you, but you didn't reply.' Zoe frowned. 'Look, something's not right, I don't know what it is but it all sounds a bit odd.' She paused for a minute, holding Tex's gaze, then nodding, as if coming to a decision. 'Look, there's something you should know. Anna made me promise not to say anything but I think that promise has been overtaken by events. I'll make you another coffee.'

Tex politely sipped his second, equally unpalatable, coffee as Zoe told him about Mark's blackmailing scheme. Tex shook his head, mumbling expletives directed at Mark and exasperations towards Anna.

'She should have told me,' he groaned. What a mess. He could have put it all right in an instant. He should have told her about Mark blackmailing him. They could have sorted it out together, sooner. It hadn't needed to come to this.

'You all right, Tex?'

'Yeah, I'm good. Everything is falling into place now.' He regarded the envelope. 'The photos are in there.'

The incredulous look on Zoe's face warranted an explanation. 'Mark was blackmailing me too. Looks liked he played us both for jerks.'

'Neither of you two told the other? How come you ended up with the photos?'

Tex exhaled. 'Trade-off. He's got secrets of his own, you know. Looks like he's had the last laugh though, sending that message.'

'It would be typically spiteful of Mark to do that.'

'But what I don't understand is why Anna didn't contact me during the week.'

'She told me she did. Sent you several texts. Tried to phone you a couple of times but your phone was always switched off. She thought you didn't want anything to do with her.'

'My phone is never off. She knows that.'

'I'm only telling you what she told me,' sighed Zoe. She leant back in the chair and absently pulled her hair into a ponytail before letting it drop back down. 'I don't understand either. Why don't you just ring her now?'

There was nothing Tex wanted to do more than to ring Anna. To see her. To take her in his arms and tell her everything would be all right. That there had been a misunderstanding. He was there to make things better. But instead, he shook his head slowly. Sad eyes looking across the table at Zoe.

'No. I'm not gonna ring her.' Now it was Zoe's turn to look confused. 'She needs to ring me.'

'Isn't that a bit childish?'

'Not at all. Look, she's been under a lot of pressure. I don't want to add to that, make her feel she owes me something. Just give her the envelope; I've put a note in, there's other stuff there too. She may not take too kindly to my interfering. If she wants me, she'll know where to find me. But it has to be because it's what she wants.'

'You're making this very difficult,' said Zoe, a slightly impatient tone creeping in.

'Please give her the stuff, and tell her just to remember what I said the last time I saw her.' Tex stood up. 'Thank you for the coffee.'

'So where will you be? How can she get hold of you?'

'She will find a way. If she really wants to.'

Chapter Thirty Five

Anna rummaged around in yet another box, in what was increasingly becoming a futile effort to find her phone charger. It was a cardboard box with the words 'work files' written across it in black marker pen. Huh! Work files, that was a laugh, she didn't exactly have a heap of it. Not since she'd resigned from Jamie's company. At the time it had seemed the only option. She couldn't face the possibility of bumping into Tex unexpectedly. Okay, it was a slim chance, but a chance all the same she wasn't prepared to take. She had to be strong now and focused. Seeing Tex had the potential to totally unnerve her.

However, the reality of resigning meant that she needed to find a new job. Thank goodness she hadn't burnt all her bridges with the translation company. Boring as it was, translating electronic manuals and property contracts was a steady income. Mark had given her some money from the house sale which, although unexpected, he had insisted upon, and she had been grateful. It took the immediate financial pressure off her, but she was responsible for paying her own rent now and she needed to be careful.

Anna closed up the work box. Her phone charger wasn't in there. Where on earth had she put the blasted thing? She'd charged her phone Friday night, leaving it in the sitting room of her new flat, but couldn't remember seeing it since. She was beginning to think it must have been scooped up with the rubbish from unpacking some of the boxes. The rubbish that was now in the communal wheelie bin downstairs. She didn't relish the thought of searching through everyone's thrown out potato peelings, leftover curry and yucky nappies just to find her phone charger.

It was now Monday and her phone had been dead since Saturday night. Anna hadn't needed to make any calls and was working on the principle that if anyone wanted to get hold of her, they would either ring back, hopefully when she'd found her charger, or they'd ring Nathan, to get him to pass on a message. Failing that, they'd come round to the flat. She'd give it until tomorrow and if the charger still hadn't turned up, well, she couldn't face the neighbours' rubbish, so she'd just have to buy a new one.

Wandering into the kitchen, Anna opened the small cardboard box that she had left on the end of the worktop. In it were a few tins and packet sauces, pasta, and a few jars that needed putting away. Luke had packed this box for her, the last-minute clearing of the kitchen cupboards at Coach House Cottages. Without much enthusiasm, she began putting them away. A tin of baked beans, Heinz of course, packet cheese and broccoli pasta, handy in an emergency, a pot noodle, yuk. Throw that out. Luke liked them but no one else did. A tin of tuna, great for baked potatoes, peanut butter, crunchy, a jar of olives. Not just any jar, but *the* jar of olives that Tex had bought. Two weeks of an olive a day and she had to admit she was actually getting used to the taste. Couldn't say she liked them, not quite, but they weren't making her screw her nose up when she popped one in her mouth any more.

The familiar pang of loss poked its sharp fingers into her heart as a wave of sadness swamped her, the olives taking her back to that wonderful week at the ranch with Tex. Anna's grip on the jar tightened. She paused. Somewhere in the back of her mind a little voice of reason was trying to make itself heard. She ignored it and held the jar to her chest with one hand, the other hand on top of the lid, then closed her eyes and leaned back on the worktop, before sliding down to the floor in a heap, the tears racing each other down her face. This was as close to Tex as she could get. All that she had left of him.

After a few minutes the voice of reason was finally making itself heard. Yes, she must pull herself together. Banish all thoughts of Tex. She needed to look forward, not back. Still, she couldn't help herself kissing the lid of the jar before dropping it into the pedal bin.

Creek Cottage, that in the past had always brought Tex peace and contentment, seemed to have lost its magic. He'd been here since Monday, having caught a flight over straight after what turned out to be lunch with Jamie and Yvonne. Usually, once he was here, any worries or concerns seemed to pale into insignificance, but not this time.

He took his black coffee outside, sitting on the wooden steps that rose to the front door. It was another hot September evening, even though the sun was just starting to dip behind the trees. Tomorrow he'd ring the UK and check everything was running smoothly at both restaurants. He knew the Guildford one was able to operate extremely smoothly without him, but he had always been close on hand to the Arundel restaurant. This would be a real test. Bookings had steadied out now after the initial surge of opening and it was running according to the business projections, so that wasn't a worry for Tex. It was just whether the staff would rise to the challenge of keeping up the high standards. He had faith in his restaurant manager and, to be honest, there was not a lot he could do about it here in Brenham.

His mind turned to other things. Well, one other thing. A person. A person who seemed to be occupying his mind pretty much all the time. Anna. The feeling that he had a lead weight chained to his heart, dragging it down continually, had been with him for so long now he couldn't remember what it felt like to be carefree and happy. Maybe coming to home hadn't been a great idea after all. It just reminded him of the last time he was here with Anna.

'Halle-bloody-lujah!' cried Zoe. 'You're a difficult one to get hold of.'

'Could say the same about you,' replied Anna, wedging her mobile between her chin and shoulder as she peeled an orange. 'How are you feeling? Better?'

'Better than what I was, but not exactly one hundred per cent. Having said that, a stomach bug does wonders for the old waistline.'

'Poor you. I called round the other day.' Anna dropped the peel into the bin and began breaking the orange up into individual segments. 'You were fast asleep and your mum seemed to have everything under control, so I didn't stay.'

'She's been an angel. Actually, Nathan has been pretty good too,' said Zoe appreciatively. 'I'm convinced it was something I ate at that anniversary party I went to at the weekend.'

'Well, if there's anything you need, just give me a shout.' Anna readjusted the phone that was threatening to slip from her shoulder.

'Actually, I need to speak to you about something. I did try to get hold of you on Sunday but your phone went straight to voicemail.'

'Oh yeah, I lost my charger. Had to buy a new one in the end,' explained Anna. 'It was quite nice in a funny sort of way, not being contactable. It was quite liberating. As soon as it was charged enough, I had Nathan ringing as he hadn't been able to get hold of me, then Mark, then work. All within an hour.'

'Mark? What did he want?'

'It's all right, don't sound so alarmed,' chuckled Anna. 'He was only seeing how I was.'

'And Luke, is he okay?'

'Yeah, he's great. Really enjoying it over there. Still it's early days. I miss him, but I'm pleased that he and Mark are at last having a proper father-son relationship. I think Luke felt a bit sorry for me. He asked me what I was doing, was I going out anywhere and had I seen Tex. A bit odd, but nice to know he's thinking of me.' Rather awkwardly, with her phone still lodged in place, Anna rinsed the juice from the orange off her fingers. 'Anyway, what did you want to talk to me about before we got sidetracked?'

'Any chance you could pop over? I don't feel up to coming out just yet. Besides, there's nothing like your own bathroom when you're feeling rough.'

Good job he was on the end of the phone a few thousand miles away, otherwise Anna wasn't sure she would be responsible for her actions. Only Mark had the power to make her feel violent.

'Anna, let me explain,' said Mark.

'Where have I heard that before? I know exactly what you were doing. How could you blackmail him?'

'Anna, I'm sorry. I was desperate. Really desperate. I wasn't thinking straight.' He was practically pleading. 'You know I've turned things around since then.'

'Why didn't you tell me Tex had the photos?'

'He didn't want you to know, and I didn't want him to blab his mouth off about my business. See, me and him, we're not that different after all.'

'Never, *ever*, compare yourself to him.' She almost spat the words out. 'And what about the text message you sent?'

'Message? What message?'

'The one you sent Tex. That night Luke ended up in hospital. The one telling him I didn't want to see him anymore. Don't pretend you don't know anything about it.'

'I honestly don't though. I certainly didn't send him a text. I mean, why would I?'

'Oh, come off it, Mark, it's so your style.'

'Anna, listen to me.' Mark sounded calm, not spiteful or vindictive like he usually did when he had been found out. 'I did not send a text to him, not on your phone, not on my phone, or anyone's phone for that matter. Absolutely, categorically, did NOT send one.'

'Well, if you didn't, then who did?' Anna stopped pacing around the coffee table. Mark's calm and convincing voice was making her doubt the accusations she had just levied at him.

'I don't know but it wasn't me. Promise. Hang on a minute. Luke, I'm just in the middle of a conversation with your mother. Why would I...?' Mark stopped and again Anna could hear him speaking to Luke. 'Can't this wait, mate? I'm just...'

She could hear Luke's voice in the background but couldn't make out what he was saying. More muffled voices as Mark must have put his hand over the mouthpiece. Then Mark's voice was clear again. 'Sorry Anna, Luke's trying to tell me something. Hang on a sec.' More indistinct dialect before Mark spoke to her again. 'Err... Anna, you better speak to Luke.'

'What? Now?' Anna began. Couldn't it wait? She was in the middle of a dingdong with Mark and now he was handing her over to Luke.

'Mum?'

'Hi, Luke. You okay?' She tried to sound upbeat.

'Yeah, err, Mum?'

'Yes?' Anna waited but there was silence. 'Is everything all right?'

'Erm, well, that message... to Tex... Dad didn't send it.'

It was a moment or two before Anna responded, totally thrown by Luke's comment. 'It's all right Luke, you don't have to back your dad up. It's nothing to do with you,' she said kindly.

'But it is,' mumbled Luke.

'Ignore us. It's not a major row, honestly.'

'No, Mum, you don't understand.' He sounded quite upset. 'It wasn't Dad who sent that text. It was.... me.'

Anna gulped. Luke? Luke sent the text? How ridiculous! Protecting his dad no doubt. 'Please, there's no need to cover up for Dad.'

'Mum! Listen! It was me. I sent it. I told Tex you didn't want to see him anymore.' Luke's confession came gushing out faster than a split water balloon. 'I wanted you and Dad to get back together. I thought if you weren't seeing Tex then Dad would stand a chance. You and Dad were arguing about him. I took your phone out of your bag when you went upstairs, and I sent a text to him. I was cross and angry. That's why I got drunk. I'm sorry.'

'Oh Luke,' sighed Anna. She could hardly believe what she was hearing. Luke had sabotaged her relationship with Tex. Silly, silly boy. Stupid boy. Poor, desperate boy. Argh, she could throttle him!

'That's not all. I changed Tex's number in your contact list. Just by one digit in the middle.' Luke sounded suitably contrite. 'I thought that way, you wouldn't notice the number was different, I mean, no one knows other people's mobile numbers off by heart, you just go by the name in the contact list. So if you sent another text to him, it wouldn't reach him and you'd never know.'

Anna closed her eyes and sunk down onto her sofa. So all her messages to Tex since that Saturday had just gone off to a random number. Tex hadn't received a single one of them. Oh God, what a mess.

'I'm sorry, Mum. I forgot all about it until the other day when I spoke to you. Trouble was, I didn't know how to tell you. And then when I heard Dad just now, I knew I had to own up. Sorry.'

Anna had to force herself to speak civilly to him. 'I can't actually believe you thought that was an okay thing to do. I am seriously peed off.'

'I am sorry.'

Anna took a deep breath, no way could she condone what Luke had done, but she didn't really want to get into a transatlantic argument with him or end the call on a bad note. 'Apology accepted. Now put your Dad on, I need to speak to him.'

Mark's voice came on the line. 'Hi again.'

'Sorry, Mark, I shouldn't have gone off on one like that, well, not about the text message anyway.'

'Hey, that's okay. I would have assumed it was me too.' There was a small silence before Mark spoke again. 'I'm sorry about all the business with the photos. I was in a real bad place, both mentally and financially. I was desperate.'

'I know that but it doesn't mean I've forgiven you. Yet.'

'I know that too. Maybe one day you can,' he said softly. Then, in an upbeat way, he added, 'Anyway, what are you doing still on the phone? Haven't you got a cowboy to track down?

Chapter Thirty Six

This was not achieving anything, sitting here moping. Anna's silence was shouting loud and clear. Tex's feeling of despair and helplessness had gradually morphed into anger and frustration over the week. Even his brothers were giving him a wide berth at the moment. Letting him get it out of his system, no doubt. If only it were that easy. He shouldn't have allowed himself to become so involved. Hadn't Jamie said at the start that Anna was complicated? Hadn't Jamie also said that the best way to get over her was to find a replacement? Perhaps that's what he needed: a no strings attached, uncomplicated, one-night stand. Maybe more than one even.

His mind almost instantly turned to Carrie, an old flame from his teenage days, part of their group that hung around high school together. Over the years the group had met up periodically with their girlfriends and boyfriends, who had later turned into their spouses, and then with their babies and children, all of whom were now grown up themselves. It was a nice, uncomplicated group of friends. Carrie had married Henry and, as it turned out, they had recently divorced. On hearing Tex was back in Brenham and alone, Carrie had wasted no time in calling by earlier in the week, making it perfectly clear that a night out, leading to a night in, a night in bed with Tex, which would involve very little sleeping, was something she was up for. And why not? He needed to get Anna out of his system and perhaps Jamie was right. Sex with someone else would be the answer. Who better than an old flame who was actually more his usual type – long brunette hair, tall and slim. Still very attractive for her age.

Yes, Carrie would do nicely.

In anticipation, Carrie had left her number scribbled on a piece of paper in the cottage. A quick call. Great. She was free tomorrow evening. He'd pick her up at seven and go into Brenham for a meal. Wine, dine, bed. Excellent.

Anna knew it would have saved time to just phone Jamie and Yvonne, but she decided that it would be harder for them to fob her off if she was there in person. She could even stage a sit-in in protest until they told her where Tex was. Anna was hoping to appeal to Yvonne, woman to woman. Jamie would be more likely to look out for Tex and not give too much away.

'Anna!' exclaimed Yvonne as she opened the door. She smiled. 'Come on in.'

Anna followed her down the hall to the kitchen, wondering whether Yvonne had been half expecting her. She had sounded more pleased than surprised when greeting her.

'Coffee? Now, is this a social visit or something to do with work? Did you want Jamie? He's about somewhere.'

'No, not especially,' said Anna, sitting down at the breakfast bar. 'It's Tex I'm after actually.' Ignoring Yvonne's raised eyebrows, Anna continued. 'Look, there's been a mix-up. I really need to find him. He's not in Arundel or Guildford and I don't know where else to try. No one at the restaurants will tell me anything, other than he is away for a few days. They don't know where or for how long.'

'Have you tried ringing him?'

'I don't have the right number. My contact list is messed up.'

Another raising of the eyebrows. Anna didn't have the time to explain about Luke's meddling, nor that she would have found out sooner had she bothered to ring back the unknown caller who had messaged her with a *Who is this?* No doubt whatever number Luke had changed Tex's to belonged to 'unknown caller'. At that moment Jamie came into the room.

'Oh, Anna.' He smiled. 'You want your job back? Only I could really do with you. The clients are missing you.'

'She's after Tex,' explained Yvonne. Anna didn't miss the look that passed between husband and wife.

'Right,' replied Jamie nonchalantly. 'Not your job then? Okay. Well, Tex, he's not here.'

'Do you know where he is?' asked Anna. She tried to keep the note of impatience out of her voice. 'Or can you just give me his number?'

'I can, but it won't do any good.' Jamie let out a sigh. 'Look, Anna, I'll be honest with you. Tex thought a lot of you. A heck of a lot. Didn't he, Yvonne?'

Yvonne nodded. 'He adored you. Never seen him like that over anyone before.'

Jamie continued, as Anna, feeling guilty, fixed her gaze on her cup. 'He's pretty cut up by everything. All this business with Mark and not divorcing him. One minute you're with Tex, the next with Mark. Or at least, that's how it appears.'

'It's not like that, honestly. I know it sounds corny but it's all been a big mix-up. Please Jamie.' She'd get down on her knees and beg if she had to. 'That's why I need to see him, or at least speak to him so I can explain.' She looked from Jamie to Yvonne and back again. 'I love him.'

'Oh, for God's sake, Jamie, give Anna his number or I will,' said Yvonne.

'Like I said, it won't do any good having his number,' said Jamie.

'He's not leaving his phone switched on. He's trying to have some time away from it all. He just checks in with work every couple of days and that's it.'

'Where is he then?' Christ, Jamie wasn't making this easy for her.

Jamie grinned. 'Can't you guess?'

The relief that swept over Anna as Jamie finally revealed Tex's whereabouts was almost overwhelming. It was obvious really, if she had thought about it. Of course Tex would go to Moonshadow Meadows. Creek Corner to be exact. His retreat.

'Here's the satnav,' said Jamie, handing the small black screen to Anna. 'I've put Tex's address in there, so you should have no trouble. Now, you've printed the plane ticket, haven't you, and your hire car form? Travel authorisation for entry into the States?'

Anna waved the e-tickets at Jamie. 'Yes. Thank you so much.' She had used Jamie's laptop to book her tickets for the following day. All she had to do now was go home and pack a few things. The taxi for the morning was all booked too.

'You're more than welcome,' smiled Yvonne, giving Anna a hug. 'I really hope you and Tex sort things out. We both do. Jamie was only being a bit difficult under Tex's instructions.'

'I know. I understand.'

'Don't forget, you can have your job back once you and Tex have sorted yourselves out,' said Jamie.

Drive for point-two miles and arrive at destination, announced the borrowed satnav. Anna gave a wry laugh. She couldn't exactly get lost on this one way track to Moonshadow Meadows. Within a couple of minutes Anna pulled up outside the gates of the ranch.

It had been a long journey and she was exhausted. On reflection, perhaps she should have booked a motel. Given herself chance to freshen up. She looked down at herself. Trousers crumpled. Stain on her t-shirt from the juice she'd spilt on the flight. Glancing at her reflection in the rear-view mirror made her mind up. She looked dreadful. She needed to look her best. She turned the hire car around on the track and headed back towards Brenham town. She'd book in to a motel she remembered seeing, near that Italian restaurant Tex had taken her to. She wanted to make herself presentable. No wait, make that irresistible.

Something made him do a double take of the sedan that had just crossed the lights in front of him. Hell, what was he thinking? Just because the driver was blonde it didn't mean it was her. Why would she be driving through town? The lights turned to green and Tex swung his brother's pick-up round the corner, heading back towards the ranch. He must stop this. Thinking about her was becoming a habit. One that he needed to get out of.

He purposefully turned his thoughts to that evening and Carrie. Yes, that was better. He'd been into town and bought himself a new shirt and trousers, together with a pair of shoes. He wanted to wear something new. Something that he couldn't associate with anything or, rather, anyone. That way he would stay focused tonight. He was a bit out of practice wooing and romancing a female. The fact that it was Carrie shouldn't make it any less of an occasion. She would at least want to feel like they had gone through the motions of a romantic evening. Even Carrie, despite the obvious green light she'd given him, would want to feel like he was making an effort and that it wasn't just for sex. Although, to all intents and purposes, that's exactly what it was.

He just needed to go home now and put some clean sheets on the bed, shower, dress, put the wine in the fridge for later, and that would give him enough time to have a quick drink with Al at Finnigan's bar in Brenham, before picking up Carrie. The table was all booked at the Colloseum Italian restaurant on South

Market Street. Perfect.

Sitting outside the gates of the ranch once again, Anna felt rather more glamorous than she had earlier that afternoon. Even though it was early evening, it was still extremely hot. She had opted for the lightweight floaty dress she had worn for her first proper date with Tex.

Okay, this was it. She opened the gate and drove through onto the track, remembering to close it behind her. She could drive straight to Creek Cottage without having to go past the main ranch house. There was a little turning on the left a bit of the way up that Tex always took. As she turned the slight bend in the track and Creek Cottage came into view, she saw a quad bike parked out the front. Her heart gave a little flutter.

She parked outside and, as she stepped out into the hot evening, she paused at the bottom of the steps leading up to the porch. Surely he had heard her car. She'd just have to knock.

No answer.

She knocked again and tried the handle. The door opened and she took a couple of steps in, calling out his name.

Nothing. Totally empty.

Her heart dropped. She had been so geared up to see him and now that feeling transformed into major disappointment.

Perhaps Jamie had it wrong. Tex wasn't here at all. She had tried to call his mobile but it had just gone straight to voicemail. She had been so sure he would come back to the ranch.

'He's gone into town.'

Anna jumped at the voice behind her. Spinning round, she was relieved to see Tex's brother standing in the doorway.

'Oh, Mikey. You startled me.'

'Hey there, Anna. You okay? I didn't know you were coming.' He smiled at her in that familiar Garcia way.

'Nor did I until yesterday,' she smiled back at him. 'Do you know where he is?'

'Not exactly, only that he's gone into Brenham.' He wiped his forehead with a handkerchief. 'Said something about meeting an old friend.'

'You wouldn't happen to know where he might go?'

'Probably Finnigan's. Come on, I'll take you there.'

Tex looked across the table at Carrie as she chatted easily to him about their mutual friends. Bringing him up to speed with what everyone was doing, where they were working or living, who had divorced, and so on. Carrie was a very beautiful woman and she was wearing a particularly low-cut dress, Tex was appreciative of the way it showed off her full cleavage to the maximum and how it fitted round her slender waist and hugged her hips like a second skin. The slightly rounded hips swung from side to side like a pendulum as she sashayed across the restaurant to the restroom. No sign of a panty line, just a smooth, well-toned butt, thought Tex. Slender legs and high heels.

'I don't think I'll have a dessert. Not good for the figure,' she said as she sat back in her seat, running her hand seductively down the side of her breast and waist, pushing her chest out and smiling at him from under her eyelashes. 'Mmmm? What are you thinking?'

Tex realised she was waiting for him to say something. Hell, he couldn't say what he was thinking – how Anna always had a dessert, said it was her favourite part of a meal. He smiled slowly, buying a bit of time, before coming up with, 'I think your figure is very good as it is.'

Carrie tittered. 'You could always ask for a closer inspection if you're not sure.'

'I may just do that,' replied Tex, unsure whom he was trying to convince more. 'Let's get a drink at Finnigan's before we go back.'

'We could just go straight to mine, it is closer.'

'It's still early. We've got all night.' Tex realised he was stalling. Why was he was putting the inevitable off? What was up with him? He really needed to stop thinking about Anna. He stood up and exhaled, as if exorcising the thought of her from his mind. Then smiling, he pulled Carrie's chair out for her and as she stood, whispered in her ear, 'Mine will be better, I have some wine waiting for us after we call by Finnigan's for a late drink.'

The bar was busier than Anna remembered. She scanned the room but couldn't see Tex.

Mikey passed her drink. 'Iced lemonade. You sure you don't wanna beer?' He then nudged her arm. 'Hey, look there's Tex... oh shit.'

Anna followed Mikey's gaze to the table by the jukebox, her eyes coming to rest on Tex. Oh shit, indeed. Her heart flipped. Several times. She could feel the rush of adrenalin surge to the tips of her fingers. He was sitting opposite Al but next to him was a woman, and Tex had his arm casually draped round the back of her chair, his fingers resting lightly on her shoulder.

Al looked up, smiled at seeing his brother, then noticing Anna, she could see him offer the same expletive that Mikey just had. Tex looked round, his eyes locking onto Anna. Every sense in Anna's body told her to turn and run. The urge to flee was overwhelming.

Hurriedly and clumsily, Anna dumped her glass on the bar, sloshing some lemonade out as she did so, before making a dash for the door. It felt as if a black mass was surrounding her, closing her in, drawing her into a dark hole of emptiness. She needed some fresh air.

Outside, Anna took big gulps of warm night air. Resting her hands on her knees, she leant forwards slightly. Gradually her breathing slowed. Standing up, she tried to think clearly. Normally, it would be at this point she jumped in her car and headed off home, beaten into surrender. Not questioning. Never knowing what if. Could she face going home, never seeing Tex again, never telling him how she felt?

Taking a final deep breath, Anna pushed open the door to the bar. All heads turned towards her but she didn't look at anyone, only at Tex. He was standing talking earnestly to the woman at his table. They stopped talking and both looked at Anna. Then the woman picked up her bag and, accompanied by Mikey, walked towards the door. She smiled as she approached Anna.

'He may have been with me in body this evening, but his mind, heart and soul have been with you, honey.' Looking over her shoulder, Carrie smiled and waved at Tex, before linking arms with Mikey and leaving.

In just a few strides Tex was across the bar, standing in front of Anna.

It was now or never. Inhaling deeply, Anna spoke, sounding almost businesslike. 'Can we talk?'

Tex nodded. Resting his hand lightly on her arm, he guided her out of the bar. 'You need a revolving door.' Just the touch of his hand seemed to burn right through her skin.

Despite the heat, she was aware that she was shaking slightly from nerves as she turned to face him. Oh how she wanted him to take her into his arms, tell her he loved her and that everything would be all right. Wasn't that supposed to happen now?

Tex was just standing there, obviously waiting for her to speak. His aftershave, that familiar citrus smell wafted in the air around them. She looked at his beautiful brown eyes, his thick lashes, his sexy mouth that she had kissed so many times, his face that she had caressed and felt against her own. She loved him so much. Whatever happened now, she wanted to remember him as he looked tonight. Beautiful. Handsome. Sexy.

'That woman, in the bar. Is she…? I mean, are you and her…?' The words stuck in her throat.

Tex shook his head gently, his eyes never leaving hers. 'I was attempting pain relief.'

'Was it effective?'

'Not one bit. I think I need open-heart surgery to stop the pain.'

Anna studied his face, working out what he was actually saying. A rush of excitement swept through her. There was still hope.

'I saw Zoe. She said you had been to see her.'

Tex nodded. He touched her wrist. 'She gave you your watch back then? Did she give you anything else?'

She cast her eyes down for a second. 'Mark said he'd send the photos out to everyone if I didn't go along with him. He was going to cause trouble for your restaurant. I had no idea he had tried to blackmail you too.' She looked up at him now. She wanted him to believe what she was about to say. 'I should have told you. I should have trusted you but…'

He put his finger to her lips and shook his head. 'You don't have to explain. I know exactly what happened.'

'The message saying I didn't want to see you. It wasn't from me. Luke sent it.'

Tex raised his eyebrows, *that* he hadn't figured out. He could hear the words catching in her throat but he let her speak.

'He changed your number in my contact list. I didn't know. I did try to contact you, I promise.'

He looked down at her hands as she nervously twiddled her fingers. There was no sign of the wedding and engagement ring she usually wore on her right hand. He lifted her hand and gently rubbed his thumb over the bare skin. So, she'd finally ditched the last remnant of her marriage. He let her hand fall away. He knew he wasn't making it easy for her but he had to be sure this was what she wanted.

She spoke again. 'Luke's gone back to California with Mark, and I've got a little flat in Chichester now.'

Another protracted pause as he looked intently at her before speaking. 'So you came all this way just to tell me that?'

'Yes. No, I mean.' He could see tears begin to gather in her eyes. 'Me and Mark are divorcing. I couldn't divorce him before. Mark said if I did he'd ruin your business. It wasn't that I didn't want to divorce him. I did. But I wanted to protect you. I'm so sorry. I should have told you.' The words were tumbling out now. 'I just wanted to tell you. To tell you that I'm sorry, I never meant to hurt you. I've missed you so much, so very much.' The tears were falling.

He held back from taking her in his arms and comforting her. She still hadn't given him enough.

She looked up at him, swallowed hard. 'I love you. More than anything.'

Then he was holding her to him, his arms wrapping tightly around her, pulling her close to his body. She'd said what he'd wanted to hear. She sobbed into his chest as he stroked her hair and kissed the top of her head.

'It's okay,' he whispered into her hair between kisses, squeezing her, holding her, caressing her. 'I love you more than you will ever know. I don't ever wanna let you go.' He pulled away and tipping her chin up with his hand, cupped her face and wiped away the tears with his thumbs. Then he kissed her. Kissed her with a passion. God, that felt so good. So right. It seemed to go on forever.

Finally, Tex pulled away and looked directly into her eyes. 'Tell me again.'

Anna laughed through her tears. 'I love you.'

'You don't know how many times I wanted to hear you say that.' He kissed her again. Longer. More urgently. More meaningfully. 'Come back to the ranch.'

'I'm booked in at the motel up the road.' She was teasing him now.

'Well, we'll just have to unbook you then.' He released her from his hold. 'Wait right there. Don't move.'

He jogged back into Finnigan's and came back out almost immediately, jangling some keys in his hand. He wrapped her in his arms again, taking time to breathe in the familiar vanilla scent, feel the curves of her body against his. She had come for him, and he knew finally he could give himself to someone. He squeezed her tighter and lifted her off her feet.

'I love you.'

'It's a mutual thing.' She kissed him.

Tex let out a groan and rested her down on the ground again. He nuzzled her neck. 'Let's stop by the motel.'

She pulled back to look at him. 'Would be a shame to waste it now I've paid for it.'

When Tex swept her up into his arms and carried her towards the pick-up truck, she was grinning like the proverbial Cheshire Cat.

'*Officer and a Gentleman*?' She laughed. 'Pah! Richard Gere, eat your heart out!'

317

9 780007 559749